"Brand, who are you?" The words sprang forth unbidden but Sybil ached to know.

He grunted and any welcome she might have imagined in his eyes disappeared into a stone-hard look. "Exactly what you see. A cowboy with a horse and a dog."

"But you must have a name besides Brand. You must be more than that."

His eyes grew harder, colder, if that were possible, and she shivered.

He might have well said, "Goodbye, this conversation is over."

She had enough for her story.

He was known only as Cowboy. He never did give a last name before he rode into the sunset. He didn't welcome any questions about his true identity. But he was the best bronc buster in the territory. A reputation well earned.

It began when he was ten…

But she wasn't satisfied.

He interrupted her thoughts. "You best get the boy back before his folks start looking for him."

She wanted to know what caused the pain she'd glimpsed before he pulled his hat lower.

Linda Ford

Winning Over
the Wrangler
&
Falling for
the Rancher Father

LOVE INSPIRED
INSPIRATIONAL ROMANCE

Recycling programs for this product may not exist in your area.

LOVE INSPIRED®
INSPIRATIONAL ROMANCE

ISBN-13: 978-1-335-44876-7

Winning Over the Wrangler & Falling for the Rancher Father

Copyright © 2021 by Harlequin Books S.A.

Winning Over the Wrangler
First published in 2014. This edition published in 2021.
Copyright © 2014 by Linda Ford

Falling for the Rancher Father
First published in 2014. This edition published in 2021.
Copyright © 2014 by Linda Ford

This edition published by arrangement with Harlequin Books S.A.

For questions and comments about the quality of this book, please contact us at CustomerService@Harlequin.com.

Love Inspired
22 Adelaide St. West, 40th Floor
Toronto, Ontario M5H 4E3, Canada
www.Harlequin.com

Printed in U.S.A.

CONTENTS

WINNING OVER THE WRANGLER   7

FALLING FOR THE RANCHER FATHER   289

Linda Ford lives on a ranch in Alberta, Canada, near enough to the Rocky Mountains that she can enjoy them on a daily basis. She and her husband raised fourteen children—four homemade, ten adopted. She currently shares her home and life with her husband, a grown son, a live-in paraplegic client, and a continual (and welcome) stream of kids, kids-in-law, grandkids, and assorted friends and relatives.

Books by Linda Ford

Love Inspired Historical

Big Sky Country

Montana Cowboy Daddy
Montana Cowboy Family
Montana Cowboy's Baby
Montana Bride by Christmas
Montana Groom of Convenience
Montana Lawman Rescuer

Montana Cowboys

The Cowboy's Ready-Made Family
The Cowboy's Baby Bond
The Cowboy's City Girl

Visit the Author Profile page
at Harlequin.com for more titles.

WINNING OVER THE WRANGLER

The Lord shall guide thee continually, and satisfy
thy soul in drought, and make fat thy bones:
and thou shalt be like a watered garden.
—*Isaiah* 58:11

Prejudice comes in many forms.
It can be against the color of your skin, your heritage or, as it is in this story, your family reputation. Although I will name no names, this book is dedicated to those of my children who deal with prejudice. May you find grace and strength in those kinds of situations and may you know the assurance of both God's love and the love of your family.

Chapter One

⌒

Eden Valley Ranch, September 1882

Stampede!

Brand knew what was happening before it took place. He saw the horses press against the corral gate, frightened by something beyond his vision. It could have been anything from a stalking cougar to a tumbling tumbleweed. Wouldn't take much to alarm a bunch of wild mustangs. Wood creaked. The gate wouldn't hold under the pressure of frightened horses.

Brand's fists tightened so hard on the reins his knuckles cracked. His heart squeezed his blood out in a flash flood.

He would shout a warning to those along the fence, tell them to stand back. But he barely had control of the horse under him, which until a few minutes ago had never been ridden.

The gate snapped. The horses reared and screamed and pushed at each other, as frightened by the noise of the breaking fence as they had been by being confined. Brand held his mount with a firm hand. The horse was not ready to ride in tight quarters, but from the first, he'd sensed a willingness in it that was absent in many of the others he'd worked with. With no choice but to trust himself and the others to the green horse, he rode in the direction of the escaped animals. He had to turn them away from the people, get them back into the pen before anyone got hurt.

He saw a little boy and one of the women who had been watching. They stood only a few feet from the kicking, screaming, twisting animals surging in their direction. Choking dust clouded the scene.

He kicked his mount, raced for a gate, slipped it open with lightning speed and galloped toward them.

The stampeding horses were ahead of him. Before them, the boy scampered toward a fence and rolled under it. But the woman stood frozen, her mouth hanging open. Brand couldn't tell if she screamed, couldn't have heard it in the uproar if she did.

Out of the corner of his eye, he caught the movement of other cowboys racing for their own horses. No one else was close enough to rescue her. Brand leaned over the horse's neck and urged him onward, closing the distance between them and the woman.

Ten more feet. He dared not look to the right or the left. All that mattered was that frightened woman.

Five feet.

One more leap of his horse and Brand reached her side. He leaned down and swept her into his arms, clutching her to his chest as they raced onward, out of the way of danger as pounding hooves thundered past and dust-laden air swirled.

He slowed, grateful the horse cooperated. "You're

okay now. You're safe." He pressed her trembling body closer.

He'd noticed her earlier as she stood by another woman, watching him at work. How could he not keep stealing glances at her? She was the most beautiful woman he'd ever seen, with her golden curls flashing in the sunshine. He could describe everything about her in detail…the autumn-gold top she wore, the brown skirt that swung about her legs as she moved. The way she walked, as if life held nothing but promise for her. The way she smiled so sweetly at others.

It had taken all his concentration not to be distracted by her presence. It was his single-minded attentiveness that gave him his reputation as the best bronc buster in the West, and he wasn't about to lose it.

And now she rested in his arms, holding his shirt-front as if it was a lifeline, and lifted her gaze to him. His world tipped at the way her cobalt-blue eyes caught his in a pleading look. How was he supposed to keep his mind off her in this situation?

Cowboys turned the herd of wild horses back to the corral amid more dust and more shouting.

"You're safe," he murmured again, as fierce protectiveness filled his insides. He wanted to promise both himself and her that he'd make sure she was always safe.

Then his world righted and reason returned. He could never make such a promise. In fact, he carried more risk than any woman deserved, and certainly more than he meant to give one. He warned himself to stay away from her before he brought danger into her life.

A mahogany-haired woman rushed toward them— the woman he'd seen earlier with his golden beauty. And then Eddie Gardiner, the ranch owner who had hired him, raced up on his horse. Already the dust had begun to settle.

"Are you hurt?" Eddie asked.

"No. I'm fine." The woman had a gentle, soft voice with a sweet English accent. A voice full of music and peace, despite the danger she'd just been in. Was her life really as peaceful and perfect as her voice caused Brand to think? From what he'd seen of her, he knew her to be a high-class lady. Likely she had never had reason in her privileged life to deal with the harsh realities of a place like his.

Realizing he still held her tight, Brand forced his arms to unfold, and lowered her to the ground, where her friend took her hand and pulled her close.

"That was exciting," the other woman said.

The golden beauty shivered. "A little too dangerous for my liking."

If she thought a herd of wild horses was dangerous, he could not imagine what she'd think if she knew the truth about him.

Eddie glanced about. "Where's Grady? Wasn't he with you?"

The woman gasped. "He was right here." She and her friend spun around, looking for him.

They must mean the boy who had wisely taken himself out of harm's way. Brand's smile formed as he looked toward where the boy had hidden.

"I'm here, Papa." The little fella crawled from under the fence and dusted himself off.

Brand would have guessed the blond-haired, blue-eyed child to be about five or six.

Grady swiped at his runny nose and looked up at Brand. "I wasn't scared."

Brand laughed at his bravado. "I was."

Grady hung his head. "Maybe I was a little."

"It's a good thing to be scared sometimes." A message he wished he could send to the woman he'd rescued and who now looked up at him with big trusting eyes.

He touched the brim of his hat and reined around. Already others had the horses contained and were moving them back into the corral. He should have checked the enclosure better. His oversight had put people at risk.

Eddie's wife raced down the hill, her skirts held in one hand. He'd seen she was in the family way, and hoped she wouldn't fall.

As soon as she was close enough, she caught Grady and sank to the ground, cradling the boy in her lap. "Thank God you're safe." She glanced up at Brand. "I saw the whole thing. You saved Sybil's life. You're very brave."

Brave! This woman was called Sybil. As if that could cancel out danger. It couldn't.

Brand wanted to ride away, avoid all this fuss, but he was surrounded by people.

He felt Sybil's gaze on him. Felt its warmth and watchfulness. He tried to avoid looking at her, knowing her blue eyes did something funny to his resolve. Made him weak and vulnerable.

"I don't think you have met Brand." Eddie pulled the woman close. "This is my wife, Linette, and my son, Grady." He turned to the other two ladies. "Mercy Newell." The darker of the pair. "And Sybil Bannerman, our guests from England. Ladies, this is Brand, best bronc buster in these parts."

"Pleased to meet you." Brand touched the brim of his hat. His dusty clothes and hat had seen better days.

Normally he didn't care, but Miss Sybil was so neat and proper, he felt grubby.

"Mr. Brand, you are indeed a hero."

Her gentle words drew his gaze and he smiled despite himself. "No hero, ma'am. Just in the right place at the right time and glad I could be." He doffed his hat and edged away.

"Wait," Linette called. "You must let me do something to show my gratitude. Please join us for supper."

"Appreciate the offer, ma'am, but I got a dog back at my campsite and he's waiting for me." Dawg would be fine on his own, but Brand grasped at any excuse to avoid joining the others. Again, he vowed to ignore Miss Sybil. Again he failed to do so. He met her gaze. She flashed a bright smile that caused his heart to shift sideways, and almost made him lose his balance.

He touched the brim of his dusty hat again and turned his attention back to his job. The horses milled about, upset at their sudden escape and equally sudden corralling. The one he rode picked up the tension. "Enough for today," he said to the men fixing the fence. "No point in trying to work with them when they are riled up like this." He dismounted and turned his horse into another pen, away from the mustangs he hadn't yet ridden.

Cal, the young cowboy who'd given Brand nothing but dark glances since he started work on the horses, looked him up and down. "Guess you think you're pretty special, having rescued Miss Sybil."

No mistaking the challenging tone in the other man's voice. "Nothing special about doing what a man can do. I'm sure you would have done the same if you'd been on a horse at the time."

"You got that right. And I could break these horses if the boss would give me a chance."

"Yup. I figure you could, all right." He had no mind to start a disagreement. "Maybe next time the boss will let ya. Seeing as I won't be back here again."

"Huh. Figures." Cal stalked away.

Brand had no idea what bothered Cal and didn't rightly care. He would be here long enough to do the job Eddie had hired him for, then be gone, never to see any of them again. It was how he must live his life.

At that knowledge, he turned and stared up the hill. Linette and Eddie, with Grady between them, entered the house, Mercy on their heels. But Sybil had paused halfway to the house and stared toward him. He couldn't see her eyes at that distance, but nevertheless, felt the intensity of her look. Wondered at it. For a moment, he couldn't tear himself away.

Then, with a great deal of effort, he pushed forward all the reasons he had to ignore her.

Dawg would be waiting for his supper. "I'll be back in the morning to work on the rest of those mustangs," he said to any of the nearby cowboys who cared to listen. He didn't glance about to see if anyone acknowledged his words.

His gaze lingered two more seconds on the beauty up the hill. Then he jerked around and strode to the clearing he'd chosen as his home away from home. Not that he had any home to be away from. Hadn't had one since his ma died six years ago. Even before that their homes had been temporary at best, as Ma tried to keep ahead of Pa and Cyrus, Brand's older half brother.

Brand had asked her often why she'd married a man who robbed houses, banks and stagecoaches. She said he hadn't done that until later, when things went wrong once too often.

"He said it didn't make sense that the rich got richer and the poor got poorer no matter how hard a poor man worked," his ma had said. "So he decided to even things out."

Only the way Pa and Cyrus went about doing it put their faces on wanted posters as the Duggan gang. And in order to protect Brand from the shame and the danger, Ma took him and fled.

At the memory he pressed his palm to his chest—the same spot where Sybil's head had rested—then jerked his hand to his side. He crossed to the fire pit he'd built out of river rock, and lit a fire. His memories flared along with the flames.

Brand had continued to run for the same reasons—to avoid the shame and the danger. He avoided friendships for the same reasons, plus more. One thing he'd learned well in his twenty-three years: associating with Brand Duggan put others at risk. Pa and Cyrus didn't hesitate to threaten his friends in order to try and force Brand to cooperate with them. Besides, simply being associated with the Duggan name spelled ruin, and shunning by decent people.

He'd once allowed himself to grow fond of a young lady, but when he'd grown bold enough to tell her his last name she had reacted in anger and firmly informed him she'd have nothing to do with a man bearing such a stained name. She'd made sure he understood all the risks and shame she could face simply by being allied with him.

And she was right. Knowing him put her at risk from his family and at risk of censure from the community.

People like Sybil, Eddie and the others at Eden Valley Ranch could live where they chose, in a big house, open and free, while he must always be on the lookout.

So Brand put down no roots, told no one his last name and didn't get close to others. Not even beautiful women like Miss Sybil. Especially not a woman like her.

Dawg had trotted toward him as he reached the clearing. Brand bent and scrubbed his fingers through the dog's silky fur now. This was all he could allow himself in the way of friendship.

He had no hope of a life full of peace and serenity. Nor did he intend to disturb Sybil's sweet world.

It took a lot of kicking clumps of dirt and throwing wood on the fire for him to persuade himself he didn't mind dealing with the truth of his life. Finally, he looked about, determined to find reasons to be grateful. Fall was in the air, filling it with deep-throated scents. Sure, it meant winter would soon be upon them, but he liked the color of the changing leaves, the cool night air and the migrating animals. He glanced up, hearing the honking of a V of geese overhead.

After a bit, his emotions back in order, Brand hunkered down beside the blazing fire, forced to sit a good distance away to avoid being scorched.

Dawg stretched out at his side.

For a time Brand stared into the flames.

"Dawg, you should have seen the commotion." He didn't know if he meant the runaway horses or the reaction to his rescue of Sybil.

"Miss Sybil just stood there as if frozen." He'd seen her eyes. Expected the fear he saw. But there was something more—a watchfulness that surprised him. There was something intriguing about the golden miss.

He dug his fingers into Dawg's fur. "Could be it's because she's such a fine looking woman that I can hardly keep my eyes off her." But his gut said it was more than that. Something that made him consider turning his back on the facts of his life and living recklessly free for a few days, just so he could enjoy spending time with her.

He reminded his gut that to do so would put her in danger. Association with a Duggan—even one not involved in the unsavory exploits of the gang—would sully her name.

Trouble with his gut was it never listened to reason.

How mortifying to be pressed so intimately close to a complete stranger. A big, strong, deep-voiced stranger. Sybil had struggled with trying to decide if she should swoon or fight, when in truth she didn't care to do either. What she'd been tempted to do was so strange, so foreign, she wondered if she'd momentarily taken leave of her senses. She wanted to look into his face and memorize every detail.

Surely her reactions were confused because of the thudding stampede of horses she felt certain would run over her.

She and Mercy had joined the cowboys crowded against the heavy rail fence cheering for the man riding the wild horse. She hadn't felt like cheering. Instead, she'd shuddered as the animal bucked and twisted and snorted in an attempt to dislodge the man on his back. How did he stay glued to the saddle? And didn't all that jolting hurt every bone in his body? Here was a man who thrived on danger. Yet, as she watched him clinging to the back of the wild horse, something tickled her insides. Excitement? Fear? Admiration? She couldn't find words to describe it. And she fancied herself a writer!

The horse had stopped bucking and stood quivering as the big man brushed his hand along its neck and murmured words she couldn't hear, but that stirred her deep inside.

Then a crack as loud as a gunshot had jolted through the air.

A dozen horses had crowded against a split gate. It swayed and then crashed to the ground. The sound of hoofbeats thundered. Frightened horses squealed. The animals were a blur of wild eyes and flying manes.

Sybil had taken a step back, her mouth dry. The noise boomed inside her chest. Dust clogged her nostrils. Uncertain which way to flee, she'd frozen in fear at the melee.

And then she'd been swept off her feet. Rescued from the screaming horses.

No wonder her heart thudded as if she'd run a mile, and she couldn't look away from his face.

But she could not avoid the truth about how unusual her reaction had been, nor could she face the others until she had herself under control. As soon as she reached the big ranch house she excused herself to go to the room down the hall from the kitchen.

Life in the West was certainly different from the one she'd known back in England.

At the thought of where she'd come from, her tension returned. She sat on the edge of her bed and pressed cool fingers to her hot cheeks. Of course she was upset. Her fear had immobilized her. She would have been trampled to death if the bronc buster hadn't swept her off her feet and pressed her to his chest.

A very broad, comforting chest.

Sybil, stop it. It doesn't matter if the chest was broad or fat or sweaty or...

But it wasn't. He smelled of leather and horses and wild grass. A very pleasing blend of aromas.

That doesn't matter. He means nothing to you and will mean nothing to you. Besides, didn't Eddie say the man would stay only long enough to break some horses? And hadn't Eddie further said the man gave no last name?

Quite the sort of fellow any woman would do well to avoid.

Not that Sybil Bannerman had any intention of doing otherwise. In her twenty years, she'd had her fill of people being snatched from her life or simply leaving of their own will, breaking off pieces of her heart in the process.

She bent over her knees as painful memories assailed her.

At only twelve years of age, Suzette, her dearest friend in the whole world, had drowned, leaving Sybil, also twelve at the time, lost, afraid and missing a very large portion of her heart.

She'd recovered enough at age sixteen to give her heart to Colin, the preacher's son. They'd spent hours talking of their hopes and plans, and dreaming of a future together. She'd finally found a soul mate to replace Suzette. She had opened her heart to Colin, expecting his attention to grow into a formal courtship. She even dreamed of the frothy white dress she'd wear at their wedding, and considered where they might live. For the first time since Suzette's death she'd felt whole and eager to share her thoughts and dreams.

No one had warned her it was temporary. Colin had never hinted that he'd changed his mind about how he felt about her, but a year after they met he left without a word of explanation. He never wrote or made any effort to keep in touch.

Another slice of her heart was cut off.

Losing her parents to fever a year and a half ago, within a few weeks of each other, had been the final blow.

From now on, she vowed, she would guard her heart, though she had very little of it left.

She sat up. Why was she having this argument with herself? It wasn't as if being rescued by Brand meant anything. As he said, he was simply in the right place at the right time. It made sense that she would feel some type of bond with a man who saved her life. But that's all it was.

Intending to calm herself, she pulled a notebook to her lap, just as Mercy rapped on the door and entered, without waiting for an invitation to do so.

Mercy nodded at the journal. "I'm guessing you're writing all about that handsome cowboy."

Her friends knew she made short notes about each day in her diary. They would never believe she wrote for publication. She'd never told them. Most people she knew didn't think a young woman should have her name mentioned in such a public way.

She didn't mind that as much as knowing most people didn't think a young woman would have anything of value or interest to say. That had been the comment of the only editor she'd been brave enough to speak to, a couple years back.

But surely Mercy would understand. She didn't share the same sense of outrage at women doing different things.

Sybil retrieved papers she'd secreted away earlier. "I'm writing a story."

"Uh-huh."

"Do you remember reading that article written by Ellis West? You know. The one that described the ship's captain from our journey here."

Mercy laughed. "He really made us see the pompous man."

"I'm Ellis West."

Mercy snorted. "Ellis West is a man."

"No. It's a pseudonym I use."

Her friend's eyes widened, then narrowed. "Are you sure?"

Sybil laughed. "Of course I'm sure. Why do you find it so hard to accept?" Was she wrong in thinking Mercy would understand?

"You?" Mercy shook her head. "It just seems so out of character."

"Look at this if you don't believe me." She held out her notes for an article about the life of a cowboy.

Mercy read them through. "You wrote this?"

Sybil sighed. "What does it take to convince you? Remember Mrs. Page on the boat? She's secretary to the editor of a newspaper back East. She saw me writing and asked about it. I showed her what I'd written about the captain. She asked if I had more. I gave her four stories I'd composed, mostly for the fun of it." Though even after the rude rejection by the one editor

Sybil had seen, the desire to write just wouldn't leave her. "She took them immediately to the editor, who offered to publish them. I gave him half a dozen stories before I left the ship." They'd been published and she'd sent several more describing the West and the inhabitants of the territory. She expected they might have already appeared in the Toronto paper. The newspapers didn't reach Edendale for several weeks after they appeared back East.

Mercy hugged her. "How exciting."

"The editor has asked me to find a bigger-than-life cowboy and write his story." He'd offered a nice sum of money for such an article.

An idea flared through her head. She'd had recent experience with a bigger-than-life cowboy, a hero, as she'd said. "Brand—best bronc breaker in the country—fits the bill to perfection."

Mercy bounced up and down on the bed. "He's exactly what you need. I say write his story."

"But how am I to get the details of his life?" Sure, Sybil could ask others what they knew. Certainly make her own observations. But the best source was the man himself.

Her skin burned. Her lungs refused to do their job. There was no way she could ever approach this man and ask personal questions. There was something about him that threatened the locks on her heart.

You're being silly. He is just a man. Observe. Ask questions. That's all you need to do. He doesn't have to know that you're writing something about him. Besides, she'd learned people were more honest, their answers more raw, if they weren't aware they were being interviewed. And who would suspect a woman of interviewing them for a story, anyway?

She could not let this opportunity pass. Or let her natural reticence—or as Mercy insisted, her fear—get in the way of this story.

"All you have to do is ask him questions. You're very good at that. People seem to trust you." Mercy flung herself back on Sybil's bed. "With good reason. You are a good person."

"It's very kind of you to say so." Sybil listened distractedly as her friend chattered on about whom she'd seen and talked to, and how she meant to pursue certain activities, until Sybil caught the words, *"learn to trick ride."*

She spun around to confront her. "Tell me I didn't hear you say you mean to learn to trick ride."

"Okay. You didn't hear me say that." Mercy grinned.

"Good. Honestly, sometimes you scare me with your rash words and even rasher actions."

Mercy regarded her with a teasing grin. "No more than you worry me with your careful way of living. Sybil, my friend, if you're not cautious you'll end up living a barren life, when there is so much to know and enjoy out here." She waved her arms in a wide circle as if encompassing the world.

"I'd sooner be safe." Sybil hoped Mercy would never learn that barrenness felt better than having your heart shredded. Besides, she experienced lots of adventures through the stories others told her. All without the risk to herself.

Mercy laughed. "And I'd sooner have fun." She draped an arm about Sybil's shoulders and rested her forehead against hers. "We are an odd pair and yet you are my best friend."

"What about Jayne?" Jayne Gardiner Collins had been good friends with her and Mercy for several years…since they'd met at a tea party given by a dowager of London society. Despite their differences in nature, they got along well, and the three of them had crossed the ocean and traveled across most of Canada together. Sybil had allowed herself these friendships, knowing from the start they wouldn't last forever. The three of them would go their separate ways. Some to marriage. Likely they would lose touch. Truth was, Sybil simply kept most of her heart safely protected from the pain she knew she'd experience by allowing any friendship to grow.

"Pshaw." Mercy waved her hand dismissively. "She's no longer any fun. She's only interested in Seth. Honestly, I get tired of 'Seth said this, Seth did that, Seth likes such and such.'"

Sybil giggled. "They're in love. What do you expect?"

Mercy laughed, too. "I'm never going to let her forget she had to shoot him to catch him."

"It was an accident," Sybil protested.

They fell back against the bed, laughing at the memory. "I tried to warn the pair of you that no good would come of shooting a gun."

"And she proved you wrong."

"I guess she did."

"Goes to show you should live a little dangerously once in a while. It's worth the risks."

Mercy left a few minutes later.

Sybil stared at the wall. Could she write Brand's

story? Yes, of course she could. The bigger question was could she do it without endangering the carefully constructed walls about her already damaged heart? The man held inherent risks for her, as she'd already discovered by her reaction to being rescued by him.

Oh, stop fretting about that. You were frightened. Snatched into the arms of a tall, dark stranger. It was an unusual experience. Of course you had an unusual reaction.

She made up her mind. She'd write the story, keeping her eyes wide-open to both her initial, surprising response and her prior knowledge that he didn't mean to stay. Eddie said the man never did. He was a born wanderer. Forewarned was forearmed. This time, unlike her unfortunate experience with Colin, she knew what to expect.

She pulled out pen and paper and wrote a letter to the publisher.

I have exactly the man for the assignment you've offered. He is a bronc rider, a quiet loner, a strong and mysterious man. Certainly bigger than life in a world that is full of strong, bold men.

She would find ways to get information about him without letting her silly reaction to being rescued cloud her good sense.

Chapter Two

Her resolve to pursue a story about this man firmly in place, Sybil went to the kitchen.

"Are you sure you weren't hurt?" Linette asked as she bustled about the large room. A big wooden table filled one corner; cupboards and shelves occupied the opposite corner. East windows on either side of the outer door allowed them to enjoy the sunrise as they ate breakfast. Another door opened to a spacious, well-stocked pantry, and a third doorway opened to the hall that led to the rest of the house. Another door, always closed, hid the formal dining room, which Linette refused to use.

Even though she expected a baby in a few months, it didn't slow her down. She never seemed to stop working.

"Frightened is all, but I'm fine now. What can I do to help?"

Mercy sliced carrots into a pot.

Roasting meat filled the room with enough aroma to make Sybil's mouth water. Food certainly tasted better when it came fresh from the garden and when she had a hand in preparing it. Something she'd never done before her arrival at the ranch.

Meeting a man like Brand—big, strong, bold—would have never happened back in England, either. The men she'd been acquainted with would pale in comparison.

Mercy paused. "That bronc buster is a fine-looking man." She gave Sybil a glance that demanded a response.

"Can't say I really noticed."

Mercy laughed. "Hard to see much with your face smashed against his shirtfront."

"He was fast enough and brave enough to rescue me. I thank God for that." Except she'd forgotten to thank Him and she made up for it on the spot, uttering silent thanks.

"I join in thanking God," Linette said as she poured water from the boiled potatoes, saving it in a jar to use later, when she made bread.

Sybil watched everything Linette did. She'd found so much satisfaction in learning to cook meals, bake bread and cookies, and even preserve garden produce for the approaching winter months. She'd only meant the trip to western Canada as a chance to start over, to rebuild her heart and strengthen the barriers around it, but she'd found so much more. She'd found purpose in doing useful things.

"I regret Mr. Brand refused to come for supper," Linette said. "But I've decided to send supper to him. Eddie said he'd be an hour yet. Would you two take a meal to Mr. Brand?"

"Of course," Mercy said.

Sybil wanted to refuse, because her heart still beat a

little too fast as she remembered being held so firmly. But it provided a chance to meet him in a less emotionally packed way and learn about him, so she could write a fine story. "Certainly we'll take a meal to him." No need for her silly reaction to repeat itself. She knew how to control her emotions.

Linette piled a plate high with what looked to Sybil like enough food to feed a family. She couldn't get used to the amount a working cowboy ate. Linette must have noticed her surprise. She chuckled. "I'm guessing a man who makes his own meals around a campfire would enjoy a home-cooked meal." She wrapped the plate in a cloth and handed the bundle to Sybil.

Sybil and Mercy left the house. They paused at the corrals, where the gate had been repaired and the wild horses had settled down. They asked where they could find Brand, and Eddie directed them to the east. They crossed the yard, the grass beaten down and brown after a summer of wear. What must it be like for Brand to eat and sleep outside as the nights grew colder? Sybil wondered. Any cowboy, not just him.

"You be sure and have a good look at him this time," Mercy said as they climbed the hill and made their way through some trees.

Sybil didn't need to give him a good look. She'd already done that and it had caused her heart to quiver. Instead, she concentrated on their surroundings. Dark pines stood like silent sentries. The golden leaves of the aspens swung to and fro, catching the sunlight in flashing brightness.

A dog growled and Mercy grabbed her arm.

"I don't fancy being torn up by a cross dog," Sybil whispered. "Maybe we should go back."

Mercy looked at the plate of food, then back down the trail.

Maybe she was doing the same as Sybil…measuring how fast they could run and considering if an angry dog would stop for the food if she dropped the plate.

"I know you're there. Come out and make yourself known," Brand called out.

Her fingers clutching the plate so hard the china would certainly crack at any moment, Sybil ventured forward. "I'll throw the food at the dog if I have to," she murmured to Mercy.

"Good idea."

They stepped into a clearing. Wood smoke shimmered in the air. The smell pinched her nose.

A dog lunged toward them. Quite the ugliest dog she'd ever seen. Dirty brown with snapping black eyes and bared yellowed teeth. Not a big animal, but still a threat to life and limb. Only Brand's hand at the animal's neck restrained him.

Sybil squeaked. At the same time, she considered what sort of man kept such a dog.

"Quiet, Dawg," Brand murmured, his voice so deep it seemed to echo the canine's growl. The animal settled into watchfulness that did nothing to ease Sybil's mind.

She swallowed hard and shifted her attention to the man. His cowboy hat was pulled low so all she saw of his face was a strong jaw and expressionless mouth.

She turned. "Come on, Mercy. No one is going to bite." She faced Brand again. "I assume I am correct in saying that." She indicated his dog, though maybe she meant more. Not that she expected Brand to bite, but he certainly filled the air with danger.

Or maybe it was her own heart calling out the silent warning.

"He won't bother you unless he thinks you're threatening me."

The dog settled back on his haunches and watched them.

Mercy laughed nervously. "And how could we do that? We're two unarmed women." She stepped closer, hesitated when Dawg growled louder, and turned her attention to the animal. "Nice doggie. I won't hurt you." She put out a hand to touch the ugly dog. It lunged with a growl.

Mercy jerked back and Sybil almost dropped the plate of food.

Brand's large hand gripped the dog by the ruff. "Stay!" He gave a tug and the dog settled.

Sybil's heartbeat hammered erratically.

"Why do you keep such a cross creature?" Mercy asked.

Brand looked at Sybil as he answered, though she could not see his eyes beneath the brim of his hat. "He's my kind of friend."

Again Mercy laughed. "I wonder what that says about you."

Sybil thought the same thing. Judging by his quick, selfless actions that day, Brand deserved better company than a cross dog. But considering how he'd declined Linette's dinner invitation, maybe he preferred it that way. That would make an interesting twist to her story.

"Read it any way you want."

Sybil narrowed her eyes and watched his face for clues.

He met her gaze. Something flickered in his eyes. An emotion she couldn't name. Perhaps he gave consideration to his chosen solitary state.

Having held a woman in his arms so recently, he longed—

No. That wasn't what she'd write.

His isolation had been momentarily disturbed by his quick actions in saving a young woman, but he quickly reverted to his usual state. He and his dog...

Her thoughts abandoned her as she tried to free herself from his gaze. The way he hid behind his hat, the set of his jaw, even eating at a campfire when he'd been invited to share a meal said he either welcomed loneliness or it had been imposed upon him for some reason. She studied him as if she might be able to discern which it was.

He dipped his head.

She drew in a sharp breath. She'd been staring. But only because she wondered about the reason for his self-imposed solitary state.

She realized she still held the plate of food. "We brought you supper. Linette decided if you wouldn't come to the house for a meal, she'd send you one."

After a moment's consideration of the offer, he nodded toward a stump. "Leave it there."

Despite his dismissive words, his solitary state called out to Sybil. She stepped past the dog to put the plate on the stump he indicated. "Do you mind if we visit a few minutes?" Would she be able to discover the reason for his loneliness? Or perhaps something about his background?

"Suit yourself. Have a seat. Lots of grass to choose

from, or pull up a log." A smile flitted across his face so fast she almost missed it.

Sybil's curiosity about the man grew. She sank to the ground. Mercy sat a few feet away, her gaze never leaving the dog.

Sybil smiled. At least her friend wouldn't be taking an inventory of Brand's looks and itemizing them for her later.

He snatched off his hat as if recalling his manners.

She stared, darted her gaze away. Against her better judgment, she brought it slowly back. Mercy was right. He was a fine-looking man, dark and mysterious. Black curly hair that was over long, deep brown eyes, a slightly crooked nose…

He met her look for a second. She saw a soul-deep sorrow that sucked at her resolve, diluted it and poured it out on the ground. She sought for reason. Perhaps she was taking her study of him too seriously…imagining how lonely it must be for him. But then, she wasn't him, so how would she know until she asked?

Before she could glance away, he shifted his attention to his dog, which was lying at his side, watching Mercy.

Sybil almost laughed aloud at the way her friend and the canine eyed each other. She'd never before seen this side of Mercy, who was usually adventuresome to the point of recklessness. At least that's how Sybil saw it, although she'd be the first to admit she was conservative in the extreme by comparison.

Still unsettled by what she'd seen in Brand's eyes, she shifted her attention back to him, wondering if she'd imagined it.

He stared at something on the ground at his feet.

She looked toward the same spot. All she saw were blades of grass.

"They say you never get bucked off a horse. Is that right?" The question had sprung from her mouth unbidden…but not unwelcome.

He chuckled, cut it off abruptly. Was he not comfortable laughing? "I guess you could say that practice makes perfect."

She smiled at how his answer said so much with so few words. "So you took a lot of spills before you got good at it?" Dawg stopped having a staring contest with Mercy and inched toward Sybil, his head between his paws. Poor thing meant no harm. He was likely as lonesome as his owner.

There you go again. Jumping to conclusions. You have no way of knowing if he's lonely or just likes to be alone.

That was part of what she hoped to discover.

"I got tossed off many times."

Remembering how she'd held her breath as he rode a bucking horse, and wondering how he could stand it, Sybil shuddered. Getting tossed off sounded even worse than riding. "Did you ever get hurt?"

Mercy leaned closer, earning her a growl from Dawg. She edged back. "It must be so exciting. I think I'll give it a try."

Sybil gasped. "Mercy, you can't be serious." She fixed a demanding, pleading look on Brand. "Tell her she could get hurt. Tell her it's foolish to think of riding a wild horse." Why did Mercy think she must do something crazy and reckless all the time?

Brand choked slightly, as if keeping back another chuckle. "Ma'am, she's right. It takes a lot of practice and lots of good fortune to survive some of the wild horses. Sure would hate to see your neck all busted up."

Mercy grinned widely. "Still, I just might see how I fare."

"Have you ever been hurt?" The words squeaked from Sybil's throat. A man with a dangerous job. Likely that explained why he was alone. A woman or a friend would face the constant risk of seeing him hurt or killed by one of those angry horses. How many women would accept that kind of life? She certainly wouldn't. She'd marry at some point, because she wanted a home and family, but she'd want security and safety when she did.

And she didn't intend to involve what was left of her heart. Colin had made her see the folly of that.

Brand answered her question. "Nothing serious, seeing as I'm still here and still riding horses."

"But you have been injured?" *Sybil, you don't need to know the particulars to see that this man should wear a big danger sign around his neck.*

Details for her story. That was the only reason she wanted to know.

"A time or two. Once when I was ten."

"Ten! You were hardly out of short pants."

"Ma'am. I never wore short pants. And it was my older brother who thought it was a lark to throw me on a horse he was trying to break. I stuck until the ornery critter stopped bucking."

Another chuckle that he made no attempt to hide. Interesting observation. It would make a nice addition to her story.

A loner of a man with a deep-throated laugh that broke out unexpectedly from time to time, surprising the cowboy as much as it did those who heard it.

"I felt so high and mighty about riding a horse my brother couldn't that I climbed to the loft and jumped out the open door."

Mercy laughed as if it was the funniest thing ever.

Sybil gasped. "Why on earth would you do that?"

"I was ten. I didn't need a reason. But I guess I thought riding a wild horse made me invincible."

Sybil laughed softly. "Let me guess. That's when you were injured."

"My brother broke my fall, but I still busted my arm." He held it out and had a good look at it.

Mercy leaned back on her hands, her gaze darting frequently to Dawg.

Sybil's mind raced with questions. How many could she ask before he refused to answer? "What happens when you get bucked off?"

"If I did get bucked off—" he made it sound like a far-fetched possibility "—I'd just get right back on and finish the job."

His answer pleased her. She liked the idea of a man finishing what he'd begun. Except, she reminded herself firmly, in this case, it meant he would break horses and move on. That's the job he'd begun.

Not that she cared one way or the other.

You're not telling yourself the truth here, Sybil.

Oh, hush. Her inner voice could be so annoying at times.

Annoyingly right, maybe? Because you wish that he'd stay around.

I do not. How could I wish for anything so foolish? A dangerous man. A leaving man. I'm paying attention only because he saved my life and I want to write a good story.

You're hiding from the truth.

Sybil wasn't interested in whatever so-called truth that annoying inner voice meant.

Chapter Three

Brand had almost forgotten about breaking his arm. But only because he hadn't seen Cyrus in a long time. Cyrus never missed a chance to remind him that he likely owed his life to his big brother, and as a result, his big brother deserved a few favors in return. Trouble was, Brand wasn't prepared to dish out the sort of favors Cyrus had in mind. A sour taste filled his mouth. Because of Cyrus and Pa, Brand could never hope for anything but a nomadic lifestyle.

"Have you ever been hurt riding a horse?" Sybil asked, her voice a melody of calm and sweetness…a marked contrast to his thoughts and the raw sounds he normally heard on a ranch. Her gaze riveted him like velvet nails, compelling him to answer.

"A few bumps and bruises. Nothing to take note of."

Dawg wriggled closer to Sybil. Well, if that didn't beat all. Brand couldn't remember when the animal had shown the least sign of interest in another human being. Dawg could spot a sly fox a mile away. Brand could only assume he could equally well spot a sweet, innocent, woodland miss. Maybe this woman warranted further interest. It wasn't like he would be around long enough to put her in danger. He eyed the plate of food. It would have to wait until the ladies left. If he dug in now, they might see it as time to leave.

"I was about to have coffee. Care to join me?" He had only two cups, but he would drink from a tin can. He filled the cups and passed one to each of the ladies.

Sybil's blue eyes held his.

He couldn't remember how to fill his lungs.

Mercy leaned forward, her expression eager. "You must have seen most of North America."

The question, posed as a comment, broke his momentary lapse and he settled back with his coffee. "Been around some."

"Have you been to the Pacific Ocean?"

"Nope. Never had no mind to see it."

She sighed. "I'd love to see it."

Sybil made a scolding noise. "Mercy is restless. Always looking for the next big adventure."

"Uh-huh." He had little interest in the excitement-craving woman. He picked up a piece of kindling and kept his attention on the rough edges of the wood. "And what are you looking for?" He meant the question for Sybil.

It was only conversation. Words to pass the time. But he raised his eyes enough to watch her from under the protection of his lashes.

Her own eyes darkened to the color of the evening sky and her lips pressed together. A very telling gesture. She wanted something she couldn't have. A man, perhaps? But what foolish man would refuse such a woman anything, including his heart and love? Unless he had the kind of life Brand did. One that didn't allow him to give heart and love to anyone. Sometimes he wondered why God had made him a Duggan. Or more correctly, given him a pa and brother like the ones he had. Seems God could have arranged things just a little better.

"I'm quite happy with my life as it is," she answered after a beat of silence.

She might think it true, but he didn't believe her.

Mercy made an exasperated sound. "Someday, Sybil Bannerman, you'll discover your life is far too safe." She fixed Brand with a daring look. "Sybil lives a very careful life. Never takes risks. Obeys all the rules."

He thought of how his pa and brother lived a lawless life. "Rules have their purpose."

"Thank you." Sybil favored him with a beaming smile. "That's what I'm always telling Mercy."

"Okay. Okay." Mercy tossed her hands in the air. "I agree to a point. But rules should not become chains. There are certain risks and adventures that don't follow rules. It's a crying shame to avoid them."

Brand stared into the fire.

He was a risk. Miss Sybil would do well to avoid him and remember the safety of her rules.

"How much longer will you be here?" Sybil asked, and his heart took off like one of those stampeding horses.

He managed to slow it some. It wasn't as if she asked because she wanted him to stay, he told himself. She was only making polite conversation.

"I'll likely finish up tomorrow, then me and Dawg will move on."

"I enjoyed watching you work today," she said. Did he see admiration in her eyes? And why did it matter? He'd move on before she learned his true identity.

Heaven forbid she'd learn it before he left and he'd see the shock and horror in her eyes. Best to change the subject.

"So how long have you ladies been in the country?"

Mercy nudged Sybil and answered his question. "A couple of months. Three of us ventured over. Jayne, the other girl, is Eddie's sister."

"So you've come to visit western Canada? Then you'll go back to your English home?" Unless they had an eye to marriage out here and with the shortage of young women in the country, they wouldn't have any trouble fulfilling such plans.

"Yes," Sybil said.

"No." Mercy shook her head. "Sybil, why would you want to go back? You have nothing left back there." She turned to Brand. "Her parents are dead. She has no other family."

He wanted to stuff a handful of grass in Mercy's mouth at the way her words sent shock waves through her friend's blue eyes.

Sybil tipped up her chin. "It's my home and I have Cousin Celia."

Mercy snorted and lifted a hand in what Brand took as exasperation. "You belong here as much as there. And here is a lot more fun."

Sybil studied her friend, her blue eyes troubled. "Your parents are expecting you to return."

Mercy shrugged. "I doubt they'll miss me."

Sybil shook her head and turned back to Brand. "I'm sorry. We shouldn't argue in front of you. It's none of your concern." Dawg had sidled closer still and she stroked his head in an absentminded way that made Brand wonder if she knew she did it.

Brand expected Dawg to object, growl, move away, slink back to Brand's side. Instead, the dog closed his eyes and looked as content as a baby in a cradle.

Brand realized his mouth had fallen open, and he forced it closed. But his surprise made him stare. Dawg never let anyone but Brand touch him. Not until this moment.

Sybil drained her cup. "Thank you for the coffee and the nice visit. Now we must be on our way." She rose to her feet in a fluid movement that reminded Brand of a deer edging from the forest. "No doubt we'll see you again."

The words were said lightheartedly, but Brand felt the promise and threat of them. Did she want to return and visit? Did she hope he'd extend an invitation? But Sybil didn't meet his eyes, so he couldn't judge her thoughts.

When Mercy scrambled to her feet, Sybil caught her arm and they hurried away.

Dawg whined as they disappeared into the trees.

Brand patted the dog's head. "Never seen you get all sappy about a girl before. Just remember, we aren't staying, so don't get too interested in her."

Words Brand knew he should tattoo on his own brain.

He couldn't stay even if he was tempted. If Pa and Cyrus saw him with Sybil, they wouldn't hesitate to threaten her. Even if they didn't catch up to him, someone would surely remember the wanted poster they'd seen somewhere, and place him as a Duggan. And if she learned his name, she'd be shocked. She'd withdraw. And who could blame her? Might as well move on and save her the trouble of telling him to leave her alone.

People would judge a person as guilty by association.
He'd grown to accept that all he could hope for in
this life was to stay ahead of the Duggan gang and avoid
the hangman's noose.

Sybil's plans to go immediately to the corrals next
morning were cut short when Linette said, "Can you
show me how to finish the edges on the baby shawl?"

"Of course." As soon as breakfast was over and the
kitchen cleaned, they went to the big room overlooking the ranch.

An hour passed before Sybil could slip away. Mercy
had disappeared to some unknown destination, so she
was forced to go alone.

Not that she *was* alone. There were cowboys everywhere. Eddie had said they were adequate chaperones
anywhere on the ranch.

When she'd first looked out the windows, only two
cowboys had been watching Brand work, but now several more gathered round the pen, and another jogged
over in a rolling, awkward gait that said riding a horse
was more his style.

Sybil found a place along the fence next to a cowboy whose name she couldn't recall. "Is he as good as
everyone says?"

"A couple of years ago, I worked on a ranch down
in Montana." The man barely glanced at Sybil as he
talked, his attention fixed on the activities in the corral. "I heard stories about a dark, nameless man who
could break the rankest animal to be found. I wondered
at the time if it was a tall tale. One of those stories told
around the campfire for entertainment. But I'm beginning to think the story held a lot of truth."

A campfire legend. Sybil liked that and would certainly include it in her story.

Already she chose words to describe it to the readers.

A man with no name, but a reputation from which legends are born. A man whose strength of character made one instinctively trust him. Whose arms—

No. She would not say that his arms made one feel safe and secure. She wouldn't even let herself believe it. This man spelled danger to her fragile heart.

But he wasn't staying around, so she didn't have to be concerned. All she had to do was write the story.

She glanced about. Strange that all the hands seemed to have gathered at the corrals this morning. Or perhaps not. Brand would finish up before long and no doubt they all wanted one last glimpse of this legend.

"That's his last horse," one of the men murmured.

"Or so he thinks," replied another, with a soft chuckle accompanying his words.

Sybil's attention kicked into full alert. "What does that mean?" she asked the second man.

He gave a wicked grin. "We found another unbroken horse."

Several of the men snickered and nudged each other.

Something about the way they acted warned her they were up to no good. Her nerves twitched with a mixture of anticipation and concern.

Brand rode the horse he was on to a standstill, then spent several minutes riding the animal around the pen, teaching it to obey the reins and the instructions signaled by the rider's legs.

"That does it." He swung from the saddle and hung a rope over the nearest post. His eyes touched her, making her forget momentarily that they were surrounded by a horde of cowboys.

He shifted his gaze around the circle.

"Where can I find Eddie?" he asked.

Sybil glanced at the assembled crew. Odd that Eddie wasn't with them. Nor the foreman or any of the other cowboys she was familiar with.

Cal answered Brand. "Boss got called away to tend a bull."

"When he returns, tell him he can find me at my campsite." Brand headed for the gate.

"Hang on. There's one more horse to go."

Sybil felt the tension radiating from the cowboys. It trickled up her spine, caused her to curl her fingers until the nails bit into her palm.

Brand stopped, studied the circle of cowboys. "There wasn't another this morning."

Cal chortled. "We found this one 'specially for you."

Only because she watched so carefully did Sybil see the way Brand's shoulders tensed and his breathing paused for a second. Then he emptied his lungs in a slow sigh.

"Special for me, you say? Let me guess. This horse is meaner than a twister, ain't never been rode, and has been known to bite, kick and generally let people know he don't intend to be."

Cal's laugh seemed a little strained despite his obvious glee. "Let's see if you can live up to your reputation. Or are ya scared to get on this horse?"

Brand tipped his hat back and slowly shifted his gaze from cowboy to cowboy. Several of them squirmed.

Then his gaze fell on her. His eyes—the color of warm chocolate—filled with resignation and a loneliness he would no doubt deny, but she felt it clear through to the bottom of her heart. "You don't have to do this," she whispered.

Acknowledgment flickered through his eyes, though he couldn't have heard her. Something shifted in his demeanor. It was as if her inaudible words encouraged him, let him know that not everyone shared Cal's wish to see him tossed into the dust.

"Bring him on." Brand jerked his hat down low, widened his stance and waited.

Three men pulled on ropes to drag in a black horse with white-rimmed eyes. The animal snorted and kicked.

Sybil held her breath.

Again, she whispered, "You don't have to do this."

But Brand never noticed.

Every eye was on that wild stallion. Every man held his breath.

"Throw on a saddle if you can." Brand's voice dared them to fail.

It took an additional two men to get a saddle blanket on the horse and then the saddle. One of them came away limping after a kick from the angry animal.

"Hold him while I get seated." Brand spoke calmly, as if the only uncertainty was the ability of the struggling cowboys to do so.

Sybil's chest hurt from holding her breath as she watched him gingerly arrange himself in the saddle.

"Let him go."

The cowboys released their ropes and raced away, throwing themselves over the fence, then scrambling around to watch the show.

Sybil could not tear her gaze from the big man on

the horse. He sat poised and ready. At first the horse simply stood quivering, then it erupted into frenzied movement. It seemed to jerk every which way at the same time. She'd watched Brand buck out a number of horses over the past two days, but nothing like this. Hooves flying toward the sky. Back twisting two different directions at the same time. Head down. Snorting. Blowing. But Brand clung to the gyrating animal.

"He's good," said the cowboy on Sybil's right.

"He ain't done yet," Cal answered, disappointment in his tone.

Then the horse stopped. It stood there quivering.

A murmur of approval circled the crowd.

"He did it," Sybil said.

"Don't think so, not yet."

And then the animal turned and tried to bite its rider. As Brand kicked away from the teeth, the horse suddenly started to buck again.

Brand fought to stay in the saddle.

The horse ran for the fence, ramming him against the boards.

Several cowboys groaned. "That's got to hurt," said one. "Be a wonder if his leg ain't broke."

The horse stampeded along the fence, several times banging Brand's leg into the boards. It bucked. It snorted.

Still he stayed on board.

And Sybil's heart swelled with pride in the man's accomplishments. Brand was far more than a campfire legend. He was the real deal. He could ride. He was a man who stuck to his decisions.

Now, where did that last thought come from? She knew nothing of his actions outside this corral.

And the feel of his arms about you as he swept you off your feet.

Nonsense. It didn't mean that much. Just that he'd saved her life and now she felt a special bond, as if she mattered to him.

Huh. I wonder if he even remembers your name.

She silenced the inner voice.

The animal trying to toss Brand to the ground finally wearied and stopped bucking.

"I'd say his reputation is well earned," Sybil said, loudly enough for several of the cowboys to hear. This story would be the best one she'd ever written.

Never once did he reveal a hint of fear as he swung into the saddle. Those watching caught a collective breath and held it, wondering who would win this contest between man and beast.

Two men jumped forward and took the horse.

Brand slipped off, leaning against the fence.

The cowboys clapped and cheered as he limped away, none louder than Sybil. Without turning, Brand waved his hand in acknowledgment. "Tell the boss he knows where to find me." He made his way across the yard and into the trees toward his campsite.

Sybil watched him leave. He had been hurt, though he hid it admirably.

At that moment, Eddie rode into the midst of the men. "I didn't find any bull needing help."

"Must have been mistaken," Cal murmured.

Eddie glanced around the group, studied the horse now turned into the bigger corral. Several of the men tried to slip away unnoticed. "Wait up."

They ground to a halt.

"Anyone care to tell me what's going on?" Eddie

leaned over the saddle horn, looking casual and relaxed. But Sybil certainly wasn't fooled by his posture, and she guessed from the shuffling of booted feet that the cowboys weren't, either.

Slim sat on a horse at the boss's side and looked about ready to give them all a good chewing out.

Eddie's gaze settled on Cal. "You sent me on a wild-goose chase. I'd like to know why. And why is that stallion in the corrals? Haven't I told you all to leave him alone? He's a man killer."

Eddie's answer confirmed her suspicion that the cowboys were all involved in this potentially dangerous challenge. She glanced to where she'd last seen Brand. How badly had he been hurt?

Cal stepped forward. "We just wanted to see how good a rider he was. After all," he said, growing bold, "you can't just take his word for it."

Eddie studied Cal long enough that the younger man squirmed. "Did he ride the stallion?"

"To a standstill," one of the others answered, when Cal hesitated.

"Then he deserves his reputation."

A murmur of agreement came from the group.

Eddie continued to study Cal. "You can shovel manure for the next month. With no help."

Without another word, the boss reined away and rode to the big house.

Sybil hid a grin at the disgruntled look on Cal's face.

Not even a wicked man killer of a horse could unseat this big, bold bronc buster. The cowboy rode the rank horse to a standstill...

Her gaze found the path where Brand had disappeared. He'd done his best to hide his pain, but she knew he'd been hurt. Did anyone care?

Brand waited at the campfire for Eddie to appear with the money he'd earned. Then he'd be on his way.

He sucked in a deep blast of air and rubbed his leg. That mean sucker of a horse had had murder in mind. Seeing as he hadn't succeeded in bucking Brand off so he could trample him, he'd meant to try and knock him off. Had banged his leg good and hard against the fence. It hurt some, but it wasn't anything he couldn't live with.

He gingerly stretched out his leg and leaned back, smiling up at the brilliant sky. He kind of enjoyed the way Sybil had watched him and clapped when he rode the horse. He snorted and pulled his hat over his eyes. No point in looking at blue skies and dreaming of possibilities.

He could never be anything more than Brand, the bronc buster.

Enough staring into nothing. Time to get something to eat. From his meager supplies he chose a can of beans and opened it. Opened a second can for Dawg.

He downed the beans cold, chasing them with hot coffee.

His thoughts wandered again to a golden gal whose blue eyes smiled so gently at him he could almost believe she cared. But how could she? She knew nothing of him. Certainly not who he really was. A Duggan. Part of an outlaw family. Even if for some reason he stayed, he could never tell her, and lose the memory of that smile.

What would it be like to return home every day to a smiling welcome like that?

Brand Duggan would never know.

His leg pained him. It wasn't broken, but bruised enough to remind him with every move that a horse had almost got the better of him. But the pain paled in light of a deeper pain that never left. Oh, sure, he sometimes managed to ignore it, push it away, pretend it didn't exist, but all his efforts were but a thin scab that could be easily dislodged.

Something about Sybil had done more than dislodge it. Her gentle manner had scrapped away the protective layer, exposing the rawness beneath.

So many things contributed to the wound. Too many to count. Besides, what was the point?

He missed Ma. He missed conversations. Heart-to-heart talks. Teasing and laughing. He missed a warm bed and a hot meal at the end of the day. He missed having a home.

Home. The word reverberated through his head, his heart and his soul. A trumpet sound of despair that he couldn't deny.

Something Ma had often said to him sprang into his mind. *God will always be with us. Always guide us to a safe place. Always. We have to trust Him.*

He'd long ago dismissed the words. He didn't see how God being with them had made any difference. Pa always ended up finding them. Yes, Ma and Brand had always slipped away, hoping to find a place where no one knew who they were. At first, Ma had urged Brand along, helping him hide, taking care of finding a place for them. Then Brand had needed no more urging. He'd helped Ma carry their meager possessions. Had sometimes been the one to find them a safe place. He'd often been the first one to hear rumors of robberies, and know Pa and Cyrus were close by and it was time to move on.

Just as he must leave here to stay ahead of the Duggan gang. But what would happen if he stayed a few more days? Not with any idea of putting down roots. No. He knew better than that. Sooner or later, Pa and Cyrus would show up.

But a few hours. A few days. What could it hurt? He wouldn't do anything rash, like attempt to court Sybil, simply enjoy a moment of her company here and there. Shoot, he'd be content to watch her from a distance. Then he'd leave, with his heart full of memories to last him a lifetime.

Memories. Nothing but memories. The word screamed through his brain, tearing a wide, aching, oozing path.

"Isn't like I have any reason to stay," he muttered to Dawg, who replied with a yawn. "Don't see anyone throwing out the welcome mat."

Brand rubbed his aching leg. At least this pain would abate and he'd soon forget it. Unlike the emotional pain.

Dawg bolted to his feet, hackles up, growling.

"I hear it." Hoofbeats thudded. Someone approaching the camp. Brand's skin prickled as it always did when he knew someone watched him. His hand crept toward his gun belt and rested on the grip of his pistol. Had his identity been discovered? Did someone seek the five-hundred-dollar reward for the capture, dead or alive, of any of the Duggan gang?

Friend or foe. He'd give his last nickel to never again have to wonder which it was every time a stranger approached. At least he didn't have to worry about whether or not he could trust a friend. He hadn't allowed himself one in a very long time.

Eddie rode into sight and air eased from Brand's lungs.

He pushed to his feet. His leg protested the change in position, but he straightened it and waited as the rancher swung from his horse.

He'd get his wages and be on his way. And if his insides twisted at the thought, he wouldn't acknowledge it. Nope. He'd move on. Forget those he left.

This time would prove more challenging than simply waving goodbye to a bunch of cowboys who spoke no more words than necessary, and would forget him as quickly as he forgot them. This time he would turn his back on a pretty young lady who had momentarily— and not of her choosing—rested in his arms.

Eddie stood before him, a grin on his face. "Got some good news for you."

Brand nodded. Only good news he could think of was the Duggan gang had disappeared into Mexico. As if it would really make a difference.

"I ran into Sam Stone today."

"Uh-huh." Whoever Sam Stone was.

"He runs the OK Ranch to the north of us."

"Oh, yeah." Still didn't make any difference to Brand. "I finished breaking the horses. Some will need a bit more handling, but they're all fit to ride. So I'll be moving on."

"Wait until you hear what I have to offer."

He waited. As if he had any choice. Eddie seemed set to drag his news out as long as possible.

"Sam sold me a herd of wild horses. Said he didn't have time or a man to deal with them." The rancher rolled back on his heels, as pleased with his announcement as any man Brand had seen. "I want you to stay on and break them for me."

Brand's shoulders jerked up. His spine pressed against his skin. Stay? Wasn't it exactly what he'd wanted? A few more days of watching Sybil. Of storing up memories. His muscles tensed at the risks it involved.

How long had it been since he'd last seen Pa and Cyrus? Longer than usual. Come to think of it, he hadn't heard mention of the Duggan gang since he'd crossed the border into Canada.

A grin crept around his heart and eased toward his mouth. Could it be that the Duggan gang didn't care to meet up with the Mounties? No doubt they'd heard the tales of how tenacious the mounted police were. How they always got their man. The grin grabbed his mouth and Brand allowed his lips to curl just a little. Maybe he could be free of them if he stayed in Canada. Even as he allowed the hope, he knew he couldn't trust it. At least not for long.

"I could stay around a few more days, I guess." His casual words disguised his eagerness.

"You're welcome to bunk with the others and eat at the cookhouse. Cookie makes a fine meal."

"I don't doubt it." He'd breathed in the rich aromas every day from the cookhouse's open windows. "But Dawg here ain't very friendly."

Right on cue, Dawg snarled at Eddie.

"He sure isn't. I wouldn't tolerate him biting anyone at the ranch."

"Never known him to bite. Mostly he threatens." Brand must make sure Eddie didn't encourage anyone to challenge Dawg. "Figure he'd only bite if he thought someone meant to harm me."

The rancher nodded. "Good enough. I'll expect you in the morning then. You want your wages for what you've already done?"

"I'll pick them up when I'm finished." No need to get them now. When he was done he'd go to town and buy some supplies and a warm winter coat. He'd plumb wore out his last one and given it to Dawg to use for a bed. Dawg had chewed it to pieces and they'd left the remnants behind a few months ago.

Eddie mounted up and rode away. And Brand allowed the waiting smile to claim his mouth. "Well, don't that beat all?"

Dawg whined, studied him with head tilted to one side.

"It's only for a short time. Then we'll be gone." A few more days wouldn't compromise their safety or Sybil's, but no point in explaining that to Dawg.

Brand settled back on the ground and smiled up at the sky. Ma's words seeped into his soul. God had led him to a safe place. Though he understood it was only temporary.

His leg twitched and he rubbed it.

How long would this place be safe?

Not long enough.

Chapter Four

Sybil's heart bucked and twisted like one of those wild horses. As if Brand meant to tame her heart, too. She shook her head. How silly. She lived a careful life that didn't need any taming. Brand filled the qualifications of a larger-than-life cowboy for her story. That was all. But she failed to still the furious pounding of her heart at having just seen him ride a rank horse, stand up to the challenge of the cowboys, and walk away as if he felt no pain. She knew otherwise and it concerned her. Would his pride and isolation cause him to neglect an injury?

She crossed to Jayne's house and knocked on the door.

"Did you see that?" she asked when Jayne called for her to enter.

"I've been busy making a shirt for Seth." Her friend held up the brown fabric. "It's proving a bit of a challenge." She let the cloth fall to her lap, and turned her attention to Sybil. "What's going on?"

"Brand rode a horse Eddie had forbidden any of them to ride." She filled in the details.

Jayne's eyes widened in horror. "Was he injured?"

"He was limping."

"Don't you think someone should check on him and make sure he's okay?" She narrowed her eyes at Sybil.

"Me?" She wanted to know he was okay, but surely someone else could take care of that. Her boundaries already felt threatened. She pulled the gates to her heart closed so she would be safe.

"Seems to me you're the one who should. Mercy says he likes you."

Why would Jayne say such a thing? Had Mercy been dreaming up stuff again? Brand had certainly never given any indication that he even noticed her. Oh, he might have let his gaze linger a bit long on her while he'd considered riding that awful horse. Simply because she was the only one to offer any sympathy at the challenge thrown before him.

"His dog might like me," she finally said. She'd petted Dawg without any growling from the animal. "It's hardly the same thing." Sybil pretended a great interest in the view from the window as her cheeks burned with—

What? It wasn't embarrassment. She had done nothing for which she should be embarrassed, except grow overly curious about a man who did not belong in her world.

Which, she reasoned, made him a perfect candidate as the hero in her story. Just not the perfect man to fill her head with all sorts of unfamiliar feelings and a thirsty longing to experience firsthand the kind of strength she'd felt when he swept her out of harm's way. She knew a deep sense of emptiness when she watched him, when she thought of him.

Surely, only because she knew a man who allowed himself no last name must be very lonely.

But, she realized, in the awareness of his loneliness there was an answering echo of loneliness in her own heart.

Of course she was lonely. Her parents were gone. She had no family except elderly Aunt Celia, who cared not whether Sybil was there. Nor did she allow anyone to fill that hollowness.

Certainly Brand couldn't be allowed to intrude into that loneliness. Only God could, and she tried to focus her thoughts on Him alone. *He is my strength and shield. A present help in time of trouble.*

The empty feeling in her heart refused to abate.

But she didn't have to let her confusion get in the way of her common sense. Someone needed to make sure Brand was okay, and if she had to be that person, so be it. She turned to face her watching and waiting friend. "You're right. Someone should check on him. Not because Mercy thinks he might like me. She is always dreaming up mad notions. But because he is alone with no one to care." She'd go with gifts, so she wouldn't wound his pride if he thought revealing an injury was a sign of weakness. "I'll beg some cinnamon buns from Cookie and take Grady with me."

"That's the spirit. Show some spunk. Take life by the horns and hang on. Just like Brand on that horse."

Sybil chuckled even as the words slapped her on the side of the head. Wasn't that exactly what she'd been thinking only moments ago? Only it had been Brand taming her heart. "I could never be like that. I don't want to be." Writing her stories was enough danger for her.

Jayne laughed. "Someday, my dear cautious friend, you will find some reason to step outside your careful boundaries."

Little did Jayne know how wobbly her boundaries were proving to be when she watched Brand and took mental notes. "Not me." She hurried across to the cookhouse and explained her request.

"I keep hearing tall tales about the man," Cookie said. "Wish he would come and visit me, but I understand he prefers his own company. He saved your life, though, and for that he has my gratitude." The big woman wrapped some fresh cinnamon rolls in a piece of brown store paper. "You tell him thanks from me and Bertie." Bertie, her husband, helped run the cookhouse.

Sybil took the buns and headed up the hill to the big house to ask Linette to let Grady accompany her.

Linette readily agreed and a few minutes later Sybil and the boy made their way toward the clearing.

Dawg's growl greeted them before they stepped from the trees.

Grady clutched Sybil's hand. "Mercy says he's got a mean dog."

"He won't hurt you." Though he certainly managed to keep most people at bay, she felt no threat from the dog.

Grady refused to take another step even when Dawg's growl became a whine of greeting.

"Come on in," Brand called.

Sybil struggled forward, her progress impeded by having to practically drag a reluctant Grady. Perhaps that was a sign she should stay away from Brand and his campsite. But now that she was here she couldn't retreat, even if she wanted to. Of course she didn't; she wanted to make sure he wasn't injured. She could do that without stepping across any invisible lines she'd drawn for herself.

She entered the clearing.

Brand lounged back on his saddlebags. He made no attempt to rise at her presence.

That alone caused concern. "Are you okay?" she asked.

"Just resting." He tried to hide it, but she heard the strain in his voice.

"Your leg must be injured."

"It's fine."

She studied him a moment, noting how the lines in his face had deepened. Why couldn't he admit he had pain? "I know you're not."

He shrugged. "It's not as if I jumped out of the loft door."

"I saw how the horse rammed you into the fence. I'm certain your leg has been bruised or worse."

"Only a bump. Nothing to be concerned about."

There seemed no point in arguing. "Grady came to say hi." She turned to the boy, who darted a look from Brand to Dawg and back again.

Sybil nudged him.

"Will your dog bite me?"

"I don't know. Let's ask him. Dawg, you gonna bite this boy?"

Dawg gave a wag of his crooked tail.

"Nope. But he's not exactly the friendly sort."

Grady carefully kept Sybil between them as Dawg wriggled closer. The nearer he got, the tighter Grady tucked himself into her other side, as if he hoped to disappear into the fabric of her skirts. She bent to pet the dog, but couldn't with her hands full, so held the brown-paper-wrapped gift out to Brand. "Cookie sent some cinnamon rolls. The best in the country. She says she regrets you never stopped in to see her."

Brand took the package. His long fingers grazed Sybil's knuckles, making her heart buck three times in quick succession.

He sniffed deeply of the aroma. "If they taste half as good as they smell…" He waved for his visitors to sit down.

Grady kept close to Sybil as they settled on a log.

The dog slunk closer to Sybil. She hesitated a second. Was Dawg as cross as Brand led everyone to believe? She had no wish to have her hand torn off. Then she saw the welcome in the animal's eyes and knew she was safe. She stroked the brown head, finding his fur surprisingly silky.

She felt Brand's gaze on her and met it. "He's a nice dog."

Brand's eyes filled with something she could only take as regret.

Did he mind that Dawg accepted her attention? She almost withdrew her hand, but couldn't deny either herself or the dog this comfort. "Eddie wasn't happy about the cowboys bringing in that wild horse."

Brand shrugged. "It happens a lot."

His words burned through her. Did he face this kind of challenge wherever he went? "Young Cal got put on manure shoveling for a month." She laughed softly. "He didn't look too happy about it."

"It's a smelly job."

"You ever had to do it?"

"Shoveled my share of the stuff."

"When? Where?"

"Here and there. Every cowboy has to do it."

She'd hoped for more explanation but he didn't offer any.

"What's the hardest job you've ever had?"

He stared into the distance. "Burying my ma."

Sybil's thoughts stalled as pain and regret clawed up her limbs. She'd expected him to talk about horses. Instead, he reminded her of her own loss and loneliness, and her chin sank forward. "I'm sorry. It's hard to be without parents."

He didn't answer.

She sucked in air to fill her tight lungs. Was he all alone? Did that explain why he drifted from place to place? Perhaps he sought for belonging. Family. Or home. "Brand, who are you?" The words sprang forth unbidden, but she ached to know.

He grunted and any welcome she might have imagined in his eyes disappeared into a stone-hard look. "Exactly what you see. A cowboy with a horse and a dog."

"But you must have a name besides Brand. You must be more than that."

His eyes grew harder, colder, if that was possible, and she shivered.

He might well have said, "Goodbye, this conversation is over."

She had enough for her story.

He was known only as Cowboy. He never did give a last name before he rode into the sunset. He didn't welcome any questions about his true identity. But he was the best bronc buster in the territory. A reputation well earned.

It began when he was ten…

But she wasn't satisfied.

He interrupted her thoughts. "You best get the boy back before his folks start looking for him."

She wanted to know what caused the pain she glimpsed before Brand pulled his hat lower. It wasn't from his leg, but a tenacious wound that she suspected went deep and needed tending.

A wound left to fester was dangerous.

She patted Dawg one last time and rose to her feet. "Goodbye. Perhaps we'll meet again."

She took Grady's hand, but faced Brand another moment. "Be sure and take care of your leg." Brand would have to find his own way of healing the deeper wound in his soul. "May God go with you and keep and protect you."

She and Grady left.

Brand would be gone in the morning. She'd never see him again. She wished she'd been able to get more information, but that did not explain the sense of loss she felt.

She had no explanation for that and forbade herself to dwell on it.

Sybil took her time returning to the ranch site. She didn't know whether to kick herself for being so direct with him, or put it down to an honest question that deserved an honest answer.

Grady ran ahead and joined his friend Billy near the foreman's house.

As Sybil passed the cookhouse, Mercy sprang to her side, causing her to jump and press her palm to her chest to calm her heart. "Where did you come from?"

Mercy tucked her hand around Sybil's arm. "Jayne

told me what happened and said you'd gone to check on Brand. How is he?"

As evasive as a turtle. But of course, Mercy meant his leg. "Said it hurt some but he'd live."

"You sound disappointed. Did you want to see him hurt?"

The words stung. "Of course not. But I had hoped he'd reveal a bit more about himself."

"Ahh. So it's all about your story?"

"Certainly. What else would it be?"

Mercy drew back and held her hands up. "I thought it might be about the man."

She *had* been thinking of the man, not the story. Not that she'd ever admit so to her friend.

"Did you get up the nerve to ask him questions?"

She had. But it wasn't nerve that prompted her question. Nor was it curiosity. She really wanted to know more about him. As a man. Best if Mercy didn't know that, however. "As soon as I asked him who he was he got all cold and distant."

Mercy grew thoughtful. "He must be running from something or maybe hiding something. Maybe he killed a man and is running from the law." She shrugged. "Or maybe he just doesn't like human company."

Sybil shrugged. "Who knows? And I guess it doesn't matter. He's leaving as soon as Eddie pays him. I'll write a story based on what I have, and that's the end of it."

"I'm sorry."

Sybil had no idea what her friend was sorry about and didn't intend to ask. No doubt Mercy would have more to say than she cared to hear.

* * *

Who are you? The question ricocheted around the inside of Brand's head.

The words that had pressed against his lips were not the words he could allow himself to utter. He was a man who longed for female company. Even more than that, for someone with whom he could share the ordinary events of his life…even his thoughts.

He shook his head at the crazy notion.

Brand stared at the cold fire. If he meant to stay here he should get some more supplies. But he didn't want to spend too much time in town. He could survive on cold beans. Had done so on more than one occasion, usually because he was trying to make time and not reveal his whereabouts with a fire.

He unwrapped Cookie's cinnamon buns and took a bite of one. It was really good. He ate all three of them.

He should have told Sybil who he was. Who he had to be. A Duggan on the run, hiding his name, hiding from his pa and brother, hiding who he really was on the inside. He couldn't change that fact. All he could do was accept it and be grateful he had been able to stay ahead of the gang.

Once Pa and Cyrus found him they became unstoppable.

How many times had Cyrus slammed him against a wall saying, "You been friends with those uppity people. Guess they must have money hidden in their house. Where is it?"

No matter how many times, or how hard Brand denied such knowledge, Cyrus would not accept it.

"Go back there and find out where they keep their

money. We'll be waiting and watching until you do," he would press his face close and growl.

"Cyrus, be nice to your brother," Pa would say. He said the right thing, but he didn't intend to let Brand go, any more than Cyrus did.

"I can't believe you're my brother." Brand had once spat the words at him.

Pa didn't intervene when Cyrus punched Brand in the gut.

Brand had learned to wrap rags around his horse's hooves and find his way out of town in midnight darkness.

The lonesome call of a coyote echoed across the dusky plains, breaking into his memories. Another call came from the opposite direction.

Brand shuffled about. Most days he enjoyed the way the coyotes called to each other, and the yip-yip-yi of their singing, but tonight the sound ached through his insides like an untreated sore, filled with painful loneliness.

Was it loneliness that had driven him to court May? He'd thought her so sweet, a real lady. He tried to recall her face, but saw only blue eyes. No, May's eyes had been brown, like her hair.

They'd met five years ago, when she came into the store where he was buying supplies, in one of the many towns he'd stayed in only long enough to keep ahead of Pa. Brand could barely recall the names of most. This one had been Lost River, Wyoming. She'd asked a few questions and got vague answers, just enough for her to guess he was alone and unsure of the future. She'd invited him to join her and her family for church and then dinner afterward, shared with her parents, a widowed aunt and a sullen younger brother. Following the meal, they'd played board games.

It was the best Sunday Brand had known since his mother died.

Sundays with May's family became a regular occurrence, as did Saturday afternoon outings. He and May spent time with her family. Sometimes they walked along the edge of town on their own.

He hadn't seen Pa and Cyrus since Ma's death, and let his guard down, thinking now Ma was gone they had no use for him.

Then he saw their names in a newspaper story. They'd robbed a bank, shot an innocent woman in the ensuing gunfight. A half-page poster accompanied the story. Duggan Gang Wanted. $500 Reward. Dead or Alive.

The ink had smudged, so it was impossible to see their likeness clearly, and no one looked at Brand with suspicion.

But he decided to tell May the truth. He planned the moment carefully. Saturday afternoon they walked to a secluded spot just out of town, where he could hope for privacy.

"That's my pa and brother," he said, knowing no other way to say it.

"Who?"

"The Duggan gang."

She'd laughed. "Don't be silly."

He laughed, too, though out of nervousness, not mirth. "I've never been part of the gang."

"Of course you haven't." She'd given him a playful push.

"How do you feel about being associated with a Duggan?" He waited, unable to pull in a satisfying breath. Then, overcome with a need to make her see it could be okay, he poured out a gush of words. "Ma and me always ran from them, but they've forgotten about me since my ma died. They'd never harm you. I wouldn't let them." He had no idea how he planned to protect her. In hindsight he knew he had deluded himself into believing they wouldn't come after him.

She'd stared at him, her eyes wide as she accepted the truth. "A Duggan. An outlaw gang."

"Not me. I've never robbed a soul." Surely she couldn't believe otherwise.

She backed away.

When he followed, she held up her hands. Her face twisted. "How dare you? What will happen if people associate my name with yours? A Duggan." She spat the word out as if it burned her tongue.

She flung about and returned to the road.

He went after her. "May, wait." He had to make her understand.

She kept walking. "Go away. I never want to see you again."

He ground to a halt. Again his life had been shattered by the Duggan name. It was a curse.

He'd returned to his job, but three days later knew he had to move on. As he saddled up, a bunch of rowdies rode into town. He'd glanced up in time to see Pa and Cyrus leading a half dozen hard-looking men.

They had come. They would always come. They would find him. Even in Canada. Brand had no doubt of it. And if he had a lick of sense he would leave now. Before they showed up. Before they put Sybil in danger. Before he had to face the same cold dismissal he'd seen in May's face.

Dawg lifted his head and growled.

Brand calmed him with a touch.

Hard voices murmured through the aspen. Hoofbeats thudded. Two horses, if he didn't miss his guess. Had the reward money brought someone to his camp? He reached for his pistol.

The sounds grew closer. He got a glimpse of two horses and riders through the leaves.

His fingers tensed on his gun. Dead or alive meant bounty hunters would just as soon shoot him as tie him up. Less trouble that way.

The trail turned. So did the riders. Not until he could no longer hear them did his grip on the gun relax.

His heartbeat slowed to normal.

How long could he stay without putting himself in danger? Worse, putting Sybil and the others in danger from the Duggan gang?

But he'd told Eddie he would break the horses, and he meant to keep his word, though it wasn't horses, Eddie or his honor that made him ignore his common sense.

It was the hope of seeing a golden-haired girl again that made him ignore all the reasons for leaving that normally proved enough to spur him on his way.

Dare he allow himself to hope Pa and Cyrus had forgotten about him?

He laughed at such high hopes.

Chapter Five

The next morning, Sybil made her customary notes in her journal, then tucked her writing pad and pencil into the deep pocket of her dress designed expressly to hide them, and left the house. She meant to walk a little distance from the buildings and find a quiet, secluded place to work on the story of the nameless cowboy. Only he wasn't exactly that. He was Brand.

But who else was he?

Her thoughts darted back and forth among the bits and pieces of information she'd gleaned. How much could she embellish to give the impression of strength and honor she sensed in him before her story grew more fanciful than actual?

So lost was she in her contemplations, she didn't realize a man worked with a horse in the corral until she reached the bunkhouse, where she had an unobstructed view.

Her feet stuttered to a stop, matching her stuttering heartbeat.

Was that Brand? She knew the answer even before the bucking horse brought him around to face her.

His head jerked back. Their gazes collided with such force she gasped and pressed both palms to her chest as if she could stop the frantic surging of her heart.

Why had he come back?

Her mind raced with a thousand possibilities, all of which ended in one question. Had he come back to tell her who he was?

The horse bucked again and Brand turned away.

She blinked back her surprise. She must move on before anyone wondered why she stood in the middle of the yard staring in Brand's direction.

Sybil hurried onward until she found a private spot and sat down, pressing her back to the sunlit poplar. She lifted the backs of her hands to her overheated cheeks and slowed her breathing to normal. Why did she feel such a peculiar leap in the depths of her heart at his return?

She shook away her stumbling confusion. Time to forget uncertainties and get to work. She pulled out her notebook and pencil and turned to the page where she had been arranging notes on Brand's story. "Who are you, Brand?" she wrote.

After thirty minutes or so all she'd put on the page besides that question were a series of doodles—circles that went round and round. Exactly how she felt as her thoughts returned again and again to the cowboy in the corrals. Why had he returned?

And why does it matter to you?

Only because I feel like it's an answer to a prayer if he changed his mind about being a nameless, root-less cowboy.

And why would that matter to you?

Annoying, persistent voice.

Because.

Yes?

She closed the notebook and put it in her pocket before she answered. Because it gives me a chance to learn more about him for my story.

Oh yes. The story. The one you haven't added a word to in half an hour of sitting here.

"I will." She silenced the inner voice by speaking aloud. "I just have to learn more about him."

She pushed herself to her feet and dusted off her skirts. She didn't know how long Brand would stay around, but she would find an excuse to visit him and talk to him and get the information she needed to flesh out her story.

Right then she returned to the house to help Linette with kitchen chores. The afternoon sped by as they made pickled beets and filled dozens of jars. The kitchen grew hot and steamy. Sybil's nose stung with the smell of vinegar.

Finally, the bottles of burgundy beets sat in neat rows on the cupboard shelves and Linette rubbed her hands together. "These will be so tasty during the winter months."

Sybil was about to excuse herself when her friend pulled out potatoes for the evening meal. She couldn't leave Linette to prepare supper on her own. They finished just as Eddie and Grady came in. Mercy followed, and they gathered around the big wooden table in the kitchen.

Sybil joined the others for the meal. Would Brand be gone by the time she got a chance to leave the house?

After supper there were dishes. Finally, she dried the last pot and hung the towels to dry. She looked around the kitchen. "I thought I'd go see if Brand is still breaking horses if you don't need me for anything more." She hoped her words sounded casual. As if it didn't matter one way or the other.

Mercy winked at Sybil. "I'll help Linette if she needs anything. You run along."

Sybil ignored her and waited for Linette's reply. "Yes, you run along." And if Linette grinned at Mercy as if they shared a secret, Sybil pretended not to notice.

As she left the house, her gaze went immediately to the corrals. No bucking horses. Was he done, and gone already? She hurried, but not enough to make anyone think she was desperate.

Brand was still there, talking to Buster, the youngest cowboy on the ranch.

Sybil moved to the fence.

"Mister," Buster said, "you know a lot about horses. Maybe you can help me with mine."

"Certainly will if I can." His words were gentle, his tone kind.

Just as she thought—a good man. A good man on the run? She shook her head. She moved closer to catch every word. Listening to this conversation might provide valuable information for her story.

"What seems to be the problem?" Brand asked the young man.

"He always backs away when I try and mount him." Buster hung his head. "Makes me look stupid in front of the others."

Brand clapped a hand to the younger man's shoulder. "Anything else?"

Sybil's throat tightened at the comfort that gesture offered. She'd certainly include that detail.

Although a loner, perhaps an outcast—she liked the word for her story, but cringed at using it to describe Brand—*the cowboy never turned his back on those who were weaker, younger, more vulnerable. Whatever had sent him on this lonesome journey, it hadn't destroyed the cowboy's compassion for others.*

Buster pushed his shoulders back at Brand's touch, then continued. "Yeah. When I try and lead him anywhere, he walks too fast, as if he's gonna run over me. Sometimes I get a little nervous."

"Sounds to me like he's trying to find out if you're the boss or not. Bring your horse here and I'll show you what to do."

Buster trotted into the barn and led out a shaggy-haired horse that indeed seemed to be pushing him rather than following.

Brand took the rope from Buster. "You can teach him to follow you by doing this."

He swung the rope in a circle in front of him as he led the horse about. Every time the animal tried to get by him, it encountered the twirling rope.

Sybil stared, mesmerized by the ease with which Brand swung the rope in a lazy loop…the poetry of motion in his limbs.

"Here, you try it." He handed the rope to Buster and let the young cowboy lead the horse.

Brand looked in Sybil's direction, his gaze direct, unblinking.

She'd wondered if he knew she watched, and now wondered if he liked having her there or—she swallowed hard—if he wished she'd leave him be.

Well, that wasn't going to happen. She had a story to write. She girded up her heart with that excuse.

Buster led his horse around the pen and soon the animal decided it was safer behind him than facing the swinging rope.

Brand slowly took his attention from Sybil and she sucked in air to relieve her starving lungs.

"Let's see you get on."

Buster saddled his horse, but when he tried to mount it backed away just as he'd said.

Brand nodded. "Let's try making it so he doesn't want to do that. Grab under his chin and make him back up. When he gets to the fence, bring him forward and do it again. Soon enough he'll decide it's easier to let you get up than to be pushed around."

As Buster followed those instructions, Brand sauntered toward Sybil. He leaned against the fence not four feet away from her.

She took it as invitation to talk. "I was surprised to find you here today."

"Eddie bought some more horses."

"I see." She scratched at a splinter on the fence and pretended her throat hadn't tightened. He'd mentioned only the horses. Of course she wasn't surprised, and certainly not disappointed.

"Look," Buster called. "He didn't back up." The young cowboy sat in his saddle, as pleased as could be. Then he jumped off and led his horse toward Brand. "Mister, you're pretty good with horses. How'd you learn that?"

The question brought Sybil's thoughts back to her purpose for being there—to get information. She watched Brand. He continued to lounge casually against the fence. Only a tightening around his eyes indicated the question struck a nerve.

"My pa was good with horses."

She caught the past tense of the question. "So your pa is dead?"

He hesitated a beat. Two. "Not that I know of."

"That's good." Buster's sad tone was a contrast to his positive words.

Sybil shifted her attention to the young man. "Buster, how old are you?"

"Sixteen, ma'am. Or I will be pretty soon."

He was barely more than a child. "Where are your parents? Why aren't you with them?"

He looked beyond her into the distance. "I left them on a farm in the Dakotas."

"You seem young to be on your own. Why did you leave?"

"They were dead, ma'am. All of them. My ma and pa and two sisters." The words were barely audible, though Sybil caught no hint of self-pity. And he certainly had every right to feel such.

Her heart twisted with knowing how alone he must feel. "I'm so sorry." She looked at Brand. His eyes darkened. His jaw muscles twitched. Compassion filled his gaze. Surely if he chose to be a recluse it wasn't because he hated people. Or even because his dog came first.

What was his secret?

She couldn't believe he was a wanted criminal, as Mercy had suggested. He simply didn't seem the type.

What do you know about the type? Have you ever met any wanted criminals?

No, but surely their hearts would be cruel.

You think him helping Buster means he's got a good heart?

Yes, of course it does. Besides, I've other evidence, such as his friendship with a dog and how he rescued me.

Aha. That kind of makes you see him with stars in your eyes, doesn't it?

Not with stars, but with certainty.

You're certain to have your heart dashed to pieces if you think it meant anything more than a man in the right place at the right time.

And willing to do the right thing. That makes him noble, if nothing else.

But are you ready to risk your heart on that?

No. She would be detached. A gatherer of information. Nothing more. She'd discover who he was. Criminal or otherwise.

Everything he did revealed an honorable heart. Those around him wondered how such a decent man had ended up being such a loner. It wasn't because he had no family. Although his mother's death had ripped away a portion of his heart, he talked affectionately of playing with an older brother, and pride filled his deep voice when he told how his father had taught him about breaking horses.

"You're doing just fine," he said to Buster, and the boy lifted his head and smiled.

"Good evening, ma'am." Buster led his horse away, swinging the rope to keep the animal behind him. Proud and sure of himself now, thanks to Brand's kindness.

Again the question raced through Sybil's mind. Who was this man?

"Did you have supper yet?" Seems he might have eaten with the others at the cookhouse.

"No, ma'am," he said, imitating Buster's formal politeness. "Me and Dawg were about to go to camp and make our supper."

"Why don't I bring you a plate of food instead? Unless you prefer your own cooking."

His laugh sent ripples of joy through her veins.

"About all I got in my pantry is beans."

"Fine. I'll be along shortly with a plate of food." She paused. Maybe she'd misunderstood. "Unless you plan to ask Cookie for a late meal."

"No, ma'am. No such plans." He watched her from under the brim of his cowboy hat.

She tried to read his expression. He revealed nothing. "You could come with me and eat in the kitchen."

He lifted his head. His face remained expressionless. His eyes darted past her to the big house, then to the woods, and finally to her. She saw a world of sorrow and regret that jarred her. Was this the look of a man who had committed a dreadful crime?

No, she couldn't believe it. Any more than she could explain the ache clenching her heart, squeezing out sorrowful tears. She gave herself a mental shake. All this talk about parents had simply reminded her of her loss.

And loneliness.

You have no reason to make so many assumptions. Sorrow, guilt or innocence all based on the way his eyes darted about and grew dark. The way he and Buster make you think of your parents.

No reason, she argued, but the witness of my heart to his. I know sorrow when I see it. I recognize it as different than guilt.

Then he blinked. "Me and Dawg will go to our camp, if it's all the same to you." He whistled for the dog, which rose from the shadows of the barn and trotted after his owner.

"I'll bring you a meal," she called.

He didn't turn, but it sounded as if he said, "Suit yourself."

God had given her a second chance with Brand and she didn't intend to waste it.

She dashed up the hill, her feet light. Just before the door, she drew to a halt. What chance did she mean— to learn more about Brand for her story or for her own sake?

Her story, she silently insisted. That's all that mattered.

That and keeping her heart safe. She knew all too well the sorrow of a leaving kind of man.

He should have told her he didn't want a meal brought to him, but he couldn't deny himself a visit from Sybil. He lifted his head as she stepped from the trees, bearing a covered plate, and thankfully saving him from having to analyze why he allowed himself to enjoy her company and ignore the warning of his gut.

Dawg bent his tail to one side—the closest thing to a wag Dawg ever managed.

"I hope there's enough food for you." She handed Brand the plate and removed the cloth.

He bent over and filled his nose with the aroma of hot beef and rich gravy. The mashed potatoes were a small mountain. "Reminds me of the meals my ma used to make." Now where had that come from? Except something more than the food reminded him of Ma. Sharing mealtime with a woman, listening to her talk, were sweet moments he'd tuck next to his heart to warm him throughout the long winter months.

"She sounds like a good woman."

"She was."

"Do you mean because she made good meals?"

He sensed Sybil's probing. It surprised him some to realize he didn't mind. It would be good to talk to someone besides Dawg for a change. Dawg might be a good enough friend but he wasn't much for carrying on a conversation. Brand would simply have to choose his words carefully and not reveal anything that would identify him as a Duggan.

"She was a good cook, all right. Sometimes there wasn't much in the pantry, but she always managed to find something and make me feel like I was privileged to have it. I guess I was. But she was so much more than that. Do you mind if I go ahead and eat?"

"By all means."

He took three bites and savored the flavors. The break gave him a chance to consider his words. "Ma never let life get her down. She used to say, 'God sends the rains that bring on the flowers.'" He fell silent. The words might sound silly to someone else.

"I like that. So your mother was a believer?"

"To her dying day." She would be disappointed to know Brand had let his faith lag.

"Are you also?"

"A believer? I am, but I don't think about it much anymore."

Sybil turned to consider him with probing blue eyes. The look went deep, knocking at closed doors, examining forbidden corners. "Why have you let it slide?"

He couldn't tell her, and shifted away from her intensity, directing his attention to the plate of food.

She turned, releasing him from her intense study, and he filled his lungs with relief.

"My parents were older when I was born," she said, her voice low as if she was lost in her memories. "They said I was a special gift from heaven, and treated me that way. They taught me my life was precious and I shouldn't waste it on foolishness." She let out a long sigh. "Mercy says I am controlled by rules, but I don't see it that way. I simply realize that life is full of dangers and risks, and yet we can do much to avoid them."

He watched her out of the corner of his eyes. She again seemed lost in thought. If she knew how much danger he posed to her and the others at the ranch, she would run back to the shelter of Eddie's home as fast as her legs would carry her. Likely she'd tell him about Brand, and Eddie would run him off the place.

Not that Brand would blame them. He already felt guilty at putting them in peril.

She nodded once as if she'd made up her mind about something. "I expected to have my parents around for a long time yet. They were only in their sixties when they died, within weeks of each other." She glanced at him, her eyes dark with sorrow. "A fever. I nursed them to the end."

Was she aware that a shiver ran up her body? "I guess it just goes to show we can't count on anyone staying around," she added.

His fingers knotted as he considered his actions, but he went ahead and pressed his hand to her forearm. "I'm sorry. It must have been very difficult."

She nodded again, slowly turning to look into his

face. Her eyes glistened with tears. "It was the hardest thing I've ever dealt with." One tear slipped from each eye. "So I understand when you say burying your mother was the hardest thing you've done."

If only he had the right to pull Sybil into his arms and comfort her. If only he could ever have the right. But being a Duggan made it impossible for eternity... a thought that scalded his insides.

She gave him a watery smile. "It's almost two years ago. You'd think I would be past the crying stage."

He lowered his hands to his knees and shifted his attention to Dawg. "Maybe there are things we should never get over." Like being a Duggan.

"Over and over my father and mother instructed me on the importance of obedience to God and living a wise life. I simply can't imagine leaving the faith of my parents." She blinked back her tears and squinted hard at him. "I can't envision what would cause anyone to neglect their faith. Was it something really awful? Was it because your mother died?"

He shifted his attention to Dawg again, unable to reply to her question because he didn't know the answer. It was a thousand little things and two major things—his brother and father. Finally, he shrugged. "Just happens, I guess."

"Then I shall pray it unhappens." She practically glowed, as if she imagined it had already occurred.

He allowed her words and her faith to warm him for two heartbeats before he gave himself a mental shake. What she thought or wanted or believed would not change the facts of his life.

He cleaned the plate and handed it back to her. "Thanks for the meal." He couldn't bring himself to tell her she'd best be going, but she must have sensed his unspoken words. Her expression flattened and she pushed herself to her feet.

"I'll be getting along." She paused to pat Dawg on the head. "Good night." She sucked back a gust of air and turned to face him. "Brand, I don't know who you are or what you're running from, but remember wherever you go, God goes with you. He loves you and protects you."

Before he could pull a word from his stunned brain, she was gone.

God loves and protects you.

Words Ma had said over and over. When had he quit believing them? He sat back and stared into the darkening sky. About the time Ma died. Or maybe when the Duggan gang—in the hopes of getting Brand to find out when the payroll was being delivered—had beat up a young man he had befriended.

Brand had learned two valuable lessons that day. Don't make friends and don't let Cyrus and Pa catch up to him.

So why was he still here?

Only a few more days and he would ride out as fast as his horse could go.

He hadn't prayed much in many years, but tonight he asked one favor of God. *Please don't let them find me while I'm here, where my presence could put Sybil in danger.*

Did God love him enough to hear the prayer?

Chapter Six

Sybil had gone to the corrals twice the following day, but Brand barely glanced her way. She told herself she wasn't disappointed. Of course he was busy. She knew that and appreciated his dedication to his job.

When he disappeared at suppertime, she prepared a plate of food again. At least he'd never refused to eat.

Yesterday she had learned wonderful things about him. He'd had a faithful Christian mother. The way he talked about her revealed a tender side. Something or someone had wounded that tender spot.

Sybil slowed her steps to savor the memory of the previous evening. She couldn't explain why she'd told him about losing her parents, but she didn't regret it. Not for a moment, because he'd touched her arm in comfort. His eyes had softened as she shed a few tears. She had almost expected him to pull her close and pat her back.

Maybe *expected* was too strong a word. She'd wished for it.

Now she could hardly wait to learn more about him.

He stood as she stepped into the clearing and handed him the plate.

"Go ahead and eat. You must be starving."

"I shouldn't be. I've eaten better the last few days than I have in months."

She waited until he sat and then chose a spot beside him, careful not to touch him lest he think her too bold.

"You worked hard today."

"Lots of horses to break," he said.

"Guess you're in a hurry to finish up and move on."

He seemed preoccupied with his food, but after a moment said, "It's what I do."

She didn't detect so much as a whiff of regret. Not that she was surprised. She'd known from the start he meant to leave. She expected it. People left. One way or another. Suzette by death. Colin by choice. Afterward Sybil could only do her best to put the pieces of her heart back together. It had never quite been whole again, so she hardened the fences around her heart now, not intending to let anyone hurt her.

"My parents weren't the only ones I lost." She didn't mean to talk about it, but the words escaped and once started, she couldn't stop. "I had a dear friend, Suzette. I knew her from as early as I can remember. We were so close." Sybil held up two fingers pressed together to indicate what she meant. Her breath jerked out and in again before she continued. "We liked to play in the bushes, making playrooms in little spaces beneath the branches." She tipped her head back as sweet memories filled her thoughts. "We had all sorts of babies. Real dolls but also pretend babies we made out of knots of wood." A tiny laugh escaped her lips. "The gardener made a swing for us at the bottom of the yard. My, we spent many happy hours on that swing. The seat was wide enough that we could sit side by side and swing together."

"Sounds nice."

She had stopped talking as she recalled the warmth and joy of those days. "It was real nice, but it ended so fast. I wish I could have stopped time before that dreadful day."

He waited, not rushing her to tell what had happened, as if he understood she could hardly bring herself to say the words.

"One day she didn't come to play as usual and Mother took me to my room. She pulled me down beside her and held me close as she told me Suzette had drowned while on an outing with her family." Sybil shook her head. "To this day I can hardly believe it."

Brand squeezed her hand gently.

She held on for dear life.

"How old was she?"

"We were both twelve."

His hand clasped hers, warm, solid, reassuring. "So young. I'm sorry for your loss."

The tension in her body slowly dissolved. "I haven't let myself think of her or talk about her since she died."

"Aren't you robbing yourself of happy memories by doing that?"

Sybil turned to look into his face.

His eyes were filled with warmth. "It seems a shame to throw out the good with the sad."

She looked deep into them, finding nothing but kindness. Something inside her shifted…a sense of being released. She sat back, stared at Dawg lying at her feet. A truth hit. "All this time I was so afraid of the pain I felt at her loss that I've buried my memories." A smile filled her heart. "I miss her terribly and always will, but my childhood was rich because of Suzette. She was full of life." Sybil told him many stories of two little girls with vivid imaginations. The games they'd played and adventures they'd had without leaving home.

Brand didn't say much, but she didn't need a lot of encouragement to continue.

Dawg stretched, turned around and settled at Sybil's feet.

She grew quiet. She'd talked for so long. How could she be so selfish and thoughtless? She'd never learn anything about him if she did all the talking. And she still held his hand, as if her life depended on it. She slipped it to her lap. "I'm sorry. I've talked about me this whole time."

"I don't mind. I'm sure your life is more interesting than mine."

"What makes you say that?"

"You lived a privileged life with all sorts of advantages."

She turned to look at him. "You make that sound like it somehow makes me different."

"It is different than my upbringing." His eyes were curtained, letting her see nothing of what he thought. "It allowed you to cross the ocean in the company of other fine women."

"Humph. Since my parents' death I've been living with my elderly aunt Celia. She's old and set in her ways. She doesn't like the curtains opened, so I spent last winter in gloom." Sybil jerked about to see his reaction. "Do you think that was a joy and privilege?"

His grin was lopsided. "Not when you put it that way."

"How did you spend last winter?" There were so many things she wanted to know about him.

"Holed up in a remote cabin on my own with Dawg."

"Sounds lonely. What did you do to pass the days?"

"I hunted game to feed us, chopped wood to keep us warm and twice ventured out to the nearest town for supplies. A man gets to crave coffee when he's been out of it for almost two weeks."

She laughed. "What I miss most about life in the West is having a grocer close enough to go every day. I could hardly believe it when I first came. But between the big gardens and generous storerooms, the ranch has its own grocer."

He joined her in laughing. "From the little I've seen this is one of the best run ranches in the territory."

"Eddie is determined it will be the best."

They sank into silence again.

"Tell me about your dog."

Brand chuckled, the sound filling her insides with pleasure at getting him to laugh. "Found him beside a trail a couple years back. Don't know if he was lost or forgotten, but his paws were raw from walking."

Dawg lifted his head and looked toward Brand as if knowing the man talked about him. His tail bent in one direction.

"I suppose he was glad to see you."

Brand laughed again. "You'd think he might be, but even then Dawg had a bad attitude. He tried to bite me."

Sybil wanted to know more. "What did you do?"

His eyebrows lifted in silent question.

"To befriend him," she added.

"Nothing. I just made camp and cooked a meal. Guess Dawg was hungry because he soon sidled toward me. Eventually he decided it was okay to be friends. Of a sort."

Sybil studied the dog. "He's not as ugly as I first judged him, but he certainly isn't a thing of beauty, either."

They sat in peaceful contentment for a moment. She'd learned much about him.

Cowboy understood how to approach wounded and frightened people and animals alike. He never pushed, never expected anything in return for the help he offered.

She realized the same patient technique that caused Dawg to judge Brand a safe friend had worked on Sybil, too. When had she ever talked so much about herself? About Suzette? But perhaps her openness would make it easier for him to speak honestly.

"Brand, tell me more about your mother."

"Why?"

She shrugged. "I heard pride and affection in your voice when you spoke of her."

"I was proud of her. Still am. She lived by high standards despite our circumstances. She did sewing to support us. I went to bed many nights with her sitting by the table, the lamp close as she sewed."

"And your pa?"

"Nothing to say about my pa."

Before she could ask the question on her lips, Brand added, "Or my brother."

She didn't press. She squeezed his hand gently and quickly withdrew before he could think her inappropriate. "I'm sorry. Whatever happened, it has hurt you deeply."

He neither acknowledged nor denied it.

She sought for something to bring back the peace she'd felt talking to him about Suzette, something to offer the same understanding he'd offered her.

"Nothing can separate us from God's love." She waited, hoping he would acknowledge her words. When he didn't, she added, "Unless we let it."

"I guess that's so."

"You make it sound like it doesn't matter. But it does."

"My ma would agree." He hung his hands over his knees and stared at them.

Sybil couldn't bring herself to say anything more for fear of adding to his dejection. Besides, it was time she returned to the house. She rose to her feet. Dawg stood, too, as if expecting to go with her. She patted him on the head, then brushed her hand across Brand's shoulder. "God is our refuge and strength, a very present help in trouble. Therefore will we not fear, though the earth be removed and though the mountains be carried into the midst of the sea." She hadn't meant to preach to him, but the words had come of their own accord. She would pray they would comfort him, whatever the cause of his discouragement.

Brand left his camp early the next day, and made his way toward the ranch. Why had Eddie bought so many wild horses? Could be he meant to sell them at a profit. But even putting in long hours, Brand wouldn't be able to leave for several more days.

A fact that should make him nervous, but failed to do so. And why shouldn't he enjoy a few days of visiting with Sybil? He'd succeeded in revealing nothing that put either of them at risk. She'd never know his pa and brother were wanted men.

Brand might not be a praying man, but his heart murmured one prayer over and over. *Please don't let Pa and Cyrus find me here. Let me get done and leave before that can happen.*

The tree before him made him think of Sybil's story of two little girls playing on a swing. It would be a perfect tree for a swing.

He reached the corrals and roped the first horse of the day. Of necessity, he must keep his mind on his task or end up facedown in the dirt. Ruining not only his clothes, but also his reputation as the bronc rider who never got thrown off. But he still found space in his thoughts to replay every word Sybil had spoken the night before. As the day progressed a plan evolved.

Partway through the morning, Sybil stepped to the fence and watched him. He nodded once in her direction, then forced himself to concentrate. Although he tried to ignore her, he knew the moment she stepped away. She and the other ladies went to the garden with baskets that they soon filled with vegetables. Then they returned to their various houses.

Only one other time did he see her, on the hill beside the ranch house, throwing out a bucket of water.

It was late afternoon when he turned loose the horse he'd finished working on. But rather than catch another, he went to the barn. With Eddie's permission, he cut a board the size he wanted and chose a length of rope, then made his way to the tree he'd noticed in the morning. In a few minutes, he had a swing hanging from a branch.

He returned to where he could see the ranch house,

and waited, hoping Sybil would come down to the corrals before suppertime. He halter broke a horse as he waited. Fifteen minutes later, she trotted down the hill.

He slipped the halter from the horse and turned it loose. This one time he would think about something besides work. Though he could never stop thinking about the Duggan gang. During the passing hours he'd convinced himself he would surely hear rumors of them long before they could reach this area of western Canada. Their reputation had a way of preceding them. He'd have time to ride away before they found him.

He was hanging the halter over a post to take care of later when he saw her approach the fence. "Howdy," he said.

"Hello." She glanced about the pen. "Are you done for the day?"

Did she sound surprised or pleased? It didn't matter. "I have something to show you."

Her eyes lit up, bright blue. "Really?"

"Yup." He vaulted over the fence. "Come and see." She kept close to his side as they crossed the yard. His grin grew to rival the sky for size.

"Where are we going?"

"You'll see." He slowed, smiled even wider when she matched his steps. How was he going to surprise her when she'd be able to see the swing as soon as they passed Seth's cabin? Only one way. Would she agree? "I need you to close your eyes."

"Why?"

"It's a surprise."

"All right." She closed her eyes.

He swallowed hard. She looked as if she waited for a kiss. Every nerve in his body sent up a red flare.

She was very kissable, but not by him. She was out of his class. She deserved better than he could ever offer her—a life on the run. Most importantly, if she discovered his identity, her eyes would snap open and fill with fear and loathing.

Nope. He'd sooner leave with memories kept sweet by hiding the truth.

"What direction am I to go?"

Her question brought him back to his purpose. "Straight ahead."

She took one step and stopped, her hands before her. "I might stumble."

He wiped his palms against his trousers and ignored the red flares of warning as he took her hand. "I'll show you the way. Trust me." His heart slammed against his ribs. Ironic assurance from a man hiding the truth.

But she rested her hand in his, following his lead without hesitation until they were within ten feet of the swing.

"Open your eyes."

She did, looking at him, her gaze so full of sweet expectation that something within him wrenched, a fierce sensation of both pleasure and pain.

He forced himself to break away from her look, and nodded toward the swing.

She looked and gasped. "Where did that come from?"

"I made it for you." He sounded too keen. "I thought of how you enjoyed swinging with Suzette, and thought you might still enjoy swinging even if your friend can't be with you." Did his explanation make him seem less eager? He didn't think so.

She clasped her hands to her chest and laughed. "A swing." Her eyes were awash with tears.

Had he made her cry? The thought slammed into him. "I thought you'd like it. I can take it down if you want."

She caught his hand. "No. It's perfect. I'm surprised and pleased that you would think to do this." She rose on tiptoe and kissed his chin. "Thank you."

Pink stained her cheeks and she rushed away to try out the swing.

Heat flooded up his neck and stung his ears. If he'd known she'd be this grateful, he might have thought twice about putting the swing up. Shoot. Who was he kidding? He didn't mind in the least. One more stolen memory. Based on hiding the truth.

What would she say if he told her he was a Duggan?

Would she laugh and say it didn't matter? Or would she look shocked and refuse to speak to him?

He couldn't risk it.

Sybil laughed, a sound of pure joy to rival the sweetest of the bird songs he often enjoyed on lonely evenings.

"I'd forgotten how much I like this." She swung back and forth. Each time she did, their gazes collided.

Every lonely night, every cold morning alone, every goodbye rolled and twisted at the bottom of his stomach. Each glance from her tempted the feelings upward, as if they wanted release. He fought them back. He fought his own longings and wishes. He almost lost when she tipped her head back and let her laughter roll out in time with the movement of the swing.

A soft laugh came from his lips. He leaned back on his heels and savored the moment. The memory of this evening would have to suffice for the rest of his life.

Thor, the fawn that hung around the place, trotted

toward him. Dawg growled, but at Brand's command backed away and sat down.

The fawn saw Sybil swinging and jumped away in playful surprise, then chased her back and forth.

Soon Sybil laughed so hard she had to stop swinging.

The sound of their play attracted Billy and Grady, the two young boys who spent time together.

"A swing," Grady said. "Who built it?"

"I did," Brand replied.

Billy looked him up and down. "I thought you broke horses."

Sybil chortled. "I guess a man can do more than one thing." The look she gave him slid right past his brain and oozed into his heart like warm syrup.

Billy nodded. "I guess so. We used to have a swing."

Sybil sobered. Her eyes dipped downward.

Brand tried to think why, but couldn't.

She got off the swing. "Do you boys want to have a turn?"

Grady hurried to get on.

For the next half hour, Brand and Sybil took turns pushing each boy on the swing, at the same time teaching them how to pump so they could make themselves go high.

As the boys grew more confident, Sybil and Brand sat nearby to watch.

"Did you wonder why Billy said he used to have a swing?" She told him how Billy and his brother and two sisters had been left orphaned. "Roper and Cassie found them and cared for them and later adopted them." The foreman and his wife lived in a new house on the Eden Valley Ranch.

"It's nice to know things work out well for some

children." Brand managed to keep his voice from showing any regret that he had not been so fortunate. But it
hadn't been so bad. He'd had a mother who cared for
him, prayed for him and protected him to the best of
her ability.

"Supper!" The call came from up the hill on one side
and within seconds echoed from Roper's house.

"Coming," the children called, and scampered away.

"I have to go, too." Sybil smiled at Brand. "You're
welcome to join us for a meal."

He hesitated a heartbeat, then shook his head. He
had already crossed too many of his boundaries. "I'll
be going."

Her smile lingered. "I can't thank you enough for
the swing. It will provide hours of pleasure not only
for me but for the others." She brushed her hand over
his arm. "Brand, you're a good man." Then she turned
and skipped toward the ranch house.

He stared after her, his heart swelling until it crowded
against his ribs. She'd said he was a good man. Then he
snorted. *Brand, it don't matter whether or not you're a
good man. You are a Duggan.*

Five hundred dollars. Dead or alive.

Sooner or later someone around here would see a
wanted poster. Then what?

Someone would come gunning for him. But worse,
far worse, he'd put Sybil in the way of danger simply
by allowing a friendship between them. Danger from
the Duggans. Danger from bounty hunters.

Would she believe him guilty?

Perhaps he would come right out and tell her who he
was. How would she react?

He slapped his forehead. It was bad enough that he

sat about expecting a woman to feed him. But now he'd crossed a line, thinking he could get away with admitting he was a Duggan. No one would believe him innocent, and just being associated with him put Sybil at risk. Cyrus wouldn't hesitate to harass or threaten her simply to get at Brand.

He knew what he must do. He returned to his campsite, saddled his horse, threw his saddlebags on the back and swung up. "Come on, Dawg." He clamped his teeth together so hard his whole head hurt. But a man must do what a man must do.

This time he didn't leave solely to protect himself from the noose. He left to protect Sybil from the Duggan gang.

Chapter Seven

Sybil did her best to hide her pleasure throughout the meal. If she gave it free rein she would smile from ear to ear and doubtless bring probing questions from her friends.

She stilled her impatience as they lingered over the meal and then did dishes at what seemed a leisurely pace.

All the while, her heart danced. Brand had made a swing for her. A sweet gesture that healed a deep fracture in her heart. As he'd said, she had been robbing herself of sweet memories because of the sadness when they came to an end. Every time she sat on the swing she would remember the joy of her friendship with Suzette.

And something more—a growing friendship with Brand.

What about your vow to never get close to someone again?

I haven't forgotten.

Seems you might be getting a little too fond of a certain cowboy. Have you forgotten Colin?

Of course not. I don't plan to be hurt again.

But she couldn't stop the smile that wrapped around her heart.

"I'll take a plate of food to Brand if you like," she told Linette, keeping her voice flat, as if it didn't matter if someone else took it.

"I do wish that man would either join us or go to the cookhouse," Linette said. "It bothers me to think of him spending every meal by himself."

Mercy snorted. "He's had company every evening since he got here. Sybil sees to that."

Sybil couldn't take offense at her friend's comment, because it was true. "Do you want to take the food to him tonight? I have no objection." After all, as her inner voice had reminded her, she didn't intend to get too fond of the man.

"I'll let you do it."

Mercy waited as Sybil filled a plate and covered it, then accompanied her down the hill. Seems Brand would have two women visiting him tonight.

Not that Sybil had any objection. Only she didn't quite convince herself of the truth of those words.

"I suppose you've been learning lots about our mysterious cowboy," Mercy said. "Where's he from? Where does he plan to go? What's his name? I can hardly wait to read your story. Will you let me read it before you send it?"

"I'm still working on it. He isn't too eager to reveal details." And yet she felt she'd learned so much about him. His caring mother, his Christian upbringing, his tenderness and consideration. "He built a swing." She pointed to it.

Mercy gave a low whistle. "The children are going

to enjoy that." She shook her head. "Seems a strange thing for him to do. Kind of out of character."

"I guess it depends on how you judge his character."

"I see him as a tough loner, likely with a dark secret that drives him." She turned to squint at Sybil. "Are you softening the man?"

Sybil widened her eyes. "I don't know what you mean." But the idea pleased her.

Mercy laughed and patted Sybil's hand. "You go soften him up some more. Maybe you can convince him to settle down. I'll see you later." She turned toward Jayne's cabin and Sybil continued onward.

She stepped into the clearing and looked to where he usually sat. "Brand?"

She swept her gaze around the clearing. No dishes. No Dawg. No Brand. Nothing. She bent over the ashes. Cold as creek rocks. She straightened. "Brand?"

His name echoed

"Brand, where are you?" She crossed the clearing and pushed through the trees to another opening that allowed her a good view to the north and west. Nothing moved except the leaves, the birds and the grass.

She retraced her steps. Surely she'd missed something to indicate where he was. She poked through the flattened grass and parted the nearby branches.

Finally she sank to the ground and faced the truth.

He was gone.

Her heart shuddered.

Not a word of goodbye.

How could it be? Less than two hours ago they had shared a special moment. Why, she'd even dared kiss his cheek.

Was that it? Did he find her too bold? Did he not want affection?

A calming thought intruded into her shock. Maybe he'd decided to join the others at the bunkhouse.

Maybe—a grin exploded on her face—maybe her sign of affection had persuaded him to abandon his reclusive ways.

She jumped to her feet, grabbed the plate, which she'd momentarily forgotten, and raced toward the ranch.

She passed Jayne's cabin and skidded to halt. Sybil could hardly rush up to the bunkhouse and ask if Brand was there. She spied Eddie talking to Slim by the corrals. She shifted direction and went toward them, standing back and waiting for a chance to talk to Eddie alone.

"Okay, boss." Slim tipped his hat toward Sybil as he left.

"Do you need something?" Eddie said.

"I took a plate of food out to Brand."

Eddie studied the still full plate. "I take it he wasn't hungry."

"Uh…" Wasn't this where Eddie said Brand had eaten at the cookhouse? "He wasn't there. I thought—" She glanced toward the bunkhouse. "Maybe he joined the others."

"No. I'm sure Slim would have said so if he did. However, he can't have gone far. He still has horses to break and he hasn't picked up his pay. Maybe he's gone hunting."

"I suppose." But she didn't believe it. Why would he take every belonging if he'd only gone hunting?

She scraped the food off the plate into the cat dish outside the barn, and half a dozen cats raced over to enjoy the meal Brand had missed. Mercy was likely still visiting Jayne, but Sybil didn't want to talk to anyone, and she slipped into the big house. She tiptoed past the living room so as not to attract Linette's attention. She passed the library full of books, a big desk and several reading chairs without even glancing in, and crossed the kitchen to her room, where she wilted at the edge of the bed. Despite all her fine talk to the contrary, she had let herself care too much.

When would she ever learn to guard her heart?

Dawg followed Brand, but as they put distance between them and the ranch, the dog stopped, turned back and whined.

"Yeah, I hear ya. She made me want to stay longer, too, but we just can't." He faced forward. Gotta keep moving. Gotta keep ahead of the Duggans.

As he rode into the afternoon sun he repeated the same words over and over. But every few minutes, other thoughts intruded.

Thoughts of a golden-haired miss whose blue eyes smiled so gently at him he could almost believe she cared. But how could she? She knew nothing of him. Certainly not who he really was. Even if for some reason he stayed, he could never tell her and lose the memory of that smile.

What would it be like to return home every day to a smiling welcome?

Brand Duggan would never know.

He found a spot with a rock cliff at his back. It wasn't a bad place as far as campsites went. He'd had worse. Tomorrow he would ride to the west, find a place deep in the mountains to hole up for the winter.

But tonight his bones ached for something more comfortable than a campsite. He ached for a place of warmth and welcome and belonging.

He shot two rabbits and dressed them, burying the entrails a few feet away, then put the rabbits on a spit to roast. A little later, he ate one and gave the other to Dawg.

He missed Ma.

Home. He dare not dream of a home of his own, shared with—

He hadn't cried for a home since the first week after he'd buried his ma. And he never let himself look back and wish for things that couldn't be his.

But tonight the ache would not leave.

Ma's oft spoken words sprang into his mind. *God will always be with us. Always guide us to a safe place. Always. We have to trust Him.*

Tonight the words wouldn't be dismissed.

He finally fell into a troubled sleep in which Pa and Cyrus chased cowboys from the ranch, while Brand tried to ride his horse through the crowd to someone beyond them. He couldn't see who it was, but terror filled him at the thought of being unable to get to the person.

He yelled at his pa to get out of the way, and his voice jerked him awake. He sat up and rubbed his face. Sweat beaded his forehead even in the cool night air.

He reached for Dawg. Found the spot empty. "Dawg?"

His senses kicked into full alert and he grabbed for his pistol. A scream rent the air and raised the hair on the back of his neck. A cougar.

"Dawg!" he bellowed. Had the fool dog gone after the animal? Dawg loved to torment cats of every size.

Brand scrambled to his feet and jammed on his boots. He grabbed up a smoldering log and trotted toward the sound, his gun ready.

A deep growl came from the dark. "Dawg, you dumb dog. Get back here."

Brand rushed onward, struggling to see with the help of the glowing hunk of wood. Despite his hurry he didn't take any chances. He didn't want to feel the sharp claws of a mountain lion tearing him apart.

Then Dawg yelped. An awful sound that tore at Brand's heart.

He fired into the air overhead, hoping to scare off the wildcat. "Dawg, where are you?"

A whimper drew him in the right direction. In three more steps he saw the dog lying in a heap, his side torn by the mountain lion. Brand held his gun at the ready, shone his light in every direction, but saw no sign of the animal. He rushed to Dawg's side and bent over him. He was torn up bad. "How many times have I told you not to chase animals bigger than you?" Had the smell of the rabbits drawn the animal? Brand should have been more careful about disposing of the remains, but thoughts of Sybil and home had made him careless. Now Dawg had paid for it.

The dog whined and tried to lick Brand's hand.

"You just lie still. I'll take care of you." He gingerly picked up his pet and carried him back to the campsite. He threw more wood on the fire until flames licked upward. Surely it would be enough to scare off any wild beasts that might be attracted to the smell of blood, and there was blood everywhere. "You got yourself tore up real good, didn't you?"

He warmed water and tried to clean the dog. "You're

going to need stitching back together." He couldn't do it alone. Dawg might be smart and cooperative and lots of other thing, but he'd react to being sewed up. He'd likely fight or bite or both.

"Don't ya dare die on me." He studied the sky. How long until morning? It was impossible to tell.

He made some strong coffee, drank two cupfuls so hot it burned his tongue. Tried to get Dawg to lap a bit of water, and waited for morning.

Then he would do what he must do.

Sunday morning arrived with late summer warmth, which did nothing to ease the cold tension wrapping about Sybil's heart. She slipped out of the house just as the eastern sky flared with pink and orange and purple. She caught her breath at the beauty, then turned her steps toward Brand's campsite. No, she didn't hope he had returned. She wasn't foolish enough to harbor empty dreams. But she needed time to adjust her thinking. She'd made a mistake by opening her heart to another man. Hadn't she learned from Colin to be more cautious?

She certainly had learned this time. This lesson would not have to be repeated for it to sink into her heart.

She sat with her back against a tree and stared at the cold ashes of Brand's campfire. Eddie expected him back to finish breaking horses and get his pay, but she didn't think he'd return. No, she thought he meant to ride away and never look back. She'd known it all along and expected it, so she had no reason to feel torn and empty inside.

It was for the best. Now she could write his story and then forget him.

She wouldn't ever forget him. Despite the knowledge that he was a man without a home who lived a life of danger—someone she would do well to avoid—she had only to close her eyes to see him. His strong features, his strong hands, his—

Oh. What was wrong with her? She knew nothing about him. Not even his name. He was only a hero in a story she continued to work on. She'd brought a copy of her notes with her and bent over the pages. Soon she'd have the story ready to send to the editor.

It didn't matter that there were so many unanswered questions in her mind. The story was good without those answers, even though she ached for more.

A sound of horse hooves startled her from her thoughts. She glanced to the right.

"Brand!" She bolted to her feet. "You've come back." Her heart threatened to explode. Her feet wanted to dance. So much for all her fine thoughts.

She sucked in a hard breath and pushed a boulder over her errant emotions. Her heart was locked solidly. Nothing would induce her to open it.

Brand didn't even bother with a hello. "It's Dawg."

She strained forward at hearing the agony in his voice.

"He's been hurt." Brand dipped his head toward the animal cradled in his arms.

Sybil tucked her notes in her pocket and rushed forward. Five feet away she saw the matted blood on Dawg's side. "What happened?"

"He figured he could take on a cougar. Dawg ain't too bright at times."

"How can you say that? Poor doggie. You were just being brave, weren't you?" She closed the distance between them and reached to pat the dog's head, then hesitated, not sure where she could touch him without hurting him.

Dawg whined.

"How bad is he?"

"Bad. I need help with him. You're the only person he's ever let touch him except for me. I thought…"

She swallowed hard. "I'll do what I can to help, but I've never done anything with an injured animal."

"You figure Eddie will let me put him in the barn?"

"Of course he will. You go on ahead. Don't wait for me. I'll get there as fast as I can."

But Brand stayed at her side as she turned toward the ranch buildings. Knowing Dawg needed immediate attention, she lifted her skirts and trotted toward the barn, pushing open the door so Brand could duck his head and ride in.

Slim stood before a workbench in dark pants and a light brown shirt, his hair slicked back, reminding Sybil it was Sunday and people at the ranch were preparing for the church service. "Is Eddie about?" She hadn't seen him on the way toward the barn.

"Last I seen of him he was taking feed to the pigs."

Even on Sunday, a day of rest, the animals had to be fed.

Slim's attention riveted on Brand. "Can I do something for you?"

"Dawg is hurt. If you could let me use a stall to doctor him up, I'd be grateful."

Slim nodded, but didn't make a move toward the dog. Like the others on the ranch, he'd learned to keep his distance. "Far pen is clean and empty. Help yourself. I'll let the boss know."

"Thanks."

Sybil followed the horse and rider down the aisle and swung the gate open. Brand slowly dismounted. Dawg growled a protest. "Sorry, old pal, but I gotta do this." He looked about. "I need the saddle blanket for him." He nodded toward the blanket still on the horse's back, beneath a large saddle.

She assumed he meant for her to get it for him, but she had no idea how. "Tell me what to do and I'll get it."

"Take off the saddle."

"I don't know how." Surely that was the weakest thing she'd ever said.

"Reach under and undo the cinch."

Reach under the horse? "He's big."

"He's used to it."

Ignoring the trembling of her insides, she did as Brand directed. She should have followed Mercy's example and learned to do these things for herself.

Slim moseyed to the pen. "Here. Let me."

Gratefully, she stepped back. She couldn't look at Brand. He'd think her useless. But she'd never ridden a horse unless it had been saddled and brought to her. As she considered the fact now, she vowed she would remedy that as soon as she had a chance.

She grabbed the saddle blanket and arranged it on a mound of hay Slim put out.

Brand gingerly lowered Dawg to the bed and knelt beside him.

Slim shook his head. "That don't look good."

Sybil caught her bottom lip between her teeth. It certainly didn't. Dawg had been torn to pieces. It looked as if clotted blood and matted hair was all that kept him together.

"He'll survive." Brand made it sound like an order. "Most of it is only skin deep."

"I'll get the supplies." Slim stepped out and returned in a moment with a box of veterinarian necessities, which he put at Brand's side.

Dawg bared his teeth and growled.

"Sure ain't discouraged his bad attitude." Slim stalked away.

Sybil knelt at Brand's side, resisted an urge to pat his hand. "What do you need me to do?"

"You want to hold him or stitch him?"

She gasped. "You're going to sew him together?"

"Got to." She felt a shudder race up Brand's body. And this time she followed her instincts and pressed her hand to his arm. Later, she would return to her vow to forget him, to remind herself that he was leaving…that he was the sort of person she should avoid if she didn't want her heart torn asunder again.

"You have to do what you can to save him. I'll help." She edged around to Dawg's head. "I'll hold him." She gave Brand an unblinking look. "We can do this."

He nodded. "He ain't gonna like it much, and as Slim said, Dawg's got a bad attitude toward most people."

"He'll be good for me, won't you, Dawg?" She scooted closer, put the animal's head between her knees. "Dawg, I'm here to help," she murmured softly. "So is Brand, but then you know that. I expect it will hurt some." She drew in a steadying breath. "But it's only because we want to help."

Dawg whined.

She cupped her hands over his head. "We're ready."

Dawg flinched as Brand pushed back the matted hair and dabbed away the blood. Then he threaded the needle and held it poised above the wound.

"He ain't gonna like it."

Sybil leaned over the animal. "Dawg, you can't fight."

"Don't put your face so close. What if he bites?"

She jerked back, her eyes widening in shock.

"I'm just saying he's a dog with an anger problem, and what I'm about to do is gonna hurt." Brand's jaw clenched and he began his task.

Dawg yelped. He snarled. He fought. He tried to free his head so he could stop Brand, but Sybil held him tight.

Brand pressed his knees to Dawg's paws to immobilize them, and continued the job.

"It's okay," Sybil crooned over and over, not certain if the words were meant for Dawg, her or Brand.

Brand paused and wiped his forehead on his shirtsleeve. He threaded the needle again, clenched his jaw so tight the muscle corded and continued sewing.

Sybil's arms began to ache from restraining the dog. Her vision blurred several times as she saw how much pain it caused the animal. She bit back a cry and had to turn away when she observed the agony on Brand's face.

Finally he finished and put everything away before he fell back on his heels.

Sybil collapsed against the wall as Brand stroked Dawg's head.

"I'm all done, old pal." He raised weary eyes to her. "I just hope it's good enough."

"You did your best."

"Thanks for your help."

She nodded, her heart bursting with so many things she couldn't even name them. Sorrow at the pain Dawg had endured. Admiration and pity at how Brand had done what was necessary. And a feeling that went deeper than any of that. A sense of having been part of something wonderful with a man who continued to earn her respect with his courage and determination.

The warning bells rang inside her head.

He'd won her admiration, even as he had earned her caution. He'd left once without a word. She knew he'd do it again, but she wouldn't let him take her heart with him when he did.

He met and held her gaze. "You asked what was the hardest thing I ever did. I'd like to change my answer. This was."

Dawg whimpered and they both sprang forward.

"Do you think he would take a drink?" she asked.

"Sure would be good if he did."

"I'll find something." She got stiffly to her feet and went in search of a dish. She found a battered tin bowl on the workbench and stepped outside to dip it in the trough, then took it back to Dawg. As she sat again, she placed it at his muzzle, but he showed no interest.

"Guess he's too exhausted at the moment." She set the bowl where he could reach it.

"He's a trooper." Brand sounded weary. "So are you."

She faced him, saw gratitude in his eyes.

His gentle smile curved his mouth and softened the skin around it. "You did real well."

She reached out and squeezed his hand. "You did the hard stuff."

He turned his hand and caught hers. "We did it together."

She couldn't move, couldn't break away from his touch nor end the look between them. It went on and on. Reaching deep corners, touching tender spots, awakening places she'd vowed to guard. She fought to regain control.

Booted footsteps sounded in the aisle and she jerked her hand free and relocked her heart.

Eddie leaned over the gate. "Heard your dog met with some kind of accident."

"A cougar."

"Sorry to hear that." The rancher made it sound like a death sentence.

Sybil immediately sat up taller. "Brand sewed him back together and did a fine job." Her voice carried more assurance than it had a few minutes ago, but Brand wasn't ready to give up on Dawg and neither was she.

"Linette sent me to say it's time for church," Eddie said. He addressed Sybil, then his gaze went to Brand, as if considering the situation. "You're welcome to join us."

He shook his head. "Thanks all the same, but I'll be staying with Dawg, if that's okay."

Eddie nodded.

Sybil rose and brushed off her skirts. She crossed to the gate, which Eddie held open for her. Then she turned back to the man and his dog. "I'll be back." It was a promise.

He flicked a glance at her in acknowledgment.

As she accompanied Eddie to the house, she made a silent vow.

She'd help Brand with Dawg. But she would not let her barriers down again.

Chapter Eight

Sybil had to hurry to change her clothes, now stained with dirt and blood. It would take a lot of scrubbing and spot removing to make the dress wearable again. She pulled a clean frock on and brushed her hair into submission, then rushed out to join the others as they made their way to the cookhouse, where church was held.

She found a seat beside Mercy and glanced around. The place was crowded. As usual, Ward and Grace and her little sister, Belle, joined them. Ward had once worked for Eden Valley Ranch, but moved to his own place after he married Grace. Ward's mother accompanied them. She had her own house on their ranch.

Jayne and Seth came across the road. Cassie, Roper and their four children joined them from the foreman's house.

Sybil adjusted her skirts and settled into a more comfortable position as Cookie rose to lead the singing. And then her husband, Bertie, spoke. Sybil had learned to appreciate his homespun talks.

After the service, as they left the cookhouse, she glanced toward the barn, but saw no sign of Brand. She couldn't slip away to see him and Dawg as everyone but the cowboys made their way to the big house, where Linette would soon serve a meal. Sybil helped with the preparations. Then she sat through the leisurely lunch and listened to visiting among old friends.

Over and over her mind skittered to the barn, where Brand and Dawg sat alone. She sought to still her thoughts. It wasn't as if Brand needed anything. Cookie had already sent over a plate of food.

Slim or one of the other cowboys would be about if Brand needed something for Dawg.

No, he certainly didn't need her, and she would do well to stay away from him as much as possible if she meant to guard her heart. But she would allow herself a visit to check on Dawg, and because she had promised to return.

However, after the meal, there were dishes to do. And the usual Sunday afternoon activities, which she normally enjoyed. Only today they seemed to go on and on. Would Brand wonder if she meant to keep her promise?

She gave a mental snort. Most likely he hadn't even paid attention to her words nor noted her absence.

Finally, the guests departed. Linette hid a yawn, then announced she'd have a nap, if no one minded.

"We're perfectly capable of entertaining ourselves," Sybil said. Now she'd be able to slip away to check on Brand. And Dawg, she insisted. "I'm going for a walk."

"I'll join you." Mercy fell in at her side. "Unless you prefer I didn't come along." She nudged Sybil.

"Now, why wouldn't I want your company?" Except her friend was right. She'd hoped to be on her own.

"Oh, I don't know. Maybe because you want to spend time with a certain cowboy."

Mercy was far too perceptive, but Sybil wouldn't give her the satisfaction of letting her know it.

"I wonder what Jayne's doing," Sybil said.

"I expect she's enjoying time with Seth. You're stuck with me."

"I don't mind."

"It's nice of you to say so." Mercy directed their steps away from the ranch house and up the hill, until they could view the road to Edendale. "It's been a long while since we went to town. Do you think we could persuade Linette it's time for a trip?"

"What do you need in town? It seems the ranch has everything you could want."

Mercy sighed. "Not everything." But she didn't elaborate. She stared in the direction of Edendale and sighed again.

Sybil recognized her friend's restlessness. But she didn't share it. "Let's go back."

"Why? There's nothing back there. Everyone has someone to spend the afternoon with."

Sybil tucked her arm around Mercy's and pulled her close. "We have each other." She couldn't leave her friend alone in this mood. "Let's walk along the river." That was one of their favorite pastimes.

Mercy shrugged. "We've done that a hundred times."

"So let's do it a hundred and one."

"Oh, very well."

Sybil knew Mercy agreed only because she could think of nothing else to do. They wandered along the river for a bit.

"This is pleasant." Sybil pointed out the birds in the trees nearby. "They sing so nicely, don't they?"

Mercy shrugged. "They're just birds."

They reached the bridge and saw Seth wave as he headed to the barn.

"He's going to do chores," Sybil said. "Let's go visit Jayne."

Mercy let herself be shepherded toward the cabin.

"Come on in and help me arrange these flowers." Jayne had a basket of golden gaillardia, white daisies and branches with clusters of red berries. She handed Sybil a blue pitcher and Mercy a tall red tin. She had a glass vase. "I love to brighten up the place."

Would the Sunday activities never end? But Sybil tucked away her impatience, chose her flowers carefully and cut the stems in various lengths. She envisioned a full, well-shaped bouquet.

Mercy grabbed an assortment of flowers and branches and stuck them in the tin, then stepped back. "I like it wild and free like that." She moved toward the door. "I'm going to practice my roping. I've got to get it down to a fine art if I'm going to catch a man that way." She laughed merrily as she closed the door behind her.

Sybil stared after her. "You don't think she really means it, do you?"

Jayne shrugged. "I can name at least two cowboys who would willingly let her rope them." She chuckled. "Not that she'd need to."

"I hope she doesn't make a foolish mistake and fall in love unwisely." Sybil paused, then added, "I can see her seeking someone wild and untamed. Wouldn't that make for a fine pair?"

Jayne held a branch of red berries and considered Sybil. "You mean like Brand?"

It was exactly what she thought, but she didn't want to admit it to either herself or her friend.

Jayne didn't wait for her to answer. "He's certainly wild and untamed, but I don't sense any spark between him and Mercy. Not like I do with you."

Sybil pushed her thoughts into submission. "What do you mean? I'd never be interested in someone like him. Why, he never stays in one place."

"He might if he had reason enough."

"He's running from something."

"Probably. But sooner or later, don't people have to stop running? I had to stop running from my fears. You need to stop running from yours. So does he. There comes a time when we need to trust God for those things."

"Me? I'm not running. What on earth do you mean?"

Jayne gave a tender smile. "You run—or maybe hide—from change. You think it's the same as danger."

Sybil drew back, her upper lip stiff. "I left home and crossed the continent to get here. That's a lot of change. And a lot of danger. So you are wrong. So very very wrong."

Jayne shrugged, her smile never fading. "Would you ever consider following a man like Brand into the wilds?"

"No." Her lungs clenched so, she couldn't breathe. She couldn't leave the safety of her life. Certainly not to follow a man who would surely ride away one day and leave her on her own.

Her friend nodded, then leaned forward and caught Sybil's arm. "Don't be so careful you rob yourself of the very thing you seek."

"Of course I won't." She said the words automatically, not sure what Jayne thought she sought. Thankfully, Jayne didn't ask, because Sybil couldn't have answered honestly. Nor could she stop her errant heart from seeing Brand as the answer to the question. Brand riding a rank horse. Brand, his leg hurt, but revealing no pain. Brand building a swing to remind her of the sweetness of time with Suzette. Brand with his injured dog cradled gently in his arms. Brand sewing up the same dog, his jaw clenched as he forced himself to do something very difficult.

"I think he's a man a person could count on." Jayne patted Sybil's arm and returned her attention to arranging her flowers.

She had voiced the very thing Sybil knew was impossible. The only thing she could count on from Brand was that he'd leave.

She took her time finishing her own flower display. Rearranged it several times even after she was satisfied. Fussed with a dry leaf, all the while knowing she did it to keep from hurrying back to the barn to check on Dawg. And Brand.

She wouldn't return. It was best if she didn't. But every time the door opened or the floor squeaked, Brand jerked his head up. Eddie came by twice. Slim brought Brand a cup of coffee and plate of food from the cookhouse. A couple other cowboys he didn't recall the names of stopped at the gate and grunted when Dawg growled at them.

Brand waited until they left to scold Dawg. "You gotta stop scaring everyone away." Guess it was Brand's fault the dog did so. He'd kind of encouraged it. Made it easier to move on if he kept everyone ten feet away.

The door opened and he knew it was Sybil even before Dawg whined in anticipation. Brand's heart took off in a wild leap, like a horse bucking. His nerves tingled. All because her quiet entrance informed him of her presence.

In the few seconds it took for her to reach the pen, he gave himself a serious scolding. Letting anyone get close to him put them in jeopardy. He would disappear into the wilds before he brought any danger to Miss Sybil. He needed to—

But before he could decide what it was he ought to do, Sybil cracked open the gate and stepped inside.

"How's he doing?" She nodded toward Dawg.

Dawg opened his eyes, but didn't lift his head.

Sybil sank down at the dog's side. "Cookie gave me some beef broth. It will give Dawg strength." She gently lifted his head and held the tin bowl to his muzzle.

Dawg whined a protest.

"Come on, try it. You'll like it. It will help you."

Brand figured Dawg lapped at the liquid simply to please Sybil. But four laps was all he managed.

Sybil lowered his head. "Good boy." She stroked him. "You're doing just fine." She leaned back against the wall next to Brand, where he sat with his knees drawn up. "How are you doing?"

"Me?" He almost jolted at her question. "I'm not the one hurt."

"But he's your dog. I know how fond you are of him."

"He'll survive."

"You're right. He's tough."

Brand chuckled, though he felt no mirth. "He's mean. Too mean to die."

She patted his hand where he pressed it to his knee. "You're talking like that because it hurts to think of him injured."

Brand stiffened. Did she have any idea how her touch flooded his insides with warmth and something sweet as honey on fresh bread? But he must resist such notions. "Says who?"

She squeezed his hand, an action that likewise squeezed his heart until he grew light-headed. "If you didn't care you wouldn't have come back and sewed him up yourself."

"A man has to take care of his beasts." No way would he admit to deeper feelings. He was Brand. A nameless, homeless cowboy who never showed a speck of emotion. He must maintain the illusion.

She laughed, the sound dancing through him. "You're more than you want people to see."

The truth of her words melted his resolve. How he longed to be more than he could allow. But it was impossible. Nothing would change the fact he was a Duggan.

Female voices came down the aisle.

Sybil glanced up. "That's Jayne and Mercy."

When two women peered over the gate of the pen, Sybil introduced Jayne.

"I heard about your misfortune," Jayne said. "So sorry."

"You'd be the other young lady who recently came from England."

"That's correct."

Mercy gave a teasing grin. "She's already married, though she had to shoot Seth to catch him."

"Mercy, at least tell the truth." Sybil's voice held shock. "I can't get over how you make things seem other than what they are."

Brand swallowed the accusation. Wasn't that exactly

what he was doing? She'd be just as shocked to learn the truth he hid.

Mercy wrinkled her nose. "It is the truth, isn't it, Jayne?"

"It's sort of true," Jayne confessed. She fixed Brand with her confident smile. "I did shoot him, though it was an accident."

Brand chuckled. "I think the three of you might put all the young men in the area at risk."

Mercy grinned. "I'd never shoot a man to catch him, but I might rope him." She swung her arm to illustrate. "I've been practicing."

Sybil sighed. "Have you got someone in mind?"

Her friend appeared to study the question. "I've got it under consideration," she finally said.

"I would never stoop to such things." Sybil's voice was filled with caution. "I'm content to let God do the work for me."

Well, that left Brand out—if he'd ever considered he was in. God would not be working out anything, not even an accidental shooting, or a roping. He grinned at his foolish thoughts.

"Sometimes God expects us to do a little work ourselves," Mercy replied.

"Well, I've no intention of shooting a man nor of roping him."

Mercy and Jayne both considered Sybil with determination in their eyes. She shifted and studied a board at the bottom of the gate as if it held important information.

The two other women turned to each other.

"There are equally effective, gentler ways, don't you think?" Jayne said.

"Oh, indeed. Some men are best caught by kindness. You know—" Mercy tipped her head toward the dog "—like helping out in a tough situation."

Sybil bolted to her feet, her cheeks red enough to ignite the hay on the floor. "I'm only..." She lifted her skirts and prepared to depart. But she hesitated at the last moment, as if reconsidering. "I'll be back to check on Dawg."

She accompanied the others down the aisle.

Brand chuckled softly. Seems her friends thought she might be a little interested in him.

He let the notion flit about in his head like a sun-struck bird, then shot it down.

Even if he hadn't been a Duggan, he had nothing to offer a fine woman like Sybil.

"You and me will do just fine together," he told Dawg, who fluttered his eyelids in acknowledgment. Or was it in disagreement? Dawg had made it clear he didn't want to leave the ranch. In fact, if it wasn't so far-fetched, Brand might think Dawg had challenged the cougar so they would be forced to return.

His dog wasn't that stupid.

And Brand wasn't dumb enough, nor reckless enough, to consider staying.

Chapter Nine

The next few days fell into a sort of pattern. Brand stayed at Dawg's side at night. During the day, he worked on the few horses left to break. If not for Dawg, Brand would have joined the other cowboys at the cookhouse for his meals. Or so he told himself. And tried to believe it.

Well, he might have if it wasn't his habit to stay away from human company as much as possible.

And—he tried to ignore the real reason—if Sybil didn't bring him supper most nights.

He was seven kinds of stupid for looking forward to her visits. Ten kinds of reckless. Should Pa or Cyrus learn of his friendship with her—

It didn't bear thinking about.

But how often did he scan the horizon, searching for any sign of them? Or listen in the hours just before dark for a familiar sound?

Each time he saw nothing, and heard nothing, he let his breath out slowly. Maybe this time they had decided to let him go.

He shook his head. He dare not hope.

The other cowboys had eaten and left the cookhouse. Eddie and Grady had disappeared inside the house some time ago. Brand waited at Dawg's side, hoping against all reason that Sybil would bring him a meal.

The time passed with all the reluctance of a winter sunrise. Maddeningly slow. Twice footsteps thudded toward the barn, but he knew they weren't hers. Too heavy. He pulled in a breath and held it, sucking back disappointment that some cowboy headed his way with a piled-high plate.

But the footsteps retreated without any offerings, and despite the growing pangs, he heaved a sigh that the cowboy didn't make it to the pen where he sat with Dawg.

And then soft footsteps approached and his heart rate picked up like a racing horse.

She stood at the pen with a plate of hot food. "Sorry I took so long. Grady was upset, because he wants a dog of his own and Eddie hasn't been able to find one, so I promised to make up a story for him."

"Wasn't counting the hours." Just the minutes. Brand took the plate. "Thanks." He tried to concentrate on only the food, but how could he when Sybil sat so close, her fingers stroking Dawg's head? And how could he envy the animal? It wasn't as if he wanted to be all tore up and sewn back together. Though he suspected when he left, his heart would feel exactly like it had been ripped by cougar claws.

Not that the knowledge should slow his departure. The sooner he left, the better. Only Dawg's injuries kept him here. If he told himself that often enough, he might actually believe it.

Sure, Dawg needed a few days to heal, but that wasn't the main reason he stayed.

Something else bounced around in his head. A welcome diversion to the insistence of his brain that he should be planning to leave. "You make up stories?"

She studied him, her eyes wide. "Doesn't everyone? Don't you?"

"Can't say I do." Sure, he sometimes thought of how things might be different. But that was as far as he got. "What sort of story did you make up for Grady?"

She looked away, pink staining her cheeks. "Just a silly little boy's story. It was nothing."

"Tell me."

Slowly, her gaze returned to his. "You'll think me foolish."

"I doubt it. Tell me." He longed to hear her story, hear her voice, enter into her imaginations. He'd love to take a story with him to warm his winter nights.

"Promise you won't laugh."

"Not unless it's funny."

"Once upon a time," she began, her eyes darkening to deepest blue as she held him in her unblinking gaze, "there was a little boy, a big dog and a bird. They lived in a world full of flowers and mountains and rivers."

She spun a tale of a boy who did heroic things, a dog with extraordinary powers and a bird who talked. They encountered challenges. The bird insisted they must obey God even when it was hard. They solved their problems, overcame obstacles, all while helping each other and those around them, and never telling a lie.

"And the boy climbed to the dog's back, the bird perched on his shoulder and they rode into the mountains, where they would encounter more adventures. The end."

Brand blinked. "That was wonderful." His food had grown cold as he listened, and he hurriedly cleaned the plate. "Have you ever considered writing the story down for others? Why, you could probably make a children's book."

Her cheeks darkened. "I couldn't do that."

"Why not? This is a story that both entertains and teaches. It's not the first you've told, is it?"

She shook her head. "I guess I have a vivid imagination."

"Why not share it?"

"No one will publish stories written by a woman."

"Really? That doesn't sound right. Who told you that?"

"An editor." She dropped her gaze to her hands, fluttering in her lap like trapped birds. "He laughed me right out of the office. Besides, my parents wouldn't approve. They said a lady's name should not be public." She brought her gaze to Brand's. "Doesn't God command us to honor our parents?"

His throat tightened at the way her eyes filled with darkness. She wanted this so badly it hurt, but she feared rejection. He caught her fluttering hands. "Things aren't always so easy and simple. Yes, we do well to obey God's rules, but when it comes to man-made rules, they aren't always in our best interests." In Brand's case, obeying his father would be to break God's law.

"Obeying is the surest way to a peaceful life."

He withdrew his hands. "I suspect it is, but life isn't always so neat and orderly. Sometimes, even when we do everything in our power to do what is right, bad things happen anyway."

"I don't mean to imply they won't. It's just…" She rolled her head back and forth, then her expression grew fierce. "I can't bear to think of my stories being mocked because they are written by a woman."

He realized they were back to talking about her writing, when his thoughts had shifted to his situation. "Well, all I can say is it's a shame you don't share your stories."

"I share them with Grady."

"He's a fortunate little boy."

"Not because of my stories. But because Linette and Eddie love him like he was their own."

"I thought he was."

She told him how Grady's father had rejected him when Linette rescued him, after his mother died on the trip across the ocean.

The story ripped through Brand. Why couldn't fathers be what God intended them to be?

Sybil squeezed his hand. "God has provided for him just as He's promised to provide for all of us."

Had Brand's expression revealed something that hinted at his distress over his pa? Was that why she offered comfort? He wanted to argue with her. Demand to know how God had provided for him. But of course God had given him an upright ma. That was all he'd needed. "Some are not as fortunate as Grady."

She nodded, her eyes wide with sorrow. "How sad that you are right."

Did she realize she clung to his hand? That her expression beseeched him to make the world better? He touched her cheek. "Don't let it sadden you. People learn to adjust to a lot of things." He trailed his fingertip to the corner of her mouth and leaned closer.

She stiffened, pulled away. "What a tragic statement about mankind. We learn to adjust to bad things." She sighed deeply. "Life should not be that way."

He jerked his hands to his lap. Had he thought to kiss her? He must be losing his mind.

For certain, he was losing his grip on the reality of his situation. He shoved rock-hard determination into his heart. He could no longer act as if he lived in a make-believe world.

He cleaned his plate and held it out to her. "Thank you for bringing it, and thank Linette for me, please."

Sybil took the plate, studied him for a heartbeat. No doubt saw he'd withdrawn, saw his dismissal. Surely she understood this was no place for a lady, and he was certainly not the kind of company a lady should keep.

With a nod, she got to her feet. "I'll tell her."

As she crossed toward the gate, he almost changed his mind and asked her to stay a little longer.

But that would be downright stupid.

She turned before she shut the gate. "Good night, Brand. Good night, Dawg. Sleep well, both of you."

"Good night," he murmured, hoping he managed to keep all regret from his voice.

He should be saying goodbye.

Sybil slipped past the occupied living room, calling out, "I'm going to bed. Good night, all."

She wondered if Mercy would trot after her, demanding to know why she didn't stop to visit, and probing her with questions about Brand, but after a few minutes, it seemed she wouldn't.

Sybil collapsed on her bed, staring at the ceiling. Brand had suggested she publish her stories. He meant the ones she told Grady. Had her heart not burned within her at his words? To be recognized as the author of the stories she published…to feel free to submit more…well, it filled her stomach with fluttering butterflies. And made her want to laugh. She was both thrilled and frightened at the idea.

Why had she not confessed she'd published stories under the Ellis West name?

She sat up and stared at her feet. Why had she not told him she wanted to write a story about him and submit it for publication?

Would he be so encouraging about her stories if she had? Would he still suggest there were times a person should step outside of safe boundaries?

She shivered—again with both fear and excitement. No doubt Brand followed his own rules. But where had that gotten him? Alone. Nameless. His only friend a dog that barely survived his wounds.

Brand was everything she didn't need or want.

What she needed and wanted was safety, security.… She pressed her lips tight and squeezed her eyes to stop the threatening tears. And the freedom to write and publish her stories under her own name.

At least she'd been able to publish as Ellis West. That was enough, she told herself.

She pulled out her notes and glanced over them. But she had very little to add.

Because, she realized with a start, in her visits to the barn she'd revealed more about herself than she'd discovered about Brand.

Tomorrow she would remedy the situation.

Questions she wanted to ask flitted through her brain, chased by the fact that she needed to be honest with him about her intention of writing his story.

Why bother telling him?

Because it feels underhanded to pretend I'm interested for any other reason.

Cough. Cough. *Wouldn't that be a lie?*

She closed her mind to the inner voice. Truth or lie, she wouldn't admit there was any other reason.

Not unless she sought for a way to have her heart fractured into a million pieces. She didn't.

Why not convince him to stay?

Huh. I never thought of that.

Well, think about it. Maybe it's time for him to put his past behind him and face the future.

The next day her plan seemed even more reasonable, and she grinned at the basin of potatoes she was scrubbing for the meal. The grin clung to the lining of her heart and tickled the corners of her mouth later as she took a plate to Brand, leaving Sam Stone from the nearby OK Ranch visiting with Eddie and the others.

Sybil handed Brand the plate of food, then sat with her back against the wall of the pen. Would he guess she meant to have a serious, and perhaps long, talk with him?

He settled down beside her and began to eat.

She shifted to study him. "Can I ask you something?"

"Don't see how I can stop you. But I don't have to answer."

She'd thought carefully about how to approach the subject. If she came at it indirectly, perhaps he wouldn't resist her questions.

"Don't you get lonely?"

* * *

His fist curled against his leg. His heart tightened so each beat hurt as if it squeezed out shards of blood. "I got Dawg."

The twitch of her eyebrows informed him she thought the answer less than adequate.

Brand looked at his plate of food. He looked at Dawg, who rested at his feet. *Lonely?* The word didn't half describe the empty hours, the silent days, the cold nights. Any more than it described the constant pressure at the back of his neck as he watched for the sudden appearance of the Duggan gang. Being alone hurt. But it sure beat having Pa and Cyrus for company.

Brand couldn't continue to ignore Sybil. Her gaze bored into him.

"Something really dreadful must have happened in your life to make you constantly run." She waited, an expectant silence in which his heart strained at its seams.

He could deny it, but knew she wouldn't believe him. "Guess you could say that."

"I'm supposing it's why you won't reveal your surname."

I'm a no-good Duggan. His nerves twitched. He'd been here longer than was wise. But he couldn't leave. Not because of the horses. Not because of Dawg. Even though he knew he might have cause to wish he wasn't so foolish, he couldn't tear himself away from her company.

Nor could he tear himself away from the look in her eyes offering hope and so much more.

She smiled so gently it loosened the cruel fist around his heart.

"You could stop running. Confront your past."

"If only I could." He touched her cheek. Soft as a dewy rose petal. Pink as an autumn sunrise. The color no doubt heightened by his bold touch. "You almost persuade me." If anything could change his circumstances he would stay. Forever. Content to be in the circle of her smile.

"I wish it could be more than almost. Think about it, won't you?" And she placed her hand over his, pressing it firmly to her cheek.

"Would it matter to you?"

She lowered her lashes to hide her eyes, then met his gaze, her eyelashes fluttering. "It matters," she whispered. "I pray you'll find what you need."

"For what?"

"To trust God with your past, your present and your future."

A present and a future of enjoying her company? Was it possible? Eddie would give him a job. He'd already offered. And then what? What about Brand's past?

Maybe Pa and Cyrus would forget about him. Maybe they already had. He sighed. Yeah, and maybe winter wouldn't come this year. The sun wouldn't rise in the east. And he could be a free man.

Not going to happen. Not with a wanted poster for the Duggans.

But with winter coming on, could he hope to remain here undetected for a few months? Would God give him a chance at a regular life? But then what?

Maybe he could have only a few weeks, a few months, but wouldn't it be worth it?

"I guess I need to let Dawg rest a few more days." It was all Brand could give her. All he could give himself.

Her eyes flickered, acknowledging that his answer wasn't what she sought. "I pray you will discover you don't need to keep running and hiding." She looked at him with such hope and assurance that his resistance disappeared like a wisp of smoke.

"You are determined to give me hope, aren't you?"

"Yes, I am." She leaned closer. "You deserve it."

He wasn't sure what she thought he deserved. More than was possible, for certain. But her sweet face begged to be kissed. And he lowered his head and caught her lips in a gentle caress.

She sat back and stared at him.

But she couldn't be any more surprised by his actions than he. His pulse took off in a wild gallop. What was there about this woman that unsettled him so much he forgot who he was, what he must do?

Brand fully expected she would rise in her dignified way and make some excuse as to why she must leave. But instead she continued to study him.

"Why did you do that?"

"Do you wish I hadn't?" He didn't regret it for one moment.

"No. But I wonder what it means."

"I don't know for sure, except you make me forget everything I should remember."

Her eyes crinkled in gentle laughter. "I'm hoping you mean that as a good thing."

"It feels right and good at the moment."

She nodded. "For me, too."

His grin widened until he thought his face might crack.

They shifted, sat with their backs to the rough wood of the pen, their shoulders touching, as Dawg snored and snorted on his bed, and Brand finished the temporarily forgotten meal.

"Gonna miss all this good cooking."

"You could enjoy Cookie's meals all winter if you wanted."

He put the empty plate aside and smiled at Sybil. "You make me wish I could. But it's not possible."

"So you keep saying. Why isn't it?" She grabbed his arm. "Why?"

"It's not, and that's all I can say." His heart lay heavy in his chest. If only things could be different.

"I don't understand."

"Sybil—" But before he could voice what he meant to say, the barn door creaked open and sunlight flared into the interior.

"Glad you could stop by." It was Eddie, bringing Mr. Stone to get his horse. Brand had been introduced to the owner of the neighboring ranch earlier, when Mr. Stone dropped by and was invited to join them for supper.

"Thanks for the meal." Sam threw the saddle blanket on his horse, then paused. "Have you heard about the recent robberies? The bank at Fort Macleod was robbed and a farmer north of there reported cash and goods had been taken while he was away from the place. Constable Allen says it's the work of the Duggan gang. He says they could be headed this direction."

Brand jolted forward, listening intently.

"I'll be watchful," Eddie said. "Thanks for the warning."

Sam led his horse out, called a goodbye and rode away.

Eddie came to the pen to check on them. "How's he doing?" He tipped his head toward Dawg.

"Almost good as new," Brand replied. Good enough to travel.

He waited for Eddie to leave, and then, his jaw hard, his voice firm, he said, "I'll be on my way in the morning." He'd collect his wages tonight.

"I hoped you would stop running." Her voice quavered.

"I can't."

"Why? Don't we all have the power to make our own choices?"

"Sounds good and noble. Doesn't always work."

"Why not? Brand, what it is you are running from?"

His gaze jerked to hers. He must deny any reason for running. Even more than that, he must deny any reason for wanting to stay. He'd been foolhardy to linger as long as he had.

"Dawg is a very fine animal, but a man needs more than a dog." Sybil swallowed hard. "Brand, would you stay if I asked you?"

He scrubbed his lips together. Pulled his gaze toward the wall. He dipped into the reservoir of strength and shook his head. "Don't ask. I can't stay."

"Can't? Or won't?"

"Same thing either way. I'll be heading off in the morning."

She sank to the floor beside his dog and petted him. "What will happen to Dawg?"

"He'll come with me. As you pointed out, he's my only companion."

"You could have more. So much more."

Brand couldn't face the pain and disapproval in her

eyes. He ached for what she offered. But the Duggan gang was too close.

If only he could stop running.

But as long as he was a Duggan, he might as well dream of finding gold in his pockets.

Sybil reached for the empty plate. He didn't want her to leave, but what was the point in asking her to stay? Every minute in her company made it that much harder to walk away without a backward look.

Brand saddled his horse at first light. Dawg limped after him, whimpering. "It's okay, old boy. I won't make you walk."

Other cowboys went in and out of the barn, ready to start their day's work. Dawg growled halfheartedly and Brand simply ignored them.

Cal grabbed a saddle, shot him a challenging look. Brand let it slide off him. Always some young buck wanting to prove something. Let him go ahead and prove whatever he thought he must. Brand wouldn't be around to dispute Cal's accomplishments.

He led his horse from the barn, lifted Dawg in front of the saddle and swung up behind him. He pulled the dog close, holding him gently.

He cast one last glance up the hill to the big house. A shadow flickered past a window. Was it Sybil? Just in case, he touched the brim of his hat. *Goodbye, sweet girl. Thanks for trying to get me to stay.*

"I'll show you who's boss." Cal's harsh words drew Brand's attention.

Cal rode a little black gelding Brand had green broke the first day. Only he jerked on the reins, sawed the bit in the horse's mouth. Brand would have called out a warning, but it was too late.

With a wild snort that signaled both pain and protest, the horse lowered his head and gave a back-cracking buck that sent Cal over his head into a mud puddle. His mount snorted and raced to the far corner.

Cal scrambled to his feet. Several cowboys watched him, but Cal zeroed in on Brand. "You." He jabbed his finger in his direction. "You got paid good money to have these horses ready to ride. And this is what we get?" He stomped off.

Brand called to him. "You're not handling the horse right. You're too hard on his mouth."

Cal shook a fist at him and stalked away.

Brand felt the study of the half dozen cowboys. Yes, the horses were ready to ride. But only if handled with a little common sense. However, the black gelding would now think he could unseat any rider.

Band watched the horse trotting around the corral, and considered his options. If he left now, he would surely be out of Pa and Cyrus's reach in a few days. However, he could not, in good conscience, leave Eddie with a horse that couldn't be ridden. Another day. No more, he vowed.

Would Sybil realize he hadn't left, and pay him a visit?

"I'll take care of that horse," he announced, and returned his horse and dog to the barn.

He spent the morning working with the horse, teaching it to obey him. He positioned himself so he could see the big house. But the sun was high overhead before he caught a glimpse of Sybil. She stepped outside, the sun pooling in her hair. She scanned the pens and corrals until her gaze stopped on him. Had she seen him?

She shielded her eyes from the glare of the sun and continued to look in his direction. Then she picked up her skirts and hustled down the hill, not slowing her steps until she reached the rail fence. "Eddie said you were still here." Her voice was breathless.

"Had to finish my job."

"That's what he said." Her gaze went deep into Brand's heart, demanding more than an excuse.

Oh, how he wished he could offer more. But nothing had changed. Except he was still here. Even though it must be temporary, he might as well make the most of it. "Want to help me walk Dawg this afternoon?" It was the weakest invite any woman ever had, but it was the best he could do.

"I would like that. If you think he's up to it."

"I figure he's up to a few steps." Half a dozen, likely, but he might be persuaded to make it as far as the trees overhanging the river, where Brand and Sybil could enjoy a few moments of privacy.

And what, you crazy man, do you intend to do with such?

He realized he was grinning like a crazy man, and forced his mouth into a more moderate smile.

She ducked her head. "I'll come back later, shall I?"

Her shyness made him feel ten feet tall. "I'll meet you at the barn." He forced his attention back to the task at hand.

When he deemed the sun was in the right position, he hustled to the barn to duck his head in the water trough, and clean his hands and face well. Then he trotted inside and pulled out a clean shirt. Nothing fancy.

Just a brown striped cotton shirt that could have used a woman's touch to iron out the wrinkles. Lacking that, he smoothed the fabric as best he could before he pulled it over his head and buttoned it.

He scrubbed a spot in the window over the workbench and tried to see his reflection. He'd have done better to stare in the water trough, but someone might notice him.

Straightening, he warned himself, as he had done all day, this was only a small treat he was stealing, to carry with him the rest of his life.

A warning thunder filled his thoughts. He was taking an awful chance, with his pa so close. But one afternoon. Only one. Was it too much to ask of life? If he was the praying man his ma had hoped to raise, he would ask God to give him this afternoon, to bless it with sunshine and kisses and make it last forever.

Knowing Sybil would soon join him, Brand stepped outside to wait. Just in time. She sauntered down the hill, her golden curls beneath a bonnet of blue. He strode from the pen and went toward her. As they drew closer, her eyes seemed to gather up the blue of her bonnet and the sky and hold it. His eyes watered at how striking she was.

He reached her side. "You look like a sunny sky."

Pink stained her cheeks. "Thank you…you do mean it as a compliment?"

He'd spoken without thinking, but replied, "Yes, it's a compliment."

She smiled. "It's a fine afternoon, isn't it?"

Finer by the moment, but all he said was, "Very nice."

He whistled for Dawg and they waited as the animal

limped toward them. The way his tail tipped to the side in a wag, Brand knew Dawg was eager for this outing.

Not half as eager as his owner.

He turned toward the river, his eyes on the goal of that little copse of trees. Their progress was slow as Dawg limped along, encouraged by both Sybil and Brand.

Finally, they reached the river, and stepped into the shelter of the gold-dappled branches.

Dawg lapped up the cool water and lay down on the leafy carpet.

Brand had waited for this moment all day, but now his tongue lay motionless in his mouth. What could he say? "Trees are pretty." Yeah, that was brilliant.

She nodded. "Mercy, Jayne and I walked along the river yesterday and saw a wonderful display of color."

A bronze leaf fluttered from the tree and landed on her shoulder.

He plucked it off. Felt her start at his touch, and he jerked back, crushing the leaf in his palm. He would never have the right to touch her.

"Shall we sit?" She waved toward a tree and they sat side by side, their backs against the trunk. "Eddie's anxious to get the cows rounded up and moved to lower pastures."

Brand didn't care about Eddie's cows. Not with Sybil at his side. If only he could stop time and stay right here. Build a cabin next to the water. Forget he was a Duggan.

Except he couldn't forget, not with news of the gang nearby. Every day made discovery more possible. Not only possible but impending. If he had any guts he would leave this minute. But he sat in the shade beside a pretty woman and discussed the weather, determinedly ignoring the increasingly loud warning bells.

She patted his hand as it lay on his knee. "If you stayed here, you might find you like it."

Liking it was the problem. It had kept him from doing what he always did and must continue to do. Ride away. Disappear. Don't look back.

Dawg rose and whined, looking toward the barn.

Sybil laughed. "Do you think he's trying to tell us something? As in he'd like to go back home?" She got to her feet. "I guess we better do as he suggests."

Thus ended his stolen afternoon.

As he gained his feet, he heard a quail cooing across the river.

Every nerve in his body fired hot lava. His heart took off at a mad gallop.

It could possibly be a quail, but Cyrus used to make that sound to signal to Brand.

Had Cyrus and Pa had found him?

He had delayed too long.

Sybil didn't seem to notice his hurry to return to the barn, and left them at the gate, saying she must get back and help Linette.

He waited until she was out of earshot before he turned to Dawg. "Dawg, we're leaving."

The dog didn't protest, but Brand's heart pounded against his ribs as if trying to get free.

Freedom was not an option for him. Either he ran or he hanged.

Chapter Ten

Brand gathered his stuff together. If that was Cyrus and Pa he'd heard, they would be watching the place. He'd slip away under cover of darkness. So he sank back on the hay-covered floor to wait, as Dawg slept. Brand planted his hat on his head, tipped it over his eyes and crossed his arms on his chest. Anyone caring to check on him would assume he slept, though the tension coursing through him made that impossible.

He woke from his pretend sleep for only one thing: Sybil delivering supper.

She sat beside him as he choked down the food.

She would be hurt that he simply disappeared. Several times he opened his mouth, and closed it again without saying the words he longed to speak. He wanted to tell her he must leave that very night. But he couldn't face an argument to stay. Nor could he risk having her try and stop him. He had no choice but to keep his plans secret.

She chattered on about Linette's intended trip to town in a few days. "She's hoping for letters from home and something from Grady's father. She is convinced the boy won't ever be happy unless that relationship is mended."

Brand had removed his hat when she joined him, and sat back at an angle so he could watch her. He had avoided developing feelings for anyone since May had made him see how dangerous that was. Even before, he'd learned to be guarded in his friendships. It was a lesson hard learned in his youth and one he should have heeded. But he regretted for less than a second the exception he'd made in this case. Yes, he had to leave. Hopefully, he could escape his brother and Pa. He'd hole up someplace for the winter as was his habit. But this winter he'd have a heart full of both regret and pleasure at this memory.

"Oh, goodness. I have talked on and on, haven't I?"

"Not a problem."

"But I must be going." She rose in a graceful move.

He scrambled to his feet and stared down at her, hoping his eyes did not reveal how thoroughly he studied every feature, knowing this would be his last time to drink in the details.

She touched the back of his hand, sending warmth racing to his heart. It took every ounce of his self-control to keep his arms crossed, his hand pressed to himself, when he ached to hold her close. Enjoy one brief moment of joy before taking up his old life again.

Perhaps sensing the hardness he must force into his heart, she stepped back. "Good night. I'll see you in the morning."

"Good night," he murmured. He waited until she left the pen before turning to watch and listen to her leave the barn. Then he hurried to the workbench and watched her through the clean spot in the window.

Not until she reached the house and stepped inside did he return to the stall.

He waited until the last of the sunset faded and stars began to pepper the sky before he led his horse from the barn, keeping carefully to soft bits of ground to muffle the sound of his departure. He carried Dawg. Any direction he took would necessitate passing an occupied building, so he must proceed with caution, but once away from the ranch he meant to ride hard in a westerly direction. He made his way past the foreman's house and up the hill. Not until he deemed he was beyond hearing did he swing into the saddle, let Dawg get comfortable in his arms. Then he galloped down the dark thread that indicated the trail.

Deepening darkness enfolded him and he had to pull the horse to a walk to see his way. He continued on for the better part of an hour. With each passing mile, his lungs filled more easily. He planned to ride through the night as long as he could make out enough of the path before him to prevent his horse from stumbling. With every step, he expected to be stopped by the Duggan gang, but he rode onward without any sign of them. Had he been mistaken in thinking they'd found him? Not that he meant to hang about and wait for that to happen.

He settled into the saddle, prepared for a long ride.

Did he hear a horse whinny? He reined in and strained to listen. It came again. Was someone camped nearby? He waited, straining to hear any sound above the heavy thump of his heart.

Suddenly a horse and rider appeared before him, a dim shadow in the darkness.

Brand's hand stole toward his gun belt and he gripped the handle of his pistol.

"We been waiting for you." Cyrus's low voice broke the fearful silence.

Brand's hand relaxed at the same time his insides clenched.

Cyrus rode closer, reined in to press close to Brand's side. "Pa said I should bring you to visit."

"Like I said before, I ain't interested."

"Now, ain't that downright unforgivin' of you. After all we done."

Yeah, like make my life unbearable. Force me to be on the run. But Brand kept his opinion to himself. He'd said it all since he was a kid. His protests had earned him a smack across the head and accusations of being ungrateful. As an adult, he'd tried again to say he wanted nothing to do with the gang. Pa had voiced his displeasure at Brand's lack of loyalty, and Cyrus had threatened to tie a licking on him. Only seeing the anger in Brand's face and his clenched fists had convinced him Brand was no longer a little brother who couldn't or wouldn't defend himself.

Cyrus pushed the horses forward. Brand considered reining away and riding until they couldn't find him. But he knew Cyrus would chase him until both horses collapsed. The man had a stubborn streak as wide as the sky.

So he let his brother edge them along. "Care to tell me where we're going?"

"I think it's time you showed Pa a little respect. I'm plumb tired of your high-and-mighty attitude. Your ma was no better than my ma, despite what she taught you."

"She never taught me anything of the sort. 'Sides, it wasn't either of our mothers who robbed innocent people. It's our pa."

"Don't you think he done it for you and your ma?"

Brand did not think so, but he knew arguing would only add fuel to the fire of Cyrus's bad attitude.

"We leave the trail here," his brother said, grabbing the reins of Brand's horse. "Just to ensure you don't change your mind," he explained, his voice full of sneering mockery.

"I don't plan to change my mind." Ever.

They crashed through the bushes with little regard for the amount of noise they made. And Cyrus certainly had no concern for the branches he pushed aside and released so that they whipped at Brand, stinging his face, bruising his arms, almost unseating him. He did what he could to protect Dawg.

Dawg hated Cyrus, but knew better than to growl at him. Cyrus wouldn't hesitate to kick Dawg, saying the animal needed to learn some respect.

Brand finally saw a campfire ahead. Made out half a dozen men lounging around it. None of them showed any concern at the approach of riders.

Only Pa rose to greet them. "Howdy, son," he said, as Brand and Cyrus rode into the circle of light. "Nice to see you again."

"Hi, Pa. Sure wish we could meet under better circumstances."

Cyrus gave a mocking laugh and ordered him off his horse.

Brand struggled to get down while still holding Dawg.

"See you still got that mangy mutt."

Dawg barred his teeth as Brand set him on the ground at his feet.

The fire flared, throwing grotesque shadows.

Cyrus saw the stitches on Dawg's side and whooped with harsh laughter. "He looks like a crazy quilt." He laughed some more.

Brand wanted nothing more than to silence that laugh with a fist to Cyrus's mouth. But he was outnumbered seven to one, and didn't trust Cyrus not to shoot Dawg out of spite, so he ignored his brother and studied his pa.

"You've lost weight," he said. The man was downright gaunt. "Don't you eat?"

"We eat real good," Cyrus answered. "Pa looks fit as a fiddle and don't you say otherwise."

The men around the fire shuffled and tried to appear disinterested.

Brand figured he didn't need to say anything more about the subject. Anyone with eyes could see how Pa's hide hung from his frame. His skin had a peculiar pale hue to it. Could he be ill? Despite the differences between them, Brand ached to think of his father dying. A man lost and on the run. *Please, God, give me a chance to speak to him.* Perhaps Brand could persuade him to stop running.

A shudder snaked across Brand's shoulders. That would mean Pa turning himself over to the authorities. He'd hang. More than once the Duggan gang had left death in the wake of their activities.

"Got any coffee?" Brand nodded toward the enamel pot hanging near the fire.

"Cyrus, get your brother some." Pa made it sound all loving and familial, even though Cyrus growled a protest as he sloshed steaming coffee into a tin mug.

Brand took it without comment. Experience told him Cyrus would object to anything, from a word of thanks to a kick in the shins. Seems he viewed every word and action with the same yellowed opinion.

One of the men took Brand's horse away, leaving him feeling exposed and helpless. But he would never reveal weakness to this brood, and he hunkered down on his heels to nurse his coffee. Dawg pressed close, keeping Brand between him and the others.

Cyrus perched on a tree stump nearby, his boots swinging back and forth inches from Brand's face.

Brand ignored him. Like Dawg, he knew better than to rise to Cyrus's invitations to trouble.

Pa sank to the ground nearby. "Hear you been doing all right fer yerself lately."

"I've been doing all right by myself most of my life." He kept all rancor from his tone, just as Pa had made his words a simple comment, when Brand knew they held a whole lot more.

"You always was ungrateful," Cyrus growled.

Pa signaled for his elder son to be still. "We been looking about, asking questions and learning lots."

"Uh-huh." Brand knew the sort of things they would be learning—who kept a stash of money in their mattress, who had valuables in the house, when the stagecoach carried a heavy strongbox.

"Some interesting things have come to light." Pa inched closer. "This Eddie Gardiner you been working for is one of the biggest ranchers in the territory." He waited for Brand to say something. When he didn't, Pa continued. "And he comes from a rich family back in England. From what I hear they practically roll in money."

"Do tell." Guess it took a certain amount of backing to get a ranch like Eden Valley going, but from what Brand had seen, Eddie and his family lived simply enough. Why, his sister, Jayne, lived in a tiny, two-room cabin with her new husband. Didn't sound like stinking rich to him.

But he knew the futility of trying to make Pa see reason.

His skin twitched to think of his pa spying on the ranch. Had he watched Sybil? Brand clenched his teeth so hard they creaked. If he'd seen them... Well, family or not, he would have shown his objection.

"You've been there some time. Guess you've learned a lot about the goings on of the ranch."

"I broke a few horses. That's all."

Pa shook his head and wagged a finger. "Ain't how I saw it."

Brand dared not react. He knew from the leer on Pa's face they'd seen him with Sybil. His head threatened to explode. His presence had put her in danger. He had known all along he should move on. But had he listened to the warning inside his head? Nope. Foolish feelings had been allowed to rule.

Cyrus laughed mockingly, his voice jarring across Brand's nerves like loud discordant music.

Pa grinned at Cyrus, sending the jarring feeling deep into Brand's gut. He knew what they would ask next. They always asked the same thing.

Could he hope to delay them? Brand set the empty cup down and yawned widely. "I'm tired."

Cyrus's boot connected to Brand's knee. "Guess that's what happens when you spend your time courting. Don't get 'nough sleep."

Brand's fists curled so tight the knuckles cracked. He saw red spots that did not come from the fire, but

from the anger rolling inside him. How dare Cyrus vio-
late an innocent friendship with his crude insinuations?
But Brand would not let him know he'd touched a raw
nerve. Ignoring both the nudge and the comment, he
yawned again.

Cyrus bolted from his post and squatted before him,
almost nose to nose. "Little brother, you can stop playing the sweet innocent boy with us. We've been watching you. What's more, we know you and that boss man
were friendly." His spit spattered on Brand's face. Brand
wiped at it with his sleeve.

"I only broke some horses for the man."

"We saw how you hung about. How the man visited
you in the barn." Cyrus leaned back with a malicious
sneer on his face.

Brand noted that the five men around the campfire
all sat up and watched. His nerves twanged with tension.

Cyrus rose and loomed above him. "We know you
got it figured out where the man keeps his money."

Brand had known what to expect, but it still turned
his blood bitter that they figured he was the same as
them. "Know nothing about it."

Cyrus's mean laugh carried no mirth. "Ya, I guess
you want us to think so. Selfish, you are. Figger to keep
it all to yerself." His eyes bored into Brand's. "We aim
to make sure you don't."

Brand didn't bother sparing a glance at Pa, knowing
he would share Cyrus's opinion.

Brand slowly rose to his feet, leaning forward, forcing Cyrus to take a step backward, which earned him
one of his brother's black looks. "I know nothing. Now
if you give me my stuff, I'd like to go to sleep."

He and Cyrus continued their staring match until the others began to shuffle nervously.

"Stu, get his bedroll," Pa said. "Brand, Cyrus, we'll finish this conversation in the morning."

Cyrus grunted. "You can count on it." When the whiskered man Pa called Stu tossed Brand his bedroll, he stretched out, hopefully giving the opinion that all he cared about was his slumber.

Dawg curled up against him. Brand closed his eyes and feigned sleep. He lay with every nerve tensed, ready for anything, knowing the battle of wits was not over.

He eventually drifted off, though he twitched awake at every little sound, and with half a dozen men snoring and Dawg's hearty snorts, there were lots of noises to waken him. At one point he sat up and looked around, hoping for a chance to escape, but a man sat near the smoldering coals, a rifle resting across his knees. He touched the brim of his hat in mocking acknowledgment of Brand's stare.

He had expected no less. Pa and Cyrus had their sights on picking off the Eden Valley Ranch.

Could he stop them?

Sleep never came, and hours later he watched dawn break reluctantly, clouds hanging low.

"Could get another storm," he mused aloud when the men stirred. Had the Duggan gang been out in the open when the last one pelted down? He kind of liked the idea of them huddled under inadequate slickers, trying to keep dry.

"A little rain never hurt no one," Cyrus mumbled, his usual cheerful self. "'Course, I know you prefer a nice warm house, with a gentle woman to serve ya meals." His laugh brought twisting tightness to Brand's chest.

"Now your ma is dead, guess you'll have to find someone else to do it for ya."

Pa slapped Cyrus's shoulder. "Don't be speaking of Brand's ma like that. She was a good woman. Better'n I deserved, for sure."

"She loved you, Pa," Brand said gently, not bothering to add that it had about killed her to see what he'd become.

Cyrus snorted. "She sure found a funny way of showing how much she cared. How often did we have to track down the pair of 'em?" he asked their pa. Then he fixed Brand with an evil look. "And then you got so's you wouldn't tell us about yer friends."

Brand had learned that lesson well. Once he discovered the interest from Pa and Cyrus was only to get information so they could rob his friends' houses, he'd stopped telling them anything.

"Come on, boys, let's have breakfast." Pa nodded for the two men who hunkered over the fire to pass around the food.

Brand ate heartily, even though he found it hard to swallow past the tension in his throat. He slipped some to Dawg. He'd no sooner scraped his plate clean before Cyrus yanked it away and handed it off.

"Now, little brother, it's time to tell us what you know."

Brand shrugged and gave him a defiant look. "I know where the horses are penned. Where the animal doctoring supplies are kept. And I know the cook who feeds the cowboys makes fine cinnamon rolls. That's about it."

Cyrus yanked on Brand's shirtfront. He would have jerked him to his feet, but Brand outweighed him.

"You always were a selfish son of a gun. Now you think ya can keep all the money to yerself." He released Brand with a shove. "Seems yer gonna take some persuading." He pulled out his pistol and aimed it at Dawg, who didn't move, but gave Cyrus a look of hatred.

"How be I shoot this cur?"

Brand's insides curled, but he simply shrugged. "He's about dead, anyway."

Pa shook his head. "Leave the poor animal alone."

Cyrus snorted and stalked off ten paces. He slowly turned to face Brand, with such a malicious grin that Brand struggled to hide a shudder. Sorrow clawed at his gut. Cyrus had once been a decent big brother. Now look what he'd become.

"Dog don't count. Saddle me a horse." He signaled to one of the men, who did as he instructed. Then Cyrus rode away.

Brand stared after him, his heart beating wild as the hooves of a mustang.

What was Cyrus up to?

Whatever it was, Brand knew it was no good.

Sybil thought longingly of her favorite spot—the place where Brand had camped. But Eddie had warned her not to stray too far. She could have found a bit of solitude in the trees next to the river where she and Brand had spent a few minutes. But her memories prevented her from going there, so she settled for a place on the hill, surrounded by trees, within a few yards of the house.

Brand! Why did she keep thinking of him? He was not what she thought.

He'd left without even saying goodbye. Or explaining

his reasons. But after Constable Allen's visit that afternoon she understood why. The Mountie had brought a wanted poster for the Duggan gang.

"Morton Duggan and his son Cyrus," the Mountie said. "They gather up ne'er-do-wells, but they're the head of the gang. Notice anything about them?"

Eddie studied the drawings of the men and groaned. "The family likeness is unmistakable." He handed the poster to Linette. Mercy and Sybil peered over her shoulders. The drawings could have been older versions of Brand.

Sybil's insides turned to ice. A wanted man. Why hadn't she listened to the warning voices in her head? Had the voices not said repeatedly that he was a dangerous man? A man who enjoyed risks?

Linette returned the poster to the Mountie. "He seemed like a decent man. Are you sure he's part of the gang?"

Constable Allen considered the poster with a serious look on his face. "From the information I have, he isn't directly involved in the robberies, but it seems he is on the scene first. It could be he garners information that he passes on to his father and brother." The officer turned to Eddie. "I hope you didn't share any information regarding your money or your valuables with him."

Eddie shook his head. "Of course not. Fact is, I didn't get more than a few words out of him, and he certainly didn't hang around socializing with the others. Except—" His gaze hit Sybil like a blow. "You spent a fair amount of time with him. Did he ask any question that in hindsight might indicate he sought information of this sort?"

Sybil's throat refused to work. She shook her head.

If they only knew it was she who'd asked the questions. Questions to which she received few answers. Now she understood why. "He said very little and asked no questions," she finally managed to say.

She'd fled the place as soon as she could, cutting short Mercy's excited rant about having a wanted man in their presence and not even knowing it.

Sybil sat on the ground now, her back pressed to a tree. The larches were bright yellow, like bits of captured sunlight. But the sight gave her no joy. Brand was part of the Duggan gang.

And she'd been silly enough to allow herself to care about him.

She pulled out her notebook. At least it would make a good story. But she stared at the page without putting down a word. How could she write about him now? He wasn't a man bigger than life. He was a common criminal. She closed her eyes and leaned her head back, letting disappointment and sorrow scratch at her insides. So much for her hard-learned lessons on guarding her heart.

But how could it be true? Was she so blind she'd missed every hint?

Her cheeks warmed as she thought of the moments they'd shared under the trees. The kiss in the barn. At least no one had seen them.

Did she hear a movement nearby? The rustle of leaves? She blew her breath out. Of course she did. The breeze made all the yellow and gold leaves move. She was just nervous, because of Eddie's warning. Knowing Linette and Eddie would worry about her, she gathered her feet under her and stood. It was time to get back.

A man stepped from the trees.

Her heart clambered up her throat, which tightened so much she couldn't even scream.

"Yer coming with me."

She thought she shook her head, but perhaps she only wanted to. She managed to stumble back a step, never taking her gaze off the leering man.

His eyes reminded her of Brand, but his expression frightened her. This was Brand's brother. Had Brand sent him?

He lurched forward.

"No." The word wailed inside her head, but came out barely a whisper. She darted to the side.

The man laughed. "Wanna play? I like that." He held out his hands and leaned one way and then the other, silently mocking her, urging her to run so he could chase her.

She lifted her skirts and took off toward the ranch. A thin sound meant to be a scream pushed past her teeth. "Help. Help." Surely someone from the ranch would see her and come to her aid. She reached the crest of the hill. Through the veil of leaves she watched Slim saddle a horse. Another cowboy sauntered toward the cookhouse. The sun glistened off the windows of the big house, making it impossible for her to see if anyone stood beyond the glass, but Linette spent much of her time in that room, often glancing out the window. Despite the bushes that partially obscured her view, Sybil lifted her arms and waved frantically. It was possible Linette would see and send help.

"Sure do like this game, but ya gone far 'nough."

Huge arms encircled her waist, sweeping her off her feet. She kicked her heels, knowing a taste of satisfaction when her captor grunted. She flailed her arms, scratched at the hands holding her. Despite his grunts, he did not loosen his grip. Instead, he carried her away from the ranch to a waiting horse.

She saw his intention and flung her head back, connecting with his chin.

His arms tightened cruelly, making it impossible to draw in a full breath, though her tight lungs had already made breathing difficult.

"Yer a regular little fighter, ain't ya? I bet Brand enjoyed that."

The mention of that name filled her with blinding fury and she fought with all her might, kicking, gouging, head butting, but Brand's brother only laughed.

"I can see yer gonna give us some fine entertainment."

She found her voice. "I'll not be entertaining the likes of you."

"Already are, sister." His laugh shuddered along her spine. His sour breath made her cringe, but only for a heartbeat. Then she fought and screamed.

He threw her facedown over the back of his horse and swung up behind her. He slapped her bottom.

She saw red. Never in her life had a man touched her in such a familiar, rude way. She would get revenge somehow. Never mind that Father said a lady should never show such emotions. She'd find a way of making him pay for this if she had to track him to her dying day.

With deliberate intent, she kicked the horse, slapped him hard, screamed and squirmed. If she could fall off… She'd sooner be killed by the tumble, trampled to death, than endure the sort of treatment she knew this man and the rest of the gang meant to inflict on her.

The horse snorted and reared. Her head swung back

hard, snapping her neck. But her captor held her by the back of her dress. She feared if she struggled any harder the fabric would tear, exposing her undergarments. The man would likely see that as invitation to do worse.

He jerked her back in place. "You can make this easy or you can make it hard. Suits me either way." He gave another of those dirty laughs.

She hung limply, weighing the possibilities. Could she pretend to cooperate and gain his trust? Bile rose in her throat at the idea. She'd sooner be hog-tied and butchered.

Did the man purposely choose a gait that bounced her so hard across the horse's spine that she wondered why she didn't vomit? Her ribs hurt. Her head hurt. Her arms grew numb. After a few minutes all she cared about was getting off that rigid spine, getting her head upright. But still the ride continued.

"Where are we going?" she demanded.

"Thought you might like to see Brand again."

"No thanks."

Another mirthless laugh. "He's gonna be surprised to see you."

She saw the legs of another horse, the boots of another rider. Had help come? She lifted her head and saw the rider. Her heart stalled. Given his expression, this man did not mean to help her.

"Got yerself a toy?"

"Keep yer hands off her. She's mine as soon as she persuades Brand to cooperate."

Sybil studied the words, but they made no sense. Except his claim that she was his. She lay still, hoping she appeared somewhat compliant. But she would not be this man's toy or trophy.

"Hey, Pa," Brand's brother called. "Lookee what I got."

Sybil lifted her head. She saw an older, thinner version of Brand, plus several very tough-looking men. Then she saw Brand and gave him a look full of all the anger that had built over the last hour of indignities.

He nodded a curt greeting, his expression stony.

So that was how it was going to be. No hint of regret or apology. But why should she think there would be? He was part of an outlaw gang. His interest in her had been solely for the purpose of learning what he could about the ranch.

"I see you've met Cyrus, my brother," Brand said. "This here's my pa. Can't remember the names of the others."

Cyrus swung down and lifted her to the ground. Her legs were wobbly, but she'd never let anyone guess. Only good manners kept her from spitting on her captor.

She swung her burning gaze at each and every one of the men, curling her lip as she looked again at Brand.

Cyrus laughed.

She'd never heard a more hateful sound.

"Thought she'd be a bit more pleased to see you, little brother."

Brand shrugged. "Could've told you she don't much care for me."

Sybil gritted her teeth. To think she'd tried to persuade him to stay. Had practically thrown herself into his arms. Thankfully, she had restrained herself.

"That ain't how I saw it." Cyrus pushed her forward. "And I'm goin' by my eyes." He stopped pushing her as they neared the campfire with a pot hanging over it. Steam escaped around the lid.

"I'm hungry." He shoved Sybil down on a log.

She sat, grateful to be off her shaking legs.

The others sat, mostly staring at her. Their looks made her shrink back, feeling soiled and exposed. One of the men filled dishes with heaping helpings of beans. All of them were so unwashed she couldn't imagine eating the food, but when she meant to refuse the plate offered her, the scowl on the cowboy's face made her swallow hard and accept it.

But she didn't say thank you.

Brand's pa edged closer. "We saw you and Brand being friendly. Ain't often a woman warms up to him." His smile was sad, regretful. "Or could be he don't often let anyone get close."

"Wouldn't know. Don't care." She took a spoonful of beans simply to discourage further conversation, and forced herself not to gag.

She felt Brand's disinterested look and shot him one that should have melted the flesh off his bones. "Where's Dawg?"

Brand tipped his head to the side. Dawg sat there with his head on his paws, his eyes alert. His tail tilted to one side at Sybil speaking his name, and he wriggled an inch closer.

"Stay," Brand ordered, and Dawg stayed.

Forks and knives clattered on the tin plates. A utensil screeched and Sybil shivered. Fear and anger and disgust raged through her.

When the men finished and handed their plates to the one who had served the food, they shifted their gaze to her. She thought her heart would leap from her chest at the way they studied her.

"Tie her up," Cyrus ordered one of the men. "Then we'll make plans."

Sybil bolted to her feet, thought to run away, but she was surrounded by hard-faced men. One reached for her and yanked her arms behind her back with no pity for how much it hurt.

Brand! She sent him a silent plea, begging him to help her.

He crossed his arms and looked away.

"To think I thought we might be friends." She spat out each bitter word. She was forced to sit with her back to a tree, trussed up hand and foot.

Cyrus laughed. "Brand don't make friends. Why, he don't even like his family much." He edged up to his brother and gave him an evil grin. He grabbed Brand's arm and dragged him away. The others followed and stood in a tight circle.

She strained to hear what the men said. She could make out only a few words. Enough to know they planned some kind of robbery and that somehow, though she'd done nothing to invite such treatment, she was to be used as a pawn. People hanged for kidnapping. She tried to find pleasure in the idea, but instead quivered so hard her teeth rattled, and she wished for a blanket to warm herself.

Please, God, rescue me.

Chapter Eleven

Brand squeezed his fists so tight he wondered if his fingers would ever straighten. He ached to break Cyrus's nose. The man did not have a decent bone in his body.

Brand knew he must keep his emotions under control. There was nothing Cyrus liked better than seeing Brand get upset about something. And nothing had upset Brand half as much as seeing Sybil dragged into the campsite hung across a horse. She must have suffered a great deal, riding like that. And knowing Cyrus, Brand had no doubt his brother had been inappropriate. The only consolation was that Sybil seemed unharmed and full of spunk. If not for the seriousness of the situation he might have smiled to see how feisty the serious little Sybil had grown.

Cyrus faced him across the tight circle. "Now, little brother, you can help us out or watch us have a little sport with that gal over there."

Brand shrugged. "She's just a young lady." He hoped to convey the impression he didn't care what happened to her. "One of the ranch owner's friends." Maybe that would give them pause.

Cyrus snorted and the others pressed closer. Pa managed to squirm a little at the idea of abusing a young lady, but their father had never stood up to Cyrus and Brand didn't expect he would start now.

"Little brother, you can't fool us. We seen you with her. I never seen you spending time with anyone before."

"You don't know a whole lot about what I do. For instance, who did I spend last winter with?" Let Cyrus mull on that for a while as Brand scrambled to think how to get Sybil away unhurt.

"Who cares? That was then. This is now." Cyrus waited.

So did Brand. Unexpectedly, he thought to ask God for help. *Lord, a good idea would be right handy about now.* But when had God ever sent a way out of his family situation? Suddenly Brand didn't care if he was a Duggan or not. *Lord, help me get Sybil out of this situation.* This prayer mattered more than any he'd ever offered. Would God answer?

"The ranchers will all be after you as soon as they discover Sybil is missing."

"Sybil is it? Now, ain't that a fine name? What do you think, Pa? You like the idea of a Sybil in the family? Sybil and Cyrus has a nice ring to it, don't ya think?"

Brand's whole body quivered with anger. But he held it in check.

"'Course I know little brother here had his sights on her first, but seems me being the oldest I should get first chance. Right, Pa?"

Pa didn't say anything.

"'Course I might just enjoy her without marrying. After all, marriage ties you down."

Brand's anger erupted. He sprang forward and landed a good hard blow to his brother's nose before the others restrained him.

Cyrus wiped his nose on his sleeve and laughed. "Knew you cared about her. Now…" his expression hardened "…let's do some negotiatin'."

Brand had little choice. "What do you want?"

"Show us where the rancher keeps his money."

Brand did some fast thinking. "It's where you'd least expect it."

"Yeah? And where would that be?"

"'Fraid I can't tell you, because then I have nothing to bargain with, do I?"

Cyrus snorted. "You ain't got nothin' anyways."

"Suit yourself." Brand leaned back on his heels and waited.

Cyrus gave him a look fit to curl the toes of a new pair of boots. The others shifted and made impatient noises.

Pa sighed. "Seems you two better work this out. Cyrus, hear what he has in mind."

Cyrus grunted, which Brand knew was as much of a yes as he could expect.

"I'll take you where the money is kept on the condition you release Sybil and see her safely home."

Cyrus shrugged. "Sure. Why not?"

Brand knew Cyrus's promise meant nothing, but Pa believed in keeping his word to his family.

Brand turned to him. "Pa?"

The old man considered for a moment, looked at Sybil straining at her ropes. "You have my word to release her once we get the money. But you better not be up to any funny business."

Brand wished he could think of something clever. But he couldn't. All he could hope for was to lead the men away and wait for a blinding bit of insight before they realized he had no idea what he was doing.

Two of the men saddled the horses and brought them forward.

Seeing Brand about to leave, Dawg whined.

"Come." Brand spoke to the dog and headed toward Sybil.

Cyrus stepped in his way. "What do you think yer gonna do?"

"Leave my dog behind. Last thing we need is him barking and giving away our presence."

"So tell him to stay."

"Sometimes Dawg don't listen too good."

"A bullet between his ears would make him obey."

"Dawg might alert us if anyone approaches the camp."

Cyrus considered the idea, the wheels turning with maddening slowness. "Okay. Leave him here."

"That's what I aim to do. I'll order him to watch Miss Sybil." Dawg, with his injuries, might not provide much protection for Sybil, but it was the most Brand could offer. He called Dawg to follow him across the clearing to her side.

"Stay," he said to Dawg, and the animal lay by Sybil.

She gave him a pleading look. "Don't do this."

"I have to do what I have to do," he whispered in reply.

Cyrus, who had been busy organizing the men, noticed Brand still at Sybil's side and chortled. "Trying to steal a little kiss?"

Brand straightened, his back to his brother, his eyes clinging to Sybil. "This is goodbye." He allowed himself a second of enjoying her face. No doubt it would be the last time he saw her. Once Cyrus and the others figured out he didn't know where there was any money, they'd shoot him on the spot. He could only hope and pray Eddie or someone would rescue Sybil before then.

The best he could hope for was to buy her time.

They left Sybil tied to the tree, Dawg at her side and a grizzle-faced man, Jock, to watch her.

"I ain't gonna stay here and be caught by no posse," he groused.

Cyrus leaped from his horse and grabbed the man's shirt. "You'll be here when we get back or I'll hunt you down and shoot you like a mad dog."

It wasn't until they'd ridden back to the faint trail along the edge of a hill that Brand knew what he must do. It was the only thing that offered any hope of success. He reined toward Edendale, praying as he had never prayed before, likely as his ma had once prayed for her husband and stepson. He prayed for help from any source. He prayed that no one would be hurt. He prayed fervently that Sybil would be released unhurt.

He didn't know the man who had been left to guard her. Jock. Dirty-looking and dirty-smelling. Brand's jaw clenched at the thought of the man going near Sybil.

"Where are we heading, little brother?" Cyrus demanded. "The ranch is that direction." He pointed to the left.

"Told you the money wasn't where you'd expect it."

Cyrus's look dripped warning. "You better not try and fool us."

"Trust me."

Pa rode on his other side. "I'm guessing Brand won't do anything stupid, because if he does, that little gal back there is fair game."

Several of the man laughed in a way that made Brand's fists coil around the reins until his knuckles shone white. He chomped back the bile that burned up his throat. "Pa, remember your promise."

"Son, I ain't forgetting the promise was in exchange for leading us to the money."

"I'm doing the best I can." Unfortunately, his best was not much. He let memories of Sybil fill his mind, giving him determination to do whatever must be done.

Sybil sitting under a tree near the ranch, bent over some book, the sunlight glistening on her golden curls.

Sybil gritting her teeth and holding Dawg while Brand sewed him up.

Sybil telling him stories she'd made up. Would she ever get a chance to get them printed?

Would he succeed in gaining her release?

The trail widened. Dust kicked up from the horses' hooves. In the distance the buildings of Edendale could be seen.

Cyrus grabbed Brand's reins and jerked them to a halt. "What kind of trick is this?"

"No trick. Money is kept in the store." Not Eddie's, but someone's was there.

Cyrus hung on to the reins as he considered the notion. "What do you think, Pa?"

Pa studied the situation. "Don't much care for riding

into a town. Too many places people can hide. Maybe it's a trap."

Brand wished it could be. "Pa, how was I to plan a trap? I didn't even know you were around. And I have only been in town twice. Once to ride through and once to get some biscuits. A young couple bakes bread and biscuits for the store, so there are always fresh ones on hand."

Still they didn't move.

Finally Pa sighed. "I keep thinking of that gal back at the camp. We watched Brand with her. Know he's fond of her. My question is would he trick us if he thought she'd suffer for it?"

Brand met his pa's gaze, letting him see the truth. He would risk his own skin before he'd let them hurt Sybil.

Pa nodded. "I don't figure he would. Come on, boys." He signaled for the others to follow. "But keep your eyes peeled."

He and Cyrus pressed close to Brand. He'd never be able to get away, call out a warning. Do anything.

He'd never felt so helpless in his life. This would surely end badly. But if Sybil escaped unharmed, he could live with the fact. Or die with it comforting him.

They rode forward slowly, watching for any sign of danger. The town appeared sleepy in the slanting afternoon sun. One horse stood in front of the store. A whirlwind of dust swept down the street. A screen door slapped in the wind. Smoke rose from the chimney of the stopping house behind the store, and the aroma of fresh bread filled the air.

They rode closer. Every nerve in Brand's body twitched. What lay ahead? He felt the same tension in Pa and Cyrus. Their hands lingered on their guns. Would he escape this day without someone being shot?

They rode up to the store and the seven of them lined up in a row, facing the closed door. Through the window, they saw a barrel, some hardware hanging from the ceiling and the counter holding an assortment of jars and tins. But not a sign of life.

"Could be he's in the back room," Brand said, his neck prickling.

"Let's go see. You can go first." Cyrus ordered two of the men to stay with the horses, then pressed his gun to Brand's back.

Their boots rang in the silence as they climbed the steps and shoved open the door. Brand paused to let his eyes adjust to the dim interior. Cyrus nudged him with his gun.

"Where's the money?"

Brand didn't know. How was he supposed to, when he was making this up? He'd never ridden a wild horse that filled him with more tension.

"Guess you need to ask the salesclerk."

Cyrus yelled, "Hello?" sending a jolt of alarm up and down Brand's spine.

A noise came from the door to the living quarters. The handle jiggled. Brand recognized the man who stepped through the door. And it wasn't Macpherson. Why was the man in civilian clothes? Brand's nerves skittered madly. Something was amiss.

"Can I help you?" Constable Allen asked.

"Yeah, mister. You can give us all the money hid here."

The Mountie lifted his arms. "Sure thing." He moved toward the counter.

Brand tensed until his bones felt brittle.

"No funny stuff," Cyrus warned.

"I'm no fool," the Mountie said, edging closer, his eyes guarded as he took in the scene before him.

Cyrus moved to keep the counter between himself and the officer, his gun steadily aimed at the Mountie's heart.

Brand wondered how the man could be so cool.

Then the Mountie flung himself out of sight behind the counter. "Now," he called.

Men burst through the doors of the storeroom and the living quarters.

The Mountie came up with a shotgun aimed at the Duggan gang. "Drop your weapons."

Cyrus and the others fired and raced for the outer door.

Brand dived for the floor.

In a few minutes the shooting was over. Brand sat up, pain burning his side. He pressed his hand to the spot and looked at the blood staining his palm. He'd been shot.

"You are under arrest," the Mountie said, and Brand got to his feet, his hands out to show he was unarmed.

He looked around. Two men lay on the floor. They'd never rob anyone again. The men who had waited outside were gone. And so were Cyrus and Pa.

"We'll find them," the Mountie said, and Brand knew it was a vow. The Mounties prided themselves on always getting their man.

Brand leaned his head against the rough wood, his hands chained to the iron rings anchored in the wall of the livery stable where Constable Allen had taken him after his arrest. He knew he would either be hanged or sentenced to hard labor for the rest of his life.

His only consolation came from having told the Mountie where to find Sybil.

His side ached.

Someone stepped into the barn. "Hello. The Mountie asked me to bring you food."

Tied hand and foot, Brand could not feed himself. Only the aroma of the meal allowed him to suffer the indignity of being fed by the other man.

"Any news from the Mountie?" Brand asked. His thoughts overflowed with worry about Sybil…worry that was not eased despite his continued prayer.

"I don't expect he'll be back until he catches up with the rest of the gang. Constable Allen is very unwavering in his pursuit of justice."

Brand didn't continue the conversation, unable to bear the idea that the Mountie neglected Sybil's rescue in favor of chasing after Cyrus and Pa. *God, keep her safe. Please, God, hear my prayer and answer it.*

Darkness fell and Brand's spirits nose-dived. Had Sybil been left out there, alone except for old Jock? Afraid? Cold?

He shivered as he thought of how vulnerable she would be.

He fell into a restless sleep and woke to find a figure silhouetted against the door. His heart skittered up his throat. Cyrus? Had he returned, intent on making Brand pay for the botched robbery?

He shuddered.

Then the figure moved. He saw it was Constable Allen and he strained against his chains. "Did you find Sybil?"

"She's safe."

He inhaled without pain for the first time in hours.

"I overtook the rest of the gang."

Something in his voice alerted Brand. "It's good news?" Then he realized good news for the Mountie would be bad news for him.

"Your father was injured. Two men are dead. Two of them escaped."

"Cyrus?" Was he dead or alive?

"He got away. I have a posse after him. He'll not get far." The Mountie's voice promised Cyrus's capture.

Brand tried to decide how he felt about it. On one hand he wanted to see the end of the Duggan gang. On the other, Pa and Cyrus were the only family he had.

The Mountie unlocked Brand's shackles and signaled for a man to bring his horse forward. "Mount up."

Brand obeyed and sat stoically on his horse while the Mountie tied his wrists together and secured a rope to lead him. He submitted without protest. He saw no point in trying to get away. Sybil was safe. He could go to his death or a jail cell content with that knowledge.

"How bad is Pa?"

"He was bleeding badly. Mrs. Gardiner is nursing him." The officer kept his attention forward, but Brand saw the way his jaw muscles tightened. "I'd like to see him stand trial for his deeds."

"Guess he will whether he lives or dies."

Constable Allen jerked his head around. "You're right. Justice will prevail either way." The Mountie rode at his side, directing him down the trail.

Brand thought of the man's desire for justice. "What if God forgives him?"

The constable considered the question for the better part of half a mile, then sighed. "As a lawman I wish to see man's justice, but I have to accept that God forgives sinners." He paused. "And I willingly confess I am a sinner saved by God's grace. I have no right to resent God extending that same grace to someone like your pa."

"Maybe you should tell him that." Brand knew Pa's salvation had been his ma's dying wish.

When they should have headed south to the fort, the Mountie indicated they should go west. They would soon reach the ranch if they continued this direction.

Perhaps the Mountie meant to let him see Pa one last time. If so he would tell Pa himself that there was forgiveness in repentance.

"No one else was hurt?"

"A cowboy in the posse got a minor flesh wound on his leg. Nothing that will slow him down."

They reached the ranch. Brand held back. Only the tug on the rope by the Mountie made him move on. He didn't want to face Eddie and the others. On the other hand, he'd give his right arm to see Sybil and know she was unharmed.

He heard a bark and looked to see Dawg limping toward him. The ropes made it impossible for Brand to reach down and pick up the animal. "Hi, Dawg."

The dog walked to his side. Seemed the old mutt would live. Guess if Brand went to jail Dawg would need a new owner.

The Mountie forced him to move forward, up the hill toward the big house. Eddie, Mercy, Linette and Sybil waited for them.

Brand and the Mountie drew to a halt in front of them.

Brand stared at his bound hands. Although the ropes were weather stained in spots, the jute strands were firm, the twists ready to defy any hope of escape. He kept his hands still, his head lowered, hiding his face as much as he could. His cheeks stung as if he'd leaned too close to open flames. What must they think of him? A Duggan. Branded with the same condemnation as his pa and brother. He expected no sympathy. No understanding of his situation. He couldn't claim innocence, so he wouldn't try.

He lifted his head a fraction, unable to deprive himself of a glance at Sybil's face. Would she be angry? Disappointed? But he couldn't tell from her expression. Seemed she didn't want him to guess at her feelings, because her face revealed nothing but disinterest. Despite understanding he had no right to speak and would likely be cut short, he let his gaze connect with hers. He schooled himself to reveal none of the regret churning his insides at the thought that this was how she would remember him—bound and headed to jail.

"Glad to see you're okay," he said to her, keeping his voice low and impersonal, while inside raged a loud protest. *I'm innocent.* But he'd made a decision and didn't intend to cry about the consequences. He had agreed to help the gang in exchange for her life. Not for a moment would he regret it. "Would you look after Dawg for me?"

A fleeting emotion flicked across her eyes. Too fast, too uncertain for him to guess what it was.

What did it matter?

She nodded. "Dawg will be safe with me."

Her words whispered across his thoughts. If only all his concerns could be so easily dealt with.

* * *

Sybil's heart hurt with every beat. Seeing Brand tied up, on his way to trial… She crossed her arms over her stomach and gripped her elbows with tense fingers. Jail or worse awaited him. She had told herself over and over to forget about those few days they had shared when she felt drawn to him. It had all been deception. Yes, she'd known he ran from something, but never in ten thousand guesses would she have suspected he was part of the infamous Duggan gang.

"Get down," Constable Allen said, holding a rope that kept Brand from considering flight.

Sybil averted her eyes, unable to bear the sight of Brand's humiliation.

Dawg leaped to his master, placed his paws on his waist and whined.

From the corner of her eyes, she saw Brand pat Dawg's head with hands bound so tightly she knew they must hurt.

She turned to the Mountie, about to ask him to loosen the ropes holding Brand, but bit back the words before she opened her mouth. Of course he must be secured. He was a common outlaw. She squeezed her hands tighter, knowing she'd have bruises on both arms.

"Down, Dawg," he murmured, and the dog dropped to all fours.

"Your father is upstairs," the Mountie said. "The Gardiners have been generous enough to allow you to visit him."

"Thank you," Brand said, his voice as flat as a thousand acres of prairie.

"Eddie will see that you are guarded until I return

to take you to the fort. I intend to find your brother and the man with him."

Sybil noted the slight shudder that twitched Brand's shoulders, but he stood tall, revealing nothing but determination. Guess he'd known this day would come sometime.

But she found no pleasure in the justice that he would face. It was easier to be angry at his deception when she couldn't see him or feel anguish at how he was bound.

The Mountie handed the rope to Eddie. "I'll be back when I'm done with this business."

He'd said Cyrus and another man had escaped. Sybil prayed the constable would find them and bring them to justice. Her face burned at the memory of Cyrus manhandling her. How could Brand and Cyrus be brothers? One so cruel? The other—

She stopped the word that sprang to her mind. He wasn't *gentle;* he was a deceiver. His name should be Jacob.

The Mountie rode away.

Linette stepped aside, indicating they should follow her indoors. "Your father is upstairs."

When Brand hesitated, Eddie tugged the rope. "Come along."

As Sybil recalled how Brand had played the innocent, convinced her that he was a worthy man, she was able to hold back any sympathy at his situation.

Brand stepped over the threshold.

Dawg sat on his haunches and waited.

Sybil hated to shut the door against him. "You wait here. I'll come feed you in a bit." She kept her back to the room, staring out the nearby window as Eddie and Linette led Brand upstairs to his pa.

Mercy grabbed Sybil's arm and dragged her to the sitting room, where she pushed her into a chair and sat facing her. "An outlaw in the house. How exciting is that?"

Sybil shuddered. "Mercy, it's not exciting at all. It's awkward and horrible. His pa is shot and lies in one of Linette's beds." Linette took in anyone in need of care. "How will she manage? Do you think it is safe for her in her condition?"

"Do you think he'd hurt her?"

"I doubt Eddie is going to leave him alone with her." Sybil shook her head. All those hours she'd spent un-accompanied with Brand, feeling safe and—she shud-dered—longing to touch him, feel his lips on hers. How could she have been so mistaken about him?

When she let emotions rule, danger followed. She'd known it all the while. Only she'd never imagined this sort of thing.

Linette entered the sitting room. "Eddie said he'd sit with Brand and his father for a bit. Then Slim will spell him off. There'll be someone guarding him day and night so we can feel safe in our beds." She sighed deeply. "I still can't believe I could be so mistaken about a man. Eddie is upset that he was, as well. He prides himself on being a good judge of people." With another sigh, she headed to the kitchen with a basin of blood-stained rags to soak.

Sybil followed. Unlike Mercy, she didn't want to speculate or rejoice in the excitement of having two outlaws upstairs.

"You must be tired," she said to Linette. "Can I help?"

Her friend brushed aside a tendril of hair. "I find it

very hard to see the pair of them. And feel the tension in the air. There's something between them that isn't quite right, and I can't put my finger on it."

Sybil wrapped an arm about her. "Could it simply be that they are common criminals and don't like being captured?"

"Maybe."

But she knew Linette wasn't convinced.

"I can't get Mr. Duggan's bleeding to stop."

The worry in her voice caught Sybil's attention. "Do you think some organ has been hit?"

Linette shook her head. "I simply don't know. The man is thin except for a pronounced potbelly, and his skin has a distinct yellowish hue."

"You mean jaundice?"

"I fear so."

Jaundice! She'd heard of it. Always spoken in dark tones. A slow, certain death. Often the sufferer would bleed to death or lose his or her mind, dying in confusion. "Does Brand know?"

"I doubt it."

"I guess it doesn't make much difference, does it?" Sybil forced indifference into her voice. "They'll either hang or rot in jail. Dying in a clean bed might be a mercy. An undeserved one."

Linette dried her hands and turned to her. "Do any of us deserve mercy? From God or man?"

"If we live a good life we don't need mercy from man, and if we seek God's forgiveness He offers His mercy."

"But it's so undeserved. And I fear none of us can claim we have not offended another."

Sybil tried to protest, but then thought of her secret.

Wasn't she being untruthful in her own way by hiding behind a pseudonym? In talking to Brand with a view to gleaning information for a story without telling him her intention?

Linette turned to meal preparation, and Sybil helped. A little later, Slim came in to relieve Eddie, and Linette served the meal. They ate in silence, as if each of them was struggling to believe the recent events.

Grady studied the sober faces around him. "Is it true? Is Brand a bad man?"

Linette and Eddie exchanged glances, while Mercy and Sybil waited for their answer.

Silent communication passed between the couple. How Sybil envied their love and security. Would she ever enjoy something similar? To her disgrace, she allowed herself to admit she'd given a few thoughts to Brand being like Eddie. How wrong she'd been.

Eddie took Grady's hands. "It would seem he is part of an outlaw gang."

Grady looked around the table, saw the same message in the nod each person gave him. He shook his head. "You're wrong. He's not a bad man. He can't be. Not when Dawg likes him so much."

No one could argue with that.

Grady's lips quivered. "Why are you all being so mean to him?"

The boy dashed out the back door.

Linette pushed herself to her feet, then looked about at the dishes to be cleaned up. She glanced upward. "They need to be fed."

Sybil made up her mind. "You go after Grady. I'll feed the prisoners and then we'll clean up."

Mercy insisted on accompanying her upstairs, and

Sybil didn't mind. She couldn't imagine facing Brand. Yet she knew she must in order to erase the false memories of the Brand she thought she had known.

She stepped into the room, Mercy on her heels. Slim sat at the doorway, leaning back in a wooden chair, a rifle across his knees. Mercy handed him a plate of food.

Slim dropped all four legs of the chair to the floor, snagged another chair and pulled it close.

Mercy sat at his side.

Slowly Sybil shifted her gaze, saw Brand's father. At their campsite she had considered him big and menacing. She hadn't taken note of the condition Linette had pointed out. Now, though, under the gray woolen blanket, he looked thin and sallow. Yellowish, just as Linette said.

"I brought dinner." Sybil held a plate of food in each hand.

Brand took one plate, his wrists still bound with thick ropes, and set it on the nearby table. But he didn't eat.

She felt his awkward waiting, but rather than relieve it, she turned to his father. "I brought you food."

He regarded her unblinkingly. "Don't think I'll be needing food where I'm going."

"I'm sure they'll feed you adequately in jail." She hated the judgmental tone of her voice, but she couldn't help it. Brand had deceived her and this man had ordered her held captive. She had every right to judge him for that.

Mr. Duggan gave a faint laugh. "No doubt the food will be better than we deserve."

She again offered him the plate.

He shifted, moaned. The blood drained from his

face, leaving his skin even more yellow. He pulled the plate closer.

She stepped back to wait, and flicked her gaze to Brand. "I don't know who you are." Every word dripped with anger, frustration and a thousand drops of pain, disappointment and shame.

He raised his eyes and lowered them again almost before she could see them. But she got a glimpse, long enough to note the indifference. He didn't even care. That was the bitterest thing of all.

"He's a Duggan." The elder man pushed away the plate, the food barely touched. "I'm done."

"Then I'll see to your dressing." She removed the plate, setting it by the door, where Mercy watched, her eyes flashing with excitement.

Sybil lowered the gray blanket to reveal a wound in the man's left side. His belly was indeed badly swollen. The dressings Linette had placed there a short time ago were blood soaked. Sybil removed them gingerly. Blood oozed from the round hole. She quickly placed pads of clean dressing on it and kept her hand firmly pressed to the area.

But warm moisture soon reached her palm.

"It's not good, is it?" Mr. Duggan said.

Her face must have given away her distress.

When she didn't answer, he asked another question. "How long do you think I have?" He turned to his son. "Brand?"

For the first time since he'd thanked her for the food she'd brought, Brand spoke. "Pa, you're tough. A little gunshot ain't going to finish you."

Pa's smile was regretful, knowing. "Boy, it ain't the bullet that will do me in. It's the rest." He patted his distended stomach. "Like Cyrus says, we eat well 'nough. But still I lose weight. Haven't hardly got energy enough to spit." He closed his eyes as if too weary to continue.

Brand had been eating his food, both hands holding the fork and going from plate to mouth. Now he shoved away the plate. "Pa, you should stop this life."

"Son, this life is gonna stop me."

Brand leaned forward, ignoring the others in the room. "Pa, repent for your sins. Make your peace with God."

"You figure God would forgive an old outlaw like me?"

"God's no respecter of persons."

Sybil observed the pair while pressing her hand to the wound in the hopes of stopping the bleeding. She didn't want to give Mr. Duggan hope. But she knew God offered hope and mercy and forgiveness. The knowledge twisted through her. Sometimes she didn't understand God's mercy. It was so undeserved.

Then her heart smote her. She might not be an outlaw, but she didn't deserve God's mercy any more than they.

Mr. Duggan shifted his gaze to her. "Is that right, miss? Do you think He'll forgive me after all I done?"

Sybil wanted to say he would burn in hell, but didn't God say He forgives all sins? Even the sinner on the cross beside Him? She had to answer Brand's father honestly despite her reluctance.

"Mr. Duggan, I believe God forgives. Didn't He say, 'Father, forgive them?' about the men who killed him?" Now, why had she added that?

Mr. Duggan closed his eyes. "I'll think on it."

"Pa!" Brand surged to his feet and leaned over the bed, bringing Slim crashing to his feet.

Brand darted a glance at the foreman, then concentrated on his father. "Pa, isn't that what you always told Ma? And then you continued on with your outlawing. Don't do it again."

The older man shifted his gaze to Sybil. "Will God forgive my son, too?"

She allowed her gaze to rest on Brand, whose attention was riveted on his father, then she drew her attention back to his pa. "God is merciful." More than she thought any of them deserved.

"You be sure and tell him." The older man closed his eyes.

"Pa." Brand shook him. "Don't keep putting it off."

But the old man did not open his eyes.

"He's sleeping," Sybil said.

Brand sank back in his chair, his hands hanging between his knees, his head bent. "He's getting weaker. I fear…" He didn't finish.

She applied a fresh dressing to the wound and pulled the blanket over Mr. Duggan, then gathered up the bandages and dishes and headed for the door. Mercy joined her as she left the room.

Sybil had hoped for an excuse from Brand for his behavior, an explanation…something that made sense. She hadn't found it. Perhaps because there wasn't one.

Like his pa said, Brand was a Duggan. The man she'd thought she saw a few days ago was nothing but a figment of her overactive imagination.

Time to face reality and bring herself in line with the rules of conduct she'd lived by all her years.

Chapter Twelve

Brand watched Sybil and Mercy leave the room, listening to Mercy's voice as they descended the stairs. He gave Slim a silent stare, then settled back in his chair.

It was the first time he'd been in a house in a very long time and it was a fine house. Pa lay on a real mattress, covered with real bedding. Likely he hadn't enjoyed such since before Ma died.

Nor had Brand enjoyed such since Ma's death. He'd been always on the run. Always hoping to stay ahead of Pa and Cyrus. Hoping no one would discover he was a Duggan.

But as Pa said to Sybil, he *was* a Duggan.

Although he'd gone along with the gang only to protect Sybil. He hadn't even held a gun during the attempted robbery. Not that he expected anyone to believe him.

There was only one more thing he wanted before he went to his short future—to see Pa accept God's forgiveness before he died.

Brand would also like to see Sybil believe his innocence. But he'd sacrificed that two days ago.

The patient stirred and Brand leaned forward to touch his arm. "Pa?" he whispered, ignoring eagle-eyed Slim's watchfulness.

Pa mumbled something Brand couldn't make out.

Brand watched his chest rise and fall, his own breathing matching the movement. So long as Pa drew breath he still had the opportunity to seek forgiveness.

Brand kept a careful vigil, waiting for him to waken.

And praying. That surprised him. His neglected, forgotten faith had been right there all the time. He only had to stop and listen to the call in his heart.

The rise and fall of Pa's chest marked off the passing minutes.

Despite his concentration, Brand knew the exact second Sybil stepped into the room. He felt her with every nerve ending that responded in eager welcome. It took every ounce of self-control to keep his gaze on his father.

She was alone, and Slim rose to accompany her to the bed, guarding her.

"The dressings will need changing again."

Pa stirred as she lifted the covers. He opened his eyes.

Brand would not let Slim and his rifle, nor Sybil and her alluring presence, stop him. He leaned over his father. "Please, Pa, before it's too late."

"Brand, stop fretting." His thin hand patted Brand's. "I done made my peace with God. Like you said, He's forgiven me."

Joy erupted in Brand's heart. He had to share this feeling with someone, and looked up into Sybil's eyes, not caring that she would likely not rejoice as deeply as he was. Why would she? Most people would think the Duggan gang deserved nothing but punishment.

Her mouth curved in a sweet smile.

His heart threatened to jolt from his chest. For one heartbeat, two, and then a thunderous third beat he let himself drown in that look. Then Pa grabbed his hand and mercifully brought him back to his senses.

"Son, I ain't long for this world. Promise me something."

He wanted to argue that Pa would recover, but he couldn't. He'd seen how Linette had earlier applied a paste of something she said an Indian woman had given her, said it would stop bleeding in normal situations.

Pa's was obviously not normal, as his wound continued to bleed. "Anything." If it was in his power to do.

"Promise me you'll tell Cyrus he can be forgiven, too."

Surprised at the request, Brand jerked his gaze toward Sybil.

She shuddered. He felt her anger.

"Brand?" Pa sounded anxious, and Brand brought his gaze back to him.

"Yes, Pa. I promise."

The old man sighed. Brand waited, but Pa had fallen asleep, his chest rising and falling rhythmically.

Brand allowed himself to lift his gaze to Sybil again. "Can God forgive my brother?"

She would not meet his eyes. "Of course."

"Can you?"

She gathered up a basin full of soiled rags. "I don't know." And she left the room.

He understood. Neither brother could expect forgiveness from her. Cyrus didn't merit it and wouldn't care.

Brand could never prove he deserved it, even though he cared so much that his throat was impossibly tight.

Sybil hurried to her room, grateful that Mercy had gone out and Linette was busy elsewhere. Sybil needed to be alone. She didn't want to forgive any of the Duggans. And it bothered her more than she cared to admit.

In an attempt to forget about the whole business, she pulled out her notebook, intending to write something imaginary that had nothing to do with outlaws and cowboys—a story for children that ended happily in victory. But her fingers went instead to the pages she'd written about Brand.

She should send the story away as it was. A nameless cowboy. Only he was more than that—less than that. A cowboy with a shameful name, a shameful life. She jammed the pages back into her drawer and flung herself facedown on her bed, burying her sobs in her pillow.

She deserved every bit of pain she would endure. All along she'd known she should avoid the man.

She and Linette, with Mercy's help, cared for Mr. Duggan the rest of the day and throughout the night, but he died as dawn broke over the horizon on Sunday morning.

Both Sybil and Linette were in the room when he breathed his last.

Brand hovered at his side, knowing the end would be soon.

Linette reached over and touched his shoulder. "He's gone. I'm sorry."

Brand sank to the chair, his face drained of all color.

Eddie, who was guarding him, went to his side and squeezed his shoulder. "I'm sorry."

For all he showed, Brand might not even have heard.

Sybil stood immobile. He'd lost his father and that had to hurt, even for an outlaw. It reminded her of her own pain and sense of loss and loneliness when her parents had died. Even her anger at Brand for his deception could not block out her concern.

She joined Eddie at Brand's side.

He lifted his head enough to see the hem of her dress. She waited, wanting more. So much more. All of which she could never have.

Slowly, his head came up until he met her eyes. She knew he tried to bank his emotions, but his eyes darkened until they were almost black. She sensed his difficulty in breathing. Her own throat constricted and her eyes stung with tears. "I'm sorry for your loss."

He nodded, his eyes narrowing, his breathing deepening. "Thank you." He turned to Linette and then Eddie. "Thank you for your hospitality."

Linette smiled. "It's what we do."

The rancher cleared his throat. "We'll give you a moment to say goodbye to your father."

Linette headed for the door. Sybil hesitated. There was so much more she wanted to say. But it was to the Brand of unknown name. Not Brand, one of the Duggan gang.

For just a moment she let herself believe he was still the former, and touched his shoulder as Eddie had. "You have my deepest sympathy." And then, lest anyone misjudge her actions, she hurried after Linette.

Eddie stayed behind, his back to Brand and his father, out of respect for Brand's loss.

That afternoon they buried Morton Duggan in the little graveyard on top of the hill.

Jayne had questioned it. "He's a criminal. Should he be buried in the same ground as these good people?" Four graves of those who had died passing through the territory stood in the small plot.

"He's a sinner saved by grace," Linette said in her decisive way. "Aren't the angels in heaven rejoicing? How can we be less than charitable?"

And so a little assembly accompanied the body to its final resting place. Most of the cowboys refused to attend on principle. Cookie and Bertie came. Jayne and Seth, Cassie and Roper joined the procession, as did Mercy and Sybil. Linette and Eddie led the way, with Brand following them.

Eddie spoke a few words over the open grave. Sybil was not the only one who wiped away a tear. Perhaps, like herself, they were recalling their own pain. Jayne had seen her fiancé shot dead before her eyes. Cassie had buried a husband and two infants. Sybil didn't know what loss the others remembered, but it seemed each had a share of pain. Her own seemed fresh in her mind—a mother and father who'd died within weeks of each other.

A best friend who had died way too young.

Despite who and what Brand was, she felt his sorrow as if it was her own.

He stood before the grave, head bowed, hat in his hands almost hiding the ropes that bound him. Seth had been appointed to carry a gun to guard him. Out of respect the others had come unarmed.

Eddie said amen. Each of them tossed in a handful of dirt then passed by Brand, uttering condolences. Sybil went last. She ached to be able to forgive his treachery and who he was. But how could she? Yet she must let him know she understood his sorrow. She'd tried earlier, but felt he was too shocked by his father's death to really hear her. "I'm sorry," she said. Such inadequate words for all she felt. "I know what it's like to lose one's father."

His gaze jerked to her, hard, glistening with tears, yet probing.

She jolted as his look rattled against the insides of her heart—an intruder, unwelcome, unsafe.

"Your father was a good man. Mine was an outlaw." His voice grated. "It's not the same."

She patted his arm. "He was your father. It's the same."

She left. Why did she say that? It didn't make sense and yet it was the truth, and somehow, she knew he needed to hear it.

Bertie went to Eddie. "Boss, he needs to be alone with his grief and loss."

"It's not a privilege I can give him."

"Give me the gun. I'll guard him but respect his need for privacy."

Eddie considered the request, then nodded to Seth, who handed the rifle to Bertie. Bertie sat on a rock a few feet away.

Brand watched the proceedings without a flicker of expression.

"Ignore me," Bertie said. "I won't bother you unless you try and escape."

Sybil joined the others as they returned to the house. She lingered at the back door, watching Brand standing over his father's grave. Dawg lay at his feet, his head on his paws, watching his master.

Mercy came to her side. "I guess you can't help feeling sorry for him even though they are outlaws."

Sybil didn't answer. She could never forgive him for being an outlaw and for hiding his identity from her. Nor would she listen to her conscience, which said she must forgive if she wished to be forgiven. Any more than she'd listen to the part of her brain that said he hadn't forced her to enjoy his company the few days he was at the ranch under false pretenses.

She turned away and put her efforts into helping Linette. Her body was usefully occupied. Too bad her heart wouldn't be diverted.

Brand stared at the hole before him. His father lay in the cold ground. He shivered. The grave would soon be covered with dirt and then a layer of snow. But Pa wasn't there. He was in heaven with Ma.

Brand wasn't sure how to deal with the sorrow that clawed at his insides. How often had he wished both Pa and Cyrus would not bother him anymore? But not like this. Death was too final.

He sighed and shifted his gaze toward the house. Was that Sybil in the shadows? Then the figure was gone. She'd expressed her regrets. Said she understood that he mourned his pa. He wished he could think she cared, that it was more than politeness, but he didn't dare allow such a thought.

He was more than grateful for the kindness shown his pa. That had to be all he could think of. Eddie had informed him he could wait in the barn for the Mountie's return. It was no more than Brand expected. He only wished the Mountie would hurry up so he could leave this place. He fought a constant fight against the sweet memories of the past few days.

"I'm done," he said to Bertie.

Bertie led him past the house, Dawg walking at his side. Brand forced himself not to look at the windows for a glimpse of Sybil. He had enough memories to carry him through his future, which would be short and end abruptly.

They went to the pen he and Dawg had recently shared. He averted his eyes from the place where Sybil had sat, her back to the rough wood as she visited with him and touched him. Silently, he submitted to being tied securely to a sturdy corner post.

"Surely hate to do this, son, but I got me orders."

"Don't worry. It's what I expect."

Bertie finished and squatted in front of him, eye to eye. "Linette says your pa made his peace with God before his death. Glad to hear that. What about you? Are you prepared to meet your maker?"

The man's gentle concern melted Brand's frozen heart and he smiled. "I am indeed. My ma was a strong believer and taught me to be the same, though truth be told, I let my faith slip for many years."

"I, too, had a believing ma and I wandered far from God for a time. My mother's prayers brought me back. Seems your ma's prayers have done the same. Do you care to send her a letter informing her of your pa's death?"

"My ma's dead, though she would have been pleased to hear of his change of heart."

"Son, I have to ask you, what led you into a path of crime?"

"I have my reasons."

"Care to tell me?"

"I wouldn't expect you to believe me."

"I'd believe you if it was true." Bertie held his gaze, demanding truth and confession.

Brand swallowed hard. If only he'd had a man like this for a father. The thought unleashed his usual reserve and loosened his tongue. "It was my brother who kidnapped Miss Sybil. He threatened…" Brand shuddered as he recalled Cyrus's ugly talk. "He said he'd do awful things unless I helped him. I figured if I went along she might be rescued." No point in mentioning Pa's promise. No one would believe Brand had trusted the word of an outlaw.

Bertie didn't even blink. "I see. Have you told Eddie this? Or the Mountie?"

"What difference would it make? I was involved in the robbery of the store. I'm a Duggan." And that said it all as far as people were concerned. It always had.

"Seems to me you're more than a Duggan. You're a good man." Bertie rose.

"I'll thank you not to repeat what I just said." Brand didn't want to be mocked for making up stories so people would think him innocent.

The other man rocked back and forth on his feet. "Are you saying you'd refuse my help?"

"I'm saying I doubt you could help, and I don't care to be considered a whiner."

Bertie patted his shoulder. "You're no whiner. Now try and be comfortable. I'll bring your supper when it's ready. You're in for a treat. My Cookie makes the best meals in the whole territory."

Brand chuckled at the man's pride. Not until Bertie

left did he realize he'd not given the promise Brand had asked for. Not that it really mattered. Nothing Bertie said would convince anyone.

Brand hadn't slept at all the night before. He settled back in the straw now, Dawg at his side, and let sleep numb his thoughts. He jerked awake as Bertie entered and bent to loosen the ropes on his wrists.

"I ain't into feeding an able-bodied man."

Brand rubbed his bruised and raw skin, then turned to the food. "You didn't exaggerate," he said after his first mouthful. "I realized that when she sent a plate out to me before." He took another bite of the tender roast beef, mashed potatoes and gravy.

Bertie grinned. Then as Brand ate, he sat and told stories of people he'd met and places he'd been. He even managed to make Brand laugh a time or two.

"Son, I'd like to read from the Bible before I go."

The idea sat well with Brand and he agreed.

Bertie read for a few minutes—stories of the Israelites as they wandered the desert.

The words gave Brand comfort, but his wanderings were soon to end and he would join his ma and pa in heaven. The comfort fled as he choked back the tightness in his throat. Tightness from an imaginary rope about his neck.

Chapter Thirteen

Sybil tossed and turned all night. She could not shake the uncertainty she felt about Brand. She rose tired and angry at herself. She did not want to think of him. He was an outlaw and would soon face justice. But he'd revealed nothing of that sort of nature while she'd kept him company, helped him sew up Dawg, nor when they'd walked to the river. Her cheeks burned with shame to think she had hoped he'd kiss her again. What was wrong with her? Never before in her life had she struggled to keep her thoughts on what was right and wise.

Realizing she was staring out the window in the direction of the barn, she jerked away and went to the library. She would take each book off the shelves and dust the place thoroughly. She sneezed as she tackled the job.

Two hours later she stood back, satisfied. Then her shoulders sagged. Now what? The job had not kept her from thinking of Brand and reliving every moment they had spent together. As it turned out, for her it was in blissful ignorance. Yet even knowing that couldn't erase those memories.

How was she to move on, with her heart so full of regrets and forbidden wishes?

She hurried from the library. The kitchen was empty. Linette must have taken Grady to visit Cassie's children. And who knew where Mercy disappeared to? The empty house echoed with Sybil's inner turmoil.

"I must forget him. Put him out of my mind," she murmured to the silent walls.

But how could she? Perhaps if she confronted him...

Her decision made, she grabbed a knit shawl and left the house, keeping her steps slow and measured, when she longed to rush down the hill.

She rehearsed what she would say: *Why did you not tell me who you are?* However, the answer was obvious. If he had, there would have been no chance of even a hint of friendship between them. Nor would he have been invited to come to the ranch in the first place.

Strange that his reputation hadn't preceded him. Everyone knew him only as a horse breaker. Why had there been no word of him being part of the Duggan gang? How did he manage to hide that and deceive so many people? Of course, his role in the gang necessitated he do exactly that. Win people's confidence, learn their secrets so the gang could rob them.

But if that was the case, why hadn't he accepted any of the invitations into the big house? Why had he shied away from any contact with others?

She pressed her palms to her temples. None of it made any sense. If she answered the questions truthfully, she couldn't see him as guilty. But was she only trying to make herself feel better about the way she had practically fallen over him?

The cookhouse lay on her left. She slowed her steps.

Would Cookie soothe her with tea and cinnamon rolls? Jayne's cabin stood on her right. Would Jayne offer wise words? Tell her she should guard her heart?

Sybil stared straight ahead. She didn't want comfort nor wise words. She wanted answers to the ache in her heart, and only Brand could offer those. Though he likely had nothing to give but more lies, more deceit.

The barn door had been pushed open, letting in the cool afternoon air and bright sunshine. Sybil paused to glance about. Noted the thinning leaves on the trees, the dusty brown piles of them gathering along the edges of the yard as if huddling together against winter. They would soon find how futile it was to try and fight the season.

Was she being equally foolish? Refusing to accept the facts?

She opened the gate of the pen in front of the barn and slipped past the bars, holding her breath lest anyone see her and wonder if she had lost her mind.

A man's voice came from the interior of the barn. Not Brand's. She paused in the doorway to listen.

"You're not so high and mighty now, are you?" Cal. She recognized his voice.

She heard no reply from Brand, and wondered whether he spoke so softly she couldn't hear, or if he didn't even bother to answer the man.

"I've half a mind to drag you outside and let all your admiring fans see who you really are." Cal laughed, a short, bitter sound. "In fact, that's what I'm going to do. The others will be showing up for supper about now."

She caught the sound of grunting and scuffling. And Dawg growling.

"Dawg, quiet." These were the only words she heard Brand speak.

"Get to your feet," Cal said harshly.

Sybil clutched at the rough wood on the door frame. Why was Cal so vindictive? What did he hope to gain by parading Brand before the others? Everyone knew he was in the barn and why. But Cal wanted to further humiliate him.

Brand had dealt with enough already. His capture. His pa's death. Enough was enough.

Ignoring the warning voice in her head that said she should stay out of this, Sybil hurried down the aisle. She reached the open gate.

Dawg whined, alerting Brand. He stood before Cal, his hands bound, a rope around his neck. He shook his head as if warning her away.

But she was beyond paying attention to a warning of any sort. "I wonder what Eddie would think of this. Or have you sent him after an imaginary sick cow again?"

Cal spun about, his eyes wide with surprise, and then they narrowed. "It was a bull and this is none of your concern."

A few minutes ago she might have agreed with him. In fact, she might have been compelled to add her own words of condemnation. But suddenly everything was so clear she wondered how she could have been confused for even a minute.

Cal gave her his back as he turned his attention to Brand. "He's an outlaw. Don't bother wasting your time on him."

She stepped into the pen. Dawg pressed to her side and she patted his head, but kept her attention fixed on

Cal. When he continued to ignore her, she grabbed his shoulder. "Who appointed you judge and jury?"

He spared her a look full of disbelief. "I could ask you the same thing."

"Sybil, leave it be." Brand obviously did not thank her for interfering.

"I have no intention of leaving it be. Cal, let him alone."

The cowboy laughed in her face. "Who's going to stop me?"

She grabbed the rope, surprising him enough that it slipped from his grip. She glowered at him. "I am."

Cal growled. "Little Miss London. Too good for the rest of us. You might just consider that you don't belong here and this is none of your business." He lunged for the rope, but Brand jerked away, pushed Sybil aside and faced Cal.

"You can call me an outlaw all you want, but you will treat Miss Bannerman like a lady."

Cal's face darkened. His fists curled.

Dawg's hackles rose and he snarled at the man.

Cal kicked at him. "Your dog is ugly and stupid." He grabbed the rope and yanked it tight.

Brand choked, fought the rope with his bound hands.

Sybil shoved Cal. He shoved back and she fell into the boards.

Dawg erupted into a ball of flying fur. He lunged at Cal, grabbed his arm and bit.

Cal shook his arm, balled his fist and—

Sybil screamed.

"Cal, that's enough." Eddie's voice stopped them midmotion. He stepped into the pen and loosened the rope around Brand's neck. "Call off your dog."

Brand croaked out two words. "Dawg, down." He clutched at his throat. Dawg released Cal and stood back, his hackles raised, his teeth bared as he growled.

Cal held his arm. "That dog attacked me for no reason. I'm going to get my gun and shoot him." He stomped toward the gate.

"Stop." Eddie spoke the order softly but with no mistake. He meant to be obeyed.

Cal halted, his back to the others.

"You can pack your bag and be off the place immediately. I wouldn't advise you to linger. I might regret letting you off so easy if I have time to think about it."

Cal turned. "I ain't done nothing wrong."

Eddie planted his fists on his hips. "I heard enough, saw enough to disagree. You aren't the sort of man I wish to have on the place." His eyebrows rose. "I'm already having second thoughts about letting you just ride out."

Cal spared Brand one hot look and then tramped out of the barn.

Eddie faced Sybil and Brand. "Are you okay?"

"I'm fine," Sybil said.

Brand nodded and backed up to the corner.

"I'm sorry," Eddie said. "Outlaw or not, you don't deserve to be treated like that. I wish I didn't have to tie you up again, but I do."

Brand simply sat down and let himself be tied to the post.

Sybil bit her lip to keep from protesting. "Eddie, do you mind if I stay here and talk to Brand?"

"I believe you're safe enough." He backed away and left the barn.

Sybil lowered herself to the floor in front of Brand and sat staring at him, uncertain what she wanted to say.

He studied her, his eyes flat, his face expressionless. Then he laughed.

She stared. "What's so funny?"

He shook his head, unable to talk.

She lifted her eyebrows, silently demanding an answer.

"You," he sputtered. "'Little Miss London.' You certainly surprised that cowboy. You looked about ready to bear wrestle him." He laughed some more.

"I don't see what's so funny. He was about to hurt you." A trickle of amusement drowned out her fear and a grin grew on her lips. "I did surprise him, didn't I?" Not half as much as she'd surprised herself. Where had the fight come from? She was normally the most agreeable, most nonaggressive person imaginable. Her actions were totally out of character.

He sobered. "Why are you here?"

Her amusement ended as quickly as it had begun. "I don't know." She studied her fingers as they intertwined in her lap. "I guess I was hoping for some answers." She lifted her head and met his look, searching for truth.

At first his eyes were hard, then she detected a softening. He sighed. "What more do you need to know? I'm a Duggan."

"I don't believe that says it all."

He looked past her. Kept his attention focused on something beyond her shoulder.

"Brand, who are you besides that?"

Slowly his gaze came to her, and she shivered at the pain she saw embedded in them. He blinked as if he hoped to erase it, but failed.

She squeezed her fingers tighter to keep from reaching for him. Her heart could not forget the few days when she'd believed in him. The way they'd laughed together, nursed Dawg together. The way they'd kissed. "Why did you kiss me?"

The pain in his eyes deepened, turning them to black coals. "I'm sorry."

She shook her head. "That's not what I want to hear." When had she become so demanding? So outspoken? She knew the answer. When she began to sort out the pieces of what she knew about Brand. "Things just don't add up. If you were staking out the place, as we're supposed to believe, why did you never visit Eddie's house? Why did you avoid everyone on the ranch except me? Why didn't you ask questions about the place? What kind of front man could you possibly be?" She grew impassioned as she spoke, lifting her hands imploringly.

She knew she wasn't mistaken in judging his attitude shifted. His shoulders relaxed. His breathing came easier.

Then he shrugged. "I'm still a Duggan and that is how I'll be judged."

"Are you saying you'll go the gallows with your only defense being that you're a Duggan? Need I point out that is no defense at all?"

He tipped his head to one side in a dismissive gesture.

"I don't understand." She sorted through the events of the past few days. "Why did Cyrus kidnap me? If you were doing the job of spying out the land, why kidnap me? Wouldn't it just bring more attention to the gang? What purpose did my kidnapping serve?"

"Apart from giving Cyrus some sport, you mean?"

It wasn't meant as a question but an answer. A truly unsatisfactory one, she decided.

"I was very angry at first. I don't like being deceived. But more and more the whole situation simply doesn't make sense."

He studied the shape of his dog's head, visually examined the grain of the wood in the wall beside him and generally pretended a great interest in everything but her demands.

"Brand. Can you not offer an explanation? Don't I deserve at least that much?"

He shifted his gaze back to her, all sign of emotion gone. "You figure one little kiss gives you the right to know everything about me?"

His harsh words drained the concern from her thoughts. She rose to her feet in a slow, self-controlled manner. "I haven't given the kiss another thought." It was as false as his pretense to be a good, kind man. Or was his falsehood in pretending to be an outlaw? She left the barn without a backward look.

But she could not shake off the feeling that things were not as they appeared, if anyone cared to look beyond the surface.

But was anyone willing to do so?

Brand waited until he knew she was long gone before he let out a low groan. "Sure hate to be mean to her," he explained to Dawg. "But what's the point in her thinking I'm innocent? The Mountie caught me in the act of robbing the store." No one would believe he was there against his will. After all, he was a Duggan. And that said it all. He'd ask for no mercy except from

God, who knew the truth and had forgiven more than one Duggan.

Lord, there's still Cyrus. Give him a chance to re-pent, too.

And thank you that Sybil wonders if I'm guilty.

Brand could die with joy tucked around his heart to know that. More than that. If he held on to the memory of her facing down Cal, he could die happy.

He sobered instantly. He did not fancy dangling at the end of a rope. But he saw no way of avoiding it.

Because the truth was, he had been involved in a robbery. He had become what he had avoided so hard for years.

He'd become a Duggan in more than name.

Unable to guess at the time except to know the sun shone in the western window of the barn, he settled down to wait, Dawg at his side.

He was roused by a shout outside. "It's the Mountie."

"Looks like he got the men."

"Nothing I like better'n to see two outlaws draped over the back of a horse."

Draped? As in dead? Cyrus was dead? Shock coursed through Brand's body. Somewhere deep in his brain he'd secretly hoped Cyrus would tell the truth about why Brand had been involved in the robbery. Now that chance was gone. Though all along he'd told himself no one would believe one Duggan over the other.

He strained upward, hoping for a glimpse of the Mountie, trying to catch more words, but he couldn't get high enough to see over the sides of the pen, nor could he hear the men as they rushed past and out of his hearing. "Dawg, I sure wish you could go find out what's going on."

Dawg stood at attention, listening to the commotion outside but choosing to stay at Brand's side.

Brand sank back, knowing he would have to wait until someone came to inform him. And wait he did, the minutes ticking by with maddening slowness.

It was Eddie who finally came. "The Mountie wants to see you." He untied Brand from the post, leaving his hands bound. "Trust you won't try and run."

Brand glanced about. "Would seem futile, seeing as every place I look there are people. 'Spect some of them would be happy enough to shoot another Duggan."

Eddie didn't reply as he led him up the hill.

Brand paused inside the door of the big house, struck once again by the size and beauty of the place. It was the right setting for a girl like Sybil.

She stood inside the room to the left of the big entryway, her eyes watchful and still begging for the truth.

He managed a flicker of a smile that went no deeper than his lips. But he wanted to somehow assure her she needn't worry about him.

Then Eddie led him down the hall to another room. They stepped inside. The Mountie sat in a big leather chair, before an oak desk. Shelves full of books encircled the room, with chairs placed in three of the corners. Just right for reading. A little table provided a place for writing. He allowed himself one mental picture of Sybil sitting there, writing her stories, before he turned his full attention to Constable Allen.

"Guess you got the others."

"I wouldn't be here if I hadn't," the Mountie replied. "They both came back dead." He indicated a chair in front of the desk, and Brand sat. "Sorry about your brother."

Brand didn't answer for several seconds, still uncertain what he thought of Cyrus's death. Finally, he said the only thing that made sense. "I hoped for a chance to tell him he could find God's mercy. Guess it's too late for that."

"Again, I'm sorry."

Sorry was a pitifully inadequate word, but he guessed there was no other.

"Cyrus had lots to say before he died."

"Cyrus always was a talker. Ma used to say his tongue was loose on both ends." Now why had he said that? As if anyone cared.

The Mountie chuckled. "I can see why she'd say that. He had some mighty interesting things to say."

Brand held his counsel. Cyrus wasn't exactly the truth-telling sort, so he couldn't begin to guess what had been said.

"I think he was afraid you'd get off scot-free, so he warned us that you might concoct a story. Even told us what it was you'd say. I found that a little odd. How would he know the details of your story? I've been asking around. Putting the information together."

"That a fact?" Whom had he been talking to and what information had he gathered?

"The facts are this. You were unarmed at the robbery. Miss Sybil says you never asked any questions that would gain you information of the sort needed for a robbery. Macpherson says you had been in the store only twice and both times hurried in and out. Eddie tells me you wouldn't even accept an invitation to the house. Seems odd if indeed you meant to rob him. Then Bertie comes to me and tells me that you were forced to go along with the robbery in order to protect Miss Bannerman. How am I doing so far?"

Brand couldn't put two words together. All those people had spoken in his defense?

The Mountie continued. "I have one question for you." He waited for a nod from Brand. "Are you guilty or innocent?"

Brand considered his answer carefully. He had no desire to hang, but neither did he want to spend the rest of his life running from the Duggan name. "I was with the gang when they tried to rob Macpherson's store, but I did not wish to be."

The Mountie smiled. "I'll take that as a plea of innocence." He closed his notebook and nodded toward Eddie. "He can go free."

The rancher untied his ropes and clapped Brand on the back. "I have to say, keeping you prisoner went against my judgment. I'm glad to see I was right in my estimation of you. Now come and join us for supper."

Brand stood, rubbing his wrists and feeling as out of place as Dawg would have. "Might be best if I move on. I'm still a Duggan."

"Nonsense. If you leave without giving us a chance to prove we believe you're innocent, you'll forever wonder whether or not we do. You want to carry that with you down the trail?"

"I guess not."

"Then come along." And before Brand could think of a reason to refuse, he found himself drawn into a big kitchen, warm with the feel of family and love, full of the smells of good home-cooked food and the smiling faces of those who lived in the house.

He stared at Sybil. He couldn't help himself. She'd

spoken on his behalf. Overwhelmed by how things had changed for the better, he lowered his gaze to the floor. "I'm grateful for—" He couldn't even say what it was, so didn't finish.

Linette sprang forward. "I never did believe you were part of the gang. Now sit here." She indicated a chair at the table, and he sat.

Everyone suddenly found chairs and settled into them. Constable Allen sat beside him, Grady beyond that. Linette and Eddie at each end of the big wooden table, Mercy and Sybil across from each other. All Brand had to do was lift his eyes and he connected with Sybil's steady blue ones. He expected his were full of shock, since he hadn't yet processed the events of the past hour. Hers brimmed with triumph.

If only he could guess what that meant. Was she happy she'd put some of the pieces together even without the Mountie's help?

Was she happy Brand wasn't going to hang?

He ducked his head. His heart raced with impossible possibilities.

Chapter Fourteen

Sybil could hardly sit through the meal. It went on and on as Eddie and Linette shared all the details of what the Mountie had discovered.

As for Mercy…well, her friend said over and over, "I can't believe you have all the adventures, while I can't find one no matter how hard I look."

Sybil only wanted the meal to end. As soon as it did she would find an opportunity to speak to Brand alone.

Constable Allen broke into the conversation and asked Brand, "Would you like to see your brother?"

"I'd appreciate it."

Eddie and Linette shared one of those secret communicative looks, then the rancher spoke. "Do you want to bury him next to your father?"

Brand did his best to hide his emotions, but Sybil felt his surprise and gratitude just as she'd felt it throughout the meal. It would appear that carrying the Duggan name had brought him nothing but regrets. Well, now he could change that.

"He was an outlaw." Brand's words were strained. "And as far as I know, he never repented."

The Mountie cleared his throat. "I don't think any of us are able to judge that matter. Cyrus did not die right away. I spoke to him once he could no longer talk nonstop. I told him he could make his peace with God."

Brand clenched his knife and fork so hard they must surely leave permanent impressions in his palm. "I expect he told you he didn't care anything for God."

"At first he did, then he asked if God could indeed forgive an outlaw. Much as I wanted to say otherwise, because I sometimes prefer a human form of justice—a man gets what he deserves for the life he's led—I had to say God accepts everyone who comes to Him in faith, seeking forgiveness."

Sybil watched Brand. Hope dawned in his eyes.

The Mountie continued. "I can't be a hundred percent certain, but I believe Cyrus asked for that forgiveness before he drew his last breath."

Brand's lungs emptied in a long sigh. "I am relieved to hear that. Thank you."

"Then it's agreed," Linette said. "You'll bury him next to his father."

"It's most generous of you," Brand said.

"Nonsense." Linette's mouth drew a firm line. "Even if Constable Allen hadn't given us this bit of assurance the offer would stand. I don't believe in living by man-imposed rules."

"Do you want to wait until tomorrow?" Eddie asked.

Brand again got that distant, half-disinterested look in his eyes as he glanced at the window. "Guess we should. It's already dark out. I'll dig the grave myself."

Eddie considered him a moment, then nodded. "I'll get you a shovel." He rose, signaling the meal was over, and Brand and the Mountie followed him outside.

Linette excused herself to put Grady to bed.

Mercy bounced to her feet. "How romantic."

Sybil turned to her as she gathered up the dishes and carried them to the washbasin. "I fail to see how knowing your family is a bunch of outlaws is the least bit romantic." Had Eddie stayed with Brand? she wondered. Or was he alone in the dark digging a hole for his brother's body?

Eddie and Constable Allen came through the door and went to the library, answering her question. They'd left him alone.

As she moved about the kitchen, she paused to glance out the window. A faint glow of a lantern shone from the little plot. She rubbed at her breastbone. A man should not be alone when dealing with his brother's death.

Mercy came to her side. "Why don't you join him?"

"I don't know if he'd welcome it." Her heart ached for his aloneness in the midst of his loss. Every so often the light dimmed as if a scoop of dirt had been tossed past it.

"I'll come with you if you want."

Sybil shook her head. She didn't want Mercy to be with her. "I'm sure he's okay."

Her friend grabbed her arm and shook her a little. "If you don't go out there, I will. The poor man has lost his father and brother. He's been accused of being part of the gang when he wasn't. Don't you think he deserves a little sympathy?"

"He deserves it, but will he welcome it?"

Linette returned to the kitchen. "What are you two arguing about?"

Mercy flung about to face her. "I think Sybil should

go up there and keep Brand company, but she doesn't think it's appropriate."

Linette joined them at the window. "I thought Eddie should have stayed with him, but he said Brand asked to be left alone. I guess we need to give him space if that's what he wants."

They watched in silence for a bit.

"Eddie insisted he spend the night in the bunkhouse. Says with Cal gone no one will give Brand a hard time."

Sybil tried to picture Brand in a bunk, with the others nearby. "Did he agree?"

"Said he'd think on it."

Which meant he'd ignore the invitation and find a place on his own.

The distant light grew brighter. Sybil could make out Brand's shadowy shape as he headed back toward the house. She grabbed her shawl. "I'm going to speak to him." She slipped out the door.

"Feel free to use the chairs by the back step," Linette called, as if knowing she wanted to be alone with him.

Sybil caught up to him in a few moments. He'd slung the shovel over his shoulder. His footsteps were weary, heavy. Digging a hole was hard work. Losing a father and brother was even harder.

She fell in at his side. Neither of them spoke. Dawg whined a greeting and she patted his head.

She couldn't say what the silence meant for Brand, but she felt no need for words. She only wanted to be with him. Let him know he wasn't alone.

"Sit and visit a spell." She indicated the chairs along the wall.

He sank down, dropped the shovel to the ground and stared at it, his hands hanging between his knees.

Dawg pressed close to his legs, though Brand didn't seem to notice.

The silence lengthened, but Sybil still could not speak until he sucked in a deep breath and sat up straight. "That's the last of my family."

She squeezed his hand. He seemed not to notice that, either.

"At least he managed to establish your innocence before he died."

"I always hoped both he and Pa would stop their outlawing, even though I knew if they did they would hang."

"Such a waste of both lives. How did your mother cope?"

Brand leaned his head back against the wall. "She prayed every day that they would repent. She tried to stay away from them just as I have. It meant always being ready to leave. Hoping no one would associate us with the Duggan gang."

"Her prayers were answered."

He stared at her. "I guess they were." He sounded both surprised and unconvinced.

"I hear Eddie invited you to stay in the bunkhouse."

"It was kind of him."

"But you aren't going to do it, are you?"

Brand shook his head. "I don't think everyone would welcome me. I'm still a Duggan...."

His fatalism made Sybil want to shake him. "The Duggan gang are dead. Isn't it time you stopped living like you're part of them?"

"I'm not. I don't. I never thought that."

"I think you do. They will never be a threat to you again, but they still have a hold over you. When will you stop looking over your shoulder to see if they've found you? When will you stop expecting others to see you as one of the Duggan gang?" She'd said far more than she should, and none of the things she'd wanted to say, but her insides burned with unnamed emotions. She rose to her feet and strode toward the door, pausing with her hand on the knob. "I'm sorry for your loss."

The others were gone and she slipped to her room and sank to the edge of her bed. What was wrong with her? She'd never been outspoken in her life and yet she couldn't seem to stop speaking her mind around Brand.

Maybe Proverbs would help her regain control. Sybil reached for her Bible and notebook. Just below, hidden by a scarf, were the pages she'd written about Brand. She pulled them out and glanced over the words, then dipped her pen in ink and wrote.

Cowboy had a name…that of a notorious outlaw gang. All his life he'd tried to distance himself from them. He'd run, he'd remained aloof from others.

She stopped there. How long would it take for him to stop living like a man on the run? Would he ever?

Despite Eddie's generous invitation, Brand took his horse and his bedroll and returned to the campsite he'd used before. Dawg turned about three times before he settled down and instantly fell asleep.

Brand knew sleep would not come as easily for him, if indeed it came at all.

Sybil had suggested he needed to stop seeing himself as part of the Duggan gang. He'd never been one of them…except in name. But she was right about one thing. It would take a long time for him to feel free of them.

Tomorrow he'd bury Cyrus, and then he'd move on before—

He was doing it again. Running from a now nonexistent danger. Perhaps the sense of impending doom would never leave him.

He wouldn't run from *them* this time. When it was time to leave, he'd just leave. Sybil's concerned face came to mind. Her laugh. Her courage in facing Cal… and him. Maybe he wouldn't be in a hurry to leave. But then he thought of Eddie and Linette's house, a beautiful home full of lovely things. Why, the staircase itself had more wood in it than most of the houses he'd lived in. He looked about. The only wood in his current *home* burned in the fire. Sybil belonged in a house like that, married to a rich landowner.

The night closed in around him and he shivered. The first snowfall would come in the mountains anytime. He'd soon have to find a place to spend the winter.

What better place than Eden Valley Ranch?

But did he have any reason to stay? Would Sybil want him to? Or was he mistaking kindness for something more, looking for hope when there was none?

The questions lingered in his mind through the night.

Next morning, Brand returned to the ranch, Dawg patiently at his side. He asked Bertie to say the final words over Cyrus, and then led the way up the hill. Cyrus's body was wrapped in a gray woolen blanket and draped over the same horse the Mountie had brought him in on. Likely most of the assembled figured it was all the outlaw deserved. Cyrus would have been the first to say it was the kind of burial he wanted.

At the hole he'd dug, Brand stopped. Constable Allen and Eddie helped him lower the body into the grave.

People gathered to one side. He glanced at them. Sybil stood front and center in a black dress and bonnet, as if in mourning.

The idea jolted through him. The only time she'd met Cyrus he'd given her no reason to mourn his death.

Brand met her gaze, felt her blue eyes bore through him, challenging him. What did she want from him? What did she expect?

Bertie cleared his throat and Brand brought his focus back to the reason for being there.

"This is not a happy occasion for us, but it's especially sad for Brand. He's buried his father and his brother in two days. There are no words to erase the sorrow he must feel."

Brand began to wish he hadn't asked Bertie to speak. The man had a way of probing at pain with his words. Pain that Brand would just as soon ignore. He did his best to block out the rest of what Bertie said until the final "amen."

Again those present passed by, tossed a handful of dirt into the yawning hole and spoke condolences. He mumbled appropriate responses, though he couldn't have told anyone what he said.

Then he stood alone at the grave, Dawg at his side.

Time to fill in the hole. He turned to grab the shovel that someone had placed nearby…and came face-to-face with Sybil.

"I thought everyone had gone."

"I couldn't leave you alone with…" She nodded at the shovel in his hand. "It doesn't seem right."

"I've been alone a long time. Every Christmas. Every beautiful spring day. Every time I rode through a town or worked at a new place. Dawg here has been about my only companion." Now why had he said all that? As if he cared. As if he wished it could be different.

"Didn't you ever wish it could be different?"

What? She could read his mind? "Not much point in wishing for stars. Might as well be content with candles." He threw in three shovelfuls of dirt.

She leaned back on her heels and watched. Seems she didn't intend to leave.

He paused to listen as she spoke.

"On the other hand, why would you stick to a flickering candle if someone offered you a handful of stars?"

He stared at her. Did she mean it as it sounded? "Are you offering stars?"

"Would you prefer to hang on to your candle?"

"Do you see a candle in my hand?" He returned to throwing dirt over Cyrus's body, trying to think of it as only filling in a hole, not saying goodbye forever to his brother.

Brand stopped and backed away from the hole. He leaned on the shovel, trying to control the way his breathing came in choked sounds. "We used to be best of friends." His words grated from a dusty throat.

Sybil moved to his side and rested her black-gloved hand on his forearm, warm and gentle. "I always wished I had a brother or sister."

"He taught me how to chop wood, how to build a fire, how to cook a meal over a campfire. He made me run hard to keep up with him. Challenged me to take chances beyond my years, rather than let him think I was afraid." Brand couldn't go on. This was the Cyrus he remembered and missed. Not the angry, hurtful man of later years.

"That's how you should remember him."

Again, she had read his mind, voiced his thoughts. How did she do that?

Brand swiped his arm across his face, hoping she would think he wiped away sweat rather than the tear that escaped the corner of his eye. For a moment it was impossible to speak. Then the words came out slowly, haltingly. "Pa and Cyrus weren't always outlaws. Not until…" He let himself remember those strain-filled days for the first time in years. "Pa bought a little farm. He was so proud of it. We had every sort of animal. I loved them all. And Pa never said no to me bringing another one home." Brand paused, gathering together his memories, sorting through them, trying to understand. "He'd had to borrow to buy the place. We lived there for four years and Pa was so proud that he always made the payments on time. 'No banker will ever take the farm,' he used to brag."

Sybil's hand rubbed up and down Brand's arm, soothing away the anger that usually accompanied the memory of those final normal days.

"Then the wheat crop got hit with hail. Lightning killed half the cows. A fire destroyed the hay crop. Pa couldn't make the payment that year and asked for leniency. He came home so angry. A new banker had come to town. He cared not for missed payments, no matter the reason. He gave Pa two weeks to come up with the money or the bank would take the farm. Pa said he'd get the money by hook or by crook. And he did. He robbed the bank that threatened to take the farm. Paid the entire amount of the loan. I think he meant for that to be the one and only time he turned to crime, but then we needed feed. Cyrus decided he needed a fancy riding horse. Pa thought Ma would enjoy a new buggy." Brand shrugged, though he felt anything but indifference.

Sybil's hand tightened on his arm. "Let me guess. Your pa had discovered he didn't have to wait for things. He thought he'd discovered a ready source of funds."

"'Fraid that's exactly what he thought. They were wanted men. Someone was killed in their third bank heist. After that, they were wanted dead or alive. I wasn't yet twelve and Ma took me and moved. We always tried to distance ourselves from the Duggan name."

"Why didn't you go by a different name?"

"We did for years. Then someone noticed my likeness to members of the Duggan gang. So we moved on. After that I never bothered telling anyone my name. Made it easier."

"Is Brand your real name?"

He smiled for the first time all day. "I have Cyrus to thank for that. When I was born, he wanted to know if Pa was going to brand me like they did the calves. Pa thought it so funny he said they'd settle for calling me Brand."

She laughed. "That's sweet." Her gaze held his, caring and searching, delving deep into his thoughts.

He tried to bank his emotions, but her probing went clear through his defenses. He blinked back the sting of tears. No way would he cry.

She reached up, touched the corner of each eye with her gloved hand. "I'm glad you have good memories to cherish."

He caught her hand and pulled it to his chest, so lost in the depths of her gaze that his head spun. "I will prize this moment."

She didn't blink. Didn't withdraw. "So will I," she whispered. "The moment when I met the real Brand Duggan."

He considered her words. Who was the real Brand Duggan? He wasn't sure he even knew. But one thing was for certain: he hoped reality included more times like this.

"Where do we go from here?" he asked, hoping she didn't think he meant to ask if they should go to the house.

She smiled so sweetly his throat constricted. "Wherever we want, I suppose. How about you finish filling in the grave. Say your final goodbye to a brother you loved, then we'll join the others for church."

He nodded in agreement and filled in the hole, smoothing the dirt into a mound. He stood at the fresh grave, head bent, Sybil at his side. "Goodbye, Cyrus. I like to think of you in heaven, your sins forgiven. You did plenty of bad things, lots of them against me. You even hurt Sybil here, and whether or not she forgives you is up to her, but I'm forgiving you. I'm sorry you ruined your life. But that's over. Goodbye, my brother." He was about to step back when Sybil caught his hand.

"Wait. I want to say something, too." She stood by the fresh dirt, looking down as if speaking to Cyrus. "I vowed I would make you pay for how you treated me. But justice belongs to God. I forgive you. Rest in peace."

She took Brand's hand again and led him down the hill to the cookhouse, where the church service was held.

He didn't realize until he stepped inside that he'd agreed to attend. By then it was too late.

Chapter Fifteen

She dropped his hand as they entered the cookhouse, but not before she felt him shudder, and guessed the cause. She might be wrong, but she believed it would be the first time he'd darkened the door of a building filled with others, especially for a Sunday service, in many years. How would it feel? Frightening, most certainly, but she hoped it also offered a breath of hope to a man used to being so alone no one even knew his whole name.

Several of the cowboys shuffled their feet as if uncertain how to react to a Duggan in their midst, attending a church service.

Brand hung back. He likely would have retreated except for her hand on his elbow, holding him firmly in place.

Bertie sprang to his feet. "Brand, I'm glad as can be to see you here. I told my wife I hoped you'd come. Darlin'?" He turned to Cookie. "This is Brand. Son, this is my wife. Everyone calls her Cookie and you no doubt know why, since you've tasted her cooking."

Cookie swept forward, grabbed Brand's hand and

pumped it up and down. "Glad to meet you. Come on in." She practically dragged him forward to a bench, and he sat because he didn't have much choice.

Sybil perched beside him, her elbow pressed to his arm. Tension vibrated from him. His hands clamped his knees and he stared at Bertie, who had moved to the front of the assembly.

Cookie led the group in two familiar hymns. Sybil sang without considering the words. Her mind was on the man next to her. She had the feeling Brand might spring to his feet and dash from the room at any moment.

Then Bertie stood and smiled at him for several seconds until Brand visibly relaxed. Only then did Bertie begin to speak. "I could tell you many stories about sinners saved by grace. I expect most, if not all of you, could add stories. Perhaps your own. But today I want to tell you a different sort of story."

They sat spellbound as he talked about how he had wandered far and been brought back by the prayers of a faithful mother. Then he closed with a prayer.

"Coffee and cinnamon buns coming right up," Cookie said. She faced Brand. "I would be greatly pleased if you'd stay. In fact, I might be offended if you left."

Eddie and several of the others laughed. "Best you don't offend her," the rancher said.

"Please stay," Sybil whispered. "Let people accept you as Brand Duggan."

He flicked a look at her, then returned his gaze to Cookie. "I've had the pleasure of tasting your cinnamon buns, and I have to say I'm not prepared to pass up a chance to enjoy them again."

She beamed at him.

Mercy sat across the table. Linette and Eddie joined them. Roper brought his family forward and introduced them, as did Ward.

"You'll figure them all out soon enough," Sybil assured Brand.

The conversation turned to general things of mutual concern to those gathered in the cookhouse, and Brand sat back, listening. Sybil wondered how he felt about it all.

As people began to leave, Linette turned to him. "We have a big dinner up at the house. I'd like you to join us."

Brand jerked to his feet. "That's most generous, but I've things to attend to." He hurried for the door.

Sybil hustled after him, catching up as he reached the outdoors. Dawg rose to follow him. "Brand, why are you rushing away?" She knew he had nothing to attend to.

He simply shook his head for an answer.

She fell in step at his side. "Promise me you won't ride away this afternoon."

He stopped, stared at her. "Why?"

She knew then that he'd planned to do so. "Because I'd like to talk to you some more." She lowered her head at her boldness. "If you leave today you will still be running. Don't you need to stop running?"

"And do what?"

He sounded truly dumbfounded, as if it was all he knew and he couldn't think of an alternative. Finally, he nodded. "I'll hang around for the day."

"Good. I'll come and visit you."

"Suit yourself." A grin tugged at his mouth before he strode away, and as he disappeared into the trees, she heard him whistling a little tune.

* * *

Brand stared at the fire as he ate cold beans right from the can. Dawg happily licked a second can clean.

Yes, he might have enjoyed a pleasant church service with Sybil at his side, but he needed time to think through this whole business. Who was he? A Duggan still. But what did that mean now? Could he make it mean what he wanted?

"Dawg, I plumb don't know what came over me. I went to church. Can you imagine that?"

Dawg didn't look up. He wasn't real good company.

Then Brand had agreed to hang about waiting for Sybil to visit. "It sure didn't take any persuading." How long before she came? Or would she think better of it? "Why would a fine lady like Sybil come out here to visit me? A Duggan?"

Stop acting as if the Duggan gang is still a threat.

Well, even if being a Duggan wasn't a problem, Brand was still just a cowboy with nothing to call his own except a dog, a horse, a saddle and a few items of clothing. Sybil was used to so much more.

He argued with himself for hours while the sun passed to midafternoon.

When Sybil never came, his thoughts went dark. She wasn't coming, he told himself. He knew she wouldn't. He wasn't disappointed. Much.

Only enough for him to jump to his feet and kick a cloud of dirt into the fire. Might just as well move on.

Dawg rose, whined and looked to the trees. Brand's heart took off at a full gallop. He slowly brought his head about, hoping it was her, and shielding his eyes under the brim of his hat lest she see his eagerness.

Against the sky-blue backdrop, Sybil stood there and

smiled. She'd changed out of her black dress into something yellow as sunshine. Her head was uncovered, her hair pulled back like a golden crown around her head.

His tongue pressed to his teeth and refused to form a word.

"Hello," she said.

When he continued to stare, she glanced about, saw the two empty bean cans and laughed, a merry sound that danced through the air.

"To think you could have enjoyed roast beef and two kinds of pie, plus all the trimmings and extras you could want. Linette and Eddie always put on a big spread on Sunday. Everyone is invited." Her eyes returned to him, burning through his well-reasoned arguments like lightning.

"Maybe you'll come to dinner next Sunday."

He forgot all about his decision to move on. "Maybe."

"Eddie says he could use you on the ranch."

"Uh-huh." Brand seemed incapable of more than grunts and one-word replies.

"Do you have other plans?"

"For what?"

"For the winter…for the future."

Had she added the last out of politeness or did she care?

He shook his head. Why would she? He looked at her mouth. Had one stolen kiss meant anything to her?

"Do you mind if I sit?" She indicated the butt end of a log.

"Sit. Sit." He snatched off his hat, waited for her to settle and fluff her skirts around her. He abused the rim of his hat.

She smiled sweet enough to melt ice. "It would be easier to talk to you if you sat as well."

He grabbed another hunk of log, placed it firmly and balanced on it.

"That's better." She folded her hands primly. "I think it's time to get to know the real you."

"Me?"

"Yes, you. Who are you, Brand Duggan, when you aren't pretending you're nobody?"

Her question slammed into him and reverberated. "I am nobody. Have been for a long time."

She leaned forward, her gaze intent, demanding. "You've never been nobody. Just running from what you feared you were."

"I've never been afraid." He tried to believe it, but remembered how his heart would leap when he thought Pa and Cyrus had found him. Like a few days ago, when he'd heard a quail call.

"There is no reason to be afraid. So tell me about yourself."

He stared. What on earth did she mean?

Her eyes flickered as if she heard his silent question. "Things like your dreams and hopes. What would people say about you if you ever let them get to know you?"

He shook his head. "There are no answers to those questions." There was one way to stop this interrogation. "What are *your* dreams and hopes?"

She drew back, shifted her gaze and considered her answer. "I guess I hope for a life of safety and security."

He waited, never taking his attention from her, knowing her answer only scratched the surface.

She smoothed her skirt and sighed. "I've always wanted to please my parents."

"They're gone. Shouldn't you do what is right for you without wondering what they would think? Seems to me that would make them proud."

Her eyes widened, filled with protest.

In this far already, he might as well go all the way. "You should listen to your own advice, Miss Sybil Bannerman. If you weren't concerned with what others would say, what would you do?"

She swallowed hard, her gaze riveted on his face. "I would try and publish my stories in my own name."

"Then do it."

"It's not that easy."

"Are you afraid of the risks?" Wasn't *he?* "This is the West. Things can be different." His words accused him. "You can make them different." Did he truly believe it? If he did, wouldn't he act on the knowledge?

Her head snapped up. "That's exactly what I've been trying to tell you. You can make people look at the Duggan name differently."

They stared at each other, her eyes blazing with challenge.

He figured his did, as well. Then the humor of the situation hit him and he laughed. "A Mexican standoff."

Her eyes widened. "What's that?"

"It usually means two gunfighters confront each other and there is no way either can win because they are evenly matched. But it can also refer to something like this, when neither party is willing to back down."

She laughed. "I expect you know a lot of cowboy stories."

He shrugged. Of course he knew a few.

"Have you ever seen a Mexican standoff where guns weren't involved?"

Grinning at the memory that sprang to mind, he said, "I once heard of one between two men on horses. Seems they both headed down a narrow alleyway at the same time, coming from opposite ends. There wasn't room for the horses to pass and neither would give in and back his horse out. They spent most of the day there until a Mountie came along and made them both back up and use a different route."

She laughed, the sound dancing across the strings of his heart. "What do you call a horse like the one Cal found for you? The one Eddie had forbidden anyone to ride."

"That's easy. An outlaw. He obeys no rules. Accepts no authority."

"Oh, I like that." She smiled as if pleased with his explanation. She studied him intently. "You said you spent last winter in a cabin? Is that how you've spent—what is it? Six winters since your mother died?"

A thousand memories, ten thousand hopes and dreams and twice as many disappointments ambushed him, leaving his lungs too tight to do their job. Outlaw lungs. Then his breath eased with a whistle and he was able to speak.

"It was December when Ma died. She'd already made plans for Christmas. She worked extra hard planning a special day. I worked, too, by cleaning out the livery barn every afternoon. Ma did laundry, took in mending and cleaned houses.

"We hadn't seen Pa and his gang in a long time. Ma said maybe they'd decided to leave us alone. I hoped it was so." He broke off and tried to slow his thoughts. "I don't know why I'm telling you this. I've put it out of my mind."

She held his gaze in a velvet grasp that made it impossible to pull away. "You've tried to forget it but you haven't. What happened to your ma?"

"Pa." One word, but it said everything he felt. "Pa and Cyrus showed up. They brought gifts. A blue taffeta dress for Ma. You should have seen her eyes light up. For me, they brought a brand-new pair of alligator boots and a leather belt. I guess my eyes lit up, too.

"But Ma put the dress back in the paper and handed it to Pa. She said she couldn't benefit from ill-gotten gains. I handed back the boots and the belt, too, though it hurt me a lot to do so." Brand paused, lost in his memories of that time. "I didn't think life could get any worse. But it did." Hearing the regret and maybe a bit of misery in his voice, he held up his hand. "Not that I'm whining. I've had a good enough life." For a Duggan.

Sybil made a disbelieving sound. Her mouth pulled down.

He didn't want sympathy. So he went on with his story. "Pa and Cyrus stormed out. A little later a neighbor rushed over to say the general store had been robbed. Many of the Christmas presents ordered by the townsfolk had been stolen or broken, and the store owner shot."

Sybil touched his hand, squeezed it. "It was your pa's gang?"

"Of course. Guess he figured to make Ma pay for refusing his gifts."

"That's dreadful."

Brand quirked his eyebrows, hoping she would read the gesture as agreement rather than the pain and shame it indicated. "That's what I've been trying to tell you. The Duggan gang was awful."

A few moments of silence passed, filled with regret and shock, before he continued. "Ma knew it was them. We packed up and escaped into the dark, with no place to go on a bitter cold night. We made camp toward morning, hiding in a stand of fir trees. Ma didn't want me to start a fire, but she was so cold I ignored her. She insisted we move on, but she was weak and grew weaker. Three days later, she could barely walk. An old couple found us and took us to their farm. She died December twentieth. They helped me dig a grave in the frozen ground and we buried her there."

"Oh, Brand. How awful."

He shrugged, though he could not dismiss the pain of those dreadful days.

"The old couple was good to me. I stayed until spring. When I heard news of the Duggan gang at work nearby, I moved on."

"And you've been moving on ever since."

"Sometimes not soon enough."

"You can make things different now." Sybil squeezed his hand.

He didn't remember turning his palm to hers, but her soft and narrow hand lay in his and he squeezed back. She offered so much hope, so much promise, but…

"Will you try?"

How could he refuse such a gentle plea? He let himself drown in her gaze and nodded, ignoring the toll of warning bells. The Duggan gang was dead, he told himself, to silence the discordant sound.

The next morning Sybil watched Brand ride into the yard, Dawg at his horse's heels. He spoke to Eddie. They shook hands and Eddie pointed toward the barn.

Brand glanced up the hill and touched the brim of his hat.

She lifted her hand in a wave before he stepped into the barn. She glanced toward the sky. *Thank you, God.* She couldn't stop smiling. Brand had decided to stay and work for Eddie.

Mercy nudged her, sending a jolt of surprise jolt thought her.

"I didn't know you were there," Sybil declared.

"I caught you mooning over that cowboy."

She knew there was no point in arguing with Mercy, especially when it was true. Still, she wasn't about to give her friend the satisfaction of agreeing. "Just admiring the nice day."

Mercy laughed. "Of course you are. Maybe you'd like to go for a walk."

Sybil longed to go to the barn and see what Brand meant to do. She'd like to ask Eddie if Brand had agreed to live in the bunkhouse. Instead, she turned from the window. "Shouldn't we help Linette with the laundry?" She headed for the kitchen, where Linette had tubs of hot water set out. Soon the three of them were up to their elbows, scrubbing and rinsing clothes.

When Eddie came to the house for dinner the laundry was all out on the line, flapping in the cold breeze.

Linette, well aware of Sybil's interest in Brand even though she'd done her best to hide it, waited until Eddie had filled his plate to ask the questions pressing at Sybil's mind.

"Did Brand say how long he meant to stay?"

Eddie glanced up from his full plate. "Said it seemed a good place to spend the winter."

Sybil barely contained her smile.

Linette beamed at her. "That sounds promising, doesn't it?"

Sybil pretended a great interest in spreading butter on a hot biscuit.

Linette turned back to her husband. "Is he going to live in the bunkhouse?"

Sybil's biscuit stopped halfway to her mouth. She couldn't make her hand go any farther as she waited for the answer.

Eddie nodded. "He asked if Dawg could spend the nights in the barn, and when I said he could, Brand threw his bedroll on an empty bunk. He took the one nearest the door." Eddie sounded as if that choice was significant, and Sybil suspected it was.

Mercy said the words for her. "Guess he wants to be able to run if he wants."

"He has no need to run," Sybil protested, even though she'd thought the same. Winter and then what? Would he move on, leaving her to pick up the pieces of her life?

"And every reason to stay." Mercy chuckled.

Linette and Eddie exchanged one of their private smiles.

Grady, quiet until now, looked up from his plate. "He likes Sybil."

All the adults except Sybil laughed. Her cheeks burned. It was on the tip of her tongue to protest, but knowing it was useless, she kept silent.

It was all she could do to keep her mind on her tasks as the afternoon hours passed. Would he come to the house and ask for her? Would he expect her to go down the hill to meet him? Or was she imagining all sorts of possibilities when there were none?

She was at the window when Eddie headed up the

hill for supper, Grady at his side. She lingered despite Mercy's knowing laugh as the cowboys hurried toward the cookhouse. Brand brought up the rear—a good ten feet behind the others. Her heart went out to him. How long would it take for him to feel comfortable around people?

He looked toward the house and again touched the brim of his hat.

Mercy chuckled. "I do believe he saw you."

"Why are you spying on me?" Sybil's voice held no rancor. Mercy was simply being Mercy. She liked adventure, liked to keep things exciting, but she didn't have an unkind bone in her body.

"Because it's so much fun."

Sybil turned from the window. "You've stuck close to the house all day."

Mercy wrapped an arm about Sybil's waist as they turned toward the kitchen. "I didn't want to miss anything."

"That's strange. You usually create your own excitement."

"Usually," Mercy agreed. "But you're much more interesting lately. Are you going to meet Brand later?"

She considered saying no just to prove her friend wrong, but then she'd feel obligated to follow through. "Maybe." *I hope so.*

Mercy laughed. "Oh, how our Sybil has changed."

Sybil jerked them to a halt. "What do you mean? I haven't changed a bit."

"You're letting yourself be friendly with an outlaw cowboy. Not too long ago you would have run from such a man."

"He's not an outlaw and never was."

Mercy just grinned and pulled her toward the kitchen. "An outlaw. A cowboy. Homeless. Likely as poor as a pauper. Sybil, so much for living a safe little life."

Mercy meant to tease, but her words stung deep inside. Sybil didn't care about his possessions or lack of them. A person's value wasn't measured in his material belongings.

By the time the evening meal was finished, dusk had fallen. Her glance went continually to the window. Would Brand come to the house? She was almost certain he wouldn't. He'd be uncomfortable. Disappointment as sharp and stinging as acrid smoke burned her eyes.

Mercy nudged her. "Do you want me to go with you?"

Sybil stalled, wanting to go down the hill and see if Brand was around, but not wanting her friend to know how desperately she ached to see him and speak to him.

Mercy dragged her to the window overlooking the ranch. Lights glowed from the buildings. A lantern hung outside the barn, and in the shadows, a lean figure lounged against the wall.

"Guess who's down there waiting for you?"

"You don't know that."

Mercy snagged shawls off the hooks in the hall and handed Sybil hers. "We haven't see Jayne all day. Let's go visit her."

Without arguing, Sybil put on her shawl.

Linette and Eddie came into the room. Linette smiled at the pair. "Going out?"

"To visit Jayne." Mercy winked and dragged Sybil to the door.

Trying to stop Mercy was as futile as trying to stop

a train racing downhill. So Sybil let herself be hustled toward Jayne's house. All the while her heart pushed against her ribs and her eyes sought out the figure leaning in the shadows.

When they reached the cookhouse, the figure stepped away from the barn and toward them. All along she'd known it was Brand.

Mercy murmured softly, "I'll see Jayne on my own." She slipped away.

Sybil barely noticed her departure as Brand moved closer. "Howdy," he said, narrowing the distance between them.

"Good evening." Was that all they had to say to each other?

He took her elbow and guided her down the moonlit path toward the river. "I decided to stay."

"I'm glad you did." They reached the bridge and stopped to lean on the handrail. They stared at the flashing silver of the water. "Are you enjoying your work?" she asked.

"Yes. And Cookie's food is great."

She saw his smile as she turned to look at him. Their elbows brushed. She could think of a hundred questions she wanted to ask him.... How had he survived his unsettled childhood? How bad did he hurt after losing his family? But she didn't want to shatter the calm between them.

He shifted, leaned on one elbow and considered her. "I imagine you growing up in England in a big fancy house somewhat like Eddie's. Fancy clothes. Fancy parties. Fine books. Am I right?"

"I was lonely."

"What about Mercy and Jayne?"

"I didn't meet them until I was considered old enough to participate in proper social events." Sybil guessed her voice conveyed her regret over the things she'd missed as a child. "Not that I didn't love my parents and enjoy their company."

"No beaux?"

There'd been Colin, but what she'd felt for him paled to insignificance. "I once fancied myself in love."

"What happened?"

"He left and never looked back." She tried to disguise the hurt in her voice. Wondered if she'd succeeded.

Brand touched her cheek. "And hurt you. And I did the same thing. I'm sorry to have added to your pain."

She couldn't push a word past her tight throat.

"Did your parents give you everything you needed or wanted?"

Her breath eased out and she could answer. "They gave me what they felt was best for me."

"You didn't agree?"

She chuckled. "It never entered my mind to disagree until…" She squelched the unfaithful thought.

He touched her elbow. "Until what?"

"My father did much of his work from his office at home. He was a lawyer and saw many of his clients there. When Mother was ill and resting, he let me stay in his office. I had to be very quiet, so he gave me paper and pencils and I amused myself."

"Let me guess. You made up stories."

"Not at first. I drew little pictures. You know the sort…a round ball with a smaller one on top. Add triangles for ears, whiskers and eyes, and I'd made a cat."

He chuckled, making her want to go on.

"I always showed them to Father. He admired them and said how clever I was. He said I must show them to Mother."

Silence descended between Sybil and Brand. A bird fluttered and chirped as if settling her babies, though the babies would have flown the nest by now. Perhaps mother birds always made comforting good-night sounds. Laughter drifted from the bunkhouse and then the mournful sound of a harmonica.

"I soon learned to read and write, and added words to my pictures," she continued. "More and more words, until finally the words grew into stories. They seemed to come from deep inside, pushing at my heart, my head and my fingers." She felt the familiar rush she did when writing.

"I continued to show them to Mother and Father. They continued to say how clever I was. Until…" She drew in a large breath to steady her voice. "Until I said I wanted to one day write stories for everyone to read. I wanted to be an author. They sat side by side as I told them. I expected they'd say how clever I was, how pleased they would be to see others enjoy my stories." She couldn't go on, feeling again the bottom fall out of her stomach, leaving her airless and slightly nauseated.

Brand caught her shoulder and squeezed gently. The warmth of his touch slowly melted the ice about her heart.

"I was so disappointed when they didn't approve, though I still don't understand why. They should have been so proud."

He pulled her closer, pressed her head to his shoulder. The steady beat of his heart vibrated through her. "And now you disappoint yourself."

She sprang back. "You're wrong." Only he wasn't.

"Really?" He leaned back. "Guess I'll never understand, so let's talk about something else. I told you about my last Christmas. Tell me about yours."

She realized he meant the year his mother had died. He saw it as his last Christmas. Six years ago. Six years of loneliness, shutting himself away from others, fearing the appearance of his pa and brother. Treating Christmas as if it didn't matter any more than any other day. And for him it hadn't, which was even sadder. Had no one ever reached out to him? Or had he turned his back on help? Either way, it was a lonely, barren life he lived. Sybil pushed back the sympathy so she could talk.

"I've been living with an elderly cousin and celebrated Christmas with her two years ago. It was very quiet." She made a sound of amusement. "Everything about her house was very quiet. Last year I spent with Jayne at her house. It's crazy there. So much coming and going I don't know how they kept track of everyone."

"And before your parents died?" Brand's low voice evaded her defenses and took her back to Christmases past.

"We always had such a good time. My parents took me to Piccadilly Circus to look at all the toys in the shops. They bought me dolls and books. They each helped me choose gifts for the other parent. I was always so excited on Christmas morning, when we ate a special breakfast of waffles sprinkled with powdered sugar and covered with clotted cream. Father passed out the gifts and we sat around enjoying them while the cook roasted a goose."

Brand turned to look at the water gurgling under the bridge. "You were a loved and adored child."

Something in his voice made her feel she had pushed him away. She tried to think what she'd done to make him grow distant. It was on the tip of her tongue to ask when he spoke.

"It's getting late." He straightened and turned to indicate they should go back. He escorted her to Jayne's house to meet Mercy. Then he hurried away with a barely murmured goodbye.

Sybil paused before the door to the cabin. Why had he retreated so quickly? Did he think she would look down on him because of the way he'd been forced to live?

As soon as she stepped inside the house, Mercy hurried to her side. "Tell us everything."

Seth bolted to his feet. "I think the horses must need something." He fled outside.

Jayne laughed. "Too many females around for him. Too much *romance*." She clasped her hands together, looking starry-eyed, then took Sybil's other hand. "Do tell us."

She allowed them to lead her to a chair. "There's nothing to report. I merely told him a few things about my childhood."

Mercy groaned. "Now there's a way to make a man feel insignificant."

"What do you mean?" Sybil had no such intention.

"You adored your father. He could do no wrong. He gave you everything you ever dreamed of. How can a homeless cowboy hope to compete with that?"

Had she made Brand feel insignificant? Perhaps she inadvertently had. Now she must find a way to fix her mistake. To make him see that it was the love of her parents that blessed her, not their gifts.

It was love she wanted. Not things. Could she make him understand that?

Chapter Sixteen

Brand took his time about returning to the bunkhouse. He needed to think. And he couldn't do it with the other cowboys asking questions or looking as if they'd die if they didn't ask one. Though to be honest, none had done either. For the most part they weren't any more interested in him than he was in them.

Sybil's words tortured his brain.

Raised with privilege and prestige. Given everything. He'd always known that, so why did it now fill him with regret? Even with his name purged of the Duggan gang guilt, he was still a nobody cowboy with nothing to offer to a gal like Sybil Bannerman.

He eased open the bunkhouse door, but it squealed like a pig. Someone ought to oil the hinges. Half a dozen heads swung toward him, then returned to what they'd been doing. He was of no interest to any of them. Just a man doing a job.

He flung himself on his bunk and turned his back to the others. He had no wish to join them in a game of cards, or sing sad songs about lonely cowboys. His own sadness throbbed in his heart. Why sing of it when he lived it?

The truth could not be denied. Sybil was out of the realm of possibility. He should leave. Move on. But her challenge to forget being a Duggan rang in his ears. He was through running from the Duggan gang. Besides, he'd given his word to Eddie, and a man was only as good as his word.

The next day he still considered his options. Perhaps he could ask Eddie to send him to the far corner of the ranch. But Eddie had already dispatched riders to bring down the cows in preparation for the soon-to-be fall roundup.

Besides, somewhere deep inside Brand a happy thought warred with the lingering idea of riding away.

If he stayed around he could hope to see more of Sybil. It was a futile, foolish idea, but what harm could possibly come of it? Her interest in him was surely no more than curiosity or politeness.

He alone would bear the pain of their final goodbye, either when he forced himself to move on or when she returned to England. There would be a pain for every pleasure, but it would be worth it.

He glanced at the house up the hill as he left the cookhouse with Slim to fix the fences of the wintering pens. Did he see someone at the window? Was it Sybil? Just in case, he touched the brim of his hat in a pretense of adjusting its position.

A few hours later he and Slim put down their tools and headed to the cookhouse for dinner.

"You done good," Slim said. "I appreciate a hard worker."

"Just doin' my job."

Slim slapped him on the back. "You'll do just fine here. Glad to have you on the crew."

Crew? As if he belonged? Could it be possible?

Brand and Slim returned to the task after a satisfying meal, and worked throughout the afternoon.

Slim didn't say much, which left Brand lots of time for thinking. Try as he did with every bit of energy he could muster to avoid one topic, his thoughts continually circled back to Sybil.

Would she again traipse down the hill after supper and spend a precious hour or two with him? He grinned in anticipation even as he told himself it was a foolish wish. Then, hoping Slim hadn't noticed his silly grin, he forced it away.

Later, as soon as he'd scraped his plate clean after two helpings of Cookie's mashed potatoes, gravy, roast beef and carrots, he left the cookhouse and parked himself by the barn door. Someone had lit the lantern hanging there and he stood at the edge of the circle of light. Sybil could see him if she cared to check. He told himself he wasn't waiting, even though his gaze was glued to the house up the hill.

When the door opened and the light flashed golden, his breath caught partway down his throat.

Dawg rose and whined eagerly. "Settle down," Brand murmured to the animal, and told himself the same.

A door slammed to his left and children's voices called out.

Both he and Dawg shifted their gaze in that direction. The foreman's three oldest children scampered down the trail toward them.

Dawg whined again.

"You like kids?" It surprised Brand, though they'd

never been around children much, so maybe the dog had always been this way.

Dawg, taking Brand's surprise for disapproval, flopped down and put his head on his paws.

"It's okay. Kids are kind of…" He had no idea what word to use. *Friendly. Innocent. Accepting.* Maybe all that and more.

The children drew abreast. Neil, the oldest boy, saw Brand first. "Hi. We're going to get Grady and play tag."

At that moment, Sybil reached the corrals. Although his attention was on the youngsters, he'd been aware of her the whole time. Every step she took closer made his heart beat stronger, until it now thumped against his ribs like a trapped animal trying to escape.

She spoke to the children, who paused long enough to respond to her greeting, then she turned toward Brand, the width of the corral separating them. "Nice evening, isn't it?"

He had paid scant attention, but now realized the full golden moon gave everything a shimmering appearance. The warm kiss of a gentle evening breeze brushed against his cheek. He inhaled the scent of fresh hay and poplar leaves. "Very nice," he murmured.

"It's a perfect evening for a walk." Her words carried warmth and welcome. "Care to join me?"

Brand jolted from the wall. He swallowed hard and forced himself to saunter, when every muscle wanted to gallop. "Sounds like a fine idea." He fumbled with the gate, his fingers stiff, and finally managed to release the latch and slip through. "Where are we going?"

Her merry laugh sang through the air, danced through his veins and vibrated in his heart. "Do we need a destination? Can't we simply enjoy the evening?"

He could have said they wouldn't need to move from this spot and the evening would be special enough to stay in his thoughts the rest of his life. Instead, he managed one word. "Sure." And fell in at her side. His arm brushed hers, sending a rush of tingles up his skin.

They walked west, toward the foreman's house. Lamplight filled the windows. They saw Roper and Cassie in matching rocking chairs talking to each other. Cassie's back was to them, but Roper faced them, a smile of pure contentment filling his expression.

"He looks happy." The words were out before Brand could stop them.

"I expect he is. He's gone from a lonely man raised in an orphanage and never knowing family, to a man loved and adored by a wife and a ready-made family."

They passed the house.

Sybil sighed. "Kind of makes you envy him, doesn't it?"

Brand had thought exactly that, but it seemed weak to say it. And why would she think such a thing? She'd been raised in a loving home. Of course, she was now an orphan. "Do you plan to return to England?"

She hesitated long enough for his lungs to ache for air.

He remembered he had to breathe.

"It's the only home I have."

You could stay here. The words hovered on the tip of his tongue, but he bit them back. He had nothing to offer her. No fine house. No abundance of books. Nothing. So he kept silent.

The children ran down the path behind them calling, "Not it." Thor, the fawn, raced after them, darting from one to the other.

They drew closer. Dawg whined and looked back.

"Do you want to play with them?" Brand asked.

The dog gave a little bark.

"Go ahead. Suit yourself." He never would have guessed Dawg would want this.

But Dawg yapped and ran toward the children, his wounds completely forgotten. The youngsters halted and waited, uncertain about Dawg's behavior. Thor bounced a safe distance away and watched the dog with wide eyes.

"He wants to play," Brand said.

Neil crouched down and held out a hand.

Dawg went eagerly, squirming with excitement. Suddenly all the children surrounded him, then backed away, calling him, as Dawg ran from one to the other, barking happily.

Daisy turned toward the adults. "Do you want to play tag?"

Sybil grabbed Brand's arm. Her fingers dug into his muscle. He couldn't tell if it signaled fear or anticipation. Was she afraid of the children? Or did she long to play with them? He was about to say no when Billy tagged Sybil.

"You're it and you can't catch me."

The children closed around them, teasing her to catch them. Brand had instinctively stepped away from her so he became part of the circle.

In the moonlight her eyes were dark and unreadable, but her lips were parted as if surprise held her immobile.

Billy darted toward her. "Catch me if you can."

She scrubbed her lips together, considering the challenge, and then darted toward the boy.

He shrieked and ran away. The other children scattered.

Brand ran, too. He'd played this game many times as a child. Often with Cyrus thudding after him. His heart clenched. He missed Cyrus. Not the man who had become part of the Duggan gang, but the big brother who had played with him. He lost his concentration and turned to look up the hill toward the little graveyard. Even if the sun shone overhead he couldn't see from where he stood, but he knew the exact location of Pa and Cyrus's final resting place. Would he see them both along with Ma in the hereafter?

He realized footsteps raced toward him, and ducked away.

They played a rowdy game of tag with the children, catching and being caught their share of times.

He was it again, having been tagged by Neil. The children raced off, disappearing in the shadows. But Sybil's golden hair caught the moonlight and gave away her position. He knew if he raced toward her, she would run the opposite direction, so he tiptoed in a round-about way until he came up behind her. She strained forward, listening for his approach, ready to take flight. For a heartbeat, two, three, he didn't move. He simply stood there taking in the fact of his freedom. For the first time in many years he could take part in a simple game of tag without glancing over his shoulder, fearing the Duggan gang.

Grinning for a dozen different reasons, he tiptoed forward.

Sybil must have heard him, for she turned just as he reached forward to tag her. His hand caught her arm. "You're it."

Was that hoarse voice his?

"Oh, you. Sneaking up on a girl like that."

"All's fair." In love and war. He felt suspended between the two. The war of outrunning Pa and Cyrus was over. But he was not ready to believe he could love and be loved. He hadn't felt that way since Ma died. Not that that was the sort of love he ached for. When had his thoughts gotten so muddled? He released her arm and called, "Sybil's it."

The children dashed by her, teasing and tempting her to chase them.

The game continued in the cool, moon-drenched evening until a rectangle of light shone from either end of the ranch and Linette and Cassie called out to their respective children. "Come in now. It's bedtime."

The little ones stopped their play and sighed. Then, calling good-night over their shoulders, they trotted home.

Sybil chuckled. "That was fun. It's the first time I played tag."

He stared at her. "You're joshing."

"No, really."

"That's positively unnatural. Tag is a favorite children's game." They fell in step, side by side, and walked to the bridge.

She shrugged one shoulder. "I had other amusements."

"Like what?"

"My books and papers. I loved making my own paper dolls."

He thought it best not to say that a normal childhood had its share of rowdy play.

"These children are very fortunate." Her voice carried a note of wistfulness.

He could name a number of ways that was true, but wanted to know what she meant, and asked her.

"They are loved by people who haven't any obligation to love them."

"That's a fact. Linette is to have a baby soon. Won't Grady feel misplaced?"

Sybil laughed gently. "Linette and Eddie aren't like that. Nor are Roper and Cassie. A child of their union won't cause them to love the other children any less."

"How can you be so certain?"

She looked into his face, studying him, perhaps wondering if there was a reason behind his question. Maybe there was. Pa had loved him, of that he was certain. But his love was on again, off again, depending on whether or not Pa felt Brand did what he wanted. And because Brand mostly hadn't, he'd often felt his father didn't really love him. Not like he did Cyrus.

Sybil rubbed her warm palm along Brand's arm. "My father taught me love is both a feeling and a choice. Even when you don't feel the emotion, you choose to love."

"That sounds pretend."

"No. It sounds real."

He decided to change the subject. "I expect there is someone back in England hoping to marry you." She'd never mentioned it, but he could imagine many suitors beat a pathway to her door.

She gave his arm a harmless tap, then withdrew her hand.

Funny how he suddenly felt cold. And alone.

"Do you really think I'd go out walking with you if someone back home had asked for my hand?"

"No. Why are you walking with me?" He wanted to slam his head against the nearest post. Why couldn't he keep his mouth shut around her?

"Why do you think?"

He turned her so the moonlight fell directly on her face. He saw uncertainty in her eyes and something more. Was it…? No. It couldn't be.

But before he could marshal a response, she tucked her arm around his elbow and drew him along the path.

"I enjoy the children here. I've never been around many before. I hope to marry someday, and have more than one child, so they wouldn't be lonely. But that's in God's hands, isn't it?"

Brand's tongue stuck to the roof of his mouth. What was in God's hands? Marriage or children?

They reached the top of the hill and stopped. She turned her face up to him with an expectant look. Did she want to be kissed? He couldn't believe that's what her glance meant. But had all this talk of children and new beginnings made her forget that Brand was a Duggan? A homeless, penniless cowboy? He'd kissed her once. Out of gratitude. If he kissed her now it would be for an entirely different reason. Would she welcome his interest? Or find him presumptuous and far too bold? He weighed his options.

She sighed and turned away. "We should be getting back."

He'd waited too long. The opportunity had passed. Probably a good thing, but he found no comfort in the thought.

He escorted her to within a few feet of the door.

"Good night," he murmured. His instinct was to run down the hill, throw himself on the back of his horse and leave, while he still had an ounce of good sense left. But he was through running from the Duggan name and his fears. He'd go only if someone made it clear he should.

In the meantime, he didn't intend to walk away until Sybil was safely indoors.

"Good night," she whispered, her hand brushing his arm. "I enjoyed the evening."

Before he could pull a word or question from his brain, she stepped inside. Did she enjoy the evening because the children played tag with them or because of their moonlit walk?

Perhaps it was best not to know. That way he could allow himself to dream a few dreams.

Sybil's thoughts tangled like knotted yarn. Did Brand care about her? How could she make him understand how she felt?

Hoping to sort out her troubled thoughts, she reached for her Bible. The book fell open at Proverbs, but she continued to turn pages until she reached the Song of Solomon…a lover's song. Surely it would answer her questions.

But after a few minutes she closed her Bible, as mixed up as ever. She wrote in her notebook. *I need wisdom from above. God, please guide my path.*

She pulled out her notes on Brand. She had so many questions, but the answers weren't for her story. They were for her heart. She studied the pages. It was a good story. One her editor would like. But she couldn't bring herself to send it. What she knew about Brand seemed like a trust he'd given her. She didn't want to dishonor that.

She put the pages back in the drawer, then lay back on the bed, recalling every moment of the evening. Playing tag had been so much fun. Seeing the children enjoying each other...

A story idea sprang into her head, and she grabbed paper and pencil and wrote for two hours before turning out the lamp and crawling into bed.

Brand had asked her about her dream of publishing her stories. She'd thought the dream had died, but found it had lain dormant as it grew and matured.

Over the next couple days Sybil found it impossible to explain this drive in her, this urgency to see Brand, to spend as much time with him as possible. She stopped trying to justify it to herself and others. She stopped trying to make excuses, and simply rushed down the hill every evening to where he waited.

Sometimes the children came out and played tag with them. Always she and Brand walked. And she asked questions. What was his favorite color?

"Gold," he said. "The same shade of gold as your hair." His answer brought pleasant warmth to her cheeks.

She wanted to know the name of every place he'd worked or lived.

He hesitated at first, then told her of the many places. Some where he'd wished he could stay longer but hadn't dared. Others where he couldn't wait to move on. Only when she pressed did he admit that not everyone welcomed a stranger who wouldn't reveal his last name.

"It didn't matter to Eddie," she said.

"Eddie is a good man, a fair boss."

Then she wanted to know about every injury he'd incurred, no matter how minor. "Like the banging your leg took when Cal brought in that outlaw horse."

Brand laughed, draped his arm around her shoulders and squeezed her close. "Sybil, bumps and bruises are an everyday part of my work, and ranch life in general. I don't take note of such minor things."

She turned to observe his face. "How about the major ones?"

At first she thought he would give the same answer, then his mouth twisted in a wry grin. "They only count if they mean I can't ride."

"Do you mean ride wild horses or ride away?"

He nodded. "Yup."

She laughed and nudged him in the ribs.

He groaned and pretended to be hurt.

"How many times have you been unable to ride?"

"Twice." She heard the regret in his voice. "Once I cut my foot on a tin can someone had carelessly tossed into a pasture. It got infected and I had to rest a few days. Even when I left, I couldn't put my boot on. Carried it over the saddle horn."

She joined him in laughing about the situation, though her insides tightened at the idea of his suffering and the risk he took riding with an unhealed foot. "And the other time?"

"Well, that was entirely my fault."

"What did you do?" She pushed her shoulder against his chest as if the movement could force the words from him.

"I let myself be distracted momentarily while working with a horse. Ended up getting kicked."

"Ouch."

"Oh, the kick didn't hurt that much. But I was mad and I got back on the horse. I was not in the frame of mind I needed to be in when dealing with a wild animal. He threw me before I found my balance. Right into the boards. Knocked me out and cut my head." Brand bent and showed her where the cut had been, just above his left ear.

She parted his hair to examine his head under the light from the lantern by the barn door. She couldn't see anything, but touching him like that made the air feel light as butterfly wings. "Glad to see you survived." Her voice was husky.

"Couldn't see straight for two days. Had a sore head for a long time."

"Ah." That was all she said.

He squinted at her. "Ah? What does that mean?"

She shrugged. "Only that it explains a few things."

He caught her elbows. "Like what?" His own voice had grown low.

She pretended to try and wriggle free, though she hoped he wouldn't take her seriously and drop his hands. "Now I understand why you act so thickheaded at times."

"When have I ever done that?"

Her thoughts stalled. Only one thing came to mind and she wasn't sure she should mention it.

He shook her gently. "Tell me."

"Well, if you insist, I'd have to say that to keep running from the Duggan gang when it no longer exists is pretty thickheaded."

He dropped his hands to his sides and studied her long and hard. "I'm through running."

She touched his arm. "I'm glad."

One more question burned to be asked. "Have you ever left a brokenhearted girl behind?"

"No. Never."

"Really? No love interests?" Sybil could hardly believe it.

"Once I thought myself in love." He told her about May.

Sybil sensed how hurt he'd been, and wrapped her arm around his as they walked along the path toward the bridge, where they stopped. She raised her face to him as she did every evening, on the pretext of deep interest in something he said. It wasn't that her interest wasn't real, but what she really hoped for was a sign of growing affection on his part.

A kiss from Brand would signal he felt the same thing.

But each time, he looked ready to accept her silent invitation...then blinked and shifted away. Perhaps he didn't share her feelings. Perhaps she was wrong in thinking he cared.

Chapter Seventeen

Being part of a crew made Brand more nervous than riding a rank horse. He was never sure what to say. He'd forgotten how to sit at a table and make conversation. Sleeping in a bunkhouse with others made his skin twitch. But it was worth it to see Sybil every day. He often observed her helping Linette or visiting with Jayne during the day. And each evening, she joined him for a walk. He'd never known such sweet moments.

She stood before him this evening, her face upturned to him. He studied her expression, memorizing every feature, branding it indelibly on his memory. As long as he lived and drew breath he would remember these evenings with joy.

He touched a wayward curl and pulled in a breath at the satiny feel of her hair. A fine lady from high-class society. And yet she smiled at him. Tipped her face toward his touch.

"Sybil?" He whispered her name. Was he misreading the invitation in her eyes?

"Brand." She lifted a hand and pressed her palm to his chest.

"You are a fine lady."

Her smile widened. "And you are a fine gentleman."

He grinned at that. "I'm just a cowboy."

"I don't think the two are mutually exclusive."

His smile spread further. "I suppose not."

Her fingers teased the hair above his ear. Tingles of anticipation flooded his brain, even as more tingles raced up his arm and pounded through his heart. Was it possible she wanted what he wanted? A kiss? And so much more. A kiss would merely signal all the things he hoped for and dared not dream of. Love, acceptance, family, home…

"Sybil." He whispered her name, again disturbing the curl on her forehead. For a moment it held his attention.

"Yes?" Her sweet breath brushed his face.

"Sybil, would you think me overly bold if I said I want to kiss you?"

"Mostly I would think it's about time."

He chuckled, delighted at her response, and slowly lowered his head, anxious to claim her lips, but wanting the moment to last forever.

She went up on her toes and met him halfway.

Her lips were warm and welcoming. Sweet as nectar.

He would have lingered, drowning in the million sensations and delights flooding through him, but he didn't want to frighten her away, so he broke off the kiss and pressed her head to his shoulder.

She sighed.

And he knew satisfaction he'd never before experienced. He wished he could find words to describe it. "I can't remember ever feeling like this." It didn't begin to say what he felt.

"What do you feel?"

"I think…" He swallowed hard, awed by the warm emotions flooding his heart and spreading to his limbs. Could this be love?

If he loved her, he would keep it secret. He didn't deserve someone like her. "Sybil, I'm just a poor lonely cowboy."

"Brand, I'm just a poor lonely English girl."

"Poor?"

"Did you think I was rich?" She leaned back to study him. "I'm not. When my parents died I was left almost penniless." She paused, her expression filled with questions. "Would it make a difference if I were rich?"

He studied the question. "You deserve a nice house and…"

"And what?"

"Everything that goes with it." What was the point of going into details? He had nothing. She deserved everything.

"You don't think I deserve love?" She didn't wait for him to answer. "Doesn't everyone?" Her voice was low, challenging.

Oh yes. He wanted to believe everyone did. Even a Duggan. "I'm just a cowboy," he said again.

"And I'm just a girl."

"Is that enough?"

"Do you want it to be?" She continued to watch him. Even in the silvery moonlight, her gaze probed until he had no defenses.

"Yes." He pulled her against his shoulder again and tilted his head to rest his cheek on her satiny curls.

She sighed. He imagined a pleased look on her face. One that would match his own.

A fire lit in his heart, warm and bright. But he must

take her home before he gave people cause to talk about her. He didn't care what they said about him. All his life he'd been talked about. But Sybil would never bear that stigma if he had anything to do with it.

He pulled her hand around his elbow and pressed it to his side.

They walked up the hill and paused before the door. She turned, lifted her face to him, her invitation clear. He needed no more and caught her lips in a gentle, chaste kiss, then broke away.

She stepped toward the door. "Good night, cowboy."

He grinned. "Good night, English girl."

Not until he reached the bunkhouse did he force the smile from his lips.

It threatened to return the next morning even when he went to work. Eddie asked him to check all the gates, a job that gave him plenty of opportunity to watch the big house.

Twice he saw Mercy carrying water, but he couldn't see the back of the house until he went to the wintering pens. Then he was able to watch Sybil hanging laundry on the line. The wind billowed her dark blue skirt around her legs, puffed out her white top and pulled pins from her curls until they rioted around her head.

He leaned back on his heels and watched.

She emptied the basket and looked about, scanning the yard to his right.

He waited, wondering if she'd search further. She did, until she found him.

The distance was too great to see her expression, but he didn't need to. His heart leaped in greeting.

She waved.

He waved back.

Neither of them moved. For sure, he wasn't going to be the first.

Something caught Sybil's attention and she turned toward the house, nodded, then picked up the basket, glancing again in his direction before she disappeared out of sight.

At that moment he made up his mind. He'd ask her out for a walk this evening and tell her he loved her.

He was ready to take the chance.

It was midafternoon when he finished his job. "All the gates are in good repair," he told Eddie. "What do you have for me to do now?"

"There's no point in starting another job this late in the day," the rancher said. "You're free to do whatever you like."

"Okay, boss." There was only one thing he wanted to do. He'd seen Sybil leave the house half an hour ago, headed in the direction of his old campsite. It seemed to be where she liked to go to be alone…where she read and wrote.

He washed up reasonably well, left Dawg in the barn and headed for the spot. This time it was about him and Sybil. He did not want Dawg to be part of what he had to say.

She sat against a tree, the golden leaves a bright backdrop. More leaves danced across the ground, fluttered in the air. She distractedly brushed one from her hair, lost in concentration as she wrote furiously.

He stood in the shadows, content to watch.

Her hand paused. She lifted her head, listening, and then glanced about.

He stepped forward so she wouldn't be alarmed. "Howdy."

She smiled, her cheeks rosy and her blue eyes glinting. "Howdy, yourself."

He crossed the clearing to her side and sat down. He hadn't thought this far ahead, hadn't planned how he'd do this. It didn't seem right to blurt out "I love you." Seemed something that important should be done properly. "What are you doing?"

"Yesterday when you talked to the boys about learning to ride wild horses, I thought of another story." She kept her head down.

"Why are you embarrassed?"

There was a beat of silence as she considered his question. "I suppose because my writing means so much to me."

"Are you going to get your stories published?"

"It's not that easy."

"Because you're still afraid of how people will react?" If the opinion of others mattered so much, how could he tell her how he felt? People would likely say unkind things if her name was linked to his. Would she let them influence her? He swallowed. This was harder than riding a wild horse.

"It's not so much that." She paused a moment, then went on. "Being published means someone has to be willing to publish my stories."

"And you wonder if anyone would be?"

She nodded. "I've never tried to publish fiction."

"Can I read your story?"

She handed him a handful of papers.

The story began well. Two daredevil boys with more guts than common sense decided to ride a wild mustang. He chuckled a few times as he read. He reached the end of the page and turned it over.

But the second page didn't seem to follow.

He was known only as Cowboy. He never did give a last name before he rode into the sunset. He didn't welcome any questions about his true identity. But he was the best bronc buster in the territory. A reputation well earned.

It began when he was ten...

This wasn't the same story. It wasn't about children. It was about a grown man who broke horses, a loner with no name and an ugly, but loyal, dog.

This was his story.

Brand stared at the pages. "Have you had other things published?" The words felt like blocks of ice on his tongue.

"A few nonfiction articles, but not under my own name."

He faced her, his eyes burning. "Is this one of those you've had published?" He shoved the pages toward her.

She glanced at them and gasped. "How did this get in there?"

He jerked to his feet. "So all the questions, all the interest was merely so you could write a story about a nameless cowboy?"

She scrambled to her feet. "No, Brand. Well, maybe at first. But—"

"I should have known. A fancy English miss and a nameless cowboy. Of course you had to have another reason."

She reached for him.

He stepped away.

"Brand, I never sent the story to the editor. I couldn't."

He slammed his hat on his head. "Well, don't let me stop you. I'm sure it's worth more than—" He would not say what he'd intended. *Me.* "I hope it earns you a lot of money." He strode away as fast as he could. He would not run, though his muscles twitched to do so.

"Brand, wait." She trotted after him.

He ignored her call and easily outdistanced her with long, hurried strides. He felt as if she'd snatched the ground from beneath his feet. All her attention had been so she could get a story. How could he trust anything he'd believed about her?

Eddie was in front of the barn. Good. That would save him from finding the man.

"Eddie, I have to leave."

"Leave? Now? Is something wrong?"

Everything. He'd been a blind, stupid fool. "I have to go. I have my reasons."

"You're sure about this? I can't change your mind?"

"My mind's made up." Brand grabbed his saddle and strode toward his horse.

"I'm sorry to hear that. I'll run up to the house and get your wages."

Brand didn't want to wait, but he would need the money to buy supplies. "I'll be at the bunkhouse collecting my things."

Eddie opened his mouth to say something more, then thought better of it and jogged away.

Brand finished saddling up, and whistled for Dawg. The dog wriggled in anticipation. Guess he was ready to move on, too. Brand led the horse from the barn.

But Sybil stood in the roadway. "Brand, please."

He pretended not to hear. Dawg hesitated, turned toward her and whined. Brand whistled and the dog trotted after him.

At the bunkhouse, Brand stuffed his things into his

saddlebag, rolled up his bedding and left the place without a backward look.

Eddie waited outside and counted out his wages. "I don't know what happened, but I saw Sybil with tears streaming down her face."

"I didn't do anything."

"Perhaps not, but there is obviously a misunderstanding that can't be resolved if you ride away."

"The misunderstanding was wholly on my part."

"Still."

Brand didn't reply.

Eddie shook his head. "If you change your mind, you're always welcome here."

"Thanks, but I won't be back."

Eddie held out his hand. "It's been a pleasure."

Brand shook the rancher's hand, wishing he could say the same, then mounted up. Dawg followed.

Not until he was beyond sight of the ranch did Brand stop, turn around and look back for a long time. Regret scratched through his veins. Another chapter over. Another lesson learned.

He headed down the trail. Dawg stood looking back until Brand called him.

Sybil hadn't been able to hide her tears from Eddie as she rushed to the house.

Linette saw her as she burst through the door and dashed down the hall, hoping to reach her bedroom before she collapsed.

"Sybil, what's wrong?" her friend called. When she didn't answer and continued her headlong rush, Linette hurried after her.

Sybil turned the corner and ran into Mercy.

"Whoa." Mercy grabbed her arms and steadied her. She looked at Sybil, saw the gushing tears. "Sybil, what's the matter?"

The only sounds she could make were the sobs she fought to stifle.

Linette wrapped an arm about her shoulders. "What's happened? Are you hurt?"

Sybil shook her head. Yes, she was hurt, but how was she to explain a pain without physical cause?

"It's Brand, isn't it?" Mercy sounded disgusted. "What did he do? Tell me. I'll find him and make him pay."

Sybil hiccuped and again shook her head. "He… didn't…" She swallowed back tears. "It's all a mistake."

"Then tell him. Whatever it is."

"I can't," she wailed. "He left."

Mercy held her at arm's length. "You mean he's gone? Ridden away?"

Sybil nodded.

Linette sighed. "Eddie will be disappointed. He liked Brand."

"Eddie's disappointed?" Mercy grunted. "What about Sybil?"

Sybil broke away from them and rushed to her room, buried her face in her pillow and wept.

Her friends followed her.

"I'm sorry," Linette said. "I didn't mean to be insensitive." Her footsteps tapped away down the hall. But not Mercy's.

Sybil wished she would go away and leave her to wallow in her misery, but instead Mercy sat beside her. "What happened?"

Sybil sat up and wiped her eyes. "I made a foolish mistake." She pointed at the notes about Brand.

Mercy barely glanced at them. "So?"

"He found these pages by accident. I meant to show him a story I had written about two little boys wanting to break wild horses. I don't know how these papers got mixed in. How could I have been so careless?"

"You're saying he wasn't happy about it? Why not? I'd think he'd be flattered."

Sybil kept her gaze on the pages, afraid if she looked at Mercy she'd be reduced to a fresh flood of tears. "I guess he thought I only cared about him to get more information."

"Did you?"

"No, of course not!" Then her defenses deflated. "Maybe a little at first, but just to start with."

"So what are you going to do?"

"I don't know." She tossed the offending papers into her drawer. "I should have never come here." Despite her pain, she couldn't regret knowing Brand.

"Oh, sure. You could still be living with Cousin Celia. My lands, child, why would you leave such a nice arrangement?" Mercy mocked Aunt Celia's voice.

Sybil shuddered. "I can't imagine going back. And yet I was happy enough there."

Her friend patted her shoulder in a motherly way. "Only because you didn't know how much more there was to life. You ought to send that." She tipped her head toward the drawer where Sybil had tossed the pages. "Brand's story is really good."

"I couldn't."

Mercy tsked. "This is a new world. We don't have to be chained by silly old rules."

Sybil sighed. Let Mercy think it was about rules and proper behavior, but she couldn't send Brand's story out without his permission. It would only verify his suspicions. She had no intention of doing that. Even if he never knew one way or the other. Pain pierced her heart like a spear. To never see him again… How would she endure it?

"Think about it." Mercy patted her arm and left the room.

Sybil stared toward the pages in the drawer. Yes, her editor would love the story, but thanks to Brand, publishing it was no longer what she wanted to do. She pulled out the children's stories she'd written and looked through them.

She wanted to publish a children's book in her own name.

But did she have the courage to do so without Brand to tell her it was the right thing to do?

She fell back on the bed. Did she even want to do it without him? She turned over to stare at the wall. His leaving had taken the sunshine from her life.

Chapter Eighteen

As Brand made breakfast, Dawg whined and paced. Breakfast didn't require a lot of work. Brand hadn't replenished his supplies, so beans were the only choice.

He offered a plateful to Dawg.

The dog sat down, stared at him and wouldn't eat.

"When did you get so particular?" he asked. Dawg gave him a baleful look. "You can forget about the kids feeding you. We won't be seeing them again." The children had started bringing table scraps to the dog.

Dawg lay down and put his head on his paws.

"Suit yourself." Brand ate the beans with the same pleasure he'd get from stabbing a fork into his thigh. Why had he let himself think he could be in love? Or maybe more accurately, why did he think Sybil's interest in him meant she loved him?

He threw away the last of the beans, downed the rest of the coffee, dowsed the fire and saddled his horse. If he rode hard and fast he could be...

Where?

He swung into the saddle and headed north, away from the ranch. The particulars of where didn't matter.

Dawg stayed by the cold campfire.

Brand whistled for him. Dawg pushed to his feet with a decided lack of enthusiasm and slunk toward Brand.

He again headed north. Dawg barked. Brand turned to see that the dog had not moved. "Come on, let's get moving."

Dawg picked up his feet and headed south.

"Wrong way, pal."

Dawg looked over his shoulder and barked.

It was a standoff. Brand meant to go north and Dawg meant to go south.

"Fine. Have it your way."

Dawg trotted away, pausing every few feet to look back and whine.

"Go. Go back to her."

Dawg yapped and took off running. The last Brand saw of him was his crooked tail disappearing down the trail.

What did a fool dog know?

Sybil had cried enough tears during the night to soak her pillow and leave her eyes puffy. She rose and washed her face. No more crying. She was done with tears. Knowing Brand had been a nice experience while it lasted. Now it was time to move on. She sighed. Words were easy and intentions were fine, but she'd never forget him.

Linette had ironing to be done so Sybil gladly stayed in the kitchen, tackling the job, while her friend sat in the front room and tended to the mending.

The stove was hot, to heat the irons, but she barely noticed the growing warmth of the room. The mindless task allowed her thoughts to constantly follow a trail north from the ranch.

Where had Brand gone? Where would he stop? Maybe he'd change his mind and return, give her a chance to explain. *Please God, send him back.* She continued ironing, knowing God could change Brand's heart, but only if Brand didn't hold stubbornly to his anger.

Outside, a dog barked, the sound urgent, demanding. Dawg? She ran down the hall, straight out the front door. "Dawg!" She fell on her knees and hugged the animal. He licked her face and wriggled from his nose to the tip of his crooked tail.

She lifted her head and looked around. There was no cowboy on the path or in front of the door. She stood and turned full circle, but still did not see Brand. "Where's your master?"

Mercy and Jayne stepped from Jayne's cabin, saw Dawg with Sybil and looked around. Then they climbed the hill to join her.

"Where is he?" Mercy asked.

"I don't know." Sybil squeezed her hands together so hard they hurt. "But Dawg wouldn't be here without him." Her throat closed off so she had to swallow twice before she could continue. "Maybe he's hurt."

Mercy shrugged. "Or maybe he sent Dawg back."

"He would never do that." Sybil fought a suffocating sense of panic.

Mercy watched her, saw her tensing, and squeezed her arm. "I'm sure there's nothing to be concerned about."

Her words barely registered with Sybil. "Where's

Eddie?" She scanned the entire ranch area visible from the hill.

Linette had joined them. "He's taken some cowboys and headed west to check on the cows."

"I have to find Brand." Sybil's voice squeaked out.

Linette took her arm on one side, Mercy on the other, and Jayne caught her hand. They led her reluctant feet back to the house and gently pushed her into a chair.

Linette hurried away and returned in a few minutes with a pot of tea and four cups and saucers. She poured them each tea. But Sybil's arms trembled so badly Linette put the cup on a nearby table.

"If you like, once Eddie returns I'll ask him to check where Brand is."

Sybil nodded. Ten thousand protests raced through her head. Brand could bleed to death waiting for Eddie to return. He could be lying somewhere unable to move. He could...

She attempted to slam the door on all the images flooding her brain. Sometimes an active imagination was an unpleasant thing.

After a few minutes she managed to drink her tea and appear calm. All the while, her thoughts raced, until she came up with a plan.

Brand rode on and on. Every mile weighed his mind until he drew his horse to a stop and stared at the narrow trail ahead. Where was he going? And more importantly, why? What difference did it make if Sybil wrote a story about someone named Cowboy? It didn't matter to him. He no longer had to run from the Duggan gang.

His horse shuffled, uncertain what to do. Brand steadied the animal. "Just thinking, boy. Just thinking."

Maybe Dawg had it right. Life was too good at the ranch to ride away.

And Sybil?

Why, she was the best thing that had ever happened to Brand. He loved her, and even if she didn't love him back, even if her interest had only been for a story...

Well, then he could still enjoy occasional glimpses of her. Enjoy hearing her sing during Sunday services. See her sauntering around the ranch. He might even follow her to her favorite spot and openly watch her if she didn't object.

Despite his brave talk, he knew that would never be enough. He couldn't believe she didn't care about him. She'd said he deserved love. She'd kissed him—a real, warm and giving kiss. It hadn't been begrudging in the least.

"Wahoo!" His shout sent the horse skittering sideways. Brand calmed him and turned him about to face south. Back to the ranch.

Back to Sybil. He meant to find out if that kiss meant she might have some sweet regard for him.

He grinned from ear to ear and barely restrained a happy song. This was the right thing. Somehow he and Sybil would work things out even if it took days, weeks, months. Nothing else mattered.

Lost in his happy thoughts, he didn't hear or see anything until a man on horseback appeared before him, blocking his path.

His eyes fell to the gleaming pistol the rider held in his hand, pointed directly at him. Brand's heart stalled and then he reined his horse in and slowly raised his hands in the air. He gave the man a quick once-over.

He was thin, rough-shaven, with dirty blond hair and a scowl fit to rot his teeth.

"I'm just a poor cowboy," he told the stranger. All he had was the wages Eddie had given him. He sure wasn't prepared to die over a few dollars. "You can have what I've got."

"Ain't interested in your money."

The skin on the back of Brand's neck tingled at the venom in the man's voice.

"Yer one of them Duggans."

Brand's nerves went into full alarm. "The Duggan gang is dead."

"Yeah. You'd like me to believe that, but I ain't fooled. I seen them firsthand and know what they look like. Get down." He waved his gun to indicate Brand should dismount.

He did so, cautiously and slowly. No telling what this man meant to do, but shooting Brand on the spot seemed highly likely.

The gun-toting man swung down at the same time and came round to face him, the pistol aimed steadily at Brand's chest.

Brand shrugged a little, which was plenty hard to do with his hands raised over his head, but he hoped to convince this man that he was harmless. "Mind telling me what this is all about?" He kept his voice low, his tone calm, just like he did when working with frightened animals. Though he wasn't sure who the frightened one was in this situation. Was the man as nervous as Brand? Not likely, seeing as he held a gun and Brand held nothing but air.

"You no-good Duggans shot my wife."

Brand stared. Pa and Cyrus were wicked and ruthless and for that, they'd got their names on a wanted poster. He'd heard of a woman getting shot. No wonder this man was angry.

"She was an innocent bystander. You Duggans didn't care who got hurt."

Brand wished the man would stop saying "you Duggans." Except he *was* a Duggan. It appeared he'd never be allowed to forget it.

"My Isabelle died right there on the street with no one to hold her hand. Without me having a chance to say goodbye."

"I'm sorry."

"Sorry don't mean a thing. You're going to pay. Where's your sidearm?"

"I'm not carrying." His gun was in his saddlebag. Since the demise of the Duggan gang he hadn't felt the need to wear it.

"That's downright stupid." The man waved his gun around, then steadied it on Brand's heart. "I should shoot you dead right here and now, just like you did my Isabelle. But that wouldn't give me no satisfaction." He indicated Brand should move away from his horse, then rifled through his saddlebags until he found Brand's gun belt.

The man emptied the gun of all but one bullet, then spun the cylinder. "There. You got a fighting chance. That's more than Isabelle had." He jammed the gun into Brand's waistband.

The man backed away. "Lower your arms."

Brand did so slowly, reluctantly, knowing what came next. He'd never get a chance to say goodbye to Sybil. Never be able to tell her he loved her. With blinding clarity he understood the other man's pain. "I'm sorry for how your Isabelle died."

"Don't you dare speak her name."

For a moment, Brand thought the man intended to shoot him.

Instead, he swallowed loudly and narrowed his eyes. "Go for your gun."

Sybil put aside her empty teacup. "I'm fine now. But I need to take care of Dawg." She pushed herself to her feet, willing strength into her shaking limbs. "Mercy, will you come with me?"

Her friend looked startled, then shrugged. "Sure. Why not?"

Dawg waited outside and wriggled a happy greeting when Sybil called him. "I'll take him to the barn. That's where he's used to staying." She waited until they reached the barn to turn to Mercy. "Help me saddle a horse."

"You? Why?"

"I'm going after Brand."

Mercy laughed.

"I'm serious."

Mercy squinted at her as if trying to bring her into focus. "You really are. Okay. I'll saddle a horse for you, but I'm coming, too."

Sybil hugged her friend. "I hoped you'd say that." She'd have to ride astride though she'd never done so. Regardless, she had to do this.

"Up you go." Mercy helped her into the saddle. It was uncomfortable, but she'd survive.

When they left the barn, Sybil glanced around. Should they tell someone? No men lingered about.

She glanced at the big house but didn't see Linette at the window. "Maybe we should tell Jayne what we're doing."

"She'll try and stop us. Do you want that?"

"No. I must do this. Let's go." So they rode north.

It didn't take long before Sybil wondered if she had been rash. She bounced with every step. Her legs cramped. Her back cried. But they kept onward, hoping for some sign of Brand.

She saw a movement through the trees. "Stop." She pulled up so hard her horse reared.

Mercy halted and waited for Sybil's mount to settle.

"Help me down." Sybil practically fell into her friend's arms, and bit her lip as her legs took her weight. "I saw someone through there." She pointed. "It has to be Brand. Wait here," she requested. "I want to see him alone."

Mercy squeezed her arm. "You go get him."

Sybil tiptoed forward, wanting to assess the situation before she confronted him. Twenty feet in she drew to a sudden halt, her heart kicking her ribs so hard it would leave a bruise.

Brand and another man faced each other. The second man held a gun aimed at Brand, and the look on his face convinced Sybil he meant business.

"Draw," the angry man ordered.

Brand didn't have a chance at outdrawing a man with a gun already in his palm.

Her legs forgot how to work and she collapsed against a tree.

Brand, she silently whispered. *Don't die. Please, God, let me get a chance to tell him how much I love him.*

Brand kept his arms stretched out at his sides as if

avoiding any indication he meant to draw. "I ain't gonna be part of this," he said, his voice firm and strong. Keeping his right hand far away from his body, he slowly reached with his left toward the gun in his waistband and tossed it aside.

Her heart beat so fast she felt dizzy. What was he thinking? Did he plan to die?

"You go ahead and take a shot if that's what will make things right in your mind. I ain't like my pa and brother. I won't shoot a man for any reason." Brand stood immobile. "If you think that's what your innocent wife would want you to do."

The stranger stared as the moments ticked by. Then he slowly lowered his gun. "You ain't no Duggan. A Duggan wouldn't miss a chance to shoot someone." He stuck his gun in his belt.

"I really am sorry," Brand said. "Kind of know how you feel. When I thought I was about to die, I had similar regrets. I thought I would do most anything to make up for past mistakes, even ones I didn't make. But you can't live life backward. Only forward."

Acknowledgment flickered through the man's eyes and then he turned, swung onto his horse and rode away.

Sybil's legs folded under her and she crashed to the ground.

At the sound Brand turned. When he saw her, his expression went from alarm to concern. He hurried to her side. "How did you get here?"

"I rode a horse." She explained how worried she'd been when Dawg returned.

Brand snorted a little laugh. "He refused to follow me, so I sent him back. Then I got to thinking. If a dog can see where he belongs, maybe I should try and be as smart."

He went down on his haunches beside her. "Sybil, I want to say something I should have said before." He scrubbed his lips together before he could go on. "For a few minutes I thought I'd never get the chance to say it."

She nodded, hopeful but uncertain. After all, she had written about him without his permission, and at first, it was why she had shown interest in him.

"Sybil Bannerman, I love you. I know you're a fine Englishwoman and I'm only a poor cowboy and a Duggan at that, but I love you. You don't have to love me back. I don't expect it, but I was afraid I'd die without ever telling you."

She wondered if he was ever going to stop. It seemed the most words he'd strung together since they'd met. She touched his lips to end his speech.

"No more apologies. Brand Duggan, I love you from the bottom of my heart."

He let out a whoop, pulled her to her feet and kissed her soundly. She kissed him right back.

Behind them, Mercy coughed.

Sybil turned without leaving Brand's arms. "I wondered how long you'd wait."

Brand held her close, filling her with pure, sweet pleasure.

Mercy drew the horses forward. "I suggest we go home before Eddie sends out a search party."

Sybil sighed and rubbed her legs. "I suppose there's only one way to get back."

Mercy's laugh rendered Sybil no sympathy. "Same way we got here. On the back of a horse." She swung up on her mount.

Brand and Sybil stood next to the other horse. She thought she had never seen such a beautiful smile as the one he wore. It sparkled in his eyes and filled her heart with joy.

"We'll take it slow," he promised.

She hoped he didn't mean their courtship. Taking it slow, being cautious, had almost cost them their chance at love.

He trailed a finger along her jaw. "The reputation of the Duggan gang might haunt me for years. Perhaps I'm not being fair to you."

"Don't you dare change your mind about loving me." She said it teasingly, having full confidence in his affections.

His laugh was short and a bit regretful, she thought. "There might be others who want to deal with the last Duggan. Like that man back on the trail."

"Then I suppose I'll have to take shooting lessons."

He chuckled then, the sound deep in his chest.

She hugged him. "I don't intend to let you go. You'll never be alone again."

He kissed her slowly, sweetly. She was learning to appreciate his gentle ways. She would always be safe with him.

"I've always wanted a little ranch where I can break and train horses."

She laughed. "I'm sure everyone will be as surprised to hear that as I am."

He grinned sheepishly. "Will you be happy as a rancher's wife? If not, we can live in town."

"Brand, it's sweet of you to offer, but I'm finding I quite like ranch life." She brushed her hand across his cheek. "I think it will be a wonderful adventure with you."

He was about to kiss her again, but suddenly drew back. "About that story you wrote about me…"

"Forget it. I decided a long time ago I wasn't sending it to the editor."

"Here's what I think. You send it in as you've written it. About a nameless cowboy. On two conditions."

"Anything you say." She waited for him to name the conditions.

He cupped her face and looked deep into her eyes. "You write more of the children's stories and sell them in your own name."

"I promise to write them, but I can't promise someone will buy them." She knew being a woman would prove a barrier to some publishers.

"Then you'll tell them to our children."

Mercy had ridden ahead and turned to call, "Are you two coming?"

"Yes," Sybil answered. To Brand she said, "I guess we better follow her."

"Not just yet." He caught her about the waist and bent his head to kiss her, with so much tenderness her eyes stung. With the promise of a growing love, the promise of a family and a bright future, they mounted up and rode back to the ranch.

Epilogue

April 1883

Sybil took one last look at the little log cabin where she and Brand had spent the winter. Eddie and the Eden Valley cowboys had built it for them as soon as Sybil said she didn't intend to wait until spring to marry.

"We both know enough about loneliness," she'd told them all last fall. "I want to share the winter with Brand even if we have to live in a tent."

Jayne's eyes had widened in shock.

Mercy had chuckled. "Whatever happened to the little Sybil who lived a safe, comfortable life?"

Sybil's smile came from the warmth of her heart. "She grew up. She found love and discovered it was worth taking risks to enjoy."

"You won't need to do that," Eddie said. "So long as you don't object to a small cabin."

"I have no objections whatsoever."

Linette had arranged for a preacher to come from the fort, and Sybil and Brand had married the last day of September. Their wedding had been simple. Just the folks from the ranch. She'd worn a new dress at Linette's and Jayne's insistence. The pair had labored over it many hours.

Sybil smiled at the remembered pleasure of that day. Honoring her wishes not to have anything fancy, her friends had made her a beautiful gown in a sunset-gold color. Its simple lines made her feel elegant.

Brand was so handsome in his white shirt and dark pants, with his hair neatly trimmed, that her eyes had stung with joy.

Her throat tightened at the thought of saying goodbye to the place where she and Brand had spent so many happy hours together.

She looked about the one-room cabin they'd shared, and prayed Brand had found their time together here as healing as she had.

The bed in the corner had been made, ready to be used by visitors. The stove was cold. She'd polished it until it was black and shiny. The shelves were almost bare. The few books and jars she left behind belonged to Linette. The unlit lamp sat in the middle of the tiny table.

"Goodbye," she whispered, and turned to wait for Brand.

He pulled a wagon to the doorstep and leaped down to lift her into his arms. He pressed a kiss to her lips before he helped her up to the seat.

Linette, Eddie, Grady and Mercy stood at the bottom of the hill. Cassie and her children waved from the foreman's house. Jayne raced out and grabbed Sybil's hands.

"You come and visit often," she said.

"And you must come and visit us." She and Brand

planned to invite the Eden Valley Ranch folks as soon as the weather permitted them to gather outside.

Amid more goodbyes, Brand and Sybil drove from the yard.

She snuggled against him, eager to share her secrets as soon as they reached their own home.

Brand had purchased land from Eddie, half an hour away to the northwest. Sybil had visited the place many times as Brand worked on their house, but she hadn't been there in several days.

If not for the joy of Brand's company and the pleasure of seeing signs of spring around them, she would have found the drive endless, so eager was she to get there.

Brand pulled the wagon to a halt at the break in the trees. "There it is. Our own place. I never thought I'd ever have the privilege of being able to settle down." He pulled her close. "Nor did I imagine I would ever have a sweet wife like you."

She kissed him and rejoiced to feel how his arms no longer carried tension in them. It had taken Brand weeks to stop looking over his shoulder for his pa and brother. But now he was finally accepting that his ordeal was over.

They continued onward. Brand pulled the wagon to the front of the new house, a log cabin with a window on either side of the welcoming door. It was three times the size of the one they'd spent the winter in, with three rooms—a big kitchen, a little sitting room and a bedroom.

"We'll add more rooms as we need them," Brand had promised.

For the many children they hoped to have. Sybil pictured little boys and girls tumbling from the doorway to greet them.

Brand lifted her down. "Welcome home." His voice deepened, indicating how much he reveled in this new stage of their lives.

"Wait a minute. I have something to show you." She retrieved the valise she'd brought from the ranch, and pulled out a book: *Western Boys and Girls,* by Sybil Bannerman.

He stared at it a moment, then understanding dawned. He whooped and swung her in a wide circle.

"I still think I should have sold it as Sybil Duggan."

"We had this argument."

"Yes, and I let you win." He thought the Duggan name might pose a barrier to her success. She'd finally relented simply because she saw how much it upset him.

"Do you still feel the same way?"

"I do. The Duggan name will always be besmirched."

She pulled his face close and kissed him soundly. "I am honored to share your name." She leaned back and studied his features. "Brand, do you think you can teach your children to be proud of their name?"

He returned her look with equal seriousness. "In time people will forget about the Duggan gang." He shrugged. "And I guess I'll learn to put it behind me, too."

"How much time do you think you'll need?"

"I can't say."

"Will six or seven months be long enough?"

His eyes stilled. "Why?"

She laughed deep in her throat. "Because in about that length of time there will be another Duggan, and

I want him or her to be proud of who they are and who their father is."

He blinked. Stared. Swallowed hard. "Another Duggan?"

She cradled her arms as if holding an infant. "A very small one."

He laughed and swept her off her feet again. "Whooee. What a day this is. A new book. A baby on the way." He crossed the threshold. "And a new home." He kissed her before he set her down inside the cabin.

"A new life together as the Duggans. We will be known as a couple—a family—that loves deeply." They'd likely be known for many more things—honesty, kindness, hospitality, and above all, joy.

"Ma used to say God will always be with us," Brand murmured. "He will always guide us to a safe place. Her words have come true this day and I thank Him."

"Me, too." Clasping hands, standing forehead to forehead, they bowed, and each prayed in gratitude for God's faithfulness and love. "Amen."

They stepped into the kitchen and the beginning of a shared life together. Brand stood behind Sybil and wrapped his arms about her. He pressed his palms to the place where their child lay in safety. "Welcome home."

She leaned against his chest, so content she didn't want to move. The anticipation of shared joys blessed every thought and eased every breath.

Life as a Duggan offered a wonderful future.

* * * * *

FALLING FOR THE RANCHER FATHER

Thou knowest my downsitting and mine uprising,
thou understandest my thought afar off.
—*Psalm* 139:2

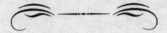

To my grandson, Julien, as he graduates
from high school. Good for you.
I know you've worked hard. We're so proud of you.

Chapter One

Eden Valley Ranch, Alberta, Canada
Fall 1882

She was gone.

His heart slammed against his ribs. He scanned the entire clearing again just to make sure but she wasn't there.

"Allie." Abel Borgard yelled his daughter's name. One minute ago the nine-year-old sat on the chair by the cabin. He'd warned her to stay there while he unloaded the supplies, but now she'd disappeared. "It's not like her," he complained aloud. Ladd, her twin brother, was a different matter. He'd set off exploring the moment they'd alighted from the wagon. Abel had warned him to stay nearby, but it didn't worry him when Ladd got out of sight. The boy had learned at a young age to be self-reliant. Allie, on the other hand, needed rest and protection. The doctor's warning reverberated through Abel's brain. "She's extremely fortunate to have survived scarlet fever, especially under the circumstances."

"Allie." He didn't bother calling this time, just muttered the word under his breath. He again turned full circle, studying his surroundings. The tiny cabin would provide temporary shelter until he could erect a larger one, which he had to do before winter. The chill in the air reminded him time was short.

The trees, a nice mix of spruce and aspen, were far enough from the buildings to allow plenty of sunshine to reach the living quarters yet provide protection and privacy. The mountains rose to the west in all their fall majesty.

He completed his inspection of the surroundings but saw no little girl. Not so much as a hint of the blue dress she wore.

Abel understood the doctor's warning. Abel had come home from a three-month absence as he sought work to discover his wife had left days before, abandoning the then eight-year-olds to care for themselves. He'd found them huddled together, hungry and afraid. According to what he could get from the children, Allie had been sick even before Ruby left. Though in all fairness, Ruby likely hadn't known at that point it was anything more than a chill. Perhaps she hadn't even meant to leave them for more than a night but she'd fallen into the river and drowned. He liked to believe it had simply been misfortune, but he guessed she'd spent too much time in the back room of the saloon sharing drinks.

He strained to catch any sound of the children. Wasn't there a thud to his right…like distant horse hooves? Every nerve in his body tensed. An intruder? Were the children in danger?

The doctor had left Abel with no misconceptions as to the seriousness of Allie's situation. "I fear she will have damaged her heart. You'll need to limit her activities for the rest of her life or…" At this point, he'd shaken his head as if expecting the worst.

Abel had vowed on the spot that Allie would be treated as gently as a fragile china doll. He couldn't lose her. If anything happened to her he would never forgive himself. Any more than he forgave himself for the fact the children had been abandoned by his wife while he went in search of work. Ruby had never wanted to settle down and from the beginning had found the children a heavy burden, while Abel discovered they gave him reason to leave off being a wastrel. He regretted having started down that wayward path in the first place. The only good thing to come of it was his children and his determination to live a responsible, careful life from now on. He was twenty-nine years old and would devote the rest of his life to the well-being of his children. Never again would he allow his foolish emotions to lead him down the slippery path into the arms of a woman. Any woman. He would not risk his children's health and happiness by trusting a woman to settle down and be wife and mother.

Another thud. No mistaking the sound. There was a horse in the nearby clearing. His heart thumped him in his ribs hard enough to cause him to catch his breath.

He broke into a gallop and headed for the spot.

If anything happened to either of the twins…

He saw Allie ahead, rocking back and forth on the balls of her feet, her hands clasped together as if she tried to contain some emotion. Already her cheeks had turned rosy—a sure indication of her excited state. A danger sign.

He raced toward her and scooped her into his arms.

He brushed strands of her long blond hair off her face. "Baby, are you okay?"

"I'm fine, Papa. Isn't she glorious?" She twisted and pointed.

Abel jerked his gaze from his precious daughter and followed the direction she indicated. His eyes lit on a woman who reminded him of those he'd seen in saloons. Only instead of bright-colored, revealing dresses, she wore a dark red shirt, fringed gloves and riding pants. It wasn't the clothes that brought those other women to mind—it was the look of sheer abandon on her face. Her mahogany-colored hair rippled down her back, held in place by a small cowboy hat secured under her chin. She sat on a beautiful palomino gelding.

She waved a hand over her head and the horse reared on its back legs.

Abel clutched Allie tight. "She's going to be hurt."

"Oh, no." Allie's voice was round with awe. "She does it on purpose. She's a trick rider. She's going to join a Wild West show."

"She is, is she?" The gal made a beautiful picture of horse and rider but she posed a threat to his children if she hung about, filling Allie's head with admiration.

The horse returned to all fours and clapping caught Abel's attention. Ladd stood on the other side of the horse, his eyes round with awe. "Can you show me how to do that?"

"It's not hard." The woman's voice rang with humor and what he could only explain as love of life.

That was all well and good. He had no objection to her joining a Wild West show, loving life or doing dangerous things on back of a horse, so long as she stayed away from his kids.

"Can you show me?" Ladd asked.

"Sure thing. All you do—"

Abel crossed the clearing to clamp his hand on Ladd's shoulder. The boy jerked, surprised, no doubt, at the sudden appearance of his father. Hopefully he was also feeling a little guilty at having brought Allie out to the woods when she was supposed to rest. "Ladd, take your sister back to the cabin. Allie, you know you shouldn't be here."

Allie patted him on the cheek. "I'm okay, Papa. You worry too much."

"Maybe I do. Maybe I don't. I only want you both to be safe." He set his daughter on her feet, patted them both on the back and sent them on their way. He didn't turn until they were out of sight.

Sucking in air, he tried to calm the way his insides rolled and bucked at how this woman had intruded on his hope of peace and quiet. He didn't want to say anything he'd later regret, so he pushed aside his inner turmoil as he slowly faced the woman. "You're trespassing."

She lounged in her saddle as if she meant to spend her entire day there. "I think you are mistaken. This land belongs to Eddie Gardiner. He's given me permission to be here."

"That might have been so at one time, but I've rented the cabin and the surrounding land from Mr. Eddie Gardiner." He planned to raise cows. His ranch would be insignificant compared to the Eden Valley Ranch, but it was all he wanted. Besides— "I want peace and quiet for my children." At the cold way she studied him, his resolve mounted a protest. "I don't want them learning reckless ways. Nor do I want my daughter overexcited by witnessing your activities. What you do in your own time and space is your business. But what you do around my children is my business."

The grin she wore plainly said she didn't take him seriously.

His spine tingled as he held back a desire to tell her exactly what he thought. He mentally counted to ten then widened his stance, narrowed his eyes and gave her his best don't-mess-with-me look, the one that made the twins jump to obey. "I suggest you leave and don't come back."

She laughed. A cheerful-enough sound, but one that dug talons into his backbone. It reminded him of Ruby and the way she laughed when he suggested she should settle down and be a mother to the children. And it filled him with something hard and cold. But before he could put words to his feelings, she spoke.

"Pleased to meet you. Nice to know there'll be a kind neighbor nearby." She reined her horse into a two-legged stand and let out a wild whoop. "I'll no doubt be seeing you around since we're neighbors." She drawled out the last word in a mocking way, then rode away at a gallop, bent over her mount's neck as they raced through the trees.

"You won't be seeing more of me and my family if I have anything to say about it," he murmured then headed for the cabin and his kids. He had to make sure they were unharmed after encountering the crazy wild woman on horseback.

Twenty-year-old Mercy Newell galloped through the trees, not slowing until she reached the barn on the Eden Valley Ranch—her home in Canada. She'd come from London to this raw new country a little more than two months ago with Eddie's sister, Jayne, and their mutual friend, Sybil. Both were now married and living in small log cabins on the ranch though both said they and their new husbands would be starting their own ranches come spring. She wished them all the best, but she didn't intend to marry and settle down. Not when there were things she wanted to do. Number one on that list was to join a Wild West show. Since the day she'd seen one in Benton, Montana, on their trip here she'd known she wanted to be part of such a show. The excitement, the thrill, the roar of the crowd's approval...

While there, she'd even managed to get a few lessons in doing the stunts and instructions on more things she could learn. Since her arrival at Eden Valley Ranch, she'd also been taking lessons from anyone who would help her.

She reined in, pulling Nugget to a halt, getting him to rear up. She jumped from the saddle before he returned to all fours and led him to the barn where she brushed and fed him.

All the while she muttered about the man in her clearing. "Who does he think he is? Telling me to leave like I was common trash. As if he has the right. He says he rented the cabin. I'm not about to take his word on it, though. But even if he did, that doesn't give him the right to chase me away."

Nugget nudged her aside as if to say he was tired of her grousing.

"Fine. You're not the only one I can talk to." Finished caring for the horse, she stalked across to Jayne and Seth's cabin. All the men were at the fall roundup except for Cookie's husband, Bertie. She didn't even spare a glance toward the cookhouse. Cookie and Bertie would both tell her to calm down and be sensible.

Mercy had no intention of doing either.

She knocked and strode in without waiting for an answer. Besides Jayne, both Sybil and Linette, Eddie's wife, sat around the table. "Good. The three of you are here. You can all hear my story at the same time." She plunked down on the only available chair. "I met the most rude man."

Sybil sat up straighter. "Where? Mercy, what have you been up to this time? I do wish you wouldn't roam about the woods as if—"

Jayne spoke as soon as Sybil paused for breath. "Please don't tell us you've met a man while out there. What kind of man? What did he do?"

Mercy waved aside their concerns. "He says he's rented that little cabin southwest of here. He informed me I was trespassing. Pfft. If he thinks he can order me around, well, he'll soon learn otherwise."

Linette waited for Mercy to run out of steam. "That must be Abel Borgard. Eddie told me he'd let him have the little cabin for himself and his children. Twins, Eddie said. A boy and a girl. Did you see them?"

She smiled. "I didn't realize they were twins. The little boy is sturdy and filled with curiosity. He wanted me to show him how to teach a horse some tricks." She ignored the way the others looked at each other and shook their heads. They simply did not understand why she had to do this. They'd asked and she'd only said it was an adventure. But it was more than that. A need deep inside. A restless itch that had to be tended to. She'd been that way most of her life. Probably since her brother died when he was eight and she, six. It was not a time in her life she liked to think about so she gladly pulled her thoughts back to her waiting friends. "The little girl is tiny but a real beauty. Her father swept her into his arms as if she was a—" She couldn't finish. She'd been about to say a precious princess. "A much younger child." She'd seen the way the little girl patted his cheeks and how his expression softened with what Mercy could only interpret as devotion. "He said I was too reckless to be around his children. Really? I am never reckless."

The others laughed.

Mercy tried to scowl but ended up laughing, as well.

Sybil sighed. "It sounds romantic. A man raising two children on his own. So protective of them."

Linette patted her rounded tummy. She was two months from having her firstborn. "Eddie will be a good father. I've already seen it in the way he treats Grady." Grady was the little boy they were raising as their own.

"Where is Grady?" Mercy asked.

"He's over at Cassie's playing with the children." Cassie and Roper and the four children they'd adopted lived beyond the barn in a house big enough for the six of them.

Linette returned immediately to Mercy's situation. "It seems to me you'll have to respect Abel's wishes and stay away from the cabin. Maybe now you'll remain at the ranch. Tell me you will. I worry about you out there on your own."

Mercy didn't bother to again say she could take care of herself. "Guess I will be practicing my riding and roping around here until I find another place. But—" She leaned forward and gave them each a demanding look. "I don't want anyone hanging about warning me about the dangers. Agreed?"

Jayne and Linette exchanged a look then together shook their heads. "We aren't agreeing to any such thing."

"Nor am I," Sybil said. "From the beginning I've opposed your dream to join a Wild West show and will continue to do so."

Mercy groaned. "I can see I'll have to find another place to practice." In the meantime, the corrals were virtually empty, with the cowboys and horses gone on the roundup. She'd be able to work on her tricks without a lot of interference. She'd simply deflect her friends' needless worry should they voice it.

The next morning she slipped from the house before Linette or Grady stirred and hurried down to the corral behind the barn. The guns she used for her fancy shooting worried the others the most so she did her gun work in the cold dawn. The pearl-handled guns, one of her greatest treasures, had been acquired through Cal, a cowboy who had worked at the Eden Valley Ranch before he'd been fired. She'd encouraged Cal to do a number of things Eddie didn't approve of. He'd even coached her roping stunts. Thankfully, it was his own actions that got him fired, and nothing she could feel responsible for.

After an hour, her wrists grew tired and she saddled Nugget and brought him out to the same area. She practiced a number of tricks—bowing, rearing up, sidestepping. Then she turned her attention to a new trick—teaching Nugget to lie on his back and let her sit on his chest.

She finally got him to lie down and roll to his back and rewarded him with a carrot.

The sun had grown warm. Her stomach growled, reminding her she'd eaten nothing but a slab of bread she'd grabbed on her way through the kitchen. Linette and Grady would be up and about by now. Time to climb the hill and find breakfast. She'd heard Cookie call good morning to Jayne a short time ago. Overhead, a flock of geese honked, and a crow called from the trees. The chickens cackled and crowed. The world had come alive.

She stepped into the house and traipsed down the hall to the kitchen.

Grady ran to her, almost tackled her. She caught him. "Whoa, cowboy. What's your hurry?"

"We got company."

Warning trickled down Mercy's spine. Surely Abel hadn't stepped into her corner of the ranch. She slowly raised her eyes. The twins sat at the table watching her. She shifted her gaze around the room until she met Linette's eyes. No one else was there.

Her breath whooshed out.

"Papa says we can stay here while he works," Allie said.

"That's nice."

The children eyed her. She eyed them back. Then they all grinned.

Linette brushed a strand of hair off her face. "I thought you might like to take the three of them out after breakfast and amuse them while I do some things around the house."

Mercy laughed, as much out of relief as amusement. She didn't mind spending time with the children. Over breakfast, she considered the day. "Who wants to watch me do some roping?"

The boys yelled yes and Allie nodded, her blue eyes sparkling.

"Good. Then finish your breakfast, help me clean up and we'll go do it."

The boys ate hurriedly but Allie picked at her food.

"Come on, Allie," Ladd said. "We can't go until you finish."

Slowly she cleaned her plate, then the three of them helped Mercy do the dishes. Ladd dried the dishes so fast they barely got introduced to the towel. He was darker than his sister, his blue eyes so dark they almost seemed black until the light hit them and the blue became evident.

Grady, five years old, carefully placed each dish on the table and dried it with both hands.

Allie dried each dish as slowly as she ate.

Ladd nudged his sister. "Go faster."

"I can't."

They studied each other. Mercy thought Ladd would press the point and then he patted her shoulder. "Do your best."

Mercy turned away and stared at the soapy dishwater. The boy's gentleness with his sister tugged at her thoughts. Had her brother, Butler, treated her with such kindness? She tried to remember. But it seemed she could only recall the loneliness of his illness and the emptiness of the house after he died. And how her parents had mourned so deeply they plumb forgot they had a daughter.

That was in the past. The future and adventure beckoned.

She handed the last dish to Ladd and dumped out the dishwater. "Are we ready?"

The boys cheered in affirmation and Allie merely nodded, but her eyes said she anticipated the outing as much as the boys.

They called goodbye to Linette and headed down the hill.

Thor, the tame fawn, saw the children and bounced over to join them, eliciting squeals of laughter from Allie.

Mercy stopped to let them enjoy the antics of the rapidly growing deer before they moved on. Soon Thor would disappear in the woods to join other deer, but she wouldn't inform the children of that fact. Let them enjoy the pet while they could.

Thor bounced away in search of amusement elsewhere and Mercy shepherded the children onward.

She had them sit against the barn and showed them how to swing the rope overhead. How to drop it over a fence post. How to spin a circle of rope just above the ground and jump in and out of it. "I have lots more to learn," she said.

"But you're pretty good," Allie said.

Ladd bounced to his feet. "You said you'd show me how to make the horse bow."

It wasn't exactly what she'd said but close enough. She'd spent a few days getting Nugget to follow the offer of a carrot until his head almost reached the ground. Then she'd taught him to pull one leg back and put the other forward. He was getting good at bowing. She figured he'd perform for Ladd and handed a carrot to the boy. "Stand here. Show him the carrot then lower it toward the ground. He'll do the rest because he knows what to expect." Nugget performed perfectly. "Now give him the carrot."

Ladd held the carrot out but drew back as the horse tried to take it.

Mercy guided his hand so Nugget got his treat.

"What else can I make him do?" Ladd asked.

"Before I show you, maybe Grady and Allie would like to do a trick." She held a hand toward the pair.

Grady jumped forward. "Can I get him to bow, too?"

"You sure can." She repeated the trick with Grady and helped the boy feed Nugget his treat.

Allie stood nearby, rocking back and forth in anticipation. "Can I do something different?"

"What would you like to do?"

"Me and Ladd saw you standing on his back. Can I do that?"

Mercy considered the request. Nugget was still saddled and he wouldn't protest, and if she held Allie, she could see no problem. The child would be perfectly safe. "I don't see why not. Come on, I'll show you how."

She lifted the featherlight child to the saddle, placing her feet so she balanced then held her hand as she straightened. "There you go. What do you think?"

Allie giggled. "I'm a bird." She held out her free arm.

A man came out of nowhere direct to Mercy's side. Although alarmed at the sudden appearance, she held Allie firmly.

He lifted Allie from the horse and stepped back. "How dare you put my child at risk?"

"You! Mr. Abel Borgard, I presume. Haven't we met before?" She didn't much care for the dark expression on his face.

"And you would be…? Just so I know to avoid you in the future."

"Mercy Newell. So pleased to make your acquaintance." But her sarcasm was wasted on him.

"Papa," Allie patted his cheek to get his attention.

"Yes, baby."

Baby! This child was no baby. Why did he call her that? Worse, why did he treat her like an infant?

"It was fun," Allie said. "And she held my hand really tight."

"It was exceedingly foolish. Ladd, didn't you think to say something?"

Ladd faced his father without a hint of fear. Or remorse. "Miss Mercy held her real good. She is smart about horses and—"

"Children are different than horses, Miss Mercy. Mrs. Gardiner knows I've come for the children. I'm taking them home." He still carried Allie in one arm and took Ladd by his free hand. "Where they'll be safe." He hurried away.

Ladd and Allie sent Mercy pleading looks. She couldn't say if they were silently apologetic or simply regretting that their enjoyment had been cut short. Regardless, something about their silent appeals released her own caution and she trotted after them, reaching Abel's side before he made it to his horse. She grabbed his shoulder and forced him to stop.

"Sir, you are mistaken if you think I was about to let something happen to your children. I was only allowing them a bit of harmless fun. Everyone should be allowed to enjoy life and not shoved into a corner."

He put Allie down and released Ladd. "You two go wait by the horse."

They scampered away and stood watching the two adults.

Abel turned his back to the children. "Miss Newell, whether or not you agree with my choices on my children's behalf is immaterial to me. But Allie has been very ill. Her heart has been damaged and the doctor says she must not get overly excited, nor can she be allowed to overexert herself. It could have very bad consequences."

There was no mistaking the agony in his voice as he spoke those words and then he strode away, swung to the back of his horse and lifted the children, Ladd behind him, Allie sheltered in his arms.

How was she to have known about Allie? The last thing she would ever do was put a child at risk.

Abel reined his horse about. He was about to leave. She couldn't let him go without trying to explain.

"Wait." She raced to the head of the horse, forcing Abel to pull up. "I'm sorry. I didn't know. But believe me, I would never put a child in danger."

Abel studied her a moment. Then he shifted his gaze to Allie. He cupped her head then reached back and pulled Ladd closer. He lifted his gaze to Mercy.

"So you say. But it is immaterial to me. My one and only concern is my children."

She fell back, struck by the depth of emotion in his eyes.

"Whatever foolish thing you choose to do with your time is your business." He rode away. Ladd lifted a hand in a wave.

Mercy stared after them, her insides churning. She knew the look in Abel's eyes. Not because she remembered ever seeing it but because she had longed for it all her life. Instead, all she'd ever seen was indifference. Seems Butler was the only child who had mattered to her parents and when he died, Mercy became a necessary nuisance. She could never do enough to get them to acknowledge her. No matter how absurd her behavior.

She shook off the feeling.

She'd hoped she'd found the acceptance she longed for when, at seventeen, she fell in love with Ambrose, the preacher's son. They'd enjoyed many adventures together. But after their romantic summer—oh, how mistaken she'd been about that—he'd introduced her to a sweet, young thing he identified as his fiancée. When Mercy confronted him, he said he couldn't live with a person like her who longed for adventure. A man wanted to come home to peace and quiet, not restlessness. Mercy realized then that men, in general, preferred a woman to be invisible in her husband's shadow. Mercy could never be that.

The circle of her thoughts widened. Wasn't the Wild West show exactly the kind of thing she'd wanted since she was sixteen years old and watching Cleopatra's Needle unveiling in London? They'd buried a time capsule beneath it that included pictures of the twelve most beautiful women. That struck her as unfair. What if a woman was born ugly? Was she to be ignored? What if she was beautiful but no one noticed? No, a person had to be able to *do* something to earn notice and value.

She would do something. She would join a Wild West show and perform for others. The audience would appreciate her skills. It didn't matter what Mr. Abel Borgard thought.

Chapter Two

Abel held Allie tight as he rode toward the cabin. He found comfort in Ladd's arms about his waist. Miss Mercy was a menace to his kids and likely to herself, though that didn't concern him. It surprised him, however, that Eddie allowed such conduct. Like his parents said, "You reap what you sow. If you sow to the wind, you reap sorrow." He'd learned the truth of their words the hard way. He'd left home at sixteen to follow a sin-filled path, thinking it meant excitement. It had led him to marriage with Ruby. She wanted to continue their wayward path but once the twins were born, Abel wanted only to provide them with safety and security. Poor Ruby hadn't signed up for that sort of life. So she paid in frustration. With an unpredictable, unreliable mother, the twins paid, too, and unable to stop the train wreck of his marriage, Abel would likely spend the rest of his life making up for his foolish decisions.

And he would not allow Miss Mercy to undo the good he aimed to achieve by settling down and giving the twins a home like they'd never known.

The children were quiet on the trip home. He let

them off in front of the cabin. "Go inside. I'll be there as soon as I take care of Sam." The faithful horse would get a few oats and some hay, which reminded him of another job awaiting him. He must find feed for the horse and the milk cow he hoped to obtain. This late in the year, locating feed would prove a challenge.

He returned to the cabin, ducking his head to enter. The inside was as inadequate as the door—barely big enough for a table, four chairs and a narrow bed. Beyond that, a corner of the roof had been damaged. He'd repaired it, but a good wind or a heavy snowfall would threaten the entire roof. He had to get a bigger, sturdier cabin built before winter set it.

Allie and Ladd stood shoulder to shoulder and watched as he hung his hat on a hook. He faced them. "What's on your mind?"

"You were rude to Miss Mercy," Allie said, her face wreathed in distress.

"Oh, honey. I was only concerned about you. Can you imagine how I felt to see you standing on the back of her horse?" His heart had punched his ribs with such force they still hurt.

"She wouldn't let me fall."

His daughter's loyalty was commendable but misplaced.

Ladd nodded. "She let me and Grady make her horse bow. She knows what she's doing. Someday she's going to be in a Wild West show and I bet she'll be the best person in the whole show."

"Don't say bet." He spoke automatically as his thoughts raced. When had the twins ever been so passionate about defending anyone? Never, in his mind, though they often refused to reveal the truth about what

Ruby had been doing in his absences. In that case he decided he preferred not to know too much so long as everyone was safe.

There seemed no point in continuing the discussion about Mercy's reliability. "Who'd like bannock and beans?"

Soberly, they both nodded. "We do."

Seeing as it was one of their favorite meals he expected slightly more enthusiasm, but he'd settle for changing the subject.

As he mixed up the ingredients for the bannock and put it in a cast-iron fry pan to bake in the oven, he told the children about his trip to the woods. "I need to get the logs in to build a nice cabin for us. Something bigger than this. And I need to chop firewood." The enormity of what he had to accomplish in the few weeks before the snow came settled heavily on his shoulders. He didn't need to deal with Mercy on top of it, yet she had become a fly buzzing about his head. He couldn't go to the woods and leave the twins alone, but obviously taking them to the ranch had been a disaster. He didn't have a lot of options open to him.

He warmed the beans and checked the bannock. "Almost ready. Anyone hungry?"

"I am." Ladd's answer was expected.

"Me, too."

Abel jerked around to stare at Allie. "You're hungry?"

"Starving."

"Well." That was good. Did it signal she would not have lasting damage from her illness? He swallowed back his reaction. He wished he could hope for her to someday be healthy, but the doctor had offered no such hope and Abel would not be taking any risks with her health.

He placed the food on the table and asked the blessing, then they dug in. Ladd ate heartily as usual but when Allie cleaned her plate and asked for seconds, Abel shook his head. "I can't believe how much you're eating. Are you okay?" His spine tightened. Did it mean she was getting better or did it signal something awful?

"I guess helping Mercy gave me an appetite."

"See, she's a good person. She made Allie feel better." Ladd grinned as much as his sister.

Abel shook his head. "She does foolish things and there is always a price for foolish choices. Doing wild things leaves a person with regrets."

The twins simultaneously put down their forks, placed their hands beside their plates and studied him with serious expressions. They turned to look at each other, then returned their gazes to him.

He felt their unasked questions and waited.

Ladd finally spoke. "Like Mama."

He wasn't sure what Ladd meant and didn't want to guess. "What do you mean?"

Allie answered. "Mama said we were nothing but a nuisance."

Ladd nodded. "A stone about her neck."

"We were the payment for your wild life, she said."

Oh, the pain he'd inflicted on these precious children. And, he admitted yet again, to Ruby. It was true. He'd changed his mind about what sort of life he wanted to live. She hadn't. But it was the twins that mattered. And always had. How could he make up to them for the choices he'd made, or would they always pay?

He pushed his chair back. "Ladd, Allie, come here."

He patted his knees and the pair scrambled into his lap. Their arms cradled his neck and he wrapped his arms about them both and held them tight.

"I love you two deeper than the ocean, higher than the sky and wider than forever. You are the very best thing that has ever happened to me. I wouldn't trade either of you for gold nuggets the size of this cabin." His voice trembled with the enormity of his love for them. "And don't you ever forget it."

"We won't," they chorused as they burrowed into his shirtfront.

He held them close as long as they would allow, but all too soon they wriggled away. "Get ready for bed while I clean the kitchen. Then I'll read to you."

A few minutes later, Ladd lay on the narrow bed he would share with Abel, and Allie crawled under the covers of the trundle bed right beside them.

"First, let's say our prayers."

The children closed their eyes and murmured their usual prayers, asking for blessings on the people in their lives. But then Ladd added, "And thank You for Mercy. I like her."

Before Abel could protest, Allie added, "Bless Miss Mercy and help her be the best Wild West person ever. Amen."

"Children, I don't think you should be including Mercy in your prayers." He hated to say it. Knew it didn't make for sound theology.

Allie gave a gentle smile. "I think God would approve. He loves her, too, you know."

What could he say? The child was right. And yet her defense of Mercy worried Abel. The woman signified danger for his children. But he simply said, "I suppose

He does at that," then opened the storybook he'd been reading to them.

This was his favorite time of the entire day. And he didn't intend to let a certain wild woman ruin it for him.

He read for a few minutes as the children grew drowsy, then closed the book and prepared to tiptoe away, though he could only move a few feet before he ran out of space.

"Papa?"

"Yes, son?"

"Mercy is the smartest woman ever and would never do anything foolish."

Abel's sense of contentment and well-being crashed. Mercy again! How had she so quickly and thoroughly beguiled his children? He had to keep her away from them. How hard could it be? Yes, he needed help with the children. But he'd take them to Linette and leave instructions that they were to stay away from Mercy and she from them.

It was simple enough. Linette would surely understand and agree. Beside, how could she refuse if he gave instructions?

The next morning, Linette and Grady were sick with colds and Linette didn't think it was wise for the twins to come for the day.

Mercy would deliver the message to Abel on her behalf, and then maybe she'd never see the man again. She could certainly live without his scorn. Yes, he had his reasons for concern over his daughter. Momentarily she felt a silly sense of longing at his affection for his kids. But more and more his final words churned inside her head. Foolish ways, indeed! Humph. He'd soon see firsthand how foolish she was when she became a star in a Wild West show. Not that she cared what he thought or whether he ever saw her perform.

She passed through the clearing that surrounded the ranch site and climbed the hill toward his cabin. Soon she entered the woods, where the cooler air made her pull her jacket tighter.

A dark shadow to her right caught her attention and as it slipped out of sight, her nerves tingled. An animal of some sort. Her pearl-handled pistols were stowed in her saddlebags, but she mostly used blanks in them. However, she had a business pistol and a rifle and both were loaded. She palmed the pistol and kept alert. Again she noticed the shadow. It passed so far to her right she wouldn't have noticed it if she hadn't been watching so carefully. Whatever it was followed her. Her skin prickled. This required further investigation. She guided Nugget off the trail, dismounted and slid through the trees toward the shadow, her gun at the ready. She paused and listened. There came a rustle of leaves as they fell to the ground to join the other yellowed and browned ones. Wind whispered through the trees. Birds cooed and called.

Then a metallic click froze her blood.

"Drop your gun and turn around real slow."

She considered the order for about two seconds. But, knowing she had few options, she obeyed and with her arms raised to indicate she didn't pose any danger, she turned to confront a man, short of stature, wide of beam with enough black whiskers to cover most of him for the winter.

"Why you sneaking up on me?" he demanded in a voice that sounded like he used his throat to store nails.

"Seems I didn't do any sneaking up on anyone."

"Only 'cause I'm better 'n you in the woods."

Her grin felt crooked. "You are that all right."

"Sure am. Now why you following me?"

"I didn't know it was you, now did I? I thought it might be a wolf."

He made a derisive sound. "And if it was, were you figuring to shoot him with that?" He nodded at her pistol on the ground.

"I figured to scare him off."

"Missy, you sure are a greenhorn. What if I'd been a bear?" He lowered the gun and hooted like he enjoyed finding someone so foolish. There was that word again. It burned clear up her throat that she'd inadvertently proved Abel's opinion of her. Not that he'd ever know.

"I guess in hindsight, I was a little careless." She let her hands fall to her side and her breath eased out when he didn't object. "Who are you?"

The man's dark eyes narrowed. "Ain't none of yer business. Just leave me alone if you know what's good for ya."

"Gladly. Now can I go?"

"Where ya going?"

"Don't see that's any of your business."

He waved the gun as if to remind her he had the upper hand.

She shrugged. "Just delivering a message to a man, then I'm going about my own business." She emphasized the final two words.

"Then git. And forget you ever saw me."

She started away.

"Not that you'll ever see me again."

"Suits me fine," she muttered when she was well

out of hearing. The woods were getting overrun with crazy men.

As she continued on her journey, something about the whiskered man bothered her. She'd seen him somewhere. But where? She couldn't place him. Had it been under good circumstances or bad? Was he a danger, or harmless except for his craziness? She shrugged. What difference did it make? He was likely only passing through.

She reached Abel's cabin. His horse stood saddled and waiting. He opened the door as she approached, the twins at his side. As soon as he saw who it was he eased the children back to the cabin and pulled the door closed.

She gritted his teeth. A person could almost think he didn't welcome her presence. Almost? It couldn't have been plainer unless he hung a big sign over the door.

"Can I help you?" he asked.

Although his words were polite enough and his tone moderate, she felt the sharp edge of each syllable, and if not for her concern for Linette and Grady she would have reined Nugget around and left him to find out on his own her reason for coming. Instead, she swallowed a huge amount of resistance. "I brought a message from Linette. She and Grady are sick with colds and she asked you not to bring the children today."

The harshness in his face fled, replaced with concern. "I trust they are not seriously ill."

"Me, too." Mercy's heart had clenched at the thought of a sick child, but Linette assured her it was only a cold and normal for this time of year.

"Thank her for letting me know. I wouldn't want Allie to get sick."

"That's what Linette said."

The door creaked open and two little heads peeked out. "Hello, Miss Mercy," the twins called.

"Hello, you two. How are you?"

"Good, thank you," Allie said.

"Papa, are you going to take us with you to the woods now?" Ladd asked.

Abel looked toward the sky. The clouds had been thickening all morning. "I can't. It looks like rain."

Or snow, Mercy added silently.

"Then what are you going to do?" Ladd's voice carried a huge dose of worry. "You said you had to get logs. Papa, we'll be okay by ourselves. Won't we, Allie?"

Allie nodded her head and looked determined.

"I'll take care of Allie." Ladd's voice carried a hefty dose of concern.

Mercy's eyes stung at Ladd's sense of loyalty and responsibility. From the far recesses of her memory came a picture. She was about four, which would make Butler six. He'd held her hand tight as he helped her cross a bridge. As she looked at the memory, she realized there had never been any danger. The bridge was plenty wide enough that she wouldn't fall off but only Butler's hand had given her the courage to venture across.

Ladd's promise to protect his sister reminded her of that moment.

Abel sighed deeply. "I really need to get those logs home."

Was he going to leave the kids alone? "How old are you?" she asked them.

"Nine," they answered together.

"But we're very responsible," Ladd assured her.

Mercy thought of the whiskered man in the woods.

"Why don't I stay with the children?" What had prompted her to make such an offer? He'd refuse without even considering it. After all, he'd made his opinion of her very plain. Foolish. The word stuck in her throat.

"Oh, please, Papa. Please." Allie clasped her hands in a beseeching gesture and rounded her blue eyes.

Mercy hid a grin. Anyone who could deny such a plea would have to have a heart of stone.

"It's an excellent idea, don't you think, Papa?" Ladd added reasonableness to the request.

Mercy chewed her lip to keep from revealing her amusement.

Abel had his back to her, considering his children. Slowly he turned and faced her. His mouth drew back in a frown. Lines gouged his cheeks.

Even before he spoke, she knew he'd refuse.

Then Ladd tugged at his arm and Abel turned back to the children.

"Papa, you know you don't have many days before winter."

"You're right, but still—" His shoulders rose and fell. He caught Allie's chin. "Baby, you have to promise to take it easy."

"I will, Papa."

He placed his hand on Ladd's head. "Sunshine, you have to promise to watch your sister." He leaned closer and lowered his voice. "And no Wild West stuff."

Mercy coughed. "Shouldn't you be giving me the instructions?"

He faced her, rather reluctantly, she figured. "I will accept your offer but only because I'm desperate. It's late in the season to be starting out and I must make up for lost time."

"My," she said, sighing as she pressed a palm to her chest, "your enthusiasm is overwhelming."

Allie giggled, then seemed to think better of it and smothered it with her hand.

Abel's eyes narrowed. They were the same dark blue as his son's, Mercy noted. And he had the same unruly dark blond hair half controlled by his hat. "You can put your horse in the pen." He nodded in the general direction. "And thank you for offering to watch the children."

His thanks was so begrudging that she laughed as she reined about and took care of Nugget.

He was in his saddle when she sauntered back to the cabin. "The children know where everything is. If you need anything, ask them." But he made no motion toward leaving.

She favored him with the most innocent, sweet look she could manage when inside she bounced back and forth between amusement and annoyance. "We'll do just fine. Don't worry." She knew full well that every minute he was gone he would worry she might do something foolish. Some rebellious portion of herself that she'd never tamed urged her to add, "I'll try not to do anything foolish."

At the look on his face, she laughed.

Ladd and Allie stood in the doorway. "We'll be good, Papa. Truly we will."

"I'll hold you to it." He rode away.

Mercy didn't wait for him to disappear from sight before she shepherded the twins inside and closed the door. "It's getting colder by the minute," she said by way of explanation for her hurry. She'd never been in the cabin before. Hadn't been the least bit interested in it. Now she glanced around taking in every detail.

Which didn't take more than a minute. The cabin was smaller than Jayne and Seth's. Only one tiny room. The small cookstove would more than heat the place on most days. She expected by the time the fire was hot enough to boil water the room would be hot enough to make a grown man drip with sweat. Only one tiny window allowed in light. The few shelves lining the wall over-flowed with books, clothing, hardware. One corner of the ceiling had a definite sway to it. She recalled notic-ing damage to the roof outside. Abel had real cause for hurry if he meant to give these children a warm, safe place for the winter and she knew he did.

"What would you like to do?" she asked the pair.

"I'm not supposed to do anything," Allie said, a little tremor in her voice.

"Your father said you were to take it easy. There are still lots of things you can do."

"Like what?" Both children leaned forward, eager-ness in every muscle.

She looked about. "Lots of things." And she'd dream them up in the next few minutes.

She'd prove to Mr. Abel Borgard that she could be trusted not to act foolishly. Not that she ever did. No matter what his opinion of her activities.

Chapter Three

Abel considered the work he'd accomplished. Trees selected for the cabin and cut down. Some firewood gathered. Despite the crisp air, he worked with his shirt-sleeves rolled up, sweat trickling down his back. Today held more urgency than just the approaching winter. Mercy was back at the cabin with his children and his nerves tingled at the idea. He'd only seen the woman twice and both times her behavior had given his heart a fit. Would he get home to find the children swinging from the rafters or jumping off the bed?

He swung his ax with renewed vigor. The best thing he could do was get as much work done in as little time as possible.

A few minutes later he paused to wipe the sweat from his brow. That's when his neck muscles twitched. Something or someone watched him. He could feel it. He jerked about. A dark shadow ducked into the bushes. But not before he'd seen enough to know it was not an animal but a squat man with a dark beard down to his chest.

His heart did a persistent two-step inside his chest, making it hard to get a decent breath.

He pretended to study a tree as if considering how best to chop it down, hoping he'd see the man again. He didn't much care for someone to be spying on him, but at least if Abel could see him he'd know the children were safe. Maybe he should forget getting logs and head back.

He warred between the urgency of his task and the need to assure himself of the children's safety.

One simple fact persuaded him to return to swinging his ax.

Mercy had a gun—he'd seen the bulge in her jacket as she returned to the cabin after penning her horse. He had no doubt she knew how to use it. Nor did he think she would hesitate to do so if the need arose. She'd probably jump at the chance.

He chuckled softly as he realized her foolish behavior provided him with a bit of comfort at the moment.

Twice more he glimpsed the dark shadow of the man. What kind of person spied on another? But after a bit he stopped worrying about the mysterious man, who did nothing to make Abel feel threatened. And as long as he was content to watch Abel, those back at the cabin were safe.

He worked steadily into the afternoon, pausing briefly only to drink from his canteen, chow down a sandwich or wipe his brow. As the shadows lengthened, he headed back to the cabin. He'd seen no sign of the intruder for the past hour and hoped the man had left the vicinity. But he wouldn't be completely at ease until he reached the cabin and saw the twins for himself.

He tended Sam first, knowing he would not want

to return to the job once he entered the cabin. He put the saddle and blanket in the little shed that offered a modicum of protection, then crossed the yard, threw open the door and ducked inside.

The aroma that greeted him filled his mouth with saliva. How pleasant to come home to a hot meal after a hard day of work. He'd always hoped Ruby would change, would someday decide she liked being married, liked being a mother, liked tending the home. It had never happened and now it was too late for dreams. He would never again risk his children's happiness for the hope of a happy home, and certainly not for the sake of a hot meal. Though it would be pleasant to have something besides beans and bannock for a change.

"The place is getting cold," Mercy said, reminding him he stood in the open doorway.

He closed the door and swung the children off their feet in a big hug. He studied each face. No guilt on either. No heightened color in Allie's cheeks. That was good. And no one mentioned a whiskered man visiting. The last of his tension slipped away.

"Your supper is ready." Mercy shrugged. "I thought you might be hungry." She slipped past him and snagged her jacket from the hook by the door. "I'll be on my way."

"Do you think Mrs. Gardiner and her son will be recovered by tomorrow?"

Mercy gave him a look so full of disbelief he felt a little foolish. "I wouldn't think so. It usually takes a few days to get over a cold, doesn't it?"

"I guess so." Abel's thoughts raced. He still had a lot of work to do and he couldn't leave the children unsupervised while he was away. He looked about again.

The children were in one piece. A meal awaited him. That left him one option. He made up his mind and had to act quickly before he thought better of it.

"Can I persuade you to work for me until such time as the children can go to the ranch again? I'll pay you a fair wage."

The children grabbed his hands and grinned up at him then turned to Mercy.

"Please, Mercy," they chorused.

He wondered if he should correct the way they addressed her but, instead, he waited for her to answer, finding himself as tense and eager as they seemed to be. Eager? No. Simply desperate.

Mercy looked at each of the children, then brought her gaze to him, regarding him steadily as if daring him to voice any objection to the way she had managed.

He couldn't and returned her look for look, noting, for the first time, the deep brown of her eyes and how her mahogany hair framed a very pretty face.

"I enjoyed spending the day with the children," she said, smiling at them. Her smile disappeared as she again looked at him. "I'd love to come as long as they need me."

"Thank you." It was only for the children, he silently repeated. She made it clear she felt the same way. Not that it mattered to him one little bit.

"I'll return in the morning then." She brushed her fingers across Allie's cheek and then Ladd's. "See you two tomorrow." And she left without a word of farewell to him.

Not that he cared, he insisted. But the tiny cabin seemed empty...a feeling that intensified after the twins went to bed.

Determined to dismiss such irrational thoughts, he pulled the Bible off the shelf and read it. His parents had raised him to look for answers to life's problem in the words of scripture and to obey unquestioningly the precepts set out there. Since the twins' births he had found strength and guidance in the pages of the Bible, just as his parents had taught.

But tonight he found no solution for the restlessness that plagued him.

Finally he gave up and prepared for bed. Thankfully the cold air and hard work of the day enabled him to fall into a sound sleep.

The next morning, the children could barely be persuaded to stay in bed long enough for him to start the fire and take the chill off the room.

"When will Mercy be here?" Allie asked for the twentieth time.

"Let's have breakfast first." He tried to corral them both to sit at the table, but they kept bouncing up to throw open the door and see if Mercy approached.

After a few such interruptions, Abel grew annoyed. "Miss Mercy is only helping for a few days. You're simply asking for trouble if you think it's anything more."

Wide-eyed and disbelieving, the twins stared at him.

"Didn't she say she meant to join a Wild West show?" he added to press home his point.

Their gazes grew wary.

"That means she'll be traveling all over the country, living with the others in the show." It sounded like a restless sort of life he wouldn't welcome. He'd tried it already and knew it offered adventure but gave only emptiness. But to each her own. "You won't see her much after that."

Allie brightened. "We could go with her."

He blinked before the eagerness in his daughter's expression. "You could not." What a dreadful, sordid life for a child.

Ladd sighed long. "She's not going for a while. She might change her mind after she gets to know us better." His shoulders sagged. "But she's very good. I guess she won't change her mind."

"There you go." Abel should be relieved that they'd accepted the facts of Mercy's friendship but, instead, he felt as if he had jerked a rug out from under their feet.

A noise against the side of the cabin snapped Abel's head in that direction. Both children bolted to their feet. "Mercy," they yelled.

He grabbed two arms and planted the pair firmly back in their chairs. "Mercy would not be rubbing against the house. Sit here and be quiet." He grabbed his rifle from over the door. If that whiskered man from the woods thought to bother Abel and his children...

"Don't shoot her," Allie whispered.

"Sit and be still." He tiptoed to the door, quietly opened it and inched out far enough to see the side of the cabin. A deer. They sure could use fresh meat, but he wouldn't shoot an animal with his children watching. Besides, this was a doe. He'd find a buck out in the woods. He signaled to the children to come and held his finger to his lips so they'd know enough to be quiet.

They joined him.

"Awww," Allie whispered, the faint noise startling the doe, who bounced into the trees and disappeared.

Allie stared after her. "What did she want?"

He shepherded them back inside though the wind was still and the air promised a warm day. "I don't know. Maybe she is curious. Maybe she's been here before when no one lived here."

"Maybe she thinks this is her house." Allie looked about ready to burst into tears.

"No, baby. I don't think so. Deer like to be among the trees. They don't live in buildings."

Allie sniffled. "You're sure?"

"Very."

Ladd had remained at the door. "Here she comes."

Abel didn't have to look up to understand he meant Mercy. Allie raced to join her brother. Abel took his time going to their side, though truthfully he was as relieved as the twins to see her ride to the cabin. But only because he needed to take advantage of the autumn weather while it lasted.

She called, "Hello," then led her horse to the corral.

Which gave him almost enough time to convince himself he only cared because he had work to do and her presence would enable him to get at it. Besides, he still wasn't persuaded the twins were completely safe with her. What if she decided to shoot her guns off? Or race her horse around with the twins on its back?

He hurried inside to get his coat and hat and leave before she entered the tiny space. They met at the doorway.

She carried a bulging gunnysack.

Both curiosity and caution stopped him in his tracks. "What's in there?" He couldn't keep the ring of suspicion from his voice.

She chuckled. "You needn't sound like you wonder if I've brought knives to let the children throw. Or guns to shoot."

He worked to hide his discomfort; she'd correctly gauged his concern. "I am their only parent."

"Yup. I figured that out. Relax. I merely brought some things to keep the children occupied. See for yourself." She opened the sack and held it out for him to peer in.

Papers, books, cookies? His mouth watered. How long since he'd had cookies? He swallowed back the saliva and nodded. "Looks harmless enough."

"I keep telling you I am not so foolish as to do something to hurt a child."

He looked at her and saw the way she tried to hide her emotion. But she didn't quite succeed. Her lips tightened slightly and her eyes were too wide.

With a stab in his gut, he realized he'd hurt her feelings. "I'm sorry. I didn't mean to suggest you would." Yet hadn't he, despite how well she'd done yesterday? The children had told him about their day in great detail. How they'd shown her all the things he'd bought before their arrival—new clothes, food and winter supplies. They'd shown her their books and their few toys. Told him how they'd played a fun game of pretend family, then she'd let them help her prepare the meals.

His suspicion was unfounded. Yet his caution must remain. He had to keep the children safe. And somehow he knew Mercy was a risk to them. And to him, too, though he couldn't say why he included himself. He had no intention of letting any woman upset the stability he'd worked so hard to establish for the children. Especially a woman whose stated goal was to join a Wild West show. He'd had enough of women who wanted only to run off for whatever reason.

His jaw creaked as he warned himself of all the dangers he invited into his life by asking Mercy to watch the children, but he didn't see what else he could do at the moment.

It would only be for a day or two, he told himself, then he'd insist Mercy stay away from all of them.

Mercy watched Abel ride from the yard, then got the children to help her clean the little cabin. When they were done she lifted the gunnysack. "I brought something for you to do."

"What? What?" Ladd jumped up and down.

"Can we see?" Allie bounced on her feet, then sighed and stood still.

Mercy wished she could tell the child to enjoy herself, but Abel said her heart might be damaged. Must the poor little girl live like an invalid all her life? Mercy had planned things to amuse both children—quiet, imaginative play for Allie, more vigorous activity for Ladd.

She pulled pieces of paper from the sack. "It doesn't look like much yet, but this is everything we need to take a long, adventuresome trip."

Both children studied the paper as if expecting a covered wagon to emerge.

The sun had already driven away the cooler night air. "It's going to be a lovely day. Let's sit outside and enjoy it while we have our adventure." She grabbed a quilt off the bed and spread it under a tree that allowed her a good view of the clearing. She hadn't seen the whiskered man again, nor had she placed him in her memories, but she meant to be cautious until she was certain he was either gone or posed no threat to them.

The three of them sat on the quilt, the children's expressions eager.

"Would you like to go on a ship?"

"Where to?" Allie asked, her eyes gleaming.

"Where would you like to go?"

They looked puzzled.

"I crossed the ocean from my home in England in order to get here." She described the ship. "Do you want to come with me?"

They both nodded, Ladd curious, Allie excited. Her porcelain cheeks had a healthy rosy tint to them. Or did the color signal heart problems? She'd asked Sybil and Linette about the child and both had warned her to watch for breathlessness, fatigue, chest pain or nausea. Sybil said she once knew a boy who had heart problems and his lips would get blue. Mercy saw none of those signs, so unless she witnessed evidence to the contrary she'd take it for natural coloring.

"I'll show you how to make boats." As she talked, she folded the paper into a boat shape and then made sailor hats for them.

"Let's get ready for an adventure." She told them of the tall smokestacks on the ship, the storms that blew and the way the waves rose so high.

She guided their play, letting Ladd climb the tree beside them and be the lookout while Allie stood on the ground acting as the captain, giving orders to Ladd.

Mercy watched Allie closely for any sign of fatigue or blueness around her lips. But the children played for a couple of hours before she felt she should direct them to quieter play.

She pulled out an atlas she had borrowed from

Linette and Eddie's library. "Let's see some of the places we could go."

For the rest of the morning they pored over the book and she told them things she knew about each country they decided to visit. It was a good thing she had paid attention to her geography and history lessons.

"Now it's time for the travelers to have something to eat."

She made sandwiches and they ate outside. "I'll make tea for us." She left them on the quilt and made tea thinned with tinned milk and rejoined them on the quilt.

The thud of approaching horse hooves and rattle of a chain jerked her to her feet and instantly at attention, but it was only Abel dragging logs into the clearing to the spot where he meant to build a new cabin.

The children rose, too.

"Papa," Allie called.

"Stay there until I finish."

He unhooked the chains, then straightened and wiped his arm across his brow. All the while, he studied the children until Mercy fought an urge to jump up and down and say she hadn't been doing anything wrong.

But she would not let his suspicious nature affect her.

His gaze settled on her. She met his look without flinching because—she told herself firmly—she had no reason to be nervous. Sunlight flashed in his eyes making them a warm blue. Their gazes held. The look went on and on until her lungs grew airless. She was overly aware of his study, of her own rapid heartbeat and of the shimmering air in the clearing.

He headed toward them and her ribs tightened so much her lungs could not work.

Ladd raced to him. "Papa, we have been having such fun."

Abel shifted his attention to the boy, and Mercy gasped in an endless breath. What had happened? Why had she felt so strange, as if the air between them pulsed with something she couldn't name?

Allie took two steps then waited for Abel to reach her and lift her to his arms. "We've traveled all over the world."

Abel lifted his eyebrows in surprise. "I sure am glad you got back before I did. I might have worried."

The twins laughed. "Oh, Papa," Allie scolded. "We were here all the time." She squirmed from his arms and ran to Mercy's side and smiled up at her. "Mercy took us on a pretend voyage. I was the captain."

"And I got to climb high and be the watchman."

"I am most glad to see you've all survived your adventure." His gaze bored into Mercy. She tried to tell herself he was warning her that the children better remain unharmed. But it wasn't suspicion she saw or felt. His look measured her, examined her and left her again struggling to fill her lungs.

"Of course everyone is safe," she murmured, then jerked away, saw the tin of cookies on the quilt and grabbed it. "Abel, we were about to have tea. Would you care to join us?" Oh no. Had she just called him by his given name? Surely another evidence of her unacceptable behavior. But it had somehow slipped out of its own accord.

"Oh, please do, Papa," Allie begged. "It's such fun."

"I think I shall." He sat cross-legged on the corner of the quilt. The children sat beside him.

His ready acceptance surprised her, made it impossible for her to think clearly. Shouldn't he be in a hurry to get his work done instead of lingering here? But for some crazy reason, she'd asked. And now she must do as she'd offered and she passed the cookies and poured milk tea from the jug she had prepared.

As he sipped from his cup, he continued to watch her.

What did he want? Why did he keep looking at her so intently? Did he like what he saw? She squirmed under his scrutiny, rearranged the five remaining cookies in the tin, set the tin on the quilt and adjusted it several times. Then, to see if he still stared at her, she lifted her gaze back to him. She blinked as her eyes collided with his blue ones.

Had he watched her all this time?

He jerked his gaze away and put his cup down. "I have to get back to work." He gained his feet in a flash. "I can get more logs hauled in this afternoon." He clamped his hat on his head and strode away.

"Bye, Papa," the twins called, then turned their attention back to their cookies and tea.

Mercy saw Abel pause at the edge of the clearing to glance their way again. His look slid past her and then returned. He shook his head as he guided the horse out of sight.

Mercy tried to analyze what had just happened. Why had he stared so long? Why had she found it so difficult to breathe? It didn't make sense. She had befriended all the cowboys at the ranch. She had been at ease with the sailors on the ship and with everyone—male or female—she met in between. But never had she felt such a strange tightness in her throat or a twitch behind her eyeballs.

Goodness. The man didn't even approve of her. He only tolerated her presence because he had no other way of providing supervision for his children. Still, she couldn't help admiring his devotion to the twins. Many children didn't ever know such approval from either parent. As for her, he made his opinion crystal clear.

She shook her head, as Abel had done, and wondered if he was as confused as she was.

What was wrong with the pair of them?

They didn't much care for each other and yet… She shook her head again.

It must be the autumn sunshine so warm and deceptive when everyone knew it could change overnight. The temporary delay had lulled them all into a make-believe state.

She turned her attention back to the children. It was time to enjoy the present and forget the unexplainable.

Chapter Four

$\sim$

Abel shook his head several times as he returned to work. What had made him stop in the middle of a sunny afternoon to share tea and cookies with Mercy and the children? He couldn't afford to waste daylight when winter was hard on his heels.

He'd observed Mercy and the children a few minutes without them seeing him. The three of them sharing a picnic. Such a domestic scene. Mercy bending her head toward Ladd and then Allie as they talked. Touching their heads and laughing. The twins drinking her in with their eyes.

His throat had tightened. This happy scene was all he'd dreamed of since the twins were born. Only he'd hoped Ruby would be the one sharing the moment with the children. And he would be right at her side.

Mercy did not fit into the picture he imagined. She wore loose trousers. All the easier to ride in. Mercy obviously did not care about following any rules in her life. Remember, he warned himself, this woman wants to join a Wild West show.

Yet as their gazes connected across the clearing, he

seemed unable to remember his arguments. He tried to pull his thoughts into order as he unhooked the logs. This woman was different from Ruby only in her upbringing. Certainly not in what she wanted from life. He and the children didn't count in her plans. He must bear that in mind.

Then her gaze had snagged his again like some kind of rope trick—demanding, probing, searching…for what he could not say, but he felt as if she reached into his chest and sought to squeeze truth from his heart. How silly. He'd been nothing but truthful with her.

He spent the rest of the afternoon working in the woods. Despite his best efforts to the contrary, his thoughts kept harking back to the cabin and the trio on the quilt enjoying the sunshine. He straightened at the truth he'd discovered—they enjoyed each other while he worked alone. He shook his head at how foolish his thoughts had grown. Of course he worked alone. And the children were safe at home. That's what he wanted. Only he felt isolated.

He bent his back to the task and swung his ax with renewed vigor. He didn't let up until the late afternoon shadows lengthened. He knew he must return if he hoped for Mercy to reach the ranch before dark.

He should warn her of the whiskered man, he realized now. Even her guns and rope would be useless if this man in the woods got the drop on her.

Anxious to get back, he hurried Sam onward. Again, as he'd done earlier in the day, he paused before those at the cabin noticed his presence. Immediately, he saw Mercy. It was hard to miss her. She rode her fancy palomino. The horse reared back on his hind legs as she twirled a rope around the pair of them.

Like Allie said, she made a glorious sight. The words *fire* and *flash* sprang to his mind.

Then he saw the children against the cabin wall, clapping. Allie's eyes were bright, her color heightened. Abel's throat clenched tight. She was overexcited. Hadn't he warned Mercy about this?

He dropped the reins and raced to Allie to scoop her into his arms. He brushed his hand across her face, swept her hair from her forehead. Was she warmer than she should be? "Come along," he said to Ladd, and strode toward the cabin. He put Allie on a chair. "Stay here." He turned to Ladd. "You stay with her." He returned outdoors.

Mercy had dismounted and led her horse toward him.

He strode toward her. His insides churned and his fists clenched at his sides. "Do you have no concern for my children? Are you interested only in an audience for your riding?" He sucked in air to refill his lungs.

She opened her mouth.

Before she could get a word out, he held his hand toward her, silencing her.

"Did you not see how excited Allie was? Did you not notice her bright cheeks?" He shook his head. "I can't believe you could be so careless. I simply can't allow you near my children."

She tilted her head and gave him a hard look.

"Have it your way," she said, her voice hard as rock. "I'm tired of explaining myself. Do you mind if I get my things?" She stalked past him without waiting for his answer.

He followed her and saw the children, wide-eyed and stiff.

Mercy knelt before them, caught their chins and pulled them to face her.

Allie, lips trembling, said, "You can't go."

Ladd gave his father a burning look, then shifted his attention to Mercy. "I like you here."

"I must go. Be good." She kissed them both on the forehead, grabbed her sack and jacket then strode from the house. She swung into her saddle and reined about. At the edge of the clearing she had the horse rear on his back legs. "Goodbye, Mr. Borgard."

This afternoon he'd been Abel, and now Mr. Borgard. Alone again. Though why he thought it had ever changed defied explanation.

He watched until she rode out of sight before he returned to the cabin and the two children watching him with wide eyes and stubborn mouths.

"What do you want for supper?"

Tears welled up in Allie's eyes. "Mercy said she'd make us vegetable soup. But now—" Her voice quivered. "You chased her away."

Ladd clattered to his feet. "She wasn't doing nothin' wrong. You're mad just 'cause she likes to do fun stuff." He glowered at Abel.

Abel sighed. "You both know how careful Allie has to be. Do you want her sick again?" He directed his question to Ladd.

The boy's anger faltered as he considered his sister. He shook his head, then faced Abel squarely. "We were only watching."

Abel didn't intend to argue with his son. "I have to do what I think is best."

"Mama said you forgot how to have fun. She was right."

Abel ignored the boy's comment. Better to let them blame him than to realize the truth that Ruby cared more about her fun than her children. "Who wants bannock and beans?"

"I want vegetable soup." Allie crossed her arms and pursed her lips.

Abel sighed. "So bannock and beans it is."

The evening did not get better and he was happy when the time came to tuck them in. They still refused to forgive him despite the fact he'd done nothing that required forgiveness.

And then he faced the lonely evening. Only then did he remember he had meant to warn Mercy of the man in the woods. He slipped outside and closed the door behind him. Had she gotten back safely? He strained to listen for any unusual noise in the woods. When he heard only coyotes howling and night birds calling he told himself he was being silly. Of course she'd gotten back safely. Surely someone would let him know otherwise.

He returned inside and prepared for bed but, despite his weariness, sleep did not come easily. How was he going to get a bigger cabin built and firewood brought in?

Still, hadn't he planned to manage on his own when he moved here? Really nothing had changed.

Only his wish that things could be different. But even that wasn't new. He'd wanted something more all his life. When he was sixteen he'd thought he'd find it in abandoning the principles his parents had taught him. When he married Ruby, he thought he'd find it with her. After the twins were born, he thought he'd find it in being a father and returning to his faith in God.

And yet... He dismissed the errant thought.

It *was* in obeying God and living a careful life and looking after the twins that he would find what he wanted.

His last thought before sleep claimed him was that Mercy had been glorious, all fire and flash. He meant to argue to the contrary but instead fell asleep with a smile on his lips.

His smile turned upside down the next day as he contemplated his work. The sky hung heavy with clouds threatening rain and making it impossible to consider taking the twins with him to the woods. That meant he must stay close to the cabin. Right after breakfast he went to the logs he had dragged in—the ones meant for firewood—and cut and stacked a supply.

The children stayed inside where they would be warm and dry. He returned to the cabin after a couple of hours to check on them and get a drink.

As he stepped through the door they both gave him accusing looks.

"There's nothing to do," Ladd said in his most disgruntled voice.

Allie nodded. "If Mercy was here she'd play games."

"Or tell good stories," Ladd added, with heavy emphasis on the word *good,* as if to say her stories were much better than any Abel had read or told.

He gave them both considered study before he said, "Or do something wild and woolly like this was part of Mr. Robert's Circus Side Show." He named a traveling circus.

Allie's eyes gleamed and pink filled her cheeks. "That was the best of all."

The mere mention of it overexcited his daughter.

"It's not good for you." He downed a dipper of water and returned to the pile of wood. He wasn't arguing with a pair of disappointed nine-year-olds. They didn't know what was good for them. Even sixteen-year-olds couldn't know. Wasn't he proof of that?

At the end of the day, the twins ate their meals in accusing silence and went to bed without being told. Ladd reached over the edge of the cot and held Allie's hand.

Their displeasure with Abel festered. But what choice did he have? He sat alone after they'd fallen asleep and faced his quandary. Without help, he would have to abandon plans to build a bigger cabin. They could spend the winter in this one just fine, if he had enough firewood to ward off the cold. On nicer days he could take the children to the woods with him, but how many nice days could he count on? As if to answer his question, the wind moaned through the treetops. *God in heaven, I'm counting on You to help me. Maybe even send*—he didn't finish the request. *Send someone to help.* Mercy certainly wasn't an answer to prayer.

He woke slowly the next morning. His eyelids didn't want to face the day. His limbs felt heavy and unresponsive. But lying abed would not solve his problems.

He sighed and rolled over. The bed beside him was empty. He patted both sides to make sure. His eyelids jerked open. Where was Ladd? In the weak light Allie looked at him from her trundle bed, eyes wide and watchful.

He scanned the cabin. Ladd wasn't there. The small quarters offered no hiding place, but he sat up and looked about again to make sure he hadn't missed the boy.

"Where's Ladd?" he asked Allie.

"Gone."

"Gone?" Any remnant of sleep vanished as his blood raced through his veins. He grabbed his trousers and pulled them on under privacy of the covers. "Where?"

"To get Mercy. We want her to look after us. 'Sides, you need her here so you can get logs." She sat in the middle of her bed and watched him as calm as could be while his arms turned leaden and he couldn't seem to get them into the sleeves of his shirt.

"Mercy? She's six miles away. When did he leave?" He peered out the window. The sun had not yet risen but cold gray light filled the clearing. Had his son ventured out in the dark? Was he lost? What about that whiskered man?

He pulled on his jacket and grabbed his rifle. But at the door he stopped. He couldn't leave Allie here alone and wouldn't take her out in the damp cold.

His lungs so tight he could hardly force in air, he faced the door. All he could do for the moment was pray. *Oh, God, keep my boy safe.* As soon as the sun drove back the chill, he would bundle Allie to her teeth and take her with him to find Ladd.

Mercy tiptoed from her room. If Abel didn't want her help with the children, that was fine. It gave her more time to practice. She wanted to be able to twirl a big enough circle with her rope that she could swing it up and down over both herself and Nugget. She'd tried the day before yesterday. That's when Abel had shown up all glower and snort. He didn't bother to take into account that the children were content to sit quietly as they watched her. Nope. He simply ordered her off the place.

She missed the children. But she surely wouldn't miss dealing with a man like Abel any more than she'd miss stabbing herself in the eye with a hot needle.

Carrying her boots so as not to disturb Linette and Grady, who were still miserable with their colds, she glided down the hall and creaked open the door. She glanced back at the stairs to make sure she hadn't wakened them and slipped through the opening.

She turned and screamed as someone stood on the step before her. Heart in her mouth, she managed to croak out a greeting. "Ladd, you gave me a fright." She looked past him as she pulled on her boots, expecting to see Abel and Allie. "Where's your papa?"

Ladd ducked his head. "He was sleeping when I left."

Mercy heard the words but they made no sense. "Left where?"

"Home."

Surely he didn't mean— "You mean the cabin?"

"Uh-huh. I promised Allie I would come and get you." He grabbed her hand. "You have to come. Please. It was so boring without you. Allie even cried a little."

She stared at the boy. "Does your papa know where you are?"

"Allie said she'd tell him."

"But it's barely light. How did you get here?"

"I followed the trail, but it was hard to see." He glanced beyond her. "Someone helped me."

Someone? So far as she knew the men were all on the roundup and the women tucked safely in their beds. Except for that whiskered man she'd seen. "What did this someone look like?"

"I don't know. I couldn't see him. He carried me and left me there." Ladd pointed toward the barn. "I might have got lost if he didn't help me. Actually, I think it was God helping."

None of what the boy said made sense. Except one thing. His father didn't know where he was. Or if he was safe.

"You must be hungry. Come in." She opened the door and herded him to the kitchen, where she sliced a thick slab of bread and spread syrup on it.

Linette came into the room as he ate. Mercy drew her into the hall and explained Ladd's presence. "I have to get him back as soon as possible. Abel will be frantic with worry. His children mean more to him than anything in the world."

"You go. And don't let the man chase you away again. He needs your help even if he won't admit it."

"And he won't." But she couldn't let her annoyance at his rude dismissal matter at the moment. She returned to Ladd's side. "While you finish eating I'm going to saddle Nugget."

He nodded. "Be sure to bring some books and maybe cookies."

She chuckled. "I'll see what I can do."

Linette followed her down the hall. "I'll keep an eye on him until you return."

"Thanks." She trotted down the hill and saddled Nugget then rode him back to the house. Ladd came out and she swung him up behind her.

They rode down the trail toward the little cabin. Every one of Mercy's senses was alert for any strangers in the woods, although she saw nothing out of the ordinary. As they neared the cabin, Abel rushed to their side. He swung Ladd down and hugged him, remaining so close to Mercy's side she couldn't dismount.

He put Ladd on his feet, then reached up and lifted Mercy down. Even though she didn't need his assistance, she saw no point in arguing with the distraught man.

He didn't release her when her feet hit the ground but hugged her equally hard as he'd hugged Ladd. Then he held her at arm's length.

"Thank you." His voice was deep with emotion.

They studied each other. She couldn't say what he thought or felt except for the way his eyes darkened, which could indicate regret or any of a dozen things.

But his firm hands on her shoulders, the unexpected solid comfort of his chest and the warmth of his breath on her cheeks as he thanked her cut a wide swath through invisible barriers she'd been unaware existed. Something made her want to return to his embrace. Strangely, she felt safe in his arms. How ridiculous! She hadn't ever needed or wanted or received such foolish comfort. Her parents had never offered it. But a little voice from her depths pleaded for more of it.

Whoa…he wasn't offering it intentionally. He merely was grateful that she'd returned his son.

She stepped back out of his reach. "He's fine."

"Ladd," Abel said. "Go see your sister. She worried." He waited until the door closed behind the boy. "Where did you find him?"

"On my doorstep."

"He made it all the way to the ranch?"

She nodded, watching the emotions on his face change from worry to disbelief. "How is that possible? It was dark and a fair hike for a child."

"He said a man picked him up and carried him."

Worry wrinkled his brow. "I've seen someone in

the woods. A short, stocky man. I meant to warn you about him."

"I've seen someone, too. A man with lots of whiskers."

"Sounds like it could be the same person." Abel scrubbed a hand over his hair, tangling it.

If she wasn't so concerned and confused at both his actions and her reactions she might have chuckled at how he messed his hair.

"I wonder who he is and what he wants," Abel said.

"I don't know, though I'm certain I've seen him somewhere before. I just can't place where or when."

"Did you get a good look at him?"

"I did. I know I should recognize him."

"Would you have seen his likeness on a wanted poster?"

She considered the question. "I don't know. I wish I could place him." She shrugged. "But if it was he who helped Ladd we can be grateful he didn't harm him instead."

Abel shuddered. "I don't like it." He messed his hair again and then, as if realizing what he'd done, he smoothed it. "The man could be crazy."

She'd momentarily shared the same thought but immediately dismissed it. A person should be judged on evidence, not on suspicion or caution. "Or maybe he likes living in the woods. Or for all we know, he has a cabin of his own."

"Wouldn't Eddie know if that is so?"

She gave silence assent.

"Has he ever mentioned this man?"

She shook her head.

"Then we'll have to be cautious and on guard."

We? When had they become we?

"Anyway. Thank you for bringing him home safely."

"You're welcome."

He smiled.

She knew her eyes widened but she couldn't help herself. His smile transformed his features and made him look...well, nice.

"Please come in."

"My horse..."

"I'll tend to him later."

She let herself be ushered to the door five steps away, let him reach around her and hold it open for her to precede him.

"Did you ask her?" Allie demanded.

Mercy knew what Allie wanted, but Abel hadn't asked.

He took her coat as she slipped her arms out. He hung it next to his and went to the stove. "Have you had breakfast?"

"No." Ladd had interrupted her plans for the day. Not that she minded.

"Then join us. We haven't eaten yet."

"Thank you."

"But first I have a son to deal with." He sat on the edge of the bed and pulled Ladd to his knee to face him. "I'm happy you're safe, but what you did was foolish and against the rules."

"Yes, Papa."

"Haven't I told you that there is a price to pay for foolish and sinful choices?"

"Yes, Papa."

"There is no escaping. The Bible says, 'Be sure your sin will find you out and whatsoever a man soweth he shall reap.' I simply want to save you the pain and sorrow of reaping a bad harvest. Do you understand?"

"Yes, Papa." Ladd spoke softly, his head bowed.

"You know I must punish you."

"I know."

Mercy wondered what form of punishment Abel had in mind. She'd witnessed how rigid he was about rules. Would he mete out unmerciful judgment?

"After breakfast, you will clean up the kitchen and do the dishes by yourself, and while you're doing it I want you to consider why I forbid you to go out on your own. You could have been hurt or lost."

"God sent a man to help me."

Mercy and Abel exchanged a look. His was full of concern and worry. For her part, she wondered how he'd deal with this.

"Son, like I said, I'm glad you're safe and sound. Let's leave it at that." He patted Ladd on the back and returned to the stove.

"Do you drink coffee?" he asked Mercy, then realized she still stood. "Please, have a seat."

She sat on one of the chairs. Allie hung over the back, her face so close to Mercy's she breathed in the sweet scent of her skin. "I like coffee fine," she answered.

He filled a new-looking coffeepot with water, ground some beans and tossed the ground coffee into the pot. In a few minutes he poured her a cupful.

She cradled her hands about the cup.

He sipped his coffee as he turned his attention back to the pot of porridge he cooked. He handed bowls to Ladd. "Set the table, please."

Mercy kept her attention on her cup as she tried to

ignore his presence. It was impossible. He was so big in such a small space. And so vital. He touched Allie's head, brushed Ladd's shoulder, smiled at them.

Her mouth went dry. She gulped coffee but the dryness remained.

The children were fortunate to know such affection and approval from their father. What had happened to their mother, she wondered?

He filled bowls, set them on the table and sat down. "Let's thank God for the food." The children bowed their heads and Abel said a prayer of thanksgiving, not only for the food but for the safety of his son.

Allie and Ladd sent silent signals to each other across the table. They ducked their heads to eat their breakfast, then looked steadfastly at their father.

Abel cleaned his bowl and drained his coffee cup. "Mercy—you don't mind if I call you that, do you?"

"I answer best to it. After all, it's my name." She knew he meant to ask her permission to use her Christian name, but some perverse imp prompted her to answer indirectly.

His smile was fleeting. "Fine. Mercy, I find myself in a quandary."

She offered him no assistance. He had gotten himself into this quandary without her help. He'd have to get out the same way.

"I need to get wood and cut logs. I can't leave the children to do it. And they are quite insistent that they want you to stay with them. Will you?"

Although she understood what he wanted, he'd been much more direct about telling her to leave. He could be equally direct about asking her to come back. "Will I what?"

His eyes narrowed. He'd correctly read her resistance.

Just as she understood that he swallowed his pride to ask her straight out. "Will you please stay with the children so I can get at my work?"

She laughed, with relief at being welcomed back and also with a touch of victory that he'd had to lessen his rigid stand. "Why, I'd be pleased to."

The children grinned. Ladd immediately set to work cleaning the table and washing dishes.

Abel pushed back from the table. "Thank you." He wrapped slices of bread and syrup in brown paper, snagged a can of beans and then grabbed his coat and hat. "I'll be on my way." He hugged the children and hurried out.

She stared at the door for a heartbeat after he left. Two and then a third. His thanks had been perfunctory. His leaving hasty. And why not? He had to prepare for winter. Had to provide the children's needs.

No reason in the world to wish he could linger a bit and talk to her. No reason at all.

In fact, it was a relief to have him gone. He was too big. He crowded the tiny room and made her uncomfortable. Whew. She released the air from her tight lungs. Now she could breathe easy without concerning herself about his reaction to what she said and did.

She rubbed her arms, remembering his solid chest and warm hands.

Why had his hug felt so good? Like it filled up an empty spot in her heart. She shook her head. Where had such foolishness come from?

Chapter Five

Abel led Sam in the general direction he planned to go but, before he ventured farther, he left the horse waiting as he scouted around the cabin. If some crazy man hung about in the vicinity he wanted to know about it. Heavy gray clouds hung low in the sky. Dampness filled the air. At least the twins would be safe and dry in Mercy's care.

Mercy! The woman seemed destined to fill his mind with confusion.

Shoot! He was crazier than any wild man. He'd hugged Mercy. Only because he was so all-fired relieved to see Ladd safe and sound. Or at least that's the excuse he gave himself and initially it had driven his actions. But he'd felt a whole lot more than relief as soon as his arms closed around her. He'd noted a number of things—how she fit just below his chin, how small yet strong she felt, how her hair filled with the scent of summer flowers and fresh-mowed hay.

Momentarily, without forethought, his arms had tightened around her and then she'd stepped back, no doubt as shocked by his actions as he'd been.

A thorough search around the cabin yielded no evidence of anyone lingering in the area. So Abel returned to Sam and left to find firewood and good logs, though building a bigger cabin before winter seemed a distant possibility.

He worked steadily all day, grateful the rain held off. Shadows filled the hollows and hung around the trees as he returned to the cabin with logs. Rather than unload immediately, he headed for the cabin, driven by far more than concern for the children. All day his thoughts had tortured him with memories of Mercy in his arms. Yet only the day before he'd considered her a menace to his children's safety.

Likely she still was, and he needed to keep that in mind. A woman interested in pursuing a wild life in a show, a woman who ignored his warnings about involving the children in her activities, a woman who rode like a man and...

He reached the cabin door and paused to listen. Laughter came from inside and he forgot to list the other things against Mercy.

Ducking his head, he stepped inside and ground to a halt. Flour covered half the surfaces in the cabin and if he wasn't mistaken, dough spatters decorated the surfaces that had been spared the flour dusting. The children wore generous amounts of both and Mercy's hair had turned gray. When had he ever seen such a mess? Was this her idea of looking after the twins? "What exploded?"

The three looked up, saw his expression and glanced around. Their gaze returned to him, guardedness replacing the laughter.

"We made cookies," Ladd said, his words solid.

"Mercy helped us." Allie sounded a little more conciliatory.

Mercy didn't say anything and her gaze dared him to object.

He swallowed hard, the aroma of cookies from the oven overwhelming his annoyance. "Cookies, huh?"

"Want some?" Allie asked.

"They smell good." He'd overlook the mess in order to enjoy the cookies. And the company of those who had baked them. Tonight he'd clean the mess. At least he'd be too busy to be bored and lonely.

He sat at the table and tried not to look too surprised at the cookies set before him. One was small and slightly black around the edges, another was the size of a saucer, several were balls and one had been shaped into— He peered more closely at it.

"It's a horse," Ladd said. "Allie made it."

Allie stood at Abel's side waiting for his approval. Who'd have thought to make a horse out of cookie dough? Probably Mercy. "It's looks very nice."

Allie beamed her approval.

Mercy handed him a cup of coffee although she didn't join him and the children at the table.

He studied her out of the corner of his eyes. Was she uncomfortable around him? He had no one but himself to blame if she was. Nor could she find this any more awkward than did he.

He downed his coffee and ate two cookies—one each child had made—pronounced them delicious, then hurried back outside to deal with the load of firewood.

A couple of hours later, he returned to the cabin. When he stepped inside, he blinked at the transformation. The flour and dough had been cleaned up and the vegetable soup Allie craved simmered on the stove. The table had been set for three. No reason he should be disappointed, he told himself. Mercy had to get going if she planned to get back while she could see the trail.

She grabbed her jacket and he followed her out the door.

"Keep alert. I don't like to think what a man is doing out in the woods."

She chuckled. "I'll keep my gun and rope ready and, if need be, use them both."

He didn't ask how she'd use them both but, no doubt, she could.

She swung into the saddle and sat there. "I don't know if you were aware that there are church services at the ranch every Sunday. There's a service tomorrow, in the cookhouse. Everyone is welcome. If you're interested."

"I'd love to come. I want the children to realize that Sunday means church. What time?"

"We meet right after breakfast." She gave the time. "See you then."

"Yes. I look forward to it." He meant both church and seeing her again. And he feared it showed in his eyes.

She smiled softly. No mocking. No challenge. "Until tomorrow then." She reined about and rode from the yard.

He watched her until he could no longer see her. A sigh rose from deep inside him. Then he shook his head. He'd once followed his heart and look where it had landed him. From now on he meant to follow his head and his head said Mercy was a pack of trouble who would turn all their lives upside down and sideways if he wasn't careful.

* * *

Mercy put on her prettiest green taffeta dress. She might be wild and unconventional, or so her friends said, but she wouldn't go to church in pants. She snorted. Despite Ambrose's opinion of her. Not even if church was in a cookhouse on a ranch.

She pulled her hair back into a twist at the back of her head. When she, Jayne and Sybil had spent the weeks on the ship crossing the ocean they had brushed and styled each other's hair. She missed it but her friends were now married. It sure hadn't taken them long. They claimed God had sent their husbands into their lives even though Jayne had accidently shot Seth and Brand had ridden in with his dog to break Eddie's horses.

Maybe God had sent Abel and the children into Mercy's life.

She dismissed the idea before it could light in her thoughts. Abel made it clear as the water in the stream that flowed by the ranch that he didn't approve of her. Not that she cared. Not a whit. She had plans that did not include a man and children…a ready-made family. Nor did she think God concerned Himself with the petty affairs of man.

She looked at the picture of her parents that sat on the dresser. What did family mean? She shook her head, dismissed the question and hurried to meet Linette and Grady.

Grady had recovered from his cold but Linette still looked pale.

"Are you sure you're up to this? And having everyone come for dinner afterward?"

Linette nodded. "I'll have lots of help." She let out

a large sigh. "I'm missing Eddie. I wish they were all back home."

"If Eddie was correct about how long it would take they'll be gone another week."

"I know." She took Mercy's arm as they walked down the hill to church. "It will be the longest week of my life." They had reached the steps to the cookhouse when Abel and the children rode into sight.

"Mercy, Mercy," the twins called, waving madly.

Abel immediately caught Allie's hand and calmed her.

Linette chuckled and withdrew her arm. "Seems your attention is requested."

Mercy smiled and waved at the twins while her gaze went unbidden to their father. The brim of his hat shaded his face so she couldn't make out the expression in his eyes and yet her lungs constricted so sharply she almost stumbled. "The children have accepted my friendship readily enough." Where did that note of regret in her voice come from? Maybe Linette wouldn't notice it.

But the way her friend studied her and patted her hand, Mercy knew she hoped in vain. "I expect their father is glad of your friendship, too."

"I didn't mean that. The last thing I need or want is a rule-bound man."

The twins continued to call out to Mercy.

Linette took Grady's hand and climbed the steps to the cookhouse door. "You best go greet your friends." Laughter rounded her voice.

Mercy opened her mouth to protest that Abel wasn't her friend and found she couldn't force the words out.

Were they friends? Or did he simply tolerate her for the sake of the children? She shrugged. What did it matter? Just because he'd hugged her…out of gratitude. Just because her heart broke into a gallop when he smiled… It meant nothing. It only indicated her growing restlessness. She needed to get back to practicing her riding and roping tricks.

They reached her side and Abel handed the children down, then swung off the horse to land at Mercy's side.

"'Morning," he said. "Are we late?"

"No. Right on time." She waited as he tied the horse to a rail. "Come and meet the others."

The children held her hands as she led the way up the stairs. "Cookie will be happy to meet you." She hesitated a moment. Maybe she should warn them of what to expect, but what could she say? She opened the door and stepped inside, the children at her side and Abel bringing up the rear.

Cookie swept across the floor toward them.

Mercy held the twins firmly. "This is Abel Borgard and his children, Allie and Ladd."

Cookie ground to a halt before the twins.

"This is Cookie."

"Welcome, welcome." The big woman opened her arms.

Ladd's grip tightened. Allie shrank against Mercy's leg.

"Shy little things, are you?" Cookie patted their heads and swung her attention to Abel. "I've been wondering when we'd get to meet you."

Abel held out his hand.

Cookie grabbed him and pulled him into a smothering hug, patting his back hard enough that the breath whooshed out of his lungs. After several pats, she released him.

Abel sucked in air and glowered at Mercy. "You could have warned me," he whispered as Cookie returned to the table.

"Would you have believed me?" she whispered back.

Abel grunted. "Likely not."

Mercy grinned.

"You don't need to enjoy it quite so much."

"Sorry." She wasn't and guessed he knew it. She indicated he should step forward and meet the others. "Bertie, Cookie's husband."

"Glad to have you with us." Bertie shook Abel's hand.

Mercy went around the circle. "Cassie and her children, Daisy, Neil, Billy and Pansy. My friends who came from England with me, Jayne and Sybil, and you know Linette." Grace and her sister, Belle, wouldn't join them today. With Ward away at the roundup Grace preferred to stay at their ranch a few miles away.

They made the rounds and found a place to sit. The twins sat on either side of Mercy, and Abel sat by Allie. His bent legs pressed Allie tight to Mercy's side. He rested a hand on the bench behind his daughter and leaned close as if sheltering her. Mercy sat very still, afraid if she shifted, she would bump into his fist or rub against his shoulder. She crossed her ankles and tucked her feet under the bench, holding herself stiff and upright, and focused her attention on Cookie, who rose to lead them in singing a few hymns.

But how could she ignore him when he sang with a

clear deep voice that made all the female voices, and indeed even Bertie's, sound mild and weak?

Did he really mean the words as firmly as he sang them?

Then Bertie stood to speak. "I know you're all missing your men." The women around Mercy murmured agreement. "It brings to mind a time when I was alone and wandering far from God. I had convinced myself that God didn't care about me. I was convinced I had no part in His great plans. It was a mighty lonely place for me to be."

Mercy didn't normally give Bertie's speeches much thought; today she clung to each word in order to stop herself from feeling Abel with every pore.

Bertie continued. "I found shelter in a church one night and happened to overhear the preacher practicing his sermon. 'Thou knowest my downsitting and mine uprising, thou understandest my thoughts afar off.' Unaware that I listened from my bed on one of the pews, the man went on to talk about how God knows and cares about every aspect of our lives. 'Too wonderful,' he said over and over." Bertie sighed deeply. "That was the day I began my journey back to God…a God who cares personally about each of us. Ladies, and Mr. Borgard, rest assured that not only does He know and care about us, He knows and cares about the men on the roundup, too."

Abel nodded.

Allie shifted to lean against her father and Abel wrapped an arm about her shoulders. His hand brushed Mercy's arm as he drew his daughter close and Mercy stiffened. She kept her eyes on Bertie though she longed to glance at Abel and see if he'd been as aware of the touch as she.

As she wondered, the service ended and Cookie invited them to share coffee and cinnamon buns. Mercy bolted to her feet at the invitation and hurried to Cookie's side. "I'll help you."

Cookie laughed. "I can manage. You go enjoy that Mr. Borgard." She leaned close. "My, he's a handsome fellow."

Mercy's cheeks burned and she couldn't look at Abel. Hopefully, he hadn't heard.

"Now go sit with your friends."

Mercy hurried to sit beside Jayne.

Her friend nudged her. "Shouldn't you make Abel feel more welcome?"

Finally she allowed herself to glance at him. He stood before the bench where they had sat together, the children at his side. The three of them looked about at the women and children, then Abel turned toward the door.

"Don't let him leave," Jayne whispered.

Mercy's awkward awareness of him vanished as she bolted to her feet and went to the trio. "Come and join the others for coffee. It's a tradition. And no one should miss out on Cookie's cinnamon rolls. There's nothing like them."

Cookie beamed her approval as Mercy took Allie's hand and urged Abel forward.

He sat across from Linette and Cassie.

Mercy sat beside him. The children crowded in next to them, pushing them shoulder to shoulder.

The sighs of enjoyment verified her claim that the cinnamon rolls shouldn't be missed.

Linette wiped her mouth. "It's also a tradition that we all go to the big house for dinner. I hope you'll consent to join us."

Mercy had been fighting awareness of every move Abel made—lifting a coffee cup to his lips, taking bites from the cinnamon rōll. Each movement caused his arm to rub along hers, sending tingles skittering up her nerves. Why was she so conscious of the man? It wasn't as if she even liked him. And certainly he didn't like her. Yet—

She closed her eyes and clamped her teeth together.

But the thought persisted. Yes, she admired certain things about him. The way he showed love for his children. How concerned he was about their welfare. It kind of reminded her of what Bertie had said about God. Abel knew his children and cared about them. Of course, Bertie had meant it about God, but she found it easier to believe about Abel because she saw the evidence.

"I don't know what to say to your kindness," Abel said.

Mercy heard the pending refusal in his voice. "I'm sure the twins would enjoy visiting with the other children," she murmured.

"Please, Papa," Allie whispered.

He shifted. She assumed he looked at Allie and turned to watch, but her gaze collided with his. She was struck by its dark blue intensity. His look went deep and long. What did he seek? Certainly nothing from her. She swallowed hard as he continued to study her. Did he want to know her opinion of him staying? The thought flared through her head. Why would it matter?

"I'm sure you'd all enjoy it," she managed with a tongue as thick as an ax handle.

A smile flickered across his face. He turned back to Linette. "Thank you for the invitation and we accept."

Ladd leaned forward to look past Mercy and grin at his father.

At that moment, little two-year-old Pansy climbed to the bench across from Abel and stared at him. "You see my papa?"

Abel shook his head. "I'm afraid I haven't."

Pansy's bottom lip trembled. "I miss my papa."

Allie sat forward on the edge of the bench. "You can share my papa if you like."

Pansy turned to study Abel with wide blue eyes.

Mercy held her breath as she waited to see how the toddler would respond. She felt Abel's arm tense, as well.

After a moment Pansy smiled. "Okay." She climbed down, trotted around the table to Abel and held out her arms. "Up."

Abel picked her up and she perched on his knee, as content as imaginable.

He smiled at Mercy and she grinned back, struck to the core by his gentle, easy way with the child. The man certainly knew how to charm little girls. She averted her eyes. Big girls weren't so easily charmed. Especially when big girls knew he didn't approve of them and their activities.

Linette rose. "Shall we go up the hill then? I need to check on the roast."

Abel and the children fell in at her side. Cassie and her children followed. Mercy joined arms with Sybil and Jayne and brought up the rear.

Jayne leaned over to whisper, "What a charming man. You didn't tell us."

Mercy shrugged. "He isn't like that with me."

"Oh, do tell." Sybil shook Mercy's arm. "How is he with you?"

Mercy wished she needn't respond but knew her friends would persist until they had an answer. She shrugged to indicate it didn't matter. "He doesn't approve of me."

They both jerked to a halt and turned to her. Sybil looked concerned. Jayne grinned.

"Why would that be, I wonder?" she asked. "Let me guess. You go out of your way to be wild and unconventional and then wonder why he is disapproving."

"I do no such thing. I am just me."

"That's what I mean." Jayne shook her head. "Always challenging life and conventional behavior." She looked at Sybil. "Why do you think she's like that?"

Sybil shrugged. "We've discussed this before and I still hold that she's trying to get her parents' attention."

Mercy let out a noisy gust of a sigh. "I am not."

"Face it, Mercy. They only notice you when you do something so outrageous they can't ignore it. So you do it again. And again."

Mercy recalled Ambrose had said much the same before he informed her he didn't care for her behavior. "You are so wrong. I simply like adventure. I'm not interested in the ordinary and expected."

Sybil grabbed her arm and clung to her side. "I might believe that if I didn't see the hunger in your eyes as you watch Abel and his children. What he has is what you want even if you won't admit it to yourself."

She ground to a halt. "And what is that, may I ask?"

"A family and a heart of love."

Mercy stared straight ahead. She hadn't expected Sybil to have an answer. Especially not an answer that cut a wide swath through her heart, leaving a trail of... fear. She swallowed hard. Fear? What utter nonsense. "I want a life of adventure. In fact, I am going to practice extra hard so I can join a Wild West show real soon."

She plowed ahead, not giving the others a chance to reply.

Inside the house, she went directly to the kitchen to help Linette. Normally, the men would visit in the front room, but Abel was the only man present so he followed the women into the kitchen.

Mercy tried to ignore his presence but every time she turned around, there he was, big and bright, watching her every move. She bit her tongue to stop from telling him she found him annoying.

"It's ready," Linette announced an hour later, catching Mercy staring into space as she plotted a way to prove she had no interest in Abel apart from his children.

Thinking of the twins brought a smile to her mouth and she allowed herself to be shepherded to the table. Only after she took her place did she realize she sat directly across from Abel. So what? He was just another cowboy and not one had ever intimidated her.

Vowing to act normally, she passed the food and ate and joined in the table conversation. Only when Abel mentioned how much he enjoyed the meal did her thoughts stutter.

"I'd forgotten what good food well served tastes like."

"But, Papa," Ladd said. "Mercy cooked us a nice meal."

Her gaze collided with Abel's. A regretful smile curved his lips. "So she did and I truly appreciated it."

Mercy made a small, disbelieving noise. "I barely know how to cook."

Linette chuckled. "When I arrived here I didn't know how to cook a thing. I learned in a hurry though I made a few mistakes." She regaled them with stories of hard beans and failed bread. "Cookie kept saying baking bread was as easy as falling off a log. I thought I'd never learn."

Neil edged forward. "Can we go play?"

"Of course," Cassie said.

"Can Ladd come?"

Abel studied his son. "Would you like to?"

Ladd nodded, his expression eager.

"Very well."

The boys clattered from the room and their calls could be heard as they ran down the hill.

"Papa?" Allie whispered.

"I'm sorry. You can't join them. You must take it easy."

"She can play with Grady's things," Linette said. "Come along, I'll show you."

Abel pushed to his feet. "I don't know…"

"It's only some carved animals. She can play quietly."

Abel reluctantly agreed. He sank back to the bench as the ladies rose to clear the table and do the dishes.

When Pansy grew fussy, her older sister, Daisy, rose to take her home and put her to bed.

Sitting there alone, Abel rubbed his legs, scratched at the table and looked about restlessly.

"Why don't you show Abel around the place," Linette whispered as she leaned close to Mercy. "Take pity on the poor man. He's uncomfortable surrounded by women."

Mercy sighed deeply. The last thing she wanted was to spend the afternoon entertaining the man, but she could hardly refuse Linette's suggestion. "Shall we?" She waved toward the door.

How could she possibly keep her errant thoughts in line while trailing about the place? She pushed her shoulders back. She could do it. She only had to remember how much he disapproved of her. Called her foolish. Accused her of being careless with his children.

A little wayward voice broke into her arguments. He praised her cooking. Hugged her, his arms warm and protective around her.

She shook her head nearly hard enough to loosen the pins in her hair.

She, Mercy Newell, cared not what Abel Borgard, or any man for that matter, thought of her.

Chapter Six

Abel let Mercy lead him from the house. Grateful as he was to escape the kitchen full of women, he glanced back, reluctant to leave. He'd seen Allie playing quietly in the corner of the living room, but would she stay there? Would the women realize she must not exert herself? Did they know of her fragile condition? Still, Linette had promised to keep her quiet. He had to trust her. He could see Ladd playing tag with the boys. His son deserved a chance for such play.

"What would you like to see?" Mercy asked.

He pulled his thoughts to the promise of the afternoon. How long had it been since he'd been able to enjoy himself without worrying about the children?

"The barn." It seemed a good enough place to start.

They traipsed down the hill and entered it. The interior was dusky and empty.

"Almost all the horses are gone with the men," she said.

"Of course." He nevertheless toured the place. "I'd like to have such a big barn someday and a nice herd of cows. Right now though, I'd be happy to have enough room for my horse and a milk cow. And a decent-sized cabin." He knew he rambled but he couldn't help it. His little rental cabin and meager supply shed seemed laughable in contrast to this ranch.

"Where's your horse?" he asked to turn his mind from such thoughts.

"He's out in the pen behind the barn along with the half-dozen horses Eddie left behind in case we need them."

She led him out the door and around to the back and whistled. Her horse trotted up to her and whinnied. She patted his neck. "He's a real good horse. So easy to train."

He scrubbed at his neck. "Why do you want to join a Wild West show?"

She laughed a little and kept her attention on her horse. "Why not?"

"What would your family say?"

She shrugged. "I doubt they'd care."

Her words stunned him. "Of course they care."

Her gaze bored into him. "I'm sorry but you simply can't say that. You don't know." She headed past the pen.

He followed on her heels. "What makes you think they don't?"

She spun about to face him. "What makes you think they do?"

"I— Well, it just figures. Family cares about family."

"Really?" She moved onward. "What happened to your wife?"

He ground to a halt at her unexpected question. "What's that got to do with anything?"

She faced him, a look of victory on her face. "Seems she's family."

"She was. A reluctant part, I confess. She'd dead. She drowned."

Shock filled her face. "That's awful. I guessed she was gone but I thought—" She lifted one shoulder. "The children said something about her that made me think she'd been ill."

"What did they say?"

She considered his question. "Something about her not looking after them. I took it to mean she wasn't able because of poor health."

He snorted. "Not because of poor health but because of disinterest. She never wanted children. Didn't want to settle down." They fell in side by side and walked along the trail, crossing a wooden bridge over the river and climbing a slight hill as they talked. "When I wanted to settle down and become a family, she accused me of trying to end her fun."

Mercy brushed her palm against his arm. "That must have been difficult."

"Yes, it was. Though I had no one to blame but myself."

"Oh, I'm sure that's not true."

They reached the top of the hill and stopped walking. "I'm afraid it is. You see, when I was sixteen, I rebelled against my parents' rules. Against God's, too. I thought the rules ruined *my* fun. By the time I realized they protected me and those I loved, I was married to Ruby and had twin babies."

She stood so close to him that he felt her stiffen.

"I'm guessing you don't agree. Maybe you think more like Ruby."

"I'm not saying rules ruin my fun, but I guess I don't think they protect me either. That makes it sound like God sees and cares what we do. That He rewards obedience and punishes disobedience."

"I'd say that was true."

"It's what you believe. Seems Bertie does, too. But I'm not convinced it matters that much to God what we do. Oh, I don't think we should hurt others or disobey the ten commandments, but beyond that, do you really think He cares?"

Her voice had grown deep with emotion.

He wondered what triggered such a response. "What happened to make you believe this?"

"Nothing." But she answered too quickly. She looked at the hills beyond them and sighed. "I never stopped to consider why I believe that way. I suppose…" She paused. "I used to have a brother."

"Used to?"

"He died when I was six. He was eight. And the light of my parents' life. When he died, it seems they did, too. Oh, they kept breathing, kept doing their work, but they were never the same."

He felt her pain though he guessed she would deny it. He brushed his knuckles across her cheek. "I'm sorry. Sorry you lost your brother and, in a way, your parents."

Denial flared in her eyes and died before she could voice it. "Sometimes I felt they didn't see me." She walked onward at a pace that forced him to lengthen his strides to keep up.

"I guess that explains the Wild West thing."

She ground to a halt and flung around to confront him. "What do you mean?"

"Performing in such a show would make certain you weren't invisible."

She harrumphed. "I'm never invisible."

He chuckled. "You make sure of that."

She turned on her heel and steamed onward.

He kept pace. "But God is not your parents."

She stopped again. "What are you talking about?"

"You aren't ever invisible to Him. That passage Bertie spoke about this morning says, 'Thou hast beset me behind and before, and laid thine hand upon me.'"

She rolled her head back and forth. "You simply hope that by keeping rules of your own making you can ensure God will take care of you and your family. Like you can buy His protection. I just can't believe God can be controlled by our behavior."

"That's not why I obey rules. Rules give us safe passage."

"So why are you raising the twins alone?"

He ground to a halt and couldn't go on. Did she have any idea how her words hurt? How they stung at his beliefs? How many times had he asked the same question? Yet, what choice did he have except to continue to do what was best and trust God for the rest?

She realized he had fallen behind and turned to study him. A flicker of compassion crossed her face, then disappeared. "If God honors those who honor Him, then why are my brother and your wife dead?" Her words ended in a whisper so filled with pain he reached for her, resting his hand on her shoulder.

"I can't explain pain except to say it should serve to push us toward God, not drive us away from Him."

She shook his hand off. "If you need rules to make

you feel safe, that's fine for you. It doesn't work for me." She faced him, her eyes wide with determination.

He longed to pull her close and pat her back, assure her that rules did keep a person safe, but he knew she would not accept either his physical comfort or his words. "Mercy, I hope and pray that someday you will find out you don't need to get anyone's attention, including God's or maybe especially God's."

"I suppose I will then become ordinary and dull."

He leaned back on his heels and laughed. "I don't think you could ever be either of those."

The fight left her eyes, replaced by uncertainty as she studied him.

He sobered and met her look for look, unblinking before her intensity. His heart hammered and he tried in vain to tell himself he didn't care what she thought, but for some unfathomable reason, he did. Only, he reasoned, because he knew the folly of living a life of flaunting rules. He wouldn't wish that for anyone.

"What have rules ever done for me?" She flung about and headed for the ranch.

He trotted after her, trying to shepherd an argument that would convince her. He sighed heavily and his steps slowed. He'd never been able to make Ruby see the truth. Why should he think he would have any more success with Mercy? She would go her own way regardless of who got hurt in the process.

One thing he'd be certain of. Neither he nor his children would be victims of her wild ways.

They crossed the bridge. The happy screams of children at play filled the air. Thor, the tame fawn, bounced across the yard chasing a crooked-tailed dog. A little girl in a blue dress ran by giggling.

"Allie."

She kidded to a halt. "Hi, Papa."

He glowered at his daughter and then looked around the yard. "Who is supervising you children?"

The happy noise stopped. Half a dozen children stared at him. He felt their fearful waiting. It wasn't their fault. "Where's Linette?"

"She fell asleep," Allie whispered.

He turned on Ladd. "You know your sister isn't supposed to be running."

Ladd hung his head. "I didn't notice her."

Abel glowered at Mercy. "Why is it every time I'm with you my children end up in danger? Children, come here." They hurried to his side, both looking fearful. "We're going home." He turned to Mercy. "Be sure and thank Linette for her hospitality."

He strode to Sam, pulled the children up with him and reined away.

The last thing he saw was the narrowed-eyed look Mercy gave him.

She had every right to wonder at his sanity. How had he gone from living such a careful life, trying to protect his children from all harm to wandering around the country with Mercy, trying to convince her his way was best.

The children were quiet, no doubt afraid he was angry at them. He wasn't. Any more than he was angry at Mercy despite his harsh words. His ire was directed toward himself. He'd allowed a woman to make him forget his duties and responsibilities. Hadn't he learned the lesson well enough already? He scrubbed a hand across his eyes. He really should go back and apologize to Mercy. No, it would have to wait. Right now it was imperative he get Allie home and tend to her. *Please, God, don't let her little lapse damage her heart further.*

As soon as they reached the cabin he took the children inside. "Allie, I want you to go directly to bed." He could only hope that rest would offset the afternoon.

"But, Papa, I'm hungry."

"I'll make something to eat in a bit." He waited as she begrudgingly changed into her nightie and crawled into her bed. "Ladd, you make sure she's okay while I tend to the chores." He hurriedly cared for Sam and gathered an armload of firewood. As he approached the cabin, he heard Ladd talking and paused to listen.

"Allie, please stop. Papa will blame me if something happens to you."

What was she doing? He shoved the door open. If he wasn't mistaken, Allie scrambled into bed as he stepped inside. He eyed her for a full thirty seconds, but she only smiled sweetly.

He shook his head and heated up soup for them.

"Papa, can I sit at the table to eat?" Allie asked as he filled bowls for each of them.

He studied his daughter. Her cheeks were pink. If he didn't know better he would say she looked the picture of health. She squirmed about until her bedcovers were tangled. Perhaps she would be more comfortable at the table. "Yes, you may sit with us."

She bounced from the bed and across the floor, perched on the edge of her chair and wriggled until he feared she'd fall off or make herself sick. But she ate the entire contents of the bowl and finished before Ladd.

Obviously the child was overexcited. "Both of you get into bed and I'll read to you." That bedtime routine usually calmed them like nothing else.

They sat cross-legged on their beds as he pulled a chair close and read. He'd finished one page when Allie started to bounce, sending her bed hopping.

He lowered the book and stared at his daughter. "Allie, what's wrong with you?"

"I don't feel like being sick all the time." Another bounce emphasized her words. "I want to ride a horse like Mercy showed me." She sprang to her feet and pretended to balance as if standing on the back of a horse. "I want to do rope tricks like Mercy." To illustrate, she swung her arms over her head.

Ladd leaped to his feet. "And I want to shoot fancy guns." He twirled pretend guns.

Abel swept Allie into his arms. "You know you can't do that. Your heart won't take it." He held her close. What had he done by exposing his children to Mercy's wild dreams? And how was he going to change it? He still needed help with the children and she'd promised to watch them.

He eventually got the children settled and then cleaned up the supper dishes, his mind twirling with confusion all the while. If he had any other choice—

He could think of no option other than taking them to Linette. And she wasn't feeling well enough, she'd said.

Sleep did not come easily as his thoughts grew more tangled. He couldn't deny he'd enjoyed Mercy's company after church. And, yes, at church, too. She listened so intently. Perhaps only because she didn't agree. Poor Mercy. To be neglected by her parents after her brother's death. Again, he vowed to always put his children first, take care of their interests before his own.

Which meant he needed to accept Mercy's help even if she did leave him confused.

Having resolved the problem, he fell asleep.

But the answer didn't seem as clear the next morning.

He and the children had eaten breakfast and they'd helped him clean up between trips to look out the door to see if Mercy came.

"Papa, maybe she's not coming. You were rude to her yesterday. Why were you so angry with her?" Ladd asked.

"I had my reasons."

"Like Mama always had her reasons for leaving?" Allie whispered.

"Not like that at all." Ruby's reasons were selfish. His were self-preservation. A whole lot of difference.

"What if she isn't going to look after us anymore?" Ladd demanded.

He sighed. He didn't need Ladd pointing out that he might have burned some bridges, an act that might put him in a jam yet again.

It seemed contact with Mercy pushed him into one difficulty after another.

"But she said she'd come." Allie's voice grew strong and certain. "So she will." Then her face crumpled with worry. "Unless something's happened to her." Her eyes widened. "Maybe a bear got her."

He patted Allie's shoulder. "Do you think she'd let a bear catch her?"

Allie's eyes shone as she shook her head. "She'd rope him."

"Or shoot him," Ladd added, and the twins grinned at one another.

But what if that man in the woods had waylaid her? What if a wild animal had pounced on her? Would anyone think to go looking for her? They'd assume she was at his cabin.

"Let's go to the ranch and see what's keeping her."

The twins hurried to pull on coats as he went to saddle Sam.

He rode slowly, scanning the trail and the trees beside them. He strained to catch any unusual sound, all the while being careful not to alert the twins to his concern.

A dark shadow flitted through the trees on his right. He slowed Sam further and watched for another glimpse yet saw nothing more. Had it been the whiskered man? Or his imagination? But he knew he'd seen something beyond the normal shapes and shadows of the woods. His heart clawed at his ribs.

If the man had taken Mercy he would find her. But he wouldn't have the twins with him. He nudged Sam into a faster pace. He must take the twins to the ranch and then he'd go looking for Mercy.

If that man had harmed her…

Mercy swung the loop of rope into a huge circle and held Nugget steady as she tried to keep it swinging over the pair of them. It was harder than it looked and took a great deal of concentration. The loop caught on her shoulder and she sighed as she coiled it back into her hand to try again.

Thanks to Abel's taunts yesterday her concentration wasn't what it should be. *Why is it every time I'm with you, my children end up in danger?* The man had a whole repertoire of insults. Good thing she'd soon be gone…a star in a Wild West show. Maybe she'd even get her picture on a poster. She could imagine herself on Nugget's back as he reared up on his hind legs while she swung a rope around them. But first she had to perfect the trick.

She swung the rope into a circle again.

Would the children miss her? She let the rope fall. She already missed them. But she didn't miss their father.

Ignoring the way her arm had begun to ache, she again swung the rope into a circle.

The hoofbeats of a horse riding into the yard made her forget the trick. Linette had gone back to bed, and Jayne and Sybil had gone for a walk. In the cookhouse Cookie and Bertie might not notice the approach of a rider. She would see who visited. She coiled up the ropes and rode past the barn.

She saw a horse approach, with three riders.

"Mercy," Ladd called. "We've been looking for you."

Abel looked up at her. Surprise shifted to relief before his face darkened with anger.

She held her ground. She'd done nothing to justify such a dark look.

He lifted the children down. "Go to Cassie's house while I talk to Mercy."

The children scampered away. He didn't even bother to tell Allie not to run, a fact that scratched up Mercy's spine.

He swung off his horse and stalked toward her.

She stared down at him, determined not to reveal any hint of trepidation while, inside, she shivered at the way he studied her.

He planted his hand around her waist and lifted her to the ground.

"How dare you?" she sputtered.

"I'm not going to look up at you while I say my piece."

"There's nothing to say." At the way his jaw muscles bunched she wondered if she should have said that.

He planted his hands on his hips and glowered at her. "Why are you here?"

"I live here."

"I suppose you're practicing your fancy tricks." Each word dripped with disapproval.

"So what if I am? I don't see that it's any of your business." She jammed her fists on her hips and met him look for look.

"Right. A strange man is wandering the woods, maybe looking for a pretty young lady to kidnap, and it's none of my business." His breathing grew ragged.

She stared. "You were worried about me?" It didn't make sense. "But you don't even like me."

He narrowed his eyes. "Who says I don't like you?"

"You." She jabbed a finger at his chest. "You call me foolish, a menace, accuse me of being a danger." She delivered every word with a jab.

He caught her hand and held it firm. His eyes darkened. He scrubbed his lips together, then opened his mouth and closed it without uttering a word "I can't afford to like a woman. My children come first. Now and always."

She shook her head. What did that have to do with liking her? Or anyone. Must the two be exclusive? He was too much like her parents. Seeing her as inconsequential. She was tired of being seen that way.

She had to get away from him before she said or did something she'd regret. She grabbed Nugget's reins and led him toward the barn.

"Where are you going?"

She ignored him.

Muttering about stubborn women, he strode after her. "We need to talk."

"I have nothing to say and I certainly don't want to hear what you have to say." She stepped inside the barn and headed down the alley.

He followed her.

She turned and glowered at him, but her anger died at the way he looked at her.

He snagged a strand of her hair and brushed it off her cheek, sending a jolt of sweetness through her veins. Oh, to receive such loving touches. She'd longed for it all her life. But he didn't even like her.

She pulled away and continued walking down the alley.

A deep sigh followed her. "Mercy, it doesn't matter what we think of each other. The children need someone to watch them so I can work. Will you please come?" The words grated as if his throat closed off at having to beg.

Did it matter what they thought of each other? His feelings were adequately clear even though she found it impossible to pull hers into any kind of sense. Of course, she didn't care for him. He was an arrogant, judgmental rule keeper. Nor did she care what he thought of her.

Only trying to convince herself made her ache like a giant festering tooth.

"Please?" He stood in the middle of the alley, his hat in hand.

It hurt to see him beg. Even if he didn't like her and she didn't care about him.

"I didn't think you'd want me back after yesterday."

"I'm sorry. I spoke in haste. I wanted to come back and apologize, but I was concerned about Allie and rushed home. Will you accept my apology now?"

The ache inside her developed a teary feel. When had anyone, apart from Sybil and Jayne, ever apologized for unkind words to her? Mostly they didn't even notice that something they said had hurt her feelings. And she'd learned to hide her reactions.

She swallowed hard and sniffed. Hiding her feelings proved more difficult at the moment than ever before. "Apology accepted, and if you're sure you trust me with the children, I will take care of them."

He struggled to answer, no doubt unable to say he trusted her.

"If you don't, then are you wise to ask me to look after them?" She intended to press the matter.

Finally, he nodded. "So long as you remember Allie's fragile health."

She sighed long and heavy. "Abel, I know the pain of losing someone because of poor health. I lost my brother, remember? I would never put Allie's health at risk."

He closed the distance between them and again brushed his knuckles across her cheek. Again, she experienced a rush of something elemental and needy.

She was not needy.

"I'm sorry about your loss."

"It's in the past."

"Your feelings are not in the past. You're still try-ing—" He shrugged. "Never mind."

What had he said yesterday? About her wanting to do things so she wasn't invisible. But he was wrong. That too was in the past. She simply liked adventure. Didn't care for an ordinary life.

"Can you come today?" he finally asked. "I can still get some work done."

"Sure, I'll come now if you like."

"I would." He gave a quick grin that caused her to catch her breath.

A few minutes later they rode toward his cabin, Ladd and Allie chattering happily. As the trail widened they rode side by side and Abel smiled at her.

It didn't matter what he thought of her, but it was pleasant to enjoy a few minutes of approval.

Chapter Seven

Four days later, Abel returned with more logs. The weather had turned cold and damp, so Mercy and the children spent the days indoors. He jogged across the yard to the cabin and ducked inside, met by warmth and the smell of coffee simmering on the back of the stove. The children glanced up and called hello. Mercy had been laughing at something the children said and the smile lingered in her eyes.

He could get used to this sort of welcome.

Scraps of paper covered the floor. He didn't care for the mess, it bringing to mind Ruby's carelessness as a mother. But so long as it was cleaned up at the end of the day he tried to not let it bother him. "What are you doing?"

"Making a treasure map," Ladd said.

"We're going on a 'venture," Allie added.

His daughter's cheeks were slightly flushed thought Mercy had lived up to her word and kept the child playing quietly. Suspicion poked in an ugly thought. Did Mercy let them do rambunctious things when she knew he wouldn't be around? No. He had promised to trust her. Relied on the fact she'd lost a brother due to illness and, because of that, understood the risks for Allie.

"What kind of treasure? And what kind of adventure?" he asked.

Ladd grew serious. "Well, you see that's part of the adventure. We don't know where we're going or what we'll find."

"I see." He quirked any eyebrow at Mercy, guessing Ladd quoted her words. "So how will you know when you're there?"

She gave a little shrug as if to indicate she understood he found their play amusing. "We'll know. First sunny, warm day we're going treasure hunting."

"Not too far, I trust."

"Trust? Hmm."

He understood her disbelief. He'd promised to trust her, so how was he to make her understand his trust only went so far? He would never let someone put his children at risk, even if it meant constant checking and supervising.

He poured himself a cup of coffee and lifted the lid on a syrup bucket that she kept filled with cookies. He snagged a handful. He sure did appreciate the cookies and hot coffee waiting when he returned. And the children were getting lots of attention.

He drank deeply of the coffee, but the warmth that encircled his heart had nothing to do with the heat of the drink and everything to do with all the good things Mercy brought into his life and the lives of his children. Despite her wild ways. He ate the cookies hurriedly. "Thank you," he murmured as he headed for the door.

She rose and followed him outside. "For what?"

He twisted his hat between his fingers. "For looking after the children." The words fell short of what he meant. "For making life good."

She blinked, then widened her eyes.

"I gotta get back to work." He strode away so fast she must wonder what bothered him. And he couldn't explain that although the words were true they scared him, like being treed by a wildcat. Which was mighty close to the truth. Mercy was as close to being a wildcat as any woman he'd met. She would never belong in his life. She meant to join a Wild West show. This was temporary and he best keep that in mind for all their sakes and his sanity. No more women. Especially the kind that didn't care to settle down.

He worked so hard the rest of the afternoon that despite the cold, damp air, he was down to his shirt with the sleeves rolled up.

When he was about ready to head back to the cabin, a snap in the woods jerked him to full attention. Someone was out there. That strange man? The hair on the back of his neck tingled. What did the man want? Was he waiting for a chance to intrude into the cabin? Would he bother Mercy? Did he want something Abel had?

Slowly, he edged around to the horse and removed his rifle. He kept it at the ready as he made his way back to the cabin. He unloaded the logs, unhooked the stoneboat and took Sam to the corral to brush and feed. All the while he secretly scanned the area around the cabin. Had the man followed him? Would he wait for Mercy to leave? His nerves twitched.

How much risk did Mercy face as she rode back and forth? If only she could stay. He snorted. That was impossible. Under any circumstances.

Finally he made his way to the cabin. A couple days

ago he'd brought in a deer, and the succulent aroma of roasting venison filled the room. He breathed deeply. "Smells good."

"Everything is ready." She snagged her coat off the hook by the door. "I'll return tomorrow if you need me."

"I do."

She hugged the children goodbye and left, with Abel following her. "Mercy, about that man in the woods…"

She saddled her horse as he continued talking.

"He was watching me again today. I don't know what he's up to and until I do, I can only assume it's not good. So be careful on the ride home. Don't let your guard down for a moment."

She stood before him. "Are you worried about me?" Her words were teasing.

He gripped her shoulders. "I don't mind saying I am. There's something strange about a man hanging about watching others."

Her eyes filled with something he could only explain as longing, which made no sense so he dismissed the idea.

"I'm pretty good at taking care of myself," she said.

He couldn't seem to release her. He wouldn't know if she got back safely until she returned the next day. It was a long time to worry and wonder. "I know you are, but if the man got the drop on you what would you do?"

"Shoot him." She said it so matter-of-factly he laughed.

"What if he pins your arms behind your back?"

She scowled. "In that case he better be prepared for some well-laid blows from my boots."

"Promise me you'll be careful."

Her eyes bored into his, demanding something he

couldn't determine. Shoot. What was wrong with him? Only one thing mattered to him—that she get back safely. And she wanted only to be allowed to continue her training for the show. "Promise!"

"I am always careful so you don't need my promise." Her grin seemed a little lopsided.

"Nevertheless, I'd feel better if you give it."

She sighed. "Very well, I promise to be alert, to watch front, back and sideways, to keep my gun at the ready, to check every shadow, to ride like the wind at the first hint of danger…" She chuckled. "And to return tomorrow to put your mind at ease."

He let out the breath he'd been holding. "I know you're jesting but if you do everything you said, I might be able to rest."

She gave his chin a playful tap. "You'll rest just fine."

He caught her hand and pulled it to his chest. "Not everything is a joke, you know."

Her eyes darkened. "So you say. You see that's where you and I differ. I'm content to think life might be for fun while you make it a serious matter."

He pulled her closer. "It is a serious matter." The words growled from his chest. He half joked but only half. Then he kissed her forehead.

She jerked back. "What are you doing?"

Shock raced through his veins. What had he been thinking? "It's what I would have done to one of the twins." Though his concern didn't feel the same. "Now go and be careful. I'll see you tomorrow."

She stared half a second then swung into her saddle and rode from the yard at a gallop. At the edge of the clearing she swung Nugget around and had him rear up on his hind legs. "Until tomorrow," she called, and with a wild whoop disappeared into the trees.

He sighed. So much for leaving quietly so as not to alert the man in the woods. Yet he grinned at the place where he last saw her.

She sure did enjoy life.

He sobered. Where did that leave him and the twins? He knew the answer. He'd lived his wild life and found it unsatisfying. Now he had the children to think of and absolutely no intention of repeating his mistakes.

Thanks to Abel's overly developed sense of caution, Mercy's nerves twitched as she rode through the lengthening shadows. She shivered and not because she was cold. If only she could remember when and where she'd seen that whiskered man. Again she scoured her memories and again came up with nothing but a vague sense of having seen him somewhere. He'd been on the edge of the scene wherever it had been. Sort of a fleeting figure. Much like he was now. She simply couldn't place him.

A rustling in the underbrush sent her thoughts into a frenzy. Her arms tensed, her hand clenched her pistol. Then a rabbit hopped away.

See that's what happens when you let fears control you. You start to see danger when there is none.

But she couldn't deny a sense of relief when she broke into the clearing around the ranch. She shuddered. All those dark shadows had filled her with wild imaginations.

Sighing, she turned toward the sun tipping the top of the mountain peaks. Abel had intentionally stopped work early enough in the afternoon to allow her to ride back before the sun dipped below the mountains. At times like this, she appreciated his caution.

She exercised caution of her own the next morning as she returned to Abel's place, though she saw nothing to make her suspect the whiskered man hung about. Perhaps Abel had been mistaken in thinking he saw him. But she doubted it. Abel was far too careful to make such mistakes.

She rode into the clearing and spotted Abel waiting outside the cabin.

He puffed out his cheeks when he saw her and stepped forward. "I don't mind admitting I worried about you all night."

"Really? So why did I bother to promise I'd be careful? Wasn't that to ensure you wouldn't worry?" She swung off Nugget's back.

Abel did not move away, forcing her to stand toe-to-toe with him. "It didn't work."

"Because you don't trust me."

"No, because I don't trust that crazy man out there." He touched her cheek.

When had he gotten so free with his touches? Of course, he touched his children all the time. Guess it simply got to be habit. But why did she let it make her heart jump with eagerness as if hoping for more? The man out in the woods wasn't the only crazy person here. She seemed to have caught the disease.

"I'm glad you're here safely."

Did she imagine his voice thickened? As if her safety really mattered? Well, of course it did. Who would look after the children if something happened to her? Braced by the thought, she edged past him and made her way to the cabin.

He followed right behind.

She hung her coat and hugged the children then turned to regard Abel. Wasn't he going to work today?

He seemed to realize he stood at the door. "I best be on my way." He jammed his hat on his head and left.

That afternoon Abel exacted another promise for her to be careful, but he did not kiss her forehead in his fatherly way. Good thing. She might have taken objection to continued familiarity. The disappointment edging her heart was only imaginary.

When she arrived the next day, Abel's welcome was full of relief. "I won't rest until I find out who that man is and what he's up to."

She was not prepared to let worry cloud her day. "Like I said before, he's only a lonely old mountain man come down to avoid the early snowfalls." She didn't believe it, though. She'd never been in the mountains and couldn't have seen him there. And she knew she'd seen him somewhere.

"Can we go outside?" Ladd asked after Abel left.

"I'd say so. We wouldn't want to waste such a lovely day. Soon winter will be here." She gave a mock shiver. "In fact, I was thinking we should have our treasure hunt today." She'd let them create a map that would keep them close to the cabin yet allow them to explore as they followed clues.

Despite Abel's opinion of her, she wasn't so foolish as to wander into the woods with two children while a strange man was out there.

For the better part of two hours, they followed clues around the edge of the clearing. Finally they discovered the treasure—a bag Mercy had hidden. Inside was a small lariat for Ladd and a pair of fringed gloves for

Allie. Mercy had also packed a lunch and blanket and they sat down to enjoy their picnic.

Abel whistled as he worked. Another pleasant day. Each one a blessing, allowing him to hope he might achieve all he wanted and needed to do before winter set in.

The only thing marring the day was the knowledge that a crazy man wandered the woods.

He quickly prepared a load of logs and headed back to the cabin, anxious for a cup of strong hot coffee. And a glimpse of Mercy and the children.

He straightened and studied that thought. Of course, he wanted to assure himself they were all safe. No need to picture a welcoming smile from Mercy and a scheme of reasons to touch her, maybe even pull her into his arms. He'd allowed himself one brief kiss of her forehead. It meant nothing.

Shaking his head to clear his thoughts, he dismissed the whole notion. How many times did he have to tell himself that she did not belong in his plans?

So he forced himself to unload the stoneboat before he went to the cabin. And if he crossed the yard with hurried steps it was only because he longed for coffee and cookies.

He flung the door open and ducked inside.

The place echoed with silence. "Hello?" The cabin provided no place to hide. He called out again, louder. "Hello? Where are you?"

He lifted a stove lid and saw glowing coals. Why had she allowed the fire to die down? Because, he reasoned, the day was warm. The pail of cookies beckoned from the shelf but he no longer imagined their sweetness, only a dusty dryness.

Surely he'd overlooked them. He turned full circle. But the cabin remained silent and empty.

"Mercy, Ladd, Allie," he bellowed, his words reverberating in the room. They were gone. He grabbed the back of the nearest chair as his legs buckled. The crazy man in the woods had taken them. Just as he feared.

He raced back to Sam, grabbed his rifle and stared at the trees. Which way would he go? He opened his mouth to yell their names again, then clamped it shut. His call would only alert the man. Best he sneak up and catch him off guard.

If only he knew what direction to go.

He studied the problems for two seconds. Probably he'd head for the mountains. Having made up his mind, he headed west, moving carefully, pausing to look for an indication they had been there. He grinned when he noticed a broken branch. Perhaps Mercy had intentionally left clues.

Another branch led him to the right, as if circling the cabin. Had the man stood here, watched the cabin for hours? Maybe even days? The skin on his arms tightened at the thought.

He slowly made his way forward as he spotted a small footprint in the fallen leaves. Or at least that's what he thought it was. And he needed the encouragement to keep going. As he moved, he prayed. *God, keep them safe. Help me find them before—*

He would not think before what.

Did he hear Allie's voice? He straightened and listened. There it was again.

He crept forward. If he could surprise the crazy man—

There! Through the trees. Ladd and Allie sitting on the edge of a blanket. Where was Mercy? And the crazy man? His mouth dried so sharply he had to hold back a cough. The things the man might do to her…he dared not contemplate them.

He edged forward an inch trying to see her. Should he sweep in and snatch up his children? Would that put Mercy in more danger?

God, please guide me.

Something cold and hard pressed to the side of his head.

"Arms in the air." A low, guttural voice half growled the words.

He raised his arms. How had it come to this? He'd done all he could to protect his children. Gone out of his way to live a careful life so they wouldn't suffer the consequences of his choices. Yet he'd fallen into the hands of a crazy man. Who would look after his children?

"Turn around slowly."

He hesitated, giving his children a farewell look. *Be safe. Know I love you.* Then he slowly turned. And gasped. "You!"

Mercy grinned at him. "You ought to know better than to sneak around the woods when there's a stranger lurking nearby. I might have shot first and asked questions later."

He stared at her. "I thought—" He rubbed at his collarbone. "I thought—" He couldn't talk. His legs turned to weak ropes and he leaned against a tree. "You're safe. You're all safe."

She nodded. "Told you to trust me. I'm not as foolish as you judge me to be."

"I repent of all the times I said anything negative." He closed his eyes and willed his heartbeat to return to normal but it refused. There was only one way to calm it. He planted his hands on Mercy's shoulders and pulled her to his chest. "Just let me hold you for a moment."

She leaned into his embrace with a little chuckle. "If it will make you feel better."

He pressed his chin to her head. "It will." He breathed deeply. She smelled of sunshine and cookies. And horse. A smell he no doubt also wore. "Do you have any idea how frightened I was to return to the cabin and find you all missing?" His arms tightened around her as he recalled the moment.

She sighed. "Someday you will learn to trust me."

"It's not that I don't..." he protested, though he knew his worry seemed to prove otherwise.

"Yes, it is. But never mind." She eased out of his embrace, causing his heart to clench. "Two children are waiting to see what I found."

He nodded. He hadn't forgotten them but now that he knew they were safe, he felt no urgency to join them. The thought made no sense and he pushed himself away from the tree.

She led the way to the clearing. "Look what I found."

The children jumped up and raced to him.

"Mercy made us promise we would sit here and not make a sound until she came back," Allie said.

"She gave me a rope." Ladd showed Abel a coiled lariat. "She said she'd show me how to use it."

"Look at my gloves." Allie lifted the fringed pair for his inspection.

Being run over by a stampede of wild horses

wouldn't have made him feel any more confused. Just when he felt overwhelming gratitude for Mercy's care of his children she did something to remind him of who she really was—a woman intent on living a wild life. He stared at the gifts, more than half tempted to order the children to give them back. "What are you doing out here?"

Both children talked at once.

He caught enough to understand they were on a treasure hunt.

"We were about to have a picnic lunch," Mercy added. "Do you care to join us?"

The twins begged him to say yes.

He might have refused Mercy—or so he tried to convince himself—but he couldn't deny his children. "You sure there's enough for me, too?"

"We'll share," the children chorused.

So with more eagerness than he should allow himself, he sat cross-legged on one corner of the blanket while Mercy sat opposite him and the twins sat between them. A sense of peace engulfed him. "I really should get back to work." It was a token protest. He had no intention of leaving them out in the woods even if they were only a few yards from the cabin. Nor did he have the heart to order them all back inside.

He knew he was in trouble when he allowed himself to ignore his sense of caution, but he'd deal with his failure after he'd eaten.

Chapter Eight

Who was this man? Mercy passed around sandwiches and freshly scrubbed carrots recently dug from the garden at Eden Valley Ranch.

Abel obviously did not trust her. Yet he'd hugged her and she'd let him, though she couldn't begin to explain why. One minute he was all business, rules and being careful. The next, he plopped down to share a picnic right in the middle of a sunny day—the perfect sort of day for working in the woods.

Why had he hugged her so tight? And why had she let him?

Because it felt good and made her feel warm and secure and cared for.

She was indeed as foolish as he accused her of being. She didn't need anyone caring for her and hadn't in a very long time.

Except—a memory refused to be dismissed—how many times had she stood in a doorway observing her parents, wondering why they never seemed to see her? One time when she was about ten and far too old to act in such a way, she'd thrown a temper tantrum right in front of them. She only wanted them to acknowledge her.

Instead, the nanny had been summoned and Mercy had been locked in the nursery. After two days she no longer cared for anything but her freedom and had stolen out the door as a maid came to change the bedding. That was the day she discovered the joy of freedom.

She didn't intend to give up that joy for anything or anyone. Though, she allowed herself to confess, she'd discovered a different kind of joy in caring for the twins and seeing Abel's gratitude at the meal she left prepared for him.

The situation was only temporary.

Besides, she'd seen the pained look in his face as he considered her gifts to the children. He didn't approve of riding, roping or anything that seemed out of the ordinary and she had no intention of giving up her joyful freedom.

No sir! She didn't intend to give up anything and if Abel thought a little hugging would change her mind—

Well, she knew how to correct that.

"Ladd, when we're done here we'll go back to the corral and I'll show you how to handle a lariat."

Abel choked back the last of his sandwich and bolted to his feet. "Mercy, can I talk to you private like?"

Taking her agreement for granted he strode into the trees.

She noticed he didn't return to the spot where he'd hugged her and where she'd stuck a gun to his head. Not that he was ever in any danger. She'd heard him coming and gone to investigate. As soon as she saw it was him, she decided she'd show him who needed to be careful.

He stopped several yards from where the children

watched with wide-eyed interest. "I don't want Ladd learning silly rope tricks."

She'd known he'd protest. "I didn't have any such thing in mind. But he's nine years old. He lives on a ranch in the West. Likely he'll be around animals a lot. A boy should know how to throw a rope around a cow, wouldn't you say?"

"I'd say he's a bit young for roping cows."

"But not too young to start learning." Her challenge stung her eyes.

He scuffed his boots in the dry leaves. He jammed his fingers in his pockets.

"Surely you wouldn't want the boy to grow up to be a sissy. Would you?"

He closed his eyes as if he was in pain and let out a long-suffering sigh.

She knew it meant he'd given in and forced herself to not smile.

"Nothing fancy, mind you. Just roping a post."

She shrugged. "It's all I had in mind." Though if the boy got it in his head to try something more, she was prepared to turn a blind eye.

"I suppose you have something in mind for Allie with those fancy gloves."

She chuckled at his suspicion. "I thought it would be cute if she and I did trick riding together."

He jerked as if she'd shot him through the heart. "It would not! I warned you—"

She cut him off with a laugh and a playful punch to his shoulder. "You are so gullible. That's what comes of being so suspicious all the time." Not waiting for him to find his voice, she headed back to the picnic site.

"I am not suspicious," he called.

"You most certainly are," she flung over her shoulder. She reached the children, folded the blanket and stuffed everything into the sack. "Come on, you two. We've got roping to do."

Like a merry parade they returned to the clearing.

He went directly to his horse and fiddled with the harness while casting suspicion-filled glances in her direction.

She led the children to the corral. Allie sat by the fence while Mercy showed Ladd how to twirl the rope over his head.

Abel continued to delay his departure.

Mercy glanced at the sky. "The light is wasting." She directed her words at him.

He turned his back to her and left.

She brought her attention back to Ladd. But somehow teaching him to toss a loop had lost some of its joy.

Abel helped the children prepare to attend the Sunday service at the ranch. He would have skipped it except he didn't want the children to think missing church was acceptable. No, he'd face Mercy and never once let her guess how she managed to keep him dancing from one extreme to the other. First, he hugged her, then he was upset with her. What had he been thinking hugging her in the first place? Relief. That was all. He'd prayed for their safety and he'd been overcome by gratitude to see them safe and sound.

How did that indicate suspicion, as Mercy had said? It didn't. Of course, he knew she hadn't referred to that when she called him suspicious. She meant the way he always jumped to the protection of his children. And he always would. It was his job.

"Are you both ready?"

The twins nodded. Both of them looked eager for the visit to the ranch. For their sakes he would try to enjoy the day.

As they approached the ranch, he forced himself to be honest. He would enjoy the day for his sake, too. Seeing Mercy in a different situation filled his mind with possibilities. Perhaps they would take a long walk together.

He lifted the twins down from the horse and threw the reins around the hitching post, then headed for the cookhouse.

Allie grabbed his hand. "There she is." She pointed toward the big house, where Mercy stepped out the door with Linette and Grady.

He didn't need either of the children to point her out. He'd seen her the moment the door opened. Wearing an emerald-green dress, her hair coiled at the back of her head, she had donned a fetching straw-colored bonnet. At the sight of her, his lungs sucked flat. She made the perfect picture of a lady.

The children waved and called her name.

Mercy lifted a gloved hand in response.

Abel's arm came up of its own accord. This Mercy caused his heart to beat faster.

"Let's wait for her," Allie said, tugging at his hand to slow his advance toward the cookhouse.

He allowed Allie to hold him back though she might have noticed it took little effort. Then both she and Ladd broke away and ran toward Mercy.

She laughed as they approached and bent to hug and kiss them. They clung to her hands as they came to join him.

"Good morning," Linette said as she passed them.

"'Morning, ma'am." He yanked his hat off and then Mercy stood before him, her eyes shining with good humor, her mouth curved in an inviting smile.

He swallowed hard.

"Good morning, Abel. Isn't it a lovely day?"

He managed to find his voice. "It is a fine day. Shall we?" He tipped his elbow toward her, inviting her to put her arm through his.

With a little nod, she did so. The twins marched behind them.

Knowing what to expect from Cookie, he braced himself as the woman hugged him and patted his back hard enough to cleanse his lungs. He held Mercy tight to his side, thinking she needed protection, but she laughed and returned Cookie's hug.

Cookie leaned over to confront the twins.

Abel feared she might break Allie if she hugged the child but instead she straightened and opened her arms to them both. They went to her ample body and let themselves be pressed to her sides.

He sat next to Mercy as Cookie led the little group in singing. It felt good and right to be singing songs of faith with Mercy at his side.

Bertie rose to speak. "I know you ladies were hoping the men would be back by now."

They murmured agreement. Four young wives missing their mates. From what Abel knew, another young woman and her sister lived nearby and her husband was also on the roundup.

Bertie continued. "I could tell you all to be patient, to trust God to take care of your men, but I figure nothing I say will make you more patient for their return so

I'm not going to bother. Instead, I'm going to tell you how I met Cookie. Eliza, as I knew her then."

Cookie waved a hand in protest. "Oh, Bertie. They don't want to know that."

Bertie grinned at his wife. "I think they might enjoy it. Would you?" he asked the audience.

Even Abel nodded.

"There you go." He leaned back, a distant look on his face. "As most of you know, I wandered far from God. But He found me and brought me back. I had a long way to come and it took some time. One Saturday found me in a little town in western Montana. Everyone I knew had gone to the saloon. I no longer had any desire for that kind of life. But what was I supposed to do on a Saturday night? I remember looking up and down the street. Lots of noise and action both inside and outside the saloon. The general store was still open and a few people went in and out. Across the street the door of the hotel opened and closed. Through the windows of the main floor I could see straight into the dining room. Maybe I could find entertainment of a decent sort there. I dusted my clothes off as best I could and strode inside and found a vacant table. I'd barely sat down when this beautiful woman appeared at my side and handed me a menu. Well, I never did get a look at the menu. My Eliza commanded my full attention." He beamed at Cookie, who ducked her head.

"To this day I can't tell you what I ate. Only that it took until closing to finish it. I sat there as she cleaned up. Finally she came to me and said I'd have to leave. I asked her where a man could worship on a Sunday. She told me of the church she attended. I told her I hadn't been in church much in the past few years but I meant to change all that."

Cookie nodded. "You surely did, too."

Bertie and Cookie gave each other such warm looks that Abel felt he intruded into something very personal.

Then Bertie returned to his story. "She invited me to accompany her the next day. Which I did. We spent the afternoon together and learned about each other. And I'm proud to say we have spent the past thirty years together." He faced his wife. "I'm looking forward to the next thirty."

Cookie grinned. "Me, too, my love."

Bertie turned his attention back to his audience. "You might wonder why I'm telling you this. It's because no matter where I wandered or how far I got from God, He had plans for me. He led me to the right town, on the right day to meet Eliza. His love never fails."

Abel nodded as Bertie finished. Hadn't he found the same thing? God had blessed him with the twins and led him here, where he could build a safe and secure life for them all. *Thank you, God. Help me to honor what You have given me.*

They again gathered around the table to share coffee and cinnamon rolls, but he sensed a restlessness in the others. The children finished and moved away to play.

Linette wandered to the window to look out. "It's snowing up higher. I can see it from here."

Sybil went to her side. "I'm sure they're all safe."

Her voice was so strained he wondered if she believed it herself.

"There are so many dangers out there," Linette said. "Snowstorms, wolves, bad men—"

Sybil laughed a little. "And young women accidently shooting innocent cowboys."

Abel turned to stare at Mercy. "Who'd you shoot?"

The others chuckled as Mercy bristled. "I didn't shoot anyone." Her eyes narrowed. "At least not yet, though I've been sorely tempted."

The laughter increased.

Jayne let out a long sigh. "It was me. I wanted to learn to shoot a gun."

Mercy shook her head. "You were supposed to keep your eyes open." She turned back to Abel. "That's how she met Seth. Poor man."

Jayne's expression grew fierce. She looked at Bertie. "I can verify what you say. The circumstances weren't good, but God used them to bring us together. I will never cease to thank Him."

"Me, too," Sybil said. She faced Abel to explain. "Brand rode in to break horses for Eddie. He was aloof and mysterious because his father and brother were part of the Duggan gang and he didn't want anything to do with them." She shuddered. "But God spared him and the Duggan gang was conquered."

Linette withdrew from the window. "I can also say that God turned an unfortunate situation into a blessing. I arrived here thinking Eddie had offered me a marriage of convenience. But he expected his former fiancée to come in answer to his letter." She looked past them, a smile wreathing her face. "He didn't think I was at all suitable but over the winter we learned we were perfect for each other." She drew in a long breath. "God is good to us all."

"Don't leave me out," Cassie said. "Look what God's done in my life. I planned to be independent, but I soon found it was nothing compared to being mother to four lovely children." She nodded toward her family playing across the room. "And a loving husband. But I do miss him. I wish they would ride in this moment." The four ladies crowded to the window looking west, where they hoped to see their men.

"I hope they're safe," Linette said as the cold wind blowing down the valley whistled past the cookhouse.

Mercy snorted softly. "You all talk about how God guided you and then you fret and worry because the men haven't returned."

Linette turned and drew the other women with her. "Mercy is absolutely right. God will protect our loved ones."

Mercy waved her hands. "Enough of this. You'll soon be in tears if you keep it up. Makes me glad I don't have a husband to worry about. Now let's plan something fun."

The women crowded around her, pushing Abel closer to her side.

"What do you have in mind?"

Seems they were all eager for something to divert them.

She lifted her hands. "Nothing specific."

"I know." Linette grew eager. "Let's plan a party for when the men return." Her suggestion was greeted with a chorus of approval and they all began to talk at once.

Before he knew it, Abel had agreed to attend and to add something to the program. "What will I do?"

The women studied him.

Mercy jabbed his ribs. "Now don't you wish you knew some roping tricks?"

"Not really." An idea had formed but he decided to keep it a secret. "I'll think of something."

They turned back to the others and their plans. The talk continued as they climbed the hill to the big house and all throughout dinner. Abel felt a little out of place after the meal. The women washed the dishes, while the children played in the front room. He didn't feel like dragging the twins away yet. Didn't want to return to the tiny cabin and his lonely thoughts.

"I could check on things around the place if you like," he offered to Linette.

"I'd truly appreciate that. Mercy, you go with him."

"Me?"

Did she have to act as if it was an insult? He was about to say he didn't need her company when Jayne shoved her forward.

"You know you're dying to get out of this hot kitchen."

Mercy laughed. "I am, indeed." She grabbed her shawl and hurried from the room.

"Don't shoot him," Jayne called.

"Or rope him like a calf." Sybil giggled.

"Girls, don't tease her," Linette interjected calmly.

Cassie followed them down the hall. "No fighting either. Half the time the two of you look ready to bite the other's head off." She sighed dramatically. "The rest of the time you look like you wish the rest of us would disappear."

Mercy glowered at her. "Can you guess what I'm wishing right now?"

Cassie laughed.

"I think it's time to leave." Abel pulled Mercy's arm though his and walked them to the door. "Let's have a look around and make sure everything is as it should be." The door closed behind them. "Do any of them know about the man in the woods?"

"I've not said anything."

"No need to worry them," he replied, "but let's take a look around."

And so they circled the place, checking for tracks or signs of the man. They reached the hill they had visited the Sunday before and paused to peruse the area.

"It's gotten cold," Mercy said, pulling her shawl tighter around her shoulders. Still she shivered.

He put an arm about her and pulled her to the shelter of his body. "Like Linette said, there is snow up higher."

"I hope it doesn't get down this far." She looked up at him. "What will you do if winter sets in before you're ready?"

He studied her upturned face, gratified to see she cared. "I can keep working unless the snow gets heavy, and I wouldn't expect that this time of year."

"I'd help you if I could."

"You are helping. Having you with the children allows me to be out in the woods."

"I meant I'd like to help you in the woods."

He tightened his arm about her shoulders. "I prefer to think of you at the cabin with the children."

She quirked her eyebrows. "Are you saying you don't think I could handle the work?"

He tipped his head to touch hers. "If I said that it would spur you to prove otherwise, wouldn't it?"

"Of course not. But I could do it."

"Be glad you don't have to."

She squirmed. "Glad?"

"Mercy, why do you have to take objection to everything I say? I'm trying to be friendly and nice here."

She softened and leaned into him a bit more. "And here I thought you were trying to turn me into your usual type of woman."

"My usual type of woman was a saloon girl. It's not something I wish to repeat."

She pressed her head to his. "I'm sorry. I didn't mean to remind you." She shifted to stare out at the landscape. "Tell me about your parents. Do you have siblings?" She drew in a sharp breath. "Look. Something's moving in the bushes."

He squinted at the spot she meant. Indeed, a shadow shifted and a four point buck slipped into the sunlight.

She chuckled. "I'm getting so I see danger in every little shadow." She told how she'd gotten all nervous at a rabbit. "It's your fault. You're so worried about that man in the woods."

"A person can never be too careful." He drew her to a grassy spot and they sat down. He thought she might withdraw but she shivered and pressed closer. For the time being, he didn't mind the cold weather.

"I have two brothers," he began. "One three years older and the other two years younger. They are both working with my father in a shipbuilding business back in Nova Scotia."

She twisted to look into his face. "Shipbuilding? I'd have never suspected."

"Why not?" Her surprise was a little off-putting.

"I don't know. Shipbuilding seems like the ultimate adventure. Didn't you want to get on one of those ships and sail around the world?"

"Shipbuilders aren't necessarily sailors. Besides—"

He shrugged, at a loss for words. He'd had big ideas but not of sailing away. He couldn't put his finger on the reason he'd been so restless. Nothing he could think of made sense now.

"What?" When he didn't answer right away, she nudged him gently. "Tell me."

"I guess I longed for adventure but I went after it the wrong way. I threw out the rules with the pursuit of excitement."

She studied him a long moment. "You believe you can't have one without the other? It's either rules or excitement?"

"Isn't it?"

"I don't think so. I don't have to enter a wayward way of living in order to enjoy my life."

He squeezed her shoulders, not wanting to argue yet uncomfortable with the direction she meant to take her life. "Frank is my older brother. He's very rigid. Everything by the book. I used to resent him for that but now I understand why he was like that. It was because in the shipbuilding business you can't afford to make mistakes."

"And your younger brother?"

"John." He knew his smile filled the word. "We used to have a lot of fun together." He didn't go on.

"What happened?"

"My father took me into the business and he and Frank made it clear there was no room for fun."

She tsked. "I can understand why you left."

"I was wrong. I needed to grow up and accept responsibility." He sighed. "But I did miss playing with John. We used to play tag, toss a ball back and forth and go on great adventures."

She sat up, allowing his arm to fall to his side. "I remember playing with Butler...that's my brother." She turned and stared at him. "I couldn't remember before now. I always wondered if we did. But we did. We played chase. I suppose it was a form of tag. I remember giggling so hard I couldn't run anymore. I'd fall down on the ground and he would lie beside me and we'd stare at the sky." She looked up as if trying to recapture the feeling. The light caught on her cheeks, revealing silvery tracks of her tears.

With a muffled groan he pulled her into his arms and pressed her face to his shoulder. His heart thumped against his ribs. "Don't cry, Mercy. Please don't cry."

She grabbed his coat front and squeezed the fabric in her fists.

How did he stop her pain? Make it go away? He tipped her head back and kissed each cheek, capturing the still silent tears.

Her eyes grew wide and...dare he think she invited more? Before he could reason a response, he captured her lips, feeling the dampness of tears, feeling her uncertainty. He had started to draw back when her arms came around his neck and she sighed. He captured the sigh and deepened the kiss.

It began as a means of comfort but grew into something more. In the back of his mind he understood he would have to explain this to himself. But he'd do it later. For now, he gave comfort and he also received it.

The kiss ended. She sighed. "I shouldn't have done that."

"Done what?"

"Cried." Relief surged through his heart. He was afraid she might have meant the kiss.

"I'm sorry if what I said was responsible."

She smiled a glorious, glowing smile. "Don't be sorry. I'm grateful for remembering my brother that way. It seems—" She shook her head. "It seems all I could remember was the deathly quiet after he was gone."

"We're more alike than one would think."

"How's that?"

"Seems fun left your life when your brother died. Mine ended when I had to grow up. Unfortunately, it led me to make some dreadful mistakes." He wanted to warn her against making similar mistakes but she bounded to her feet.

"I hear the warning in your voice—don't say it. Don't ruin the moment." She reached down and held her hands out to him.

He let her pull him to his feet and retained her hands, edging her close so he looked down into her dark eyes.

They were so different—she craved adventure; he lived carefully.

But they'd found a special closeness between them today. Though he knew it could only be temporary, he didn't want to spoil it.

Chapter Nine

Mercy's throat clogged with tears. Butler had become a happy memory. She remembered laughing and playing with him. Abel would never understand the beautiful gift he'd given her in causing her to remember Butler this way. Not even his disapproval could mar the joy.

He touched his forehead to hers. "I wouldn't think of spoiling the moment." His voice had grown husky.

She rested against him, so filled with quivering softness she knew she would sob if she tried to talk. The wind tugged at her shawl and he drew it more closely around her shoulders.

"I must take the children home before it gets any colder." But he did not move for two more heartbeats. Then he pulled her to his side...to protect her from the wind, she assured herself.

They went down the hill and got Sam.

She had to say something. Let him know how much she appreciated all he'd done. "Thank you for the nice day." Such inadequate words.

"I made you cry."

"They were good tears."

He touched her cheeks with his cool fingertip. "You're sure?"

"I'm sure." She squeezed his hand and pressed it to her cheek, wanting to plant a kiss in his palm but afraid of her trembling emotions. She had no desire to start crying in earnest.

He pulled her to his side again as they led the horse up the hill. They paused outside the door and as he looked down at her, his gaze drifted across her face, lingered on her lips, then came to her eyes. His smile seemed full of regret.

"I have to go."

She nodded and stepped to the door.

He followed and called the children. "See you tomorrow?"

"Of course."

He and the twins were soon on Sam's back. He wrapped a blanket about the pair and tucked them close to him.

She smiled. One thing about Abel—he would always take care of those he loved. Her eyes stung as she watched them leave. She had not known such loving care from her parents but thanks to Abel, she remembered when life had been kinder.

Cassie shepherded her children out the door. "My goodness, that wind has a nasty bite."

Linette stood at the window, holding Grady's hand. Mercy knew she wouldn't be able to relax until she saw Eddie and hugged him.

Mercy slipped past and went to the kitchen, where Jayne and Sybil visited.

Sybil studied her hard. "You have the look of a woman who's been kissed. Well kissed."

Heat flamed Mercy's cheeks. She would not confess she and Abel had kissed. How would her friends interpret it? *She* didn't even know what to think. "Abel told me how he and his brother played tag and chased each other. It made me recall Butler playing with me." She sucked in air. "I'd forgotten everything but the tiptoeing quiet of his illness and the deathly stillness that followed." She shuddered a sob. "I miss my brother."

Both Jayne and Sybil rushed to her side and wrapped arms about her. They patted her back and made soothing noises as Mercy struggled to contain her emotions. After a few minutes she was able to breathe normally and she gave a tight chuckle. "I'm fine."

The girls pulled chairs close and sat holding her hands.

Jayne spoke. "It's like Bertie said, God brings people into our lives at just the right time. He's sent Abel into yours to help you remember good times."

Sybil chuckled. "I think God might have brought him into Mercy's life for more reason than that."

Mercy made a protesting noise. "He doesn't approve of me."

Jayne drew back, her mouth open in mock surprise. "You don't say!"

Sybil patted Mercy's hands. "There's a difference between not approving of some of your activities and not approving of you." She nodded as if her sage advice should make all the difference in the world when it made little sense to Mercy.

Determined not to rob herself of the comfort Abel had provided as she cried, she refused to analyze why it had felt so good to be in his arms and why she had accepted his kiss.

And even more. Why had she offered a kiss in return?

The questions remained unanswered the next morning as she watched Linette return again and again to look out the window.

The cold wind continued, giving Linette cause to worry about the men.

"Do you want me to stay?" Mercy asked.

"No, no. I'm fine." Linette sighed. "Or at least I will be as soon as I can see and hold Eddie again. I miss that man so much I feel ill."

Mercy wrapped an arm about Linette's waist. "You should rest."

"I know. I'll be okay. Truly." As if to prove it to them both, she sat in her green wingback chair and pulled out a little garment she'd been stitching.

But Mercy knew she could see the trail coming in from the west as clearly from her chair as she could standing at the window.

"You go look after those children. And don't worry about me. There's only one thing that will make me feel better and that's Eddie striding through the door." Linette's voice caught and she ducked her head to concentrate on her sewing.

Mercy guessed she wanted to hide her trembling lips and teary eyes. Staying here would do nothing to ease Linette's lonesomeness. Only Eddie could do that, so Mercy donned a heavy winter coat and headed for the door. "I'll be back before dark. Perhaps the men will return before I do."

Linette nodded. "Be careful."

"I always am."

Sybil and Jayne both stood at the window of their cabins as Mercy rode by. She waved, knowing they didn't watch for her. All the women were so tense. It made her glad she didn't have to worry about a man returning.

Alert to any danger as she rode through the woods, she nevertheless smiled just recalling the previous day. Abel had been so solicitous. Her smile faded and she narrowed her eyes. Did he see her as a responsibility? Like one of his children? She snorted. If so, he would soon enough learn she didn't need looking after, though she acknowledged a tiny argument to the contrary. It had felt good to be sheltered in his arms.

She reached the cabin. Abel must have been watching for her for he strode from the cabin as she swung from Nugget's back. "You came."

"Any reason I wouldn't?" After all, she'd said she would.

"I guess not."

"There you go again. Always so suspicious." Her words were sharp but she didn't care. Must they always circle his lack of trust in her? "You're always certain I'm going to fail or disappoint."

"I am not. It's just that it's cold. I thought you might think you…we…should stay in where it's warm."

She gave him a hard look, not believing his excuse. "What I thought is that I said I would come, so I did. What I thought was you need to get things done while you can, so here I am."

He couldn't quite meet her eyes.

She grabbed his elbow and shook him. "Admit it. You don't trust easily."

He brought his gaze to hers. Dark blue misery. "Mercy," he growled. "I don't trust myself."

"What?"

"I've made such foolish mistakes. I live with the consequences but so do my children." His voice deepened. "So did Ruby." He shook his head. "I can't let my emotions guide my decisions. That's how I get led astray."

She dropped his arm. "Are you saying if you like something it's automatically wrong?"

"Of course not." He shrugged. "Maybe."

"Sounds to me like you think having fun is wrong."

He shuffled his feet. "Maybe not wrong, but risky."

"Guess that includes me." She flung Nugget's saddle over a sawhorse and stomped past him toward the cabin.

He raced after her. "I have to live by rules if I want the twins to be safe."

She paused to give him another hard look. "Safe or overprotected?"

He drew back.

But she wasn't done. "Be careful you don't make them afraid to face life."

His look could have burned a hole in wood. "You forget I have a daughter who must be taught to be very careful or the consequences could be fatal."

"I know that. Though—" She'd wondered a time or two and now that he'd brought it up, she might as well say it. "Could the doctor have been mistaken?"

He jabbed his finger at her. "You will not take it upon yourself to presume to know more than the doctor."

"I could promise I would never put her at risk, but seeing as you don't trust my promises there isn't much point. However, maybe you should get another opinion. Take her to another doctor. Or are you afraid?"

He snorted and ground about to head back to the corral. Before she closed the door behind her, he thundered from the yard.

She sighed. How had she gone from anticipation at seeing him and being reminded of the closeness she thought they'd enjoyed yesterday and her even being thankful to him, to this churning resentment?

She pushed away her mental turmoil and turned her attention to the eager children.

He didn't return until late afternoon, when it was time for her to leave. She told herself she didn't care. Tried to convince herself she wasn't getting as bad as Linette, glancing out the window every few minutes to see if he rode into the yard.

She slipped on her coat and headed for the corral before he unloaded his logs.

When he saw her intention of leaving before he got to the cabin, he jogged over.

The time had come. She closed her eyes. All day she'd wondered if she'd pushed too far, feared he would ask her to stay away from him and the twins.

"I want to apologize," he said. "You're right. I'm far too suspicious. But it's only because I don't trust my own judgment." He smiled a little. "I can't afford to repeat my mistakes."

She had expected a scolding. Not an apology. Especially when she'd told herself all day she deserved one. "It's my fault. I need to learn to mind my own business."

If she thought her apology would relieve him, his stubborn expression convinced her otherwise. "I know you care about the children and they care about you, so I can't ask you not to voice your opinion about them."

She blinked. "You're saying you don't mind?" She shook her head. "You're sure?"

He nodded, a little sheepish. "I'm not saying I won't continue to be—"

"Suspicious?" she supplied.

"It's not a nice word but, to my embarrassment, I have to admit it's accurate. I'll try to do better. Can you be patient with me?"

What had happened to this man? Had he spent time out in the woods thinking about her accusations? While she indulged in misery in the cabin thinking she had overstepped the boundaries and he would never forgive her?

He touched her cheek. "Friends?"

"Of course." She nodded, too confused to do otherwise.

He lowered his hand to her shoulder and squeezed. "Thank you."

"You're welcome."

A warm smile curved his lips. His eyes darkened. He leaned toward her to plant a quick kiss on her mouth, then pulled back before she could react. "Now be on your way before it gets dark."

She didn't move, too stunned by this sudden change in him and by the way relief surged through her veins.

He turned her toward Nugget. "Will I see you tomorrow?"

She swung into the saddle and looked down at him. "I'll be back." A little bubble of laughter left her lungs, riding the wind as she headed toward the woods.

* * *

Abel could not explain his actions. She wasn't right for him. She represented all he'd once been and had vowed never to be gain—wild, undisciplined. And yes, he found himself reluctantly attracted to her. But never again would he go down that path and therefore he did his best to drive her away. Except every time he tried to do so, he hated himself for hurting her and missed her before she'd even left.

God, help me. Give me strength to do the right thing.

Not that he could even say what the right thing was anymore.

He made his way to the cabin. The kids played contentedly on the bed with little animals created from folded paper.

Savory hash was ready for his supper.

This side of Mercy he enjoyed and appreciated.

They ate and cleaned up, then he read to them. Allie insisted on taking the fringed gloves to bed with her.

If only Mercy would abandon her plans to join the Western show. Maybe then he could begin to trust his feelings for her. Maybe then he wouldn't have to quell his eagerness for her to return the next morning. He forced himself to sit at the table and wait for her even after he heard her ride into the yard.

Allie and Ladd raced for the door.

"Wait here. It's cold out there."

"But we want to see Mercy," his daughter said. "She said she'd bring us a game."

"Wait." He'd allowed not only himself but the twins to grow too fond of her, too anxious for her return each morning.

Her boots sounded on the wooden step outside. The

twins hovered at the door. It took all his rigid self-control to remain at the table.

She flung the door open, her face wreathed in happy greeting. "Good morning." She hugged the twins before turning her face toward Abel.

"The men returned last night just before dark. You have never seen so much hugging and kissing and crying." She laughed. "What a commotion. The men were as bad as the women."

"They cried?" Ladd sounded incredulous.

Mercy chuckled. "No, but they sure did laugh."

"There were glad to see each other." Allie sighed with the joy of the idea. "I'd be like that, too." She turned to Abel. "Were you and Mama like that?"

Abel's mouth fell open. He'd been thinking of how glad he was to see Mercy come each morning. Ruby had not even entered his thoughts. "I was always glad to get home and see you two." He felt the twins studying him.

Ladd sighed. "Mama and Papa weren't like that."

"Mama never hugged us either. How come?" Allie looked about ready to cry.

"You've just forgotten," Abel said, but the stubborn look on both little faces said otherwise.

Mercy hung her coat and turned back to the room. "Linette says we'll have a great big party on Friday. Everyone is invited. She wants us all to celebrate."

He could have hugged her for diverting the children from regrets about their mother. "We'll certainly be there, won't we?"

The twins nodded.

"Have we ever been to a party?" Ladd asked.

Abel scrubbed at his hair. "Why, I don't know. Didn't Mama take you to any?"

Their two heads shook a negative response.

"Mama went to her parties by herself," Ladd said.

This conversation threatened to take him down paths in his memory he didn't care to travel. His parties had been wild, wicked events. He'd never gone to one after the twins were born, while Ruby had never quit. "I need to get to work." He shrugged into his heavy woolen coat. "Will you be okay?" He looked at Mercy, wondering if she would be able to handle the questions the children would likely voice about their mother.

She grinned at him. "You can trust me. Remember?"

Her teasing reminder lifted his concerns and he grinned back. "I do. Remember?" He scuffed his fist across her chin and walked out the door, singing one of the hymns from the Sunday service as he left.

Mercy's laughter rang out, following him from the yard. It continued in his heart as he worked.

Realizing he had gone from resolving to guard his heart to smiling at a shared few minutes, he bent his back to the work of the day. He must get a cabin built and firewood stacked.

Several hours later, he straightened to wipe his brow and stretch his aching back. He downed half the water in his canteen. As he recapped the container, a crackling noise drew his attention to the right. Was that strange man watching him again?

The crazy man posed danger to himself and those back at the cabin. Every day as Mercy rode back and forth, the risk of who he was and what he wanted haunted her ride. Anger raced up Abel's spine and pooled behind his eyes. "Who are you? What do you want?" He roared the words. "Come out and identify yourself."

Only silence, as heavy as a January snowstorm, answered him. His horse whinnied and shook his head. Sam, too, sensed the strangeness of someone watching them.

"Show yourself," Abel called again. He listened and waited, hearing nothing but his own heartbeat. The man must have left.

Abel returned to his work, his nerves twitching with every real or imagined sound. An hour earlier than normal, he packed it in and headed back to the cabin.

Not until he stepped into the warm interior and counted three happy, surprised occupants did he finally relax.

Sooner or later he was going to track down the man in the woods and confront him. Not until then would he be at ease.

Mercy came to his side. "You're back early. Is something wrong?"

He lowered his voice so the twins wouldn't hear him. "I heard that man in the woods again. I won't feel safe until I find out who he is and what he's doing."

She nodded, though her eyes remained skeptical. "I'll head for home then. Linette will be up to her ears in plans. I can help her. I've left you a pot roast and vegetables cooking. It will be ready whenever you are."

He followed her outside. "I know you don't need the warning—nevertheless, I have to say it. Be careful. There's danger out there."

She grinned at him. "So you are fond of saying. But like I've said time and again, I am always careful. I am not going to live my life in fear." Imitating his action, she brushed her fist across his chin. "Life is too short to waste it worrying about what might happen."

"My experience has given me reasons to worry that people won't get home safely."

"I'm not Ruby."

"I know you're not." There were differences between the two women, significant ones. Mercy loved spending time with the children. She made the cabin smell like home. She had always come when she said she would. But there were similarities, too. That wild streak. Not wanting to settle down and be ordinary.

She began to saddle Nugget. "Tomorrow then?"

"If you can come. I need to get my work done before the snow comes."

She swung into the saddle and rode away.

What he hadn't said was he wanted her to return even if he didn't have logs to get. But soon winter would be here and there'd be no need of it.

The thought shivered through his mind like a cold winter wind.

Chapter Ten

A͟bel repeatedly told himself he must not care about Mercy, but every time he had himself convinced of this fact she would do something that made him forget his decision.

Like the next day when she had the children draw pictures and post them all over the cabin.

"You remember this, Papa?" Ladd asked, leading him to the picture beside the table.

Abel leaned closer to examine the drawing. It looked like a little house with a brown door and a body of water behind it. "What's this?"

"'Member the house we lived in by the lake?"

He nodded. "I do. You and Allie were five years old. I had to warn you to stay away from the water."

"We learned to swim."

Abel straightened to study his son, then shifted his gaze to Allie. "You did?"

"Mama said we could play in the water when you weren't home."

Abel lifted his gaze to Mercy. He knew his eyes were filled with so many things…regrets, mostly. But also a touch of anger that Ruby had ignored his wishes. Not that he should have been surprised.

Mercy smiled gently. "Learning to swim is a good thing."

"I guess so." That wasn't the point, but he didn't expect her to understand.

Allie tugged at his hand. "I drew this one. It's Mama in her prettiest dress."

A stick woman wore a bright red dress, her yellow hair tied with a matching bow. He wished he could forget that outfit. It had a revealing neckline and whenever Ruby put it on she got a faraway look in her eyes. He knew it meant she would soon be taking one of her trips. "What else do you have?"

Allie pointed to the next picture.

"A ball?" A blue one with white stripes.

"You gave me and Ladd balls for Christmas when we were little."

"So I did." He hugged the pair to his side. "You played with them for days. What happened to them?"

Ladd sighed heavily. "We lost them."

Allie shook her head. "No, we forgot them when we moved. They were in the backyard."

Ladd nodded. "I wonder if someone else found them."

Abel shifted to the next picture. Mercy stood nearby and as he held her gaze, he felt a jolt of sympathy from her. He vowed he would not let his emotions show in his face. She didn't need to know the depth of his hurt at Ruby's failure to be a parent or a wife.

Ladd directed his attention to the picture.

"A plate of cookies?" he guessed.

"Gramma Lee used to live next door and she would bring us cookies for special occasions."

"I didn't know that."

"You weren't home. And Mama was gone a lot."

Silent accusations filled his heart, draining it of everything but regret. He knew Ruby didn't stay home all day every day, but only recently had he realized how frequently she'd been absent.

The twins drew him to the next picture. A stick girl in a bed with a brown cover.

"It's Allie," Ladd said. "When she was sick. I was so scared. Mama was gone. I wished Gramma Lee still lived next door, but we'd moved."

The three of them stared at the picture. If Abel was a child or a woman he might have cried. Instead, he sucked back sorrow as sharp against his throat as steel filings and clamped his teeth together. The air about them seemed fragile. He could hear the twins breathing, and his own breath cut through his lungs.

He couldn't take the memories, the pain and the regrets any longer. He spun around and hurried out the door, closing it quietly behind him.

His emotions drove his legs like pistons as he strode to the edge of the clearing and stared into the trees.

The click of the cabin door informed him someone had come out. Mercy was then at his side, and she brushed his arm.

"I didn't mean for the pictures to upset you. I suggested the children draw things to decorate the cabin. It was meant to be a surprise for you. They wanted to know what to draw. I said draw some of their favorite things or things they remembered…" Her voice trailed off.

"I'm not blaming you. I'm blaming myself. I knew Ruby wasn't taking care of them as she should but I kept hoping things would improve."

She pressed her hand to his arm. "I'm sure you did what you thought best."

He no longer believed it or excused himself. "We moved a lot," he said. "I told myself it was necessary so I could find work, but mostly it was to satisfy Ruby's restlessness." He closed his eyes against the pain of his past. "It was all so futile."

Her hand tightened against his forearm. "There's no value in blaming yourself for the past. Nor in letting regrets cripple you. I'm certain you did what you thought best at the time."

The warmth of her hand slipped up his arm and sent calming blood to his heart. "I suppose I did." It was small comfort considering how everything had turned out, but even small comfort was welcome.

He faced her. "I will never put the children at risk again. Not for anything."

She drew back and dropped her hand from his arm, leaving him cold and alone. "Why do I get the feeling you're saying that as a warning to me?"

"No more to you than myself. I found it far too easy in the past to think my decisions wouldn't affect others. I was so wrong."

"Perhaps you were." She took a step away, then stopped. "But there is a risk of swinging too far in the other direction, don't you think?"

They studied each other. At times like this, Abel realized how far apart their philosophies were. He wished it could be otherwise but unless she changed...

Because he would not.

After she left, he went to the woodpile and lifted his ax. Wood needed to be split for the winter. Chop. Chop. Chop. Bits of yellow, pine-fragrant wood scattered at his feet. He pressed his boot to the length of log and chopped until the log disappeared into a mangled pile of wood chips. He tried to remember how careful he must be but her laughter weakened his defenses, making it difficult to think of her as merely a friend.

Finally spent, he wiped his brow and returned to the cabin and care of the children but the wood chopping had not helped clear his thoughts.

He looked forward to her return tomorrow for more than just the children's sake.

The day of the party arrived. Abel was grateful Mercy wasn't coming to watch the children. The past two days had been a strain for him as he fought an internal battle. Her absence made it possible for him to get his thoughts under control.

Or so he hoped. But the twins couldn't seem to hold a conversation without bringing her name into it.

"Can we go now?" Ladd asked.

"Not yet. Do you want to draw another picture?"

"No. I want to see Mercy." The children spoke the same words at the same time. They got their coats and put them on a chair as if it would make the time go faster.

He couldn't stand to confront their silent demands any more than he could ignore his own impatience to see Mercy. "I'm going to chop wood. You two stay inside. I'll be back soon."

"And then we can go?" Allie asked, rocking back and forth on her feet.

"You're flushed." He pressed a palm to her forehead. "Are you okay?"

"I just want to go."

"Then you better lie down until it's time to leave. We aren't going anywhere if you're sick."

"I'm fine." Her bottom lip came out and she crossed her arms.

"Nevertheless…" He pointed toward the bed.

She looked ready to defy him, then marched over and flung herself on the bed.

"I'll watch her," Ladd offered.

Abel hesitated. He didn't want to disappoint them. He'd been looking forward to the afternoon of fun as much as they, but if Allie—

"Papa, I'm okay." Her voice interrupted his thoughts, ringing with unfamiliar firmness. "Ladd's cheeks get red too when he's excited and you never say anything to him."

Abel studied his son. His cheeks were indeed flushed. Why had he never noticed it before? What kind of parent was he? He knew the answer. He was a father who had made mistakes in the past and seemed destined to continue making them. But, he promised himself, he would not make the same mistakes twice.

"Ladd's never been sick," he explained to Allie. Needing to sort himself out, he left the pair and went outside to chop and stack firewood.

Two hours later, Ladd appeared before him.

Abel slammed the ax into the chopping block. "Is Allie sick?"

"No, Papa. She's hungry. Can we eat now?"

Abel glanced toward the sky. It wasn't noon yet but— "Why not?"

He returned to the cabin. Allie perched on the bed, her innocent expression and flushed cheeks did not convince him she had been resting since he left. He made sandwiches and poured them glasses of water. He hadn't found a milk cow yet.

Another of his many failings.

The children ate their sandwiches so fast he wondered they didn't choke. They cleaned the table before he could drink his coffee.

"We're ready," Ladd said, his coat on. Allie waited impatiently at his side, her coat buttoned to her chin.

"I give up." He hurried out to saddle Sam and was barely finished before the twins were at his side. He insisted on wrapping a blanket around Allie's shoulders and tucked two more in the saddlebags in case it turned cold.

As they rode toward the ranch the twins tried to get him to gallop the horse, requests that he steadfastly refused. "We'll get there soon enough."

Still, their excitement was contagious. At least that's how he explained his growing impatience. When before had six miles seemed so long?

Even though it was too early for them to appear, Mercy's gaze went often toward the trail that would bring Abel and the children. Already people from around the area had arrived. Hands from the OK Ranch and the owner, Sam Stone, his foreman, Ollie Oake, and Ollie's sister, Amanda, were there.

Some of the townspeople from Edendale had ridden in a few minutes ago.

It had been such a strange week. Mercy felt as if she rode a bucking horse every time she and Abel were in the same room. One minute he was warm and welcoming, making her insides fill with sweetness. Then he grew fierce and disapproving. Seeing his reaction to the twins' drawings had made her ache for him. He blamed himself for things he shouldn't feel responsible for. As far as she could tell from what he'd said to her, he'd done his best for his children and even for Ruby. His wife's decisions and choices were beyond his control.

She'd told herself again and again that it didn't matter what Abel thought. The children had drawn the pictures they wanted to draw. So what if they reminded Abel of his wife? Or if they made his jaw muscles tighten visibly? Or if he suddenly grew fierce as if remembering he lived by rules, and squinted at her to remind her she did not?

Yet despite the bucking ride he sent her on, she continued to check the trail.

Ward, Grace and Belle rode into the yard. Billy and Grady raced over to greet their friend Belle.

Linette hugged Grace. "I'm so glad you're here. And isn't it wonderful that the weather turned warm so we can be outdoors for the entertainment and picnic?"

Long tables had been set up, laden with food that Linette and Cookie had been busy cooking for two days, along with Mercy's help. Sybil and Jayne would contribute food, as well as Grace, who had brought a covered dish.

Mercy hugged Grace and Belle after Linette stepped back.

"Do you need anything else?" she asked Linette.

"I think we're ready. Run along."

Mercy glanced toward the trail again.

"Go on and meet them," Linette said.

Jayne and Seth's door opened and in an attempt to persuade Linette she wasn't anxious for Abel to appear Mercy ran toward them.

Jayne took Mercy's arm. Mercy spared a brief glance toward the opening in the trees. Still no one.

"They'll be here," Jayne said.

"Who?"

Jayne laughed. "I won't even answer that."

A horse bearing a man and two children broke into sight.

"Mercy, Mercy," the twins called. Allie shrugged from the blanket covering her. Her golden hair shone from beneath a knit hat. Her blue eyes glistened. Her cheeks glowed with healthy pink excitement.

Ladd leaned around his father, waving. Handsome little lad.

Abel's smile caught her heart and held it captive. The man certainly looked glad to see her. She tried to control the eager leap of her heart and failed.

"Oh my," Jayne whispered. "I don't know which of you has it worse."

"I don't know what you're talking about." She looked away from the welcome she imagined in Abel's smile.

"What don't you know?" Sybil walked over and joined arms with Mercy, as well.

Jayne chuckled. "Look at them. What do you think?"

Sybil gave Mercy her full attention, then studied Abel. She chuckled. "I think I see another wedding coming up."

Mercy shook off their hands. "You are both crazy. The children like me. He does not."

Her friends laughed.

Abel and the children were now close enough to hear them and she gave both her friends a quelling look.

Laughing, they left arm in arm. She faced Abel alone.

He lifted the children down. "Can you watch them while I take care of the horse?"

"Surely." She held her hands out to the twins and led them toward the growing crowd, without—she congratulated herself—glancing back at Abel.

She found a spot on the slope overlooking the open area that had been set up for the program. She made sure to squeeze in between Jayne and Sybil. But if she thought that would save her from sitting beside Abel, she was wrong. As soon as he crossed toward them both Sybil and Jayne moved and waved him over.

He jogged to her side. Ladd shifted to make room for Abel between them. Great. So much for proving to her friends that Abel didn't care for her.

So much for proving to herself she didn't care about him.

Eddie stepped to the center of the stage area. "Welcome, friends. My wife wanted everyone to be able to celebrate the end of the roundup."

"And having you back home," Linette added, bringing laughter from those assembled.

Eddie held out a hand, inviting Linette to join him, pressing her to his side when she did. "We won't have many more opportunities to gather like this before winter sets in, so let's enjoy ourselves."

Linette signaled to Jayne, who stepped forward and recited a poem. One by one, others followed. Buster, the youngest cowboy on the ranch, juggled five balls and earned a roar of approval. There were solos and duets. Bertie recited Psalm 147 with such conviction Mercy's heart was stirred.

"'He telleth the number of the stars; he calleth them all by their names.'"

She'd never thought of that before. God cared enough about stars to name them. Did that mean He cared for her the same way? Or did He only want her unquestioning obedience?

Two gray-headed cowboys from the OK Ranch limped to the center. One pulled out a mouth organ and started a fast tune. The other danced a jig, so lively and quick Mercy guessed she wasn't the only one who was surprised at the man's grace. Soon everyone clapped along.

Then Linette signaled Abel. He and the children went to the center. He held each child by their hand, grinned down at them and then they faced the audience and began to sing.

Jesus shall reign where'er the sun
Does his successive journeys run;
His kingdom stretch from shore to shore,
Till moons shall wax and wane no more.

Allie's sweet clear voice, Ladd's uncertain one and Abel's deep tones filled the air with conviction. It was the sweetest sound Mercy had ever heard. Jesus did reign across the world. That meant He reigned right here at Eden Valley Ranch. Mercy blinked back tears.

Jayne squeezed her hand on one side, Sybil on the other.

Mercy scrambled to her feet and rushed away. She did not look back to see Abel's reaction.

She hurried to the barn, where she'd left her costume, and ducked into the tack room to change into trousers and a fringed shirt.

A few minutes later, she rode Nugget into the performance ring. She had him rear on his hind legs and waved, the fringes of her gloves fluttering.

The crowd burst into cheers and clapping. Their approval continued as she did some rope tricks, then twirled her pearl-handled guns. To conclude, she had Nugget bow, then she rode back to the barn.

Only once had she glanced toward Abel and the children. The twins cheered and clapped. Abel sat with his hat pulled low and clapped halfheartedly. After that she would not look in his direction. She knew he didn't approve. Just as she knew he would never trust her.

What difference did it make? She knew what she wanted and it wasn't a man full of unbending rules with a ready-made family.

Chapter Eleven

"Oh, Papa," Allie gushed. "Didn't I tell you she was glorious? The most glorious thing I ever saw. Wasn't she?"

"Oh yes," Ladd answered. "The best ever."

The twins turned to him. "Papa, don't you think so?"

Fire and flame. That was what he'd seen when he'd looked at her. Her hair streaming down her back, her face shining with pure joy and excitement.

His gaze went to the barn. Beauty and boldness. It was the final word he focused on. Boldness that overlooked rules and safety. He could not, would not ever go back to that sort of life, or that sort of woman.

"Allie, you're flushed. Calm down or we'll have to leave."

Allie's expression flattened as if he'd slapped her. His heart stung at the joy he'd taken from her, but she must not get overexcited, and watching Mercy perform had already achieved that.

"There she is." Ladd pointed to Mercy as she sauntered over to the crowd. Men and women alike reached out to congratulate her.

Abel held the twins back or they would have run to her side. Instead, he steered them toward the tables where the ladies were still piling mounds of food.

"Mercy," Ladd called. "Over here."

People pressed on either side and at his back, while the table penned him in the front. Abel could not escape. Slowly he faced Mercy.

Thankfully the twins had her attention, giving him time to calm his thoughts.

"Oh, Mercy," Allie said. "You were so glorious."

If Abel heard the word one more time he would leave.

"You will be the best person ever in a Wild West show," Ladd assured her.

Several others clapped her back or shook her hand.

She fairly glowed at their praise. Her gaze claimed his, brown and demanding.

He felt her silent question but he couldn't answer it.

Then the twins claimed her attention again.

"Did you like our song?" Allie asked.

She hugged them both. "It was beautiful." She grabbed a plate and led them by the table, filling her plate and guiding Allie and Ladd in selecting food. He followed the twins, doing the same.

Thankfully, he didn't need to worry about carrying on a conversation with her as others continually stopped to visit with both of them.

He hadn't met Ward before and immediately liked the man and his redheaded wife, Grace. He soon learned their little girl, Belle, was Grace's sister and they lived on a small ranch to the west. "My mother and brothers live there, too, but Mother wasn't feeling well so didn't come. I thought the boys would come but they said something about going to town instead."

Ward told him about the two cabins on his place and gave some advice about construction.

Eddie and Sam Stone talked about a work bee to get the church built and soon everyone offered to help.

Abel hesitated. He had his own building project but a church would be nice, though he had no objection to the meeting held in the cookhouse. He wondered what Bertie and Cookie would think and noticed that they nodded their approval.

Conversation shifted to how to obtain a preacher. Then Eddie said, "I'd like to see a doctor in the area, too. We've certainly had need of one several times in the past."

The Mountie, Constable Allen, was in attendance and offered to send messages to the different forts and towns in hopes of stirring up some interest.

Abel paid close attention to all the discussion, more, he admitted, to avoid facing Mercy and his troubled feelings than because of an overwhelming interest in the proceedings. He figured the others would go ahead with plans with or without his help. His own buildings must be erected first.

Eventually the party ended. The food was whisked away. Wagons and horses departed. He headed for the corral and Sam. If he left soon he could avoid time alone with Mercy.

He should have known he couldn't hope for that. She followed him.

"Abel, aren't you going to say anything about my riding?"

He faced her, knowing his lips were pulled back in disapproval.

Her shoulders sagged. "Of course you don't approve."

To him her performance signified she still wanted to leave. "I'm sorry, but why do you do such...such—"

"Foolish things?"

"I was thinking unpredictable." Among several other things.

She shrugged. "It's who I am. And you live by rules."

"Well, rules keep you safe."

"I tried the rules. Tried to do everything right." Her voice grew harsh. "But only when I did something unpredictable did anyone notice me."

Ahh. So now it became clear. "Are you talking about your parents?" Hadn't she said they didn't see her after her brother died?

She shook her head but her eyes said yes.

"I'm sorry. Sorry you never felt important to them. Sorry you still feel the need to do unusual things before anyone will notice you."

She closed her eyes, but it did not hide the pain in her face.

He didn't want to add to that pain and caught her shoulders and eased her toward him. When she didn't protest, he wrapped his arms about her and held her tight.

"You don't need to get people to notice you anymore. Don't the children appreciate you even when you're ordinary?" Though he couldn't imagine her ever being ordinary. Nor did he think he'd like her any better that way despite all his talk to the contrary. "I know I do."

A twitch shivered through her. He held her tighter,

wondering how she'd respond to his words. He hadn't planned them. If he had he wouldn't have said them. Fire and flame. Beauty and boldness. Only she didn't seem so bold now as she clung to him. He liked her this way. Maybe she would believe him that she didn't need to try and get attention from anyone, especially him.

Jayne and Sybil waited for Mercy as she wandered back to the thinning crowd.

"You've gotten really good at riding and roping," Jayne said.

"And handling guns." Sybil shivered. "I will never like guns." She tipped her head to consider Mercy. "Are you still planning to join a Wild West show?"

"Yes." Abel had held her and assured her he liked her just the way she was. "No." Did he mean it or was he trying to convince her to change—maybe abandon her plans. "Maybe." Would she forget about joining a show if he asked her to? "I don't know."

Jayne and Sybil looked at each other and laughed.

"What?" Mercy demanded.

"We both remember that feeling." Jayne's smile seemed condescending.

"What feeling?"

Sybil pressed her hand to Mercy's arm in a soothing gesture. "The feeling that you aren't sure which way is right anymore. You aren't even sure what you want."

Mercy denied it flatly. "I know exactly what I want." But did she?

She tossed the question around throughout the rest of the evening and still mulled it over the next morning as she rode to the cabin.

Maybe, she finally decided, if he came right out and

asked her to consider staying, she'd give it serious consideration. She arrived at the cabin and Abel stepped outside. Her breath stuck in the back of her throat. Was he planning to make his wishes clear?

"Good morning," he said, trotting toward the corral.

She headed the same direction and swung off Nugget's back. Sam was already harnessed. Was Abel in a rush to leave? Because of her? Had he said more than he intended? More than he felt?

"The twins are anxious to see you," he said, leading Sam from the enclosure. With a barely there wave, he left the yard.

"At least someone is," she muttered. It certainly wasn't Abel, who couldn't wait to get away from her.

She entered the cabin.

"Mercy, Mercy." Allie rushed to her side. "Do you think I can learn to ride fancy like you?" She dipped her head. "Maybe like you showed me before. You know, standing on Nugget's back?"

"I've been practicing with the lariat," Ladd said, his voice cautious yet hopeful.

Mercy sighed. They both wanted to imitate her. No doubt their eagerness explained Abel's withdrawal. "Allie, you know you can't do those kinds of things."

"What about me?" Ladd asked.

The resignation in his tone bothered Mercy, reminding her of her own childhood. Ladd was often expected to curtail his activities in order to protect Allie. Did anyone ask him if he minded the sacrifice? Or if he felt insignificant?

She pulled them both close and kissed the tops of their heads. "Ladd, I think you can keep swinging your rope. Someday you'll get really good. Now what shall we do?"

"Can we go exploring?" Ladd asked.

The sun had moved over the treetops and sent warmth into the clearing. Like Eddie said yesterday, they wouldn't enjoy too many more nice days. "That's a good idea."

Ladd glowed at her approval.

She vowed she would go out of her way to give him more attention.

They wrapped up in warm coats and hats and ran outside. She chased Ladd through the trees while Allie laughed at them.

"Can you chase me?" she asked when Mercy caught Ladd and held him tight.

Mercy shook her head. "I wouldn't want to make you ill." She wondered if Allie knew her heart might have been damaged. A cold breeze tugged her coat. "We better go indoors. It's getting cold."

She hurried them inside as the wind increased. "Let's make some soup." She always let the twins help even though it took longer and generally made a mess. She'd noticed the pained look on Abel's face when he saw the mess and promised herself to have it cleaned up before he returned.

The soup was ready, the table set, but Abel didn't ride into the yard. She delayed half an hour while the children begged to eat and she finally gave in. They finished and still Abel didn't come.

The children played with the collection of paper animals she'd helped them create, leaving Mercy free to listen to her thoughts. Had she really expected Abel to ask her to stay? Even worse, she'd foolishly allowed herself to think he might want to make this arrangement permanent. It was all because Jayne and Sybil had said they foresaw a wedding. Pshaw. They lived with their vision clouded by their own romances.

The afternoon dragged on, but she had no doubt he'd return soon. In the meantime she decided to make the place welcoming. "Let's bake cookies."

Two hours later the cookies cooled on a tea towel. She'd cleaned the place so not a bit of flour dusted anything. And she waited. And waited.

Then the truth hit her. Abel hadn't said he liked her just as she was. He'd said he approved of her as ordinary. Huh! Who wanted to be ordinary? A perfect little woman, cooking and cleaning and washing clothes. Not her sort of life at all. He was just like Ambrose.

The children ate cookies and drank milk tea.

Yet wasn't that exactly what she did every day? And she enjoyed it because she cared about the twins. And yes, she cared about Abel. Though she couldn't explain why.

The twins joined her at the window. "Where's Papa?" Allie's voice sounded thin with worry. "Why isn't he back?"

"He'll be along any minute." Already the shadows lengthened enough that it would be dark before she returned to the ranch.

"It's just like Mama." Ladd sounded resigned to the fact.

She drew the pair away from the window. "How is it like your mama?"

"Mama went away and didn't come back."

She nodded. "Your papa will come back."

"Mama would be gone for days." Ladd clung to her hand.

"But now she's never coming back." Allie cuddled close.

Mercy wrapped her arms about them. "Don't worry. Your papa would never leave you."

The three of them sat huddled together as the minutes ticked past with painful slowness.

Mercy slipped away from the pair and returned to the window. Dusk filled the clearing. Abel would never be so late at returning unless something happened. She curled her fingers into her palms as she counted off the many risks. A bear. A wildcat. A crazy, whiskered man. A wandering outlaw. A—

She spun away from the window and hurried to the stove to stick in another piece of wood. She pushed the kettle back and forth and shook the coffeepot. Aware the children watched her every move, she forced herself to smile and act as if everything was perfectly fine. But her insides burned with worry.

Someone should go looking for him. But she was the only adult who knew he should be back by now. Only she could help him. "Children, bundle up. I'm taking you to the ranch."

"You're worried about Papa, aren't you?" Ladd asked.

"He should have been back by now. I need to go see if he needs help." While they dressed in warm clothes, she hurried out to get Nugget. The cold had deepened. If Abel was out there hurt—

She would find him and bring him home.

She grabbed a lantern from inside the little shed and led Nugget to the cabin. The children joined her on the horse and she wrapped them in blankets, knowing if either of them got sick, Abel would hold her personally responsible.

As they rode toward the ranch, she held Allie close and made certain Ladd held on tight. She rode right up to the big house and handed the children down to Linette, who came immediately to the door.

"I need to leave the children here," Mercy said.

"Where's Abel?"

"I don't know but I intend to find out." Ignoring Linette's protests, she rode down the hill and across the yard.

Jayne had seen her ride in and stepped from her cabin as Mercy rode past. She called out something, but Mercy ignored her. She knew they would all try to dissuade her. Advise her to wait for the men to return and one of them would go look for Abel. She didn't intend to wait for anyone.

The growing darkness forced her to make her way slowly back to the cabin. She passed it without stopping and took the trail Abel had created. Her slow pace gave her plenty of time to think. If something had happened to him—

She swallowed a lump so sharp it scratched her throat. The twins would be heartbroken. How would they survive?

She couldn't imagine life without him. Her mind flooded with pictures of him—holding Allie close, stroking Ladd's hair, the three of them singing together.

Being a star in a Wild West show lost its appeal. In

comparison to what she'd found with Abel and the children, it seemed a foolish goal. Foolish, just as Abel said.

Ordinary, he liked. He'd said he appreciated her when she was ordinary.

She rode through the trees, pausing often to call his name. But she heard nothing except the rustle of the branches in the wind, the squawk of birds disturbed by her noise and the whistle of her own breath.

She'd show him she could be ordinary. If only she would get another chance. *Please, God, he's a father. Keep him safe for the children's sake.* And mine. But she did not pray the final words. Why would God care for her sake?

She reached a place where he'd chopped down trees and dismounted to look around more closely.

"Abel. Where are you?"

Not a sound indicated his presence. Where could he be? Tension clawed at her throat. What if—

She dare not finish the question

Abel's mind cleared long enough for him to know he was in serious trouble. And so cold he ached. The cold might be responsible for the fact he couldn't feel his legs. He prayed it was so.

He faded. Couldn't tell how much time had passed except to note the sun dipped to the west. How long had he lain out here? He tried to move his legs. Nothing. He reached down to see why they wouldn't respond and felt the log that lay across them.

That's right. The chain had slipped. The tree had rolled and caught him. He recalled falling and his head whacking the ground. Probably explained the pain in his head. How long ago was it? He couldn't remember for certain but it seemed it had been early morning. He squinted at the sky. And now it was late afternoon. Almost dark. Would anyone look for him? Would Mercy? Of course she would. Darkness wouldn't stop her any more than she'd let the man in the woods make her too fearful to search for him.

Mercy would come.

He lay back and tried to relax. Cold seeped into his bones like a disease.

His mind clouded over and he dreamed. In his reverie Mercy stood at his side, a plate of cookies in her hand. Behind her the children beckoned for him to come. He hesitated, wanting Mercy to go with him.

"Mercy." His cry jerked him awake. He shivered. "Mercy," he called again in desperation.

Off to the side, he saw and heard the tall bushes being crushed to one side. He closed his eyes. If a wild animal meant to eat him, he prayed it would be swift.

"Abel?"

Wild animals didn't say his name in Mercy's voice. He looked up. "Mercy?"

"There you are." She broke through the trees. "I would have gone right by you if you hadn't called."

"I'm pinned."

"Let's have a look." She held a lantern up and made her way around him. "Yup. You're pinned. Where's Sam?"

"Haven't seen him since the log broke away. How bad is it?"

She wouldn't look at him.

"Mercy, is it real bad?"

She squatted by his head. "Truthfully I can't tell.

Won't be able to until I pull the log off you." She didn't move. "It's likely going to hurt some."

"Just do it."

Still she didn't move.

"What's wrong?" He squeezed the words past his shivers.

"I'm afraid of what I might find when I pull the log off."

He struggled to suck in air. "Me, too, but I don't intend to lie here forever."

She chuckled though he thought the sound rather strained. Then she touched his brow. "Then let's do it." She rose. "I need to find Sam. Nugget isn't strong enough to move this log. Don't go anywhere."

He clamped his teeth together to stop shivering. And to stop himself from calling at her not to leave. He unclenched them long enough to say, "I'll be right here when you get back."

"Sam, Sam." She whistled and called, beat her way through the underbrush.

He strained to hear her, and caught enough rustling and grunts to be comforted that she hadn't left him. A few minutes later—or what seemed so, but his mind faded in and out so he couldn't be sure—he heard the rattle of a chain. She'd found Sam.

Then the light of her lantern flickered. "You're back." He couldn't say for certain if he spoke the words aloud or only in his mind. It didn't matter. She'd returned. She'd get him out of this predicament.

She returned to his side, tucked two blankets in around his body. "As soon as I get you home, I'll get you warm."

"Where are the twins?"

"I took them to the ranch. Linette is watching them."

He wanted to ask why she hadn't gotten Eddie or one of the cowboys to look for him, but he couldn't quell the relief he felt as seeing her. He would trust his life to her hands.

She led Sam to the butt end of the log and hooked the chain around it. She picked up a smaller log and wedged it under the downward side of the one pinning him to the ground. "I don't want it to roll back on you if Sam slips or something."

Good to know.

"I'm going to put a log on this side, too. I want the one on your legs to roll off without doing more damage." She adjusted the chain, checked the wedge, then squatted at his side. "It could hurt."

"Just do it."

She brushed her knuckles across his cheek. He caught her hand and pressed it to his face. Brought it to his mouth and kissed the palm. She wore gloves so he was unable to feel her flesh. Nevertheless, he found strength and courage in holding her hand close for a moment.

She withdrew, leaving him cold and alone. "I'll holler when I start to pull."

He grunted a reply, not trusting himself to speak calmly.

She skirted around the log. "Ready? Here we go." She guided Sam forward. The chain snapped into place. He could imagine Sam leaning into the harness. The log pressed harder into his legs. He stifled a moan. And then it eased off as it rode up on the logs she'd put in place.

And as the pressure eased, the pain began, sharp as

a deep knife cut, digging into his shin until he wished she'd put the log back in place.

The pain grew, swelled, until it consumed him. He squeezed his lips tight, determined not to cry out, but a moan welled up from someplace deep inside, a reservoir of pain he'd never before uncovered. It escaped past his clamped teeth and rent the air.

"Almost done," she called.

A moment later she hurried back to his side. "I have to look at your legs and see what kind of damage you've done."

He grabbed her hand and held on like a drowning man.

She seemed to know what he needed and squeezed back, stroked his forehead and made comforting noises. "I need to check your legs in case you're bleeding."

He forced his hands to release her.

She moved to his feet. Cold touched his flesh as she exposed his legs. But he *felt* the cold, which surely was a good sign.

She grunted. "No bleeding." She straightened and looked about. "I have to get you out of here. I'll get Nugget."

"I'll ride Sam." His voice squeaked, giving away the depth of his pain.

She stood over him. "I don't know how you'll get on his back."

"I'll do it."

"Very well." She brought Sam forward, then leaned down to offer him a hand.

He wanted to refuse. To do it himself. He managed to sit up fine despite the pain clawing at his brain. "My head." He would have pressed his hands to the back of his head but needed them to keep himself upright.

"Let's have a look." She held the lantern behind him and ran gentle fingers against his scalp.

He grunted when she touched the bruise.

"There's a nasty lump here but no bleeding. You must have banged your head."

He heard the worry in her voice and could offer little in the way of assurance. Truth be told, his head felt like someone had attacked him with an ax handle.

Her soft touch lingered a moment more, smoothed his hair, then left him hurting more than he had before.

He pulled his blurry thoughts back to the need to get home. Which meant getting to Sam's back. He tried to put his feet under him, but his muscles turned to pudding.

"Put your arms around my neck and I'll pull you to your feet."

With little option except to obey, he put his arms about her, breathing in her comforting warmth. To his embarrassment, he clung to her like a baby.

She wrapped her arms about his waist. "On the count of three. One, two, three." She leaned back and he did what he could to help. Somehow she managed to right herself despite his weight, and steady him. "Grab the horse."

He gritted his teeth and forced himself to release her even though he wanted nothing more than to hold her tight and feel her strength and determination. But he must get home.

Gathering together every remaining ounce of his waning strength, he pulled himself upward, clawing his way to Sam's back while she lifted his legs. Somehow they managed to get him on the horse. The exertion was so intense he swayed.

She grabbed him and steadied him. "Can you stay there?"

"I'll stay here."

"Then let's go." She led him through the trees back to the trail, where Nugget waited patiently. She called him to follow, then swung up behind Abel. "I'll hold you." Her arms came around him and took the reins. He buried his fingers in Sam's mane and hung on.

"We'll soon be home." Her voice carried a sharpness that jerked his head up. Had he fallen asleep? Passed out? He righted himself and blinked his eyes hard.

"I'll be okay." How far did they have to go? He didn't recall having gone such a distance from the cabin.

The trail was dark. He shivered and not just from being cold. A thousand dangers hovered in the dark trees. Like that crazy mountain man. "I hope you're praying," he croaked.

"I have been since I set out to find you."

"Guess God answered your prayers."

"Yup. I have to say I am as surprised as you."

"Who said I was surprised?" Talking helped keep him alert.

She chuckled, the sound reverberating up his spine. "You didn't have to say it."

"Are we almost there?" He didn't care that he sounded like Ladd.

"We're here." She guided Sam to the door and slipped to the ground. "Let's get you inside."

How did she figure to do that? He doubted he could stand and she couldn't carry him.

She helped him swing one leg over the horse until he

sat sideways. "I'm braced against the door," she said. "I can hold you. Come on, get down."

Knowing he would crash to the ground but not seeing any alternative, he reached for the door frame, held it as tight as he could and launched himself off Sam.

He fell into her with a barely muffed groan.

Grunting under his weight, she grabbed him about the waist and steadied him. Once she had him fairly well balanced, she reached for the doorknob and they staggered inside.

The narrow space of the cabin seemed to yawn before him. But somehow, between the two of them, he dragged himself across the room and fell on the bed.

Home sweet home.

Chapter Twelve

Mercy tucked blankets around Abel, who shivered like a wind-struck leaf. His skin was icy. She hurried to add wood to the fire and to fill the kettle, then turned back to Abel. His boots needed to come off.

Explaining what she meant to do, she began to ease off the first boot. His groan shivered up her spine. She closed her eyes, gritted her teeth and would not allow herself to look at him as she removed one boot and then the other and dropped them to the floor. "Done." She breathed hard, swiped at beads of sweat on her brow. She set the lamp on a shelf above the bed. "I want to have a better look at your legs." In the woods, she'd worried about bleeding and how she'd stop it. Now she meant to check for broken bones. She picked up the edge of the blanket and bent closer, touching each shin-bone, moving each foot. Her guess was his legs were badly bruised but not broken. "God watched over you."

She recalled a verse Bertie had recited the day before…was it only a day ago? She felt she'd lived several days in the past few hours. He'd said it was Psalm 147. *God delights not in the strength of the horse, nor is His pleasure in the legs of a man.* She repeated the words to Abel. "Seems God cared enough about your legs to keep you safe."

Abel grunted.

Mercy moved closer to his head. His eyes were dark with pain. "Where do you hurt most?"

"My head." His words were thick, almost garbled.

She tried to remember what Linette had said about the time Eddie had been unconscious with a head wound. Was there anything special she did? Or—her brain froze—had she said all they could do was wait and see?

Abel's eyes closed.

"Abel? Are you okay?"

He didn't open his eyes. Didn't respond.

"Abel." She shook him a little.

His eyes cracked open so briefly she would have missed it if she hadn't been straining to see some response. After that he slept. Or was he unconscious? She couldn't tell.

What if something happened to him?

She fell on her knees beside the bed. "Abel, don't you die. You've got Allie and Ladd to think about." Why had she thought adventure was so important? All she wanted now fit into this small cabin. Abel alive and standing on his feet, the twins clinging to his hands as the three of them smiled at her.

"Lord God, I've never been one to call on You much. I've always figured I could take care of everything myself. But now I can't. Abel's head is hurt. I don't know how bad it is or what to do. Please, let him be okay."

She remained on her knees half praying as she watched Abel's chest rise and fall. The *clop clop* of horse hooves jolted her to her feet. She was alone except for an injured man. She grabbed Abel's rifle and faced the door. No one would be allowed to harm him.

"Mercy," a familiar voice called from the other side of the door.

"Jayne?" She rushed over and flung the door open. "What are you doing here?"

"Seth brought me. He'll be here as soon as he tends the horses. Abel's horse and Nugget were wandering about the yard."

She'd completely forgotten the horses. "Come in." A cold wind shivered across the floor. "Why are you here?"

"Because you need us. Linette told us about Abel being missing. As soon as he heard, Seth saddled horses for us both and here we are."

Seth stepped into the room. "Are you okay?"

She nodded. "I don't know about Abel though." She explained how she'd found him trapped by a log. As she recalled those anxious moments when she couldn't find him and then when she wondered what she'd discover when she pulled the log off, her legs refused to hold her weight and she sank into a chair.

Jayne wrapped an arm about her shoulders.

Mercy sucked in air and held it until her strength returned. "I think his legs are okay but he hurt his head." She led them to Abel's bedside and showed them his legs.

"I don't think there's any reason to be concerned about his legs," Seth said, after examining them. "How long has he been unresponsive?"

"He's not." She shook him and called his name.

But Abel didn't open his eyes.

Mercy grabbed the edge of the bed to hold herself upright. "Is he—?" She would not give words to her worries.

"He can't be left alone," Jayne said.

Mercy had no intention of leaving his side until she saw him standing and his mind clear.

"We'll stay with you," Jayne added.

"We'll pray." Seth bowed his head. "God in heaven, You care about sparrows but we know You care about us a lot more. Because You love us, we humbly ask that You heal Abel's wounds. Amen."

Seth and Jayne looked at each other, eyes so full of trust and assurance that Mercy straightened her legs. Abel would recover. He had to.

"Have you eaten?" Jayne asked.

Mercy shook her head. "I'm not hungry."

Jayne made tea and sandwiches and insisted Mercy leave Abel's bedside and sit with them at the table. To placate her friend, Mercy nibbled at a sandwich and drank a cup of tea. Then she pulled her chair to Abel's bedside. "Abel, if you can hear me, I want you to know you have to get better. For Ladd and Allie." She repeated the words again and again. Inside her head, she added, *And for me. I have so much I need to tell you. Changes I need to make. But I need a chance to make them.*

Jayne and Seth moved about the room almost soundlessly, pausing often to glance down at Abel, then returning to the table where they spoke quietly. Mercy didn't listen to them. Every thought, every word, every breath concentrated on willing Abel to get better. Silent prayer followed every lungful of air. *God, please heal him. Make him as good as new.*

"We brought bedrolls," Jayne whispered. "We'll sleep by the table. Why don't you pull out the trundle bed and put it against the wall and try and get some rest?"

"I'll stay here." She meant to stay at his bedside until he opened his eyes and recognized her. "You can have Allie's bed."

Jayne chuckled softly. "It's too small for Seth, and I intend to sleep with him. There's nothing you can do except wait. You'll hear him if he calls out." Jayne pulled her from the chair and tugged out the bed. She shifted it away from Abel's side and pushed it against the wall. "You need to rest."

Rather than argue, Mercy stretched out on the tiny bed, but as soon as she heard Jayne's and Seth's breathing deepen she slipped from the bed and returned to Abel's side, where she sat in a chair to guard him. She watched his face in the lowered lamplight, waiting and praying for him to wake up.

"Mercy." A hoarse voice jerked her alert. Had she fallen asleep? How long since she'd last checked on Abel?

She blinked to focus and looked at him. His eyes were open and he looked at her.

"Mercy." The word whispered from his lips into her heart.

She leaned close and spoke softly so as to not disturb Seth and Jayne. "How are you feeling?"

"My head hurts and my legs ache, but I am grateful to be here." He swallowed hard. "Can I have a drink?"

She hurried to fill a cup with water and hold it to his lips.

He drank eagerly then settled against the pillow.

For a moment she wondered if he'd fallen asleep or drifted into unconsciousness, but then his eyelids came up. "I am grateful to be alive."

She squeezed his hand. "Me, too."

His grip on her fingers was surprisingly strong. The fact filled her with encouragement. Surely it meant he was going to be just fine.

"Thank you for coming to find me."

She grinned. "You must have known I would."

He smiled softly. "I counted on it."

She stroked his brow with her free hand. "You've given me enough adventure to last a lifetime." Would he understand what she meant?

"I'm tired," he murmured as he pressed her hand to his chest. In no time his breathing deepened. He'd fallen asleep. But when she tried to remove her hand, his eyes jerked open. "Don't go," he whispered.

"I won't."

A few hours later, daylight crept into the window. Seth and Jayne scrambled to their feet. Jayne rushed to Mercy's side. "How is he?"

Mercy had tried several times to slip her hand away, but he held it firm even in his sleep. "He woke and was clear in his head. I think he's just sleeping."

Jayne patted her shoulder. "He's lucid enough to know to hang on to the person who rescued him."

Seth rolled up the bedding, built a fire and joined them at Abel's bedside. "His color is good. His breathing is even."

Abel opened his eyes. "I'm fine."

Mercy tugged her hand away lest her friends read more into the way Abel held it than they should. She couldn't say what it meant. And until she could...

Abel pushed himself to a sitting position. The color left his face.

"You need to take it easy," Seth said.

"I'll be fine." Every breath Abel took rasped into his lungs.

Mercy's lungs felt impossibly tight before they released with a whoosh as his color returned. She'd never seen anything so beautiful in her life as the way his eyes focused, clear as a cloudless sky. He smiled at each of them in turn. Mercy thought he looked at her several seconds longer and it wasn't imagination or gratitude that made her think his smile was wider as he regarded her.

"Are you hungry?" Jayne asked.

"A cup of coffee would be mighty nice."

She slipped away to make some. Seth followed his wife, leaving Mercy alone with Abel.

Her smile felt too wide for her face, but she couldn't help it. He was alive and well.

Life felt wonderful and exciting and promising all at once.

Despite the pounding of a cattle stampede in his head, Abel couldn't stop looking at Mercy, afraid she'd disappear if he blinked. How many times had he wakened shaking with the fear of being alone and each time he'd found her at his side? She'd rescued him just as he knew she would.

"Thank God," he murmured.

"Amen," she whispered back.

He wondered at the way she blinked until he realized she'd been up all night. Most likely she had a hard time keeping her eyes open.

He shifted, preparing to put his legs over the side of the bed, but the movement sent a stabbing pain into his head. He leaned against the wall and waited for it to end.

"I have coffee ready." Jayne held a cup toward him.

"I'll sit at the table." He had to get back on his feet.

Seth appeared at his side. "Don't you think you should take it easy for a day or two?"

"I can't. The twins will be worried about me." He knew from the way Mercy dipped her head and avoided his eyes that she agreed with him.

Seth patted Abel's shoulder. "I suppose they will. How about if I ride back and get them after we've eaten?"

Abel tried to nod but it hurt too much. "I have to get up. I don't want them to see me like this."

Mercy leaned forward. "Why not leave them at the ranch until you feel stronger? As long as they know you're all right they'll enjoy it."

He settled back. His arguments had all been dealt with. "So long as they aren't worried. Especially Allie."

"We'll look after them," Seth promised. "You rest and get strong so you can take care of them."

His lungs spasmed. His ears ached from the noise inside his head. He grabbed at his chest.

"Abel, what's wrong?" Mercy asked, her voice strained.

"The children." The words grated from his throat. He grabbed Mercy's hands, his eyes stinging. "Promise me you will take care of them if something happens to me."

Mercy drew her lips together. Either her eyes filled with tears or he only saw through his own tears.

"Of course I will, but you're fine. Nothing is going to happen to you."

He nodded and fell back, weakened by his surging emotions. "Thank you."

"Come on, Mercy." Jayne drew her toward the table.

Abel drank his coffee and lay back on the bed, shivering from that little bit of exertion.

"I'll ride to the ranch and tell the children." Seth's voice came to him as if through a long tunnel. "Jayne will stay here with you."

He heard Mercy's familiar voice like a wordless lullaby answer her friend before sleep claimed him.

When he wakened, he blinked to drive back the pain behind his eyeballs. He shifted to his side and that's when he saw Mercy asleep in the trundle bed against the far wall. Her dark lashes fanned across her porcelain cheeks. Her mahogany curls spread across the pillow in wild disarray. His heart filled with a hundred different emotions, all of which made him smile. He remembered her strength as she had held him on the back of the horse, her steadying presence at his bedside, how he'd clung to her hand. His smile widened. He saw her dusted in flour as she'd helped the children, recalled their eagerness as they watched her return every morning. Eagerness that matched his own.

Her eyelids fluttered open. Their gazes connected in a steady, unblinking look. He opened his heart to her and let her look deep. Felt her silent search. He wanted her to know how grateful he was for her, how much he admired her and trusted her.

"Hi," he murmured.

She jerked to a sitting position and rubbed her eyes. "What time is it?"

"Midafternoon." Jayne sat at the table and answered the question.

Abel sat up, as well. His head protested with a sharp stab, which he ignored as he looked about the cabin. He'd forgotten about Jayne and Seth. Seth wasn't there. Then he recalled Seth had ridden back to the ranch to tell the children Abel was okay. How long ago was that? He couldn't say. "Has Seth returned?"

"Not yet. I expect him soon." She rose and went to the stove. "Can I get you something to eat or drink?"

"Water would be nice."

She brought him a cupful and stood at his side as he drank it. Over the rim of the cup he watched Mercy as she rose and smoothed her riding skirt. She ran her fingers over her curls trying to tame them, he supposed. She straightened the bedding and shoved the bed back under his, then faced him. "How are you? How are your head and legs?"

"Better, I think." He handed the cup to Jayne. "I'd like to try getting up."

Jayne shook her head. "Not until Seth is here to help."

Abel leaned back against the wall. He could wait a few more minutes.

A little later a horse rode into the yard and Seth called out a greeting before he strode into the cabin. He didn't wait for questions. "The children are just fine. Enjoying their time at the ranch. They wanted to come and see you for themselves—I said you were tired and needed to rest. I promised them I'd let them know when you were ready to have them come home."

Abel shifted his legs over the edge of the bed. "I'm going to get up."

Seth tossed his coat and hat on a hook and hurried to Abel's side.

Abel waved him away. "Let me do it on my own." Dizziness filled his head, but he willed it away and took a step. His legs hurt, though the pain was nothing he couldn't deal with. Finally the dizziness lessened. "The twins need to see for themselves that I'm fine. And I need to have them with me." He made it to the table and sank into a chair. Mercy sat across from him, her gaze following his every move. He guessed at her concern and sent her a reassuring smile that he knew drew his lips narrow as he concentrated on his breathing.

Jayne poured them all tea and set a plate of cookies in the middle of the table.

He didn't feel up to eating, but the tea felt good going down.

"How was church?" Jayne asked.

Abel had forgotten it was Sunday. By the way Mercy jerked back he guessed she'd forgotten, as well.

"When Bertie heard about your accident he changed his mind about what he meant to say and reminded us all of how God watches over even sparrows who are sold two for a penny. 'How much more are we worth?' he said." Seth turned to Jayne. "My wife told me the same thing. She made me see how much God values me." The two of them smiled at each other in a way that filled Abel with a thousand regrets. This couple had what he wanted from a marriage. Not the regrets and accusations he'd experienced with Ruby. Nor the loneliness.

Seth spoke again, bringing Abel's thoughts from that regretful place. "Bertie prayed a very nice prayer for you though he was careful not to say anything to alarm the children. Everyone sends their prayers."

"It could have been so much worse." Abel's words were soft. "Thank God it wasn't."

"Amen," the three said.

"Belle said to tell you that it was God who made sure everyone was in the right place at the right time."

"Belle? But she's only a little girl." She was a year younger than the twins.

"A little girl who has experienced a whole lot of sorrow and trouble." Jayne and Seth told him how Ward had rescued Belle and Grace from a man who held them captive. How afraid Belle was of everyone to begin with but how she soon learned not every man was bad. "She fell in love with Ward before Grace did. Or at least before she would admit it." Jayne reached for Seth's hand. "God has brought so many people together at the ranch. First Linette and Eddie, then Cassie and Roper, then Ward and Grace, us, and more recently, Sybil and Brand." She chuckled.

Jayne fixed Mercy with a wide smile. "And now you."

Mercy bolted to her feet. "I'm going to make soup for supper." She hurried to the stove.

Laughing, Jayne and Seth regarded each other and nodded as if they shared a secret.

Abel shifted to watch Mercy. Did Jayne and Seth think he should marry her? Right now he could think of nothing he'd like better, but despite his thumping head he wasn't about to let his emotions rule his actions.

He remained sitting at the table as Jayne and Mercy made soup. He listened halfheartedly to Seth's talk about a work bee for the church in Edendale.

A little later, he accepted a bowl of soup and ate it. Not because he had any appetite but to prove to the three watching him so carefully that he was fine. He finished his bowl and pushed it aside. The others were done before him.

"Are you going to bring the children home?" He addressed Seth.

"If you're sure you're up to it."

Abel nodded.

"Right then." Seth grabbed his hat. "I'll get them."

"I'll stay with Mercy," Jayne said.

Seth kissed his wife and left.

Mercy waited until the door closed behind Seth. "Abel, I know you want to prove to us that you're fit as a fiddle, but I can tell your head hurts. Why don't you rest until the children return?"

He shook his head, the movement making his eyes hurt.

"Come on." She took his hand and urged him toward his bed. "Just until they get here."

He must have dozed off, because he roused when Mercy tapped his shoulder. "Abel, Seth is back." She stayed at his side as he sat up.

He barely made it to his feet before the door burst open and the twins ran to him.

"Papa," Allie shouted. "What happened?" They both clung to him as he hugged them.

Ladd let go first. "Are you okay?"

"I'm fine. Very glad to see the pair of you."

"Tell us what happened."

He led them to the bed, glad to sit on the edge as he told them. "A log fell and pinned me to the ground. I couldn't free myself, but Mercy found me and got

Sam to pull the log off. Then she brought me home safe and sound." He hugged them both again. Nothing mattered half as much as staying safe so he could take care of them.

Allie sighed. "She's glorious. Didn't I tell you?"

At the moment, Abel had no argument to the contrary.

Glorious and brave.

A warning flashed in his brain. Wasn't it simply the flip side of wild and free? But tonight he didn't care.

Chapter Thirteen

Mercy glanced over her shoulder half a dozen times as they left the yard. She didn't want to leave Abel and the children, knowing she would worry about him all night. But he assured them he was fine. And he squeezed her hand secretly before she left. She wished for a few minutes alone with him.

For what? she chided herself. Did she think he would thank her with a kiss?

Well, if he didn't, she'd kiss him just because she was so grateful he had survived his accident.

She didn't care what differences they had. Those no longer held any significance. The only thing that mattered was he was safe and sound. She'd never been so grateful for anything in her life.

Her gratitude made her take more time than normal the next morning. She pulled on a dark blue woolen skirt and demure white blouse. She looked through her jewelry until she found a brooch her mother had given her one Christmas. At the time it had been much too heavy and grown-up for Mercy and she knew her mother had given little thought to the gift, but now the purple amethyst set in a gold setting and surrounded by natural pearls said Mercy was grown-up and serious.

She drew her hair into a roll at the back of her head and pinned it in place, securing it firmly with a plain and ordinary tortoiseshell comb.

She stepped back to study herself in the looking glass. Yes, indeed, she looked exactly right. Serious. Mature. Ready to be ordinary.

A strand of hair escaped and she tucked it back in place. Only a bonnet would hold it secure on the ride and she chose a plain one.

If Linette and Eddie thought anything unusual about her outfit, they refrained from saying so.

Perhaps because they were excited about their own news.

"We've decided to help Abel with his cabin before we work on the church," Eddie said.

"It's a fine idea." Linette glowed with approval. "He's been trying so hard to do it on his own, but the accident will slow him down." She turned to Mercy. "Don't tell him. We want it to be a surprise."

"It's a lovely idea." Of course it was. He'd get his cabin ready before winter. He and the children would be safe and warm. So why did a protest sting her tongue so hard that she had to cool it with a gulp of cold water?

How much time would she have to show him her change if his cabin was built? She gathered up a few things and went out to saddle Nugget. She might wear skirts and pin her hair up, but she refused to ride side-saddle.

She arrived at the clearing and waited. The cool air was so still she could hear tumbling water in the distant river. A twist of smoke came from the chimney.

Sam stood at the corral fence. It looked like he hadn't even been fed yet.

No one opened the door to greet her.

Her heart tumbled against her ribs. Was Abel…? She turned Nugget loose in the corral without bothering to unsaddle him and, lifting her skirts, ran for the door. Why had she decided to wear all these petticoats today? If Abel had gotten worse, he wouldn't even notice.

She flung back the door and stepped inside.

Three pairs of eyes looked up from the table.

Abel skidded his chair back. "Is there something wrong?"

"No." Her breath jerked in and out of her lungs. "But when no one came to greet me—" She slammed her mouth closed before she could give her fears a voice. "I just wanted to make sure you were okay. All of you."

Their surprise overcome, the twins ran over and hugged her. "Papa was telling us how God answered his prayer and sent you."

She lifted her gaze to Abel. Did he really mean that? Of course he meant when she'd found him in the dark. Not, as her overactive imagination first thought, in a general, everyday way.

"I prayed, too," she said, her gaze still holding his. Both surprise and welcome filled his eyes. She shook her head, chastising her overactive imagination again. She took her long coat off and hung it on the nearby hook.

"You're wearing a dress."

Did he sound approving or only surprised? She couldn't tell and untied her bonnet and hung it over the coat.

He studied her hair and opened his mouth to speak, then closed it without uttering a word.

What had he been about to say? That he liked her hair up? Or did he wonder what it meant? She hoped he'd soon figure it out on his own.

From now on she meant to be ordinary.

The dishes still sat on the table, thick porridge lining the edges of the white bowls. Glasses stood before the twins' bowls and a blue porcelain mug before Abel. "Are you finished with your breakfast?"

Three heads nodded.

"I'll clean up." She gathered the dishes into a pile and checked the kettle. Finding it empty, she filled it and set it to boil. She glanced around. Today she meant to begin proving how well she managed as a housewife. *Wife.* The word echoed through her head even though she mentally denied she had such hope.

She made the two beds, pushed the trundle bed away and picked the children's clothing off the floor. All stuff they normally did themselves, but there was no need for them to do it anymore. She would take care of them and their needs. She took the paper animals off the shelf and arranged them on the bed for the children to play with.

"Mercy."

Abel's soft words stopped her. She turned to face him. He sat alone at the table and she joined him.

"How are you? Did you have a good night?" She kept her voice low so the children wouldn't hear and worry.

"Apart from a bruise or two, I'm fine. How are you? You seem different this morning."

So he'd noticed. But she couldn't tell what he thought about the change. It was on the tip of her tongue to ask but she wouldn't. Let him see that she could be the sort of woman he needed—ordinary.

The kettle hissed and she bounded to her feet, poured the water in the dishpan and tackled the dishes.

He rose and reached for his coat. "I still have that log to get home."

Her hands stilled, her lungs stopped and her heart blasted against her ribs and clung there. "You can't." The words crackled from her lips. She shook her head. She'd worry about him every minute. "You might... You aren't..." Swallowing hard, she dried her hands and followed him to the door. "Couldn't you rest one more day?" Just then she recalled that Eddie and the men would soon arrive to help him. Let one of them get the log and any more logs they needed. "Please."

He stood with his hand on the latch. "Winter will soon be upon us."

All sorts of arguments sprang to her mind. Winter would come whether or not he was ready. If he hurt himself he would never be ready. And if his injuries were serious—

She couldn't finish the thought.

"Hello, the house." The call made them both jump.

"Who can that be?" he asked.

She pretended innocence. "It sounds like Eddie. You better see what he wants."

He stepped outside and she followed. There stood Eddie, Seth, Brand, Roper, Slim and half a dozen cowboys from Eden Valley Ranch, along with Ward and, if she wasn't mistaken, some hands from the OK Ranch.

"What is this?" Abel sounded confused.

"I believe it's a work bee," she replied from behind him.

Abel jerked back, forcing Mercy to sidestep. He grabbed her arm. "Whose idea is this?"

"I think it's Eddie's. Why?"

"I can't accept all this help."

She grinned at him. "Try telling that to all those men. They've come to help because they know you need it and deserve it."

"But they hardly know me."

"You're a friend and a neighbor. That's all that matters. I've learned that out west people pull together. It's one of the best things about this country." That, and the freedom allowed woman.

Abel stared at the men, who were now dismounting. "I don't know what to do."

"I'd suggest you go out there and welcome them and thank them." She shoved him in the right direction.

He glanced at her over his shoulder. "Did anyone ever tell you you're bossy?"

"Nope. Not a soul. Best if you don't either."

Chuckling, he crossed to Eddie's side.

The sun shone warm and bright. The light breeze stirred the treetops. The air sang with the smell of autumn leaves and woodsmoke.

Mercy watched the men with a smile on her face. It was going to be a fine day.

Eddie clapped Abel on the back and indicated the men. Each carried an ax or saw or hammer or sometimes two or three tools.

The children joined Mercy and she explained the men had come to put up a new cabin for them.

"Like Papa wants?" Ladd asked.

"Exactly like your papa wants."

They asked to watch. "Put on your coats and stay close. I don't want you getting in their way."

She would like to watch, too, but she had work to do.

She browned meat and peeled vegetables for a stew. Linette had informed her the men would bring their own lunches, but she meant for Abel and the children to have a hot, nourishing dinner.

As the stew simmered, she slipped outside to check on the twins. They sat against the cabin watching the beehive of activity. Some of the men shaped logs, chips of wood flying in every direction as the axes rose and fell. The aroma of new wood filled the air.

Others peeled new logs, the bark peeling off in long strands.

A crew laid logs into place. Already she could see the shape of the cabin. It would be considerably larger than the current one. Roomy enough for a family.

Families had needs. She turned back inside and set to work wiping the logs of the old cabin. Even if it wouldn't be a home for them much longer, they deserved the cleanest, warmest, best-run home in the country.

But again and again, she was drawn to the door to see how the building progressed.

She looked for Abel. He stood by Eddie discussing something. She nodded her satisfaction. Knowing about Abel's injuries, especially the blow to his head, Eddie would somehow divert Abel from doing anything heavy.

Returning indoors, she glanced around. What did a person—a housewife—do in such small quarters? Normally Monday meant laundry, but the morning had flown by. It was too late to start washing clothes. However, she could prepare to do it tomorrow and she went outside to retrieve the copper boiler hanging on the side of the cabin. Still, if she put it on the stove now, the water would half boil away before morning. With a sigh, she hung it back on the nail.

"What are you doing?"

Abel's voice came unexpectedly from behind her, sending her blood to her heart in such a hurry she gasped. She turned slowly. "I was thinking about laundry."

"You seem restless. It's not necessary for you to be here. I can watch the children."

Was the man blind? How could he have so completely misinterpreted the change in her? "Oh, no. I've no place else to be. Nothing else I want to do."

He didn't speak. Didn't nod or shake his head. He simply studied her, his eyes revealing nothing more than confusion. "Why have you been avoiding looking at the new cabin?"

She rubbed a spot on her nose and slowed her breath. All the while she'd been trying to prove she could be a good and efficient housewife, he'd been thinking she wasn't interested in the construction work. "I've been busy. That's all."

"In that case, why don't you come over now and have a look." He crooked his elbow toward her as if she needed assistance crossing the yard. Let him think so. She tucked her hand about his arm and let him lead her.

"It's much bigger and will be sounder than the little cabin. There will be a bedroom, kitchen and living room." He pointed out where each would be. "The loft will have two rooms for the twins."

She could see it all. The table and chairs there. A wide bed there. The cupboards and stove over there. Little beds with bright quilts in the loft. In fact, she saw it much too clearly. She saw herself at the table rolling out biscuits, at the stove stirring a pot, smoothing the bedding on all three beds. She even pictured herself making the quilts for each of the twins' beds.

She shouldn't have come with him. Shouldn't have listened to his description of the rooms.

"I can't quite decide where to put the window in the kitchen." He stared at the area meant for that room. "Is it better by the door, do you think?"

She saw it over the table. But before she could answer, he spoke again.

"I'm sorry. I know it doesn't matter to you. You'll soon be on your way to join a show." He patted her hand as it lay on his arm. "I just—"

"Abel," Slim called. "Show me where the wall will go."

"Be right there." He removed his arm so her hand fell to her side. "Feel free to look around."

But her thoughts burned within her. How much clearer could he be than to remind her that she'd said she planned to be a trick roper and rider? Had he even realized she'd changed her mind?

It was up to her to make him see it. She glanced at the shape of the future cabin, then returned to the present one.

She stepped inside and leaned against the door. As she reviewed what had just happened, she groaned. She hadn't even asked him how he felt. How did that prove anything but selfishness?

Straightening, she squared her shoulders. She could change and she would. He'd soon be able to see it clearly.

Although Abel paid attention to each word Slim spoke, he knew every step Mercy took back to the cabin. His thoughts moved a little slower today because of his headache, but Mercy was different. She'd worn a dress for one thing and pulled her hair back into a roll. Not that she hadn't done so before, but only on Sundays. Normally he would have expected to see her watching the construction work. Or amusing the children with games and pretend play. But today she stayed inside the little cabin. Why? He wished he knew what it meant.

Or maybe he didn't want to know.

After she'd rescued him and stayed at his side until she thought he was no longer in danger, he believed a new understanding, a closeness of sorts, had developed between them.

Obviously he only imagined it because of his vulnerable state. Something that no longer existed. He must guard his thoughts and actions lest he make another mistake.

But an hour later, he wished she would come outside and offer a few suggestions. He could use a woman's point of view on some of the decisions.

"Let's have dinner," Eddie called.

The men threw down their tools and jogged to their saddlebags to pull out the lunches they'd brought with them.

Abel didn't have a prepared lunch so he strode toward the cabin, his steps slowing as he neared the place.

He could hear the twins talking inside, could hear Mercy respond though he could not make out her words.

He would soon have a new cabin. There would be no need for her to come and watch the children. He almost wished Eddie would take his crew and go home.

Realizing how foolish a thought that was, he put it down to his headache. Of course, he was grateful. He and the twins would have a safe, warm, solid home for the winter…for those long cold days and even colder nights when he would lie alone in his bed while the children slept in the loft. He'd rise to a cold room. The loneliness of the prospect scratched at him. But he had the twins. That's all that mattered.

If only he believed it… But having had Mercy's company for these past three weeks, he knew he'd wish every day for more than safe and warm.

There must be a solution. One that would satisfy them both.

But she wanted to leave. And he wanted a woman who would stay.

He stepped inside and breathed in the savory aroma of stew. "I feel guilty eating a hot meal while everyone else eats cold sandwiches."

"You aren't everyone else." Mercy filled four bowls and then sat across the table from him.

What did she mean?

"You need extra nourishment after your accident."

Oh. Only that. He dipped his head to hide his disappointment. "I'll say grace." He took a moment to collect his thoughts before he prayed. After his amen, he silently asked God to guard his heart and mind. But an inadmissible thought followed. *God, could You make it possible for Mercy to stay a little longer?* Maybe until it would be too late for her to join a crazy show. Maybe until she changed her mind.

The children plied him with questions throughout the meal. Good thing, as Mercy seemed interested only in her bowl of food. He thanked her for the meal and thanked her again when she filled his coffee cup for the third time. She smiled nice enough but seemed to be faraway in her thoughts.

His coffee grew bitter and he pushed the half-empty cup away. No doubt she wondered when she'd be able to fulfill her commitment to help with the children so she could pursue her own activities. A Wild West show. What did he have to offer to compare with that? Nothing but two children who needed lots of attention, a cabin under construction and his own demands... food, coffee, laundry. No wonder she grew restless and distant.

Yet he couldn't imagine her leaving. Would she stay if he asked?

He bolted to his feet. "I hear the men back at work." He fled the cabin. But, despite the blow of ax against wood, the pound of hammers, the shrill of saws, his thoughts circled the same question over and over.

He could ask her to stay until the new cabin was finished. That meant windows in, partitions up, the floor finished, the chimney built. It would mean her riding back and forth every day. How long could he reasonably consider that feasible? Once the cabin was finished, then what?

He picked up a saw that leaned against a log and examined it, ran his finger along the teeth. Then what? The question rattled against the inside of his head. Then what?

Eventually he had to say goodbye. Let her go.

Because the only alternative wasn't something he dared think about. Mercy was too much like Ruby. Unprepared to settle down.

Someone called him and he set aside the saw and went to see what was wanted.

Would she stay if he asked her? If only until the new cabin was finished and ready to live in?

He could offer neither of them any longer than that.

By late afternoon, the cabin walls were halfway up.

Eddie called a halt to the work. "We'll be back in the morning. I'll escort Mercy home."

"I truly appreciate your help," Abel replied. But he couldn't help feeling disappointed that he would not get a chance to ask Mercy to consider returning every day until the new cabin was livable.

As she rode away with Eddie, he realized he didn't know if she meant to return in the morning.

Why hadn't he thought to ask?

The question plagued him throughout the evening as he served the children more of the stew that grew more flavorful the longer it simmered.

He tried to stay awake after the children went to bed to figure out what he wanted to do about Mercy, but his body demanded otherwise and he crawled between the covers and fell instantly asleep.

The children woke him the next morning. Not often did he sleep longer than they did. Every bone in his body felt the effects of his accident and he groaned as he got up.

Allie watched him carefully. "Are you okay, Papa?"

He straightened and hid his pain. "I'm fine." It was later than he usually got up. "We better hurry with breakfast or the men will be here. They'll think we do nothing but sleep."

Ladd poured water in the kettle. "The fire is going."

Abel stared at his son. When had he grown so independent?

"Mercy showed us what to do and said it was okay so long as there was an adult present."

He guessed being asleep while Ladd tended the stove qualified as having an adult present. But he didn't know if he should be concerned or pleased at Ladd's ability.

One thing he knew for certain, if he didn't get moving the men would be back before he did his chores. He sliced bread and set out syrup to spread on it. Knowing it would never get him through the morning, he opened a can of beans and another of peaches.

Allie sighed. "I wish Mercy would make breakfast for us."

"Well, she can't be here in time. Eat up. I have chores to do." He downed his food and rushed outside to feed Sam while the twins still ate.

He was returning to the cabin with an armload of firewood when Eddie rode in with a crew. Abel's lungs sucked in air laden with the smell of wood and fall leaves and warm sunshine when he saw Mercy riding at Eddie's side. She'd come back.

She swung down and handed her horse to Eddie, then followed Abel to the house. "How are you?" She studied him. "Seems to me you're limping a little."

"It's only bruises. I'm fine." Even the remnants of his headache had vanished with her arrival.

She paused to take the copper boiler from the hook and carried it to the stove. "I'll get the water heating." She headed to the well with two buckets.

Why would she do the laundry? She'd never done it before. He'd managed on his own, scrubbing a few things as they were needed. But before he could ask her, Eddie called and he had to leave.

So many things about Mercy had changed. She again wore a dress and had her hair pinned up. She seemed set on remaining indoors despite the brilliant sunshine. What was wrong with her? Was this her way of preparing to say a final goodbye?

The walls of the new cabin rose steadily.

"We'll get the basic shell up today," Eddie predicted. "Tomorrow we'll put on a roof."

"I can manage the shakes on my own," Abel said. "And the inside finishing."

"Good, because I assured Linette we'd get the church up this fall."

"I'll help with the church."

"Not until you're ready." Eddie clapped Abel's shoulder. "There'll be lots of people at the church raising. It will be a major community event if Linette has her way."

As Abel watched the walls go up, he made up his mind. He would ask Mercy to watch the children until they moved into the new cabin. It was the most he could allow himself. Even that might be beyond his reach if she had her heart set on joining a Wild West show before winter. Any show in this part of the country would soon be heading south to miss the bad weather. Unless… He smiled. He might need her so long she missed joining before they'd left.

He shook his head. He knew the folly of hoping a person would give up their dreams because of contrary circumstances. Hadn't he learned his lesson with Ruby? And his own choices?

But a delay was acceptable.

Having made up his mind, he discovered how difficult it was to find an opportunity to ask the question. He'd insisted he should join the men eating sandwiches outdoors at dinnertime. Mercy and the children ate indoors. He'd expected her to join the men. The fact she hadn't had him half convinced she was ill.

But she rushed about hanging wet clothes on a line she'd suspended between the cabin and a nearby tree. Later, she took each item off the line and carried it indoors showing no sign of illness.

Then, before he knew it, Eddie called out, "That's it, boys. The walls are up."

Abel went from man to man shaking hands and thanking them. "I appreciate everything."

When he turned to speak to Mercy, she was already sitting on Nugget's back at Eddie's side, waiting to leave.

"I'll bring a crew tomorrow to do the roof," Eddie called as they rode away.

Abel stared after until Ladd asked, "Papa, what's the matter?"

He turned away. "Nothing wrong, son. I'm just thinking how grateful I am for the help. We'll soon be in a big, warm cabin."

"This cabin is warm," Ladd said.

"Except when the wind blows, then the roof rattles and the cold shrieks through the chinks in the wall." It would be plenty hard to stay warm come winter, but now he could get the new cabin ready, fill in every space between the logs so tightly no wind would ever sneak through.

Tomorrow, he vowed, he'd ask Mercy to keep coming. If she didn't return tomorrow, he'd go to the ranch and ask her.

That night he lay awake after the twins fell asleep and he prayed. He prayed for things he knew were in the children's best interests, like safety and love. But he also wished for things he doubted were in any of their best interests.

Wishes were harmless enough so long as he didn't let them rule his choices.

He was up early the next day and put coffee to boil. The sun had not yet appeared over the eastern horizon but the sky turned steely gray, indicating it would soon appear. Abel opened the door, on the excuse of getting more wood. He paused to listen. No thud of approaching horses. He lingered, straining for a sound. Sighing, he returned inside. The coffee boiled over and he reached for it, remembered just in time to wrap a cloth around his hand. He shook the pot and stared at the mess on the stove.

The children crawled out of bed and dressed, then they sat at the table.

"Papa, are we going to eat?" Allie asked.

He jerked his attention from the coffeepot. How long had he been staring at it, wondering?

"Of course, we'll eat." He dragged out a fry pan, threw in a spoonful of bacon fat and sliced in leftover potatoes before he began another pot of coffee.

Ladd rushed to the stove and pushed the pan aside.

"Ladd, stay away from the stove."

"Papa, the potatoes are burning."

"Sorry. I got distracted." And his lack of concentration wouldn't end until he knew if Mercy would come this morning. Maybe not then even. Not until he asked her to stay and got the response he wanted.

A short time later, horses rode into the yard.

Abel hurried for the door and flung it open. His lungs filled with ease for the first time all morning at the sight of Mercy beside Eddie. Half a dozen men accompanied them, but he didn't even look at them. He couldn't have said who they were.

He and Mercy smiled and said hello. They passed each other as he joined the men and she went inside the cabin. It took almost more self-discipline than he could muster not to follow her and ask her on the spot. Perhaps, at the same time, he'd ask why she'd been acting so differently if he ever got a chance to speak to her without cowboys or the twins or both hanging over his shoulder, listening to every word.

By midmorning, he could wait no longer and, murmuring some excuse, he climbed from the roof and headed for the cabin. He opened the door. Mercy sat with a basket of mending on her lap and a needle and thread in her hand.

On the floor before her sat Allie, also with a needle and thread. She held a piece of fabric in her hand. A handkerchief. She took stitches to hem it.

Ladd sat beside her cutting pictures from a magazine.

Abel's heart threatened to melt out the soles of his boots. This was what he'd wanted since the twins were born. A welcoming home. A happy family. A woman who glanced at him and smiled.

Then reality slammed into his thoughts and he swallowed hard. He had no more room for useless dreams. All he wanted, all he could allow himself, was a few more days of pretending.

Chapter Fourteen

Mercy sewed a button on a pair of Ladd's trousers. She'd done laundry, ironed the clothes. She now worked on the mending. Wasn't she being ordinary? But Abel only said she seemed different.

Different as night from day, if he cared to notice.

The door opened and he stared at the three of them. She couldn't read his expression. Did he approve? Did he even notice?

"Ladd, Allie," he said. "Run outside and play for a bit. Mind you don't bother the men."

The twins set aside their projects and dashed outside without arguing. Mercy watched them go. They were such good children. What did Abel have to say that couldn't be said in front of them? She kept her head bent over the button. The new cabin was almost finished. Likely he'd come to tell her he no longer needed her to come. She would not let him guess how desperately she wished he could see the change in her and understand what it meant.

He remained just inside the door and twisted his hat

round and round. "I know you've got your heart set on joining a Wild West show."

"That's been my plan. I haven't minded delaying though." *I could be persuaded to change my mind if you offered an alternative.*

The hat went round and round. Then paused. "You're good at it."

He meant her trick riding, she supposed. "Thank you." He'd had little enough to say at the time. Why now? She tied off the thread and shook out Ladd's shirt. One more garment mended.

Abel shifted from one foot to the other. "The new cabin is looking good."

"Indeed." The subject she'd been expecting and dreading.

"Of course, I still have a lot of work to do. More firewood to get in. The inside of the cabin to finish. The cracks to fill."

"Mmm-hmm." She selected one of Allie's dark pinafores whose seam needed repairing. She cut off a length of navy thread. The little girl needed someone to dress her up and do her hair, she thought absently. Not that Abel didn't do the best he could.

He jerked a chair from the table and plunked it in front of her, his knees only inches from hers. He leaned forward until she felt him with every breath.

She lifted her head and met his eyes, blinked before his demanding look. She lowered her hands to her lap, scrubbed her lips together. Had she done something wrong? Something to earn his displeasure? But she couldn't think of what it could be. Why, these past few days she'd been so perfectly behaved she thought she'd perish of boredom. How did Linette, and Jayne and Grace manage? Sybil, she could understand. All Sybil had ever wanted was to live by rules.

"Mercy." Abel's voice jerked her nerves like a taut rope. "What I'm about to say…ask…is big. I know it is. But I hope you'll consider it carefully before you give a response." He scratched at a snag on his trouser's leg. If he kept it up there'd be another mending job.

"Of course." He was certainly being mysterious and her nerves began to twitch in time to his scratching.

He pressed his hand against his leg as if realizing the damage he did. "I would like to ask you to consider coming a bit longer." He sprang to his feet. "There, I've said it." He crossed to the stove, picked up the coffeepot and set it down again, then returned to the chair, swinging it around and straddling the seat. He leaned over the back. "I could get my work done so much faster if I didn't have to watch the twins and they really enjoy having you here."

That she knew to be true. But what did he think of her presence? She dared not ask. "I enjoy keeping them company."

"So you'll think about it?"

It was a beginning. More time would allow him to see how ordinary she could be. "I don't need to. My answer is yes."

He jumped to his feet and stood by her chair. "That's great."

She took her time inserting the threaded needle into the fabric she held. Carefully, she folded it, keeping the needle visible on top, and set it on the basket of other items to be mended. Only then did she lift her gaze to him.

He grinned widely. She wondered if his eyes revealed approval or only relief.

Drawn by the look in his gaze, she rose to face him.

"I'm glad." He smiled at her.

"Me, too." She returned his smile.

The air shimmered between them until she had to blink to keep her eyes from tearing. If only she could read his thoughts. Was he grateful only for the sake of the children? Or did that gleam in his eyes say he was happy for his sake, as well? He scrubbed his lips together. Shifted on his feet. His gaze dipped to her mouth.

Her breath stuck midway up her throat. Without forethought, she leaned toward him.

He leaned in…then he blinked, patted her shoulder and headed for the door.

She lifted a hand, thinking to call him back. For a moment she'd thought he meant to kiss her.

She pressed her fingers to her mouth as he ducked out the door. Next time she'd make sure he followed through on that thought.

The next morning Abel sat at the table pretending he wasn't as anxious to see Mercy as were the twins. Wearing their coats, they waited at the door for the sound of her horse. The morning air was chilly, and he'd insisted they keep the door closed until she arrived.

"I hear her," Ladd yelled, and the pair rushed outside.

Abel slipped into his coat and followed.

"Mercy," Allie called. "Papa made us wait until you got here before we could look inside the new cabin."

They trooped after her to the corral, where she unsaddled Nugget and turned him loose.

"He did, did he?" She took Allie's hand on one side and Ladd's on the other, and the three of them waited for Abel to catch up. "Now why would you do that?"

"It was as much their idea to wait as mine."

"I see."

If only he knew what she saw. She'd agreed readily enough to help for a few more days. Would it be long enough for him to provide reason for her to...

What? Make it permanent?

He'd wasted enough of his life chasing after dreams and he saw how that had turned out. All his life he'd wanted...

He couldn't even say. Only that he hadn't found it at home building ships; nor had he found the elusive something living a wild and free life. He certainly hadn't found it in his marriage to Ruby.

The only thing that had ever given him satisfaction was the twins. He loved them and vowed to devote his life to them.

Yet his insides ached for more.

When they reached the cabin, he opened the door and waved them in with a wide sweep of his arm.

The twins dashed in and circled the room at a run. Mercy entered more slowly and stood at Abel's side. "Eddie insisted on putting up the walls for the bedroom and the loft floor. I have yet to put in the chimney and get glass for the windows." He took her arm and led her forward. "I plan to put the stove here. And the table will go beneath the window so we can see out as we eat." Thankfully, she didn't seem to notice his use of the word "we" or she assumed he meant himself and the twins. But he'd been picturing Mercy at the table across from him, enjoying a cup of coffee as the sun shone through the glass.

Ladd and Allie faced them. "Papa, where is Mercy going to sleep?"

"Me?" He noticed a jolt run up her arm. She touched the two little heads. "I am only coming to help until your papa doesn't need me."

Confusion crowded their faces and then disappointment. Ladd led Allie away. Just before the door closed behind them, Abel caught Allie's whispered words. "She doesn't want to stay with us. Just like Mama."

Had Mercy heard the words? He slanted a look at her. If she'd heard she gave no indication.

"It will be a very nice home," she said.

"It's missing only one thing." He hadn't meant to say the words aloud but now that he had, he didn't regret it. Now he would get a chance to say what was in his heart.

He ignored the little warning voice in the back of his brain telling him to listen to his head not his heart.

She turned to face him. "What's it missing?" Her eyes were watchful and, dare he believe, hopeful?

"A mother."

She raised her eyebrows and her eyes filled with disbelief. "Wouldn't that mean you'd have to take a wife?" She stepped away as if to check the view out the window. "And as I recall, you've decided you would never marry again."

He crossed to her side, struggling to find words to express both his desire and his uncertainty. "I think what I said, or at least what I meant, is I would never marry a woman who wasn't devoted to the twins." Suddenly a rush of words flooded his mouth. "Ruby found them a nuisance. It didn't matter to her if they were properly supervised or even adequately fed and clothed. I'll never put them through that again. Never."

"Nor should you."

Her silent waiting sucked at his thoughts. Did she mean—

"Papa!" Ladd's fear-filled yell jerked Abel toward the door. He rushed outside to discover the twins between the cabin and the corrals, staring into the woods. Allie gripped Ladd's hand, her face white and drawn.

"What's wrong?" he asked as he reached them, Mercy hard on his heels.

Ladd answered, "There's something out there."

Abel and Mercy glanced at each other. In her eyes was the acknowledgment of the same thing he feared. The man in the woods.

"You two go to the old cabin and stay inside with Mercy." He shepherded them toward the door.

"Papa," Allie's voice was a thin whisper. "It was a kitty cat."

No kitty cats wandered about the woods, but he'd let her believe it rather than frighten her. Inside, he grabbed his rifle and turned to Mercy. "Do you have your gun?"

She shook her head and avoided meeting his gaze.

How strange. Wasn't she afraid of the man out there? "Where is it? I'll get it for you." He turned on his heel, expecting she'd say he'd find her gun on her saddle.

"I quit carrying it."

His jaw fell lax. He blinked at her. "I must have misunderstood. I thought you said you didn't carry a gun anymore."

"That's what I said."

"What a time to be without a gun." Especially with

a wild man in the woods. "Keep the children with you. Don't wander about in the woods. Call if you need help."

He closed the door behind him and skirted the woods around the cabin, but he saw nothing that made him think either a man or a kitty cat had been there. Perhaps the twins had been mistaken.

The tension slipped from his shoulders. Why would Mercy stop carrying a gun? His shoulders tightened again. Didn't she realize the dangers of riding back and forth through the woods without protection? Kitty cat or crazy man, it was but a fraction of the dangers that faced her.

If something were to happen to her—

It would be partially his fault for asking her to make the journey twice a day.

Assured no wild animals or wild men stalked his family, Abel went to the new cabin. It was time to start on the chimney. Time to get his new home ready for the winter.

He'd been about to ask Mercy to stay on. In the back of his mind, he supposed he meant to ask her to marry him. But he understood a man with two kids and a desire to live a calm, ordinary life held no appeal to her. It was a good thing Allie and Ladd had interrupted their conversation.

He would not think of the long, lonely days. His only concern had to be the welfare of the twins.

The next day Mercy came prepared to give the children school lessons. She'd used every opportunity to teach them math and reading skills. When they helped with a recipe she had them measure, add and subtract the ingredients. When they had a treasure hunt or played sailing on a ship, she let them read from one of the many books she borrowed from Eddie's large library.

But now she needed to be more purposeful about it. She meant to show Abel she could be a responsible mother figure. He'd said he wanted a mother for his children. Well, he'd soon learn she could be that. Would she be willing to settle for nothing more? Of course. Who needed more? Lots of women had loveless marriages and lived for their children. Wasn't Abel satisfied with being a father and nothing more? Yet her answer failed to satisfy an ache deep inside, in a forbidden place behind her heart. A place with solid steel doors for which she'd thrown away the key. Yet somehow the doors managed to creak open a bit each time she thought of Abel.

As soon as the cabin was clean and soup simmered on the back of the stove, she brought out pencils and paper for the children. Linette had supplied her with texts suitable for the twins. "Allie, Ladd, today we are going to start school lessons."

Ladd stared at the books. "I don't like school."

"The others make fun of us because we can't read as good as they do," Allie said, with a tremble in her voice.

No doubt they had missed much school if they moved around as often as Abel said and if Ruby hadn't made sure they attended. Mercy wanted to gather the children in her arms and assure them she would never neglect them. But she didn't have the right.

"Then why don't we work to catch up?"

They reluctantly sat at the table. She explained the lesson to them and guided them to answer the questions.

She knew they had the skills for basic arithmetic, but they stalled at completing the work.

Ladd dropped his pencil and chased it across the floor.

Allie followed his lead.

Mercy tried to corral them back to the table, but Ladd climbed on the bed and pulled down their collection of paper animals.

It gave Mercy an idea. Perhaps they weren't ready for formal lessons, but that didn't mean she would give up.

"Ladd, if each of us made three more animals, how many more would we have?"

The twins looked at her as if she'd asked them to number the stars.

"Look. There's three of us and if we each make three animals…" She laid out three piles of three. "How many more would you have?"

"Nine," Allie shouted.

"Right. Now how many all together if you add nine?"

Ladd answered first, pleased at figuring it out.

She went around the house, naming objects. "How many legs in total do four chairs have? How many cans of beans in half a dozen cases?"

Soon the children were asking each other and shouting out answers.

She guided them back to the table. "Let's see how fast you can come up with the answers on your worksheets."

At first she thought they would balk, but when Allie bent over her page, so did Ladd. They finished within seconds of each other.

Mercy checked the answers. "A hundred percent for

both of you. Good job." Now to shift to writing. "Let's practice handwriting."

Two bottom lips came out.

"How can you send letters if you can't write?"

Ladd gave her a look of disbelief. "Who would we send letters to?"

"Why don't you write to your grandparents?" She had no idea if Abel was in contact with them, but he'd never said anything to lead her to suspect otherwise.

So she helped them pen simple little letters, suggesting they tell about the new cabin.

"I want to tell about you riding in a Wild West show," Allie said.

"Let's leave that for another day." If the grandparents were anything like Abel, they would be shocked he had a woman like her—someone who had taught the twins about trick riding—caring for the children.

The twins did not like her answer.

"Why don't you write pretend stories about whatever you want? We could put them in a scrapbook and save them? Wouldn't it be fun to read them to your own children?"

Ladd and Allie laughed so hard they almost fell off their chairs.

She chuckled, too. "I'm sure your papa would like to keep your stories."

They nodded and bent over the sheets of paper she gave them. She had to spell many words for them and show them how to shape some of their letters. Half an hour later they had finished their stories.

Just in time as Abel came through the door. "What's going on here?"

"We're having school," Ladd said.

"We wrote to Grandma and Grandpa," Allie added.

"You did?"

Mercy watched his expression, saw it go from curious to surprised to pleased and she hugged her success to herself.

"We wrote stories, too," Ladd said.

"Do you want to read mine?" Allie held out her piece of paper.

Mercy's heart clenched. Allie had written about a young girl who was the star in a Wild West show.

Abel took the piece of paper. His jaw tightened as he read. It tightened further when he read Ladd's story about a boy who roped a wild horse and tamed it.

Mercy crossed her arms about her. Her success had been swallowed up in defeat.

"Very adventuresome," Abel said as he crossed to the stove.

By adventuresome he meant foolish. Risky. He didn't have to explain; she knew.

"Dinner is ready." She gathered the school supplies together, careful with the pages the twins had written. If he didn't want to save them, she would. And maybe now that they knew how to write a letter they'd write her once she left.

She pressed a hand to her middle and stifled a groan. She did not want to leave them. Any of them. Still, it seemed less and less possible Abel would ever see how much she'd changed.

But as she served soup and then cleaned up, she made up her mind. She wasn't prepared to give up yet.

She decided to seek counsel from her friends. Later, when she returned home, she took care of Nugget and looked up the hill toward the big house. But rather than head in that direction she crossed to Jayne's cabin.

Jayne welcomed her. "I see so little of you lately. How are Abel and the children?"

"They're fine." She crossed to the window and glanced out without seeing past the glass, then spun around and went to the table to run her finger along the surface.

"How is the new cabin coming?" Jayne asked, watching her from her chair.

Mercy shrugged. "They'll soon be moving in." She dropped to a chair facing Jayne. "Are you happy?"

Showing no surprise at the change in conversation, Jayne smiled. "Supremely. Seth is wonderful."

Mercy shook her head. "I don't mean Seth. I mean this." She waved her hand around the room.

"This cabin is only temporary. We'll have something bigger. Not that we need it right now."

Mercy couldn't deny the serenity of both Jayne's smile and words. "I don't mean the cabin. I mean this life. You hardly leave the cabin. You spend most of your days cooking and sewing. Is it enough?"

"It is for me because it's who I am."

Mercy studied her hands as they twisted together in her lap. Realizing Jayne might read more into the gesture than she cared to explain, she folded her hands together and forced them to be still. "I don't know who I am."

"I think you do. I've watched you these past few days. You've changed. That might be good. You've been far too adventuresome, as if trying to fill up a need in your life. But remember, you can't be what you think someone else wants you to be. You will only be happy if you are true to who you are, who God meant for you to be."

"I expect you're right." She stayed and visited a few more minutes then left. She wanted to change so Abel would approve of her. Did that mean she was trying to be someone she wasn't? Or was she trying to become the person she was meant to be?

It was all so confusing. She trotted the last few yards to the house and rushed indoors to see Linette and Grady.

Linette seemed content. So much so that Mercy envied her. But hadn't she had to change to fit into ranch life? Mercy had heard tales of how Linette struggled to learn how to bake bread, make meals and prove to Eddie that she could be a proper ranch wife. That had worked out well. Both of them were so happy.

She drew in a long, slow breath. She would prove her ability to change, as well.

Would Abel then notice and approve?

Would he grow to love her?

Chapter Fifteen

Abel brushed Allie's hair and fixed a bow on it. Over the past few days Mercy had spent time on the child's hair. It made him think he should give the chore a little more thought. At least with Ladd all he had to do was make sure the boy washed behind his ears. And did his wrists. He smiled as he recalled his own mother checking those very places.

His smile flattened and his brow tightened. Mercy had changed. And he didn't mean solely that she had worn a dress every day of the past week and had done her best to keep her hair pinned up. He chuckled softly as he thought how the curls escaped long before she left each day.

"What's so funny, Papa?" Allie asked.

"I was just thinking."

"Of Mercy?"

"Now why would you think that?"

"I was thinking of her and how she braided my hair after she washed it. Do you like it all crimpy like this?"

"It's beautiful. Just like you."

"Oh, Papa." But Allie smiled, pleased at the compliment.

He straightened and shifted to look out the window. Was Mercy acting differently to get his approval? Just as she did wild things to get attention?

He wished he knew what the change in her meant. He wasn't sure how he felt about it. He had spoken his disapproval of her adventuresome nature because he feared the children would be hurt.

And, he silently acknowledged, because it reminded him painfully of Ruby.

But the new Mercy didn't quite fit.

Fit what? asked an inner voice.

"Are we going, Papa?" Ladd asked, cutting into his thoughts.

The twins stood at the door waiting to go to the ranch for church.

Grateful to be pulled from his musings, his answerless questions and his vague sense of disappointment, he lifted them to Sam's back and turned to the trail.

They arrived at the ranch just as Mercy headed down the hill ahead of Linette and Eddie and young Grady.

The twins slipped to the ground and raced to greet her. Abel took his time, tending Sam and trying to sort out his feelings. This was Mercy, who had tended the children and cooked welcome meals for several weeks now. Mercy, who rode like a man, roped better than many and twirled guns like they were toys. Mercy, who taught his children their sums and letters, who made him aware of the emptiness of his heart in a way that sucked reason from his thoughts time after time.

He shifted to study the scene around him. Without forethought, his gaze followed the direction he and

Mercy had gone so many days ago, up the hill to the crown of trees. He'd kissed her there. To comfort her, he assured himself. But despite his reservations and internal words of caution, he was drawn to her. He continued to be drawn. But things had changed. And he didn't mean only Mercy.

Until he could sort everything out, he must guard his heart.

"Papa?"

He turned at Allie's call and came face-to-face with Mercy, a twin clinging to each hand. "'Morning."

She smiled. "Yes, it is."

Her simple mocking observation eased his troubled mind and he grinned.

"A nice day for church."

She chuckled. "A nice day for anything."

They crossed to the cookhouse and climbed the steps. He braced himself for Cookie's exuberant greeting then led the children to one of the benches.

Mercy hung back.

He tipped his head to indicate she should join them.

She nodded, a smile lighting her eyes.

The smile landed in his heart with a gentle plop. Whatever else was going on, he did enjoy sharing Sunday services with her.

As Cookie led them in several hymns, her voice joined his, with the children singing loud and clear. Bertie spoke about the joy of obedience to God. Abel nodded. Obedience provided a safe route. Then those in attendance gathered round the tables for the usual cinnamon rolls and coffee.

The talk immediately shifted to plans for a building bee for the church in Edendale.

"So we're agreed, next Saturday?" Eddie said. "I'll let others in the area know."

"We women will bring plenty of food," Linette said. "It will be a great community gathering." She gave Eddie an adoring look. "I've been waiting a long time for this day."

He pulled her close. "I'm sorry you had to wait so long."

"I'm not complaining."

The children ran out to play.

"Papa, can I go, too?" Allie asked, her eyes big with pleading.

"You can watch but not run."

She sighed softly and shuffled to the door.

Mercy watched her leave, her eyes dipping down at the corners. She glanced at him.

He knew from her look and from things she'd said that she felt sorry for Allie always being excluded from the joyful play of the other children.

If only he knew whether her heart had been damaged. But the doctor had warned him not to take chances.

When proffered, he accepted Linette's invitation to dinner.

"It will be ready in a couple of hours. In the meantime, why doesn't everyone enjoy the beautiful weather?"

"I'll help." Mercy started to follow Linette.

"No need."

She halted.

Abel could feel her uncertainty across the room and blamed himself. He'd been so tense around her the past few days that he'd made her nervous. He went to her side. "Would you care to go for a walk?" The others made enough noise they wouldn't hear his question.

She nodded and they left, retracing their steps of a few weeks ago. They reached the top of the hill and stood side by side, looking out on the landscape.

"The leaves are almost gone." Was that the best he could do? But everything else he thought of offered far more than he knew he could give.

"Winter will soon be here. You'll have a nice warm home. Soon you'll be moving in. The twins will sleep upstairs in the loft."

She spoke quickly, sharply, saying things she was aware he already knew. Was she nervous, too?

"I would like to make quilts for their beds if you have no objection."

He didn't get a chance to say one way or the other as she rushed on.

"Linette says she has scraps I can use. She offered to help me. It would be nice for them to have something to remember—" She swallowed hard. "For them to have something warm and cozy on their new beds." She crossed her arms and stared at the distant mountaintops.

"I think it would be very nice if you made quilts for them." He couldn't help wondering if she would have time to finish them before she rode off to join a show. A thought slammed into his brain. Did the changes in her mean she might have decided against that?

He pulled her around to face him, keeping his hands on her arms. "Remember last time we were here?"

She studied the front of his shirt. "I believe I cried a little."

He chuckled. "I believe you did." He urged her closer. "And I believe I kissed the tears away."

She nodded, her gaze still chest level.

"And if I'm not mistaken, you kissed me back."

Her head jerked up. Her gaze riveted him, full of hot denial. She opened her mouth, closed it without speaking as the protest fled. A tiny smile curved her mouth. "Maybe."

"Maybe? Hmm. That needs a little clarification, I'd say." He bent closer, giving her plenty of time to withdraw. When she didn't, he claimed her lips. Felt their cool resistance that melted like a sudden spring thaw. Her hands came up and caught his shoulders.

He splayed his hands across her back and held her to him. She melted into his embrace. His heart swelled with joy until he wondered how his ribs contained it.

Reluctantly he withdrew.

She eased back without leaving the shelter of his arms.

They studied each other. He guessed she would see both eagerness and caution in his eyes. Even as he saw it in hers.

He dropped his hands to her arms. The kiss had been fine and good. But he could not allow it to mean all he wanted. Not so long as she was set on joining a Wild West show.

"We should go," Mercy said, stepping out of his arms. "Dinner will be ready soon."

Questions tangled in Mercy's thoughts as they sauntered down the hill. Exactly what did his kiss mean?

Neither of them seemed to be in a hurry. Was he analyzing the situation, as well? She gave a silent chuckle. Abel was far more likely to be trying to figure out what it meant and where it fit in his plans than she.

They arrived at the big house and joined the others around the table. She continued to push aside her inner turmoil enough to listen to and respond to the conversation.

Would he ask her to walk with him again after the meal? But the dishes were barely done when he thanked Linette and Eddie for their hospitality. "I don't like how flushed Allie is. I better take her home."

Mercy hugged the twins goodbye. She stepped back before she lifted her gaze to Abel. He nodded, whether as goodbye or to inform her he shared her confusion, she couldn't say.

Ladd waved as they entered the trees but Abel didn't turn. She stared after them until they disappeared from sight.

Her limbs twitched. Her brain churned. Restlessness filled her. She turned and rushed to her bedroom, changed into her riding trousers and shirt. "I'm going riding," she announced to the women lingering in the kitchen.

She trotted down the hill and caught up Nugget. "It is going to be so good to ride like the wind and practice all our tricks again." No one but the horse heard her words. Within minutes she galloped out of the yard.

But half an hour later she reined to a halt. The questions she'd been ignoring had followed her.

Why had Abel kissed her? Did it mean he had begun to see how much she'd changed and he approved? What next? Would he ask her to stay on? Or, like Ambrose, did he find her too unsettling despite her attempt to be otherwise?

She swallowed hard and stared straight ahead though she saw nothing. She'd once thought she could marry him to be a mother to his children.

She no longer believed it. She wanted more. The depth of her longing twisted inside her, making her squeeze her hands until her gloves threatened to split at the seams. The longing felt frightening, like how she'd felt as she watched her parents and wished they would notice her. She'd outgrown such neediness and had no desire to substitute another situation that made her feel that way.

She had Nugget rear back. She swung a rope over his head and circled it around them both. They practiced his bowing. She twirled her pearl-handled guns.

But nothing she did drove away the restless ache of her heart.

"Papa, I'm not sick." Allie said it several times as they rode toward the cabin.

"Maybe you aren't. But I don't intend to take chances." Not with her health and not with his heart, Abel silently added. He'd almost welcomed the excuse to leave Eden Valley Ranch early. Why did he let himself kiss Mercy when he knew she didn't fit in his world?

Or was she saying with the changes he'd recently seen that she did?

If he hadn't been so distracted by his thoughts he would have paid more attention to his surroundings. He might have noticed the clues before he rode into the clearing and saw the man from the woods standing near the new cabin.

The man looked at him, then darted to the trees.

Abel didn't say anything, not wanting to frighten the children. But he pulled Sam to a stop and watched to see if the man would reappear or simply melt into the woods as he usually did.

When he didn't see him again, Abel took the children with him to the corral as he tended Sam. He carried Allie to the cabin, every sense alert to any sign of danger. Inside, he didn't put her down immediately. "Ladd, stay right there." He pointed to the door. Not until he could be certain there was nothing to be concerned about would he let them go in.

He looked about slowly. The bed was unruffled. The clothing on the hooks undisturbed. The supplies on the shelves appeared exactly as he'd left them. Even his used coffee cup stood on the cupboard exactly where he'd left it.

He put Allie on her feet. She stared up at him.

"Papa, what's the matter?"

"Nothing." At least indoors. "I'm going to do a few things outside. You two stay here. Don't go outside. Don't open the door."

Ladd and Allie exchanged glances. "Something's wrong, isn't it?" Ladd said.

Abel didn't want to alarm them but he couldn't lie to them, either. "I thought I saw something when we rode up. I'll check around to make sure there's nothing out there. Stay here." He left before they could pepper him with questions.

Slowly, methodically, he circled both cabins. He examined every inch of the clearing before entering the new cabin. Apart from a few barely distinguishable footprints that surely belonged to the intruder, he saw nothing to alarm him.

This couldn't continue. He would not live in fear wondering about that crazy wild man.

Tomorrow he would track him down, confront him and put an end to his lurking about. Only then would he feel his family was safe.

True to his word, the next morning, he packed enough supplies to last the day. This mystery man had vanished in the woods at the blink of an eye. Abel anticipated needing the whole day to track him down.

When they heard Mercy ride up, he told the children to stay inside. "I need to talk to Mercy alone for a moment."

Ladd rolled his eyes and Allie clasped her hands and looked dreamy.

He groaned. "I'm only going to tell her my plans for the day." He ducked out before either of them could reply, and joined Mercy at the corral, where she tended her horse.

He told her about discovering the wild man in the yard when he returned Sunday. "I'm going to find him and see what he's doing here. I might suggest he find somewhere else to hang around."

She kept her attention on putting her horse away. "Be sure to give him the benefit of the doubt."

"I won't shoot first and ask questions later, but I can't think what good reason the man could have for hanging around. It's downright spooky. I feel I need to check around every corner and constantly watch over my shoulder."

She straightened and faced him. "Just because he's different doesn't mean he's dangerous."

He recognized her protest for what it was—a defense of her own behavior—and touched her cool cheek. "I know and I promise I will bear it in mind."

A smile lit her eyes. "See that you do."

As he rode away he contemplated the conversations. Was it possible that though she was different, she wasn't a danger to his family? But could he believe that thought, or trust it? Because whatever he did affected his children. He could not simply follow his heart.

Leaving Sam behind so he could more effectively follow the tracks, he searched the woods surrounding the cabins, starting at the uncertain footprint he'd found the day before. The man surely wore moccasins because he left little in the way of tracks. He checked the branches and the leaves. There was little for Abel to follow, but he found a bent branch in a couple of places and an old log with moss brushed off it. The work was time consuming and slow, but he climbed to thicker trees. He paused to stretch his back and wipe sweat from his brow. The day had grown unseasonably warm now that the sun hung at its zenith.

He pulled sandwiches from his pack and swilled back some water. Then he moved on. No telling how far the man had gone since yesterday and Abel wanted to find him and return early enough for Mercy to get home before dark.

He tracked for two more hours, finding more evidence, and guessed the man had spent a good deal of time in that area. He straightened and listened, hoping for a sound to indicate the man's presence even though he knew the man was too smart to reveal himself in any way.

The skin on the back of his neck tingled. Someone watched him. He lifted his rifle for easy access and slowly looked around. At first he saw nothing, then he heard a deep-throated growl and the hair on his arms rose. He jerked back. Not twenty feet away, on a branch above his head, a mountain lion snarled, revealing fangs that could rip him to pieces in a matter of minutes.

He edged the rifle upward.

The big cat crouched and snarled.

His fingers twitched. He held his breath to steady his muscles. He had two children at home who needed him. A wild animal would not rob them of a father. Nor rob him of a chance to have a real family. Could he hope to get a shot off before the animal sprang? He sucked in air and forced every move to be slow and steady, but it happened before he could get a shot off.

Chapter Sixteen

Mercy squeezed her fingers together until they hurt. She pressed her knees tight to stop her legs from bouncing. Somehow she must remain in her chair talking about sums when all the while she wanted to rush to the window for a glimpse of Abel. In fact, if she could follow her instincts, she would swing to Nugget's back and ride out to find him.

Although he'd said he would be gone most of the day, every hour that passed wound her nerves more taut. She didn't even have to close her eyes to picture him pinned under a log. And this time he'd gone carrying a rifle to look for a wild man who lived in the woods. Abel must be crazy. And she as well for not stopping him.

She bounced to her feet. The wide-eyed twins watched her. Crossing to the stove, she shifted the coffeepot six inches to the right and then back to its original spot.

"Where's Papa?" Allie asked.

"Gone to the woods." Mercy and Abel had agreed not to give the children any details of his plan.

Ladd pushed from his chair. "When will he be back?"

Realizing the twins had picked up on her restlessness, Mercy pushed aside her worries. "It's early. He won't be back for another hour or so."

She took one quick glance out the window and returned to the table. "If you're done your sums, let's do some reading." She'd brought some easy reading books and listened with a fraction of her hearing as the twins took turns reading aloud.

Did she hear something outside? She jumped to her feet and dashed to the door. Before she opened it she thought of the man in the woods and stopped. She went to the window but saw nothing. The sound came again, jerking her attention to the corral. Only Nugget and Sam chasing each other around. Mercy sighed.

"Why are you so scared?" Ladd asked.

"I'm not." But her skin felt too tight for her arms and she rubbed to loosen it. If only Abel would return. If something happened to him...

She closed her eyes and pressed her palm to her chest, unable to contemplate the possibility.

Did she hear a thud outside? She would not jerk the way she had before. Instead, she edged closer to the window so she could sneak a look. A movement in the trees caught her attention and she raced for the door.

"Stay here," she told the twins. If Abel was hurt she didn't want them seeing it.

Picking up her annoying skirts, she ran from the cabin, across the yard.

Abel waited at the edge of the clearing. He opened his arms and she went straight to him, pausing only long enough to run her gaze over him. Seeing no sign of blood or injury she caught his face in her hands.

"Are you okay?"

"I'm fine." He pulled her into his arms and rested his cheek on her head. "Just fine."

She wrapped her arms around his waist and clung to him. "I was so worried. What if that crazy man attacked you?"

His chuckle reverberated in his chest and echoed in hers. "What happened to assuming the man was harmless?"

"It's easy enough to say that when he's far away." And Abel was close at hand.

"Are the twins okay?"

"They've been wondering why I kept looking out the window so often." She rested her head against his chest, not eager to let him go. He kept his arms tight about her as if he might feel the same way.

"I found the man."

"You did?" She looked into his face, surprised at the way he smiled.

"Rightfully you could say he found me."

Her arms tightened around him. "What happened?"

"I was tracking him when something made me aware I was being watched. I turned slowly but it wasn't a man I saw. It was a mountain lion overhead ready to pounce."

Her mouth dried so abruptly she couldn't swallow.

He smiled down at her. "Before I could even lift my rifle, a shot rang out and the cat fell to the ground." He brushed a strand of hair off her cheek. "I spun around and saw the man I sought. All whiskered and wild looking, but his eyes were calm and kind. He nodded once and slipped into the trees. I called out. 'Who are you?' but he never turned." Abel brushed his knuckles along her jawline, sending happy little dances up and down her nerves.

"He saved your life."

"Yes, he did. I wish I could do something for him."

"Like what?"

He shrugged. "I don't know. But I hate to think of him out there alone."

"Might be he prefers it that way."

"Could be."

"I wish I could remember where I've seen him before." In her memory, she had fleeting images that she could never pin down to a certain place and time.

Abel's gaze swept across her face and lingered on her lips.

Her heart hammered against her ribs and she lifted her face, meeting him halfway. Their lips touched lightly. Then his arms tightened and he claimed her mouth. She leaned into his embrace. He was back safe and sound and she returned his kiss with a heart full of gratitude.

He lifted his head and looked deep into her eyes, searching her thoughts, her heart, her very soul.

She opened herself to him, allowing the steel doors to her heart to swing wider.

"That's a very nice welcome home."

She grinned. "Glad you enjoyed it."

He chuckled. "No more or less than you, I think."

"The twins are waiting."

He laughed and pulled her to his side. "Then by all means, let's go see them."

She stayed at his side until they reached the cabin,

then slipped away, not ready to let the children see their father and her together. They'd ask questions she couldn't answer because she didn't know what the kiss meant.

Gratitude for his safe return?

On his part, reaction to being spared an attack by the big cat?

"Do you suppose that's what Allie meant when she said she saw a cat?" she asked him.

"I figure it is. I had a look around and saw some cat tracks. I wonder if the man in the woods has been chasing the cat away from us. I think we owe him a lot."

As he shoved open the door, the twins rushed to him.

"Mercy's been worried about you," Ladd said.

"Is that a fact? Well, it's nice someone cares." Abel sent her a teasing grin.

"We care." Allie insisted Abel pick her up. He sat down and pulled Ladd to his knee.

"So what have you being doing all day?"

"We did sums."

"We read a story."

The twins told him the details of their day.

Mercy hung back. She should be on her way, but Abel had just returned and she didn't want to leave. She wanted to stay and share supper with them, help tuck the children into bed and later, after they were settled, talk to Abel about his day and hers.

Did he want it, too? He seemed focused on the children.

She turned to put on her coat.

Abel set the twins to one side. "You two stay here while I go to the corral with Mercy."

She turned to face the door as a grin widened her lips. He'd never wanted to accompany her before.

He fell in at her side. "I'm glad you can get home before dark. Be careful."

"I thought you'd decided that whiskered man was friendly."

He grabbed her hand and pulled her to face him. "There might be another mountain lion out there or a bear." He shuddered. "I sure wouldn't want you to run into anything like that."

"Nor would I."

"Do you have a gun with you?"

She wanted him to think she'd changed. That she no longer wanted to live a wild, undisciplined life. From now on she meant to be ordinary. But she'd felt naked and vulnerable without a firearm and stuck a pistol in her saddlebag. "I might have a gun with me."

"From now on, be sure you have a rifle at the very least."

She didn't say anything, surprised by his change of opinion.

He shook her a little. "Promise me you will."

She searched his eyes. Did the claiming way he looked at her signify a special kind of caring…or simply responsibility like he'd feel if the twins did something risky?

She couldn't tell and afraid of how desperately she wished it was the former, she said, "Very well. I promise." Then she continued her walk to the corral.

He kept in step with her. As she put the bridle on Nugget, he lifted the blanket and saddle to the horse's back.

She watched him tighten the cinch. "I can do that, you know."

He grinned over his shoulder. "I know you can." He finished and straightened. "Do you object to me helping?"

"No. But why do you want to?"

He closed the distance between them. "It seemed the right thing to do."

"Why?" She'd been coming for weeks and he'd never offered before.

"I thought of doing it before but figured you'd kick up a protest. But lately you seem different." He searched her face, his look again going much deeper.

He'd realized she'd changed exactly as she'd hoped. She shivered. She'd have to be careful not to do anything to make him question it.

He quirked his eyebrows. "Or maybe it's me who is different. Looking at a snarling cat and knowing he could rip you to pieces makes a person value life even more."

She nodded. "I expect it does."

He caught her shoulders, planted a quick kiss on her mouth, then stepped back so she could mount up and ride away.

She stopped at the edge of the clearing and turned around to wave at him. A smile tugged at her heart at the grin blazing on his face.

Her smile remained all the way home.

For the next week she anticipated his welcome smile when she returned to his cabin every morning. Often she'd look at him and find his gaze on her mouth. Each time her heart would lurch like a wild horse ride. She wanted to jump on Nugget's back and do some crazy tricks, swing her rope in a big loop and dance in and out of the circle.

He stayed close by, working on the cabin. "It will soon be done," he said.

Shouldn't he have been happier at the idea? She would no longer come. There'd be no need. Unless—

But he'd given no indication of wanting more. Said nothing to make her think anything other than that this would end when the new cabin was finished.

"I'll be joining the church work bee on Saturday," he said over dinner one day.

"Are you taking the twins?"

They leaned forward, anxious for his answer. "Are you wanting to go to the bee?" he asked her.

"Linette says everyone is going to be there."

"Then by all means, you should go. I'll take the children."

Ladd and Allie cheered.

Abel shifted his attention to his daughter. "You'll have to play quietly."

She hung her head. "I know."

"I'll watch her." Mercy decided then and there she would make sure Allie had fun despite her restrictions. She kept her gaze on her empty dish. She'd do her best to show Abel they could all have fun together with her being an ordinary person.

"Are we almost there?" Allie asked Abel yet again.

"Soon." Edendale was not far away, but Allie and Ladd were excited about going to town and spending the day with friends and neighbors. Abel hid it much better, though he looked forward to the day, as well. Yes, he would enjoy meeting more of the community, but mostly he longed to see Mercy in a different situation. Apart from a few Sundays and one event at Eden

Valley Ranch that left him struggling to decide if it had been a good experience or a disappointment, he'd only seen her at meal times and a bit in between at the ranch.

This work bee would give him a chance to spend time with her in a social setting.

Town came into sight and in his excitement to see everything, Ladd leaned over so far Abel had to grab him by the back of his coat to keep him from falling off the horse and tumbling to the ground. Thankfully Mercy had offered to watch Allie because he didn't figure Ladd would do a good job today. He was too anxious to run and play.

He studied those already assembled. Many came from Eden Valley Ranch. He recognized a few from OK Ranch, Macpherson from the store, the Mortons who ran the stopping house and a handful of others. But he didn't see Mercy. His heart battered his ribs. Had he misunderstood her intention to attend?

As the circle of women shifted, his breath whooshed out. There she was. Wearing a pretty, dark red dress, her hair coiled about her head. No trousers. No fringed shirt. When was the last time he'd seen her dressed in such a fashion? She'd dressed in her fanciest riding duds for the celebration at the ranch when she'd done her showy riding and roping tricks.

Since then? He nodded. He hadn't seen her dressed in her outlandish outfits since before the night she'd rescued him. He couldn't say what she wore that night. Were the two facts connected? He couldn't see how they were and yet, for some reason, he felt they were. Would she explain if he asked her?

As always, the children slipped to the ground and raced to her side. She hugged them, then followed the direction Ladd pointed and waved at Abel. He gave a little salute before he went to join the men around a stack of lumber. It was a pretty spot. The mountains to the west were crowned with fresh snow. A few golden leaves clung to the deciduous trees. Darker pine and spruce covered much of the hills. The flash of running water indicated the river behind the store.

Eddie made introductions. "How many of you have experience with a building this size?"

Two men put up their hands. Several said they hadn't built anything bigger than a shack.

"I've worked on ships," Abel said.

"That's good news," Eddie said. "We'll be needing your expertise."

But Eddie was the foreman and soon had the crowd of men organized. Abel readily saw that the man knew how to get a job done and get others to help.

He glanced around to check on the twins. A crowd of children chased each other up and down the street. He straightened. Where was Allie? He scanned the area. Because he couldn't see her, he laid down his hammer to search for her. Then he saw the red of Mercy's dress and beside her, Allie, sitting and watching the children. Mercy pointed at something and they laughed.

He wished he could hear what Mercy said but at least Allie was safe with her. He picked up his hammer and returned to work.

By noon they had made significant progress. "All we can hope for today is to get the shell up."

Eddie nodded. "Once it's that far we can work on it bit by bit, one or two men at a time."

The women had set out piles of food on a long table made of sawhorses and lengths of wood.

When the men joined their womenfolk and children for the meal, Abel went to Mercy's side, the twins beside them.

Eddie stood at the end of the table. He removed his hat. The other men did likewise. "I'd like to say a few words."

The crowd grew quiet.

"As most of you know, this church is Linette's idea. And what Linette wants, she gets. I'm proof of that." He pulled his wife to his side as those assembled chuckled. "However, by the good turnout today, I'd say all of us agree with getting a church built for the community."

A round of applause signaled agreement.

"We are truly becoming a solid community. When I came out here there were people at the Eden Valley Ranch, those at OK and Macpherson here. Now look at us. We're a growing, thriving community."

"Eddie," someone called. "Don't we need a preacher?"

"Constable Allen said he'd ask at the fort. Said he'd ask about a doctor, too." Eddie glanced at Linette and Abel guessed he wished for a doctor nearby should anything go wrong with the birth of their little one.

Miss Oake from the OK Ranch waved to get Eddie's attention. "I recently heard from a cousin from back east who is a doctor. He's on his way to visit us. I don't know if he plans to set up practice here or just visit but he'll be here for a while."

More applause, then Eddie said grace. "Let's enjoy the abundance."

Mercy supplied Abel and the children with plates and they filed past the food.

"There's so much," Allie said, her eyes wide. "How can I taste everything?"

Mercy chuckled. "You might have to make some choices."

"But I want to try it all."

Mercy and Abel looked at each and laughed. Something sweet filled his heart at the shared joy over his daughter.

When they reached the end of the table, Allie eyed the desserts and sighed loudly.

Abel laughed. "I remember when she was ill and I couldn't get her to take more than a spoonful of broth," he said to Mercy.

"I'm all better now," Allie assured him.

Ladd asked if he could sit with Billy and Neil, and Abel gave him permission. Allie sighed again and didn't even ask though she looked longingly at a circle of little girls.

As they sat and ate, Abel glanced about. And felt something deep inside him unfurl. He'd always longed for this sort of thing—community, acceptance and belonging. Many times throughout the morning men had asked his advice regarding the building and he had given it. They'd accepted him. His family belonged here.

Family. He truly felt like family for the first time in his adult life. Even though it was temporary.

Unless he made it permanent.

He studied Mercy out of the corner of his eyes. She certainly seemed to care about the twins. Did she feel anything for him? Fondness at least? He examined his own feelings. Yes, he was fond of her. Very fond. His insides tightened and his fingers clenched the edge of the plate. He'd been fond of Ruby and married her—and that had been a mistake.

He didn't intend to make any more mistakes. No matter what he felt, how fond he was of her.

But hadn't Mercy changed for the better?

Then again, why had she changed? Was it for real or simply a reaction to something? He needed to ask her. He needed to know what she felt about him. About family life. About settling down.

This community gathering would not give him a chance to speak privately with her.

He needed to make such an opportunity.

By the next morning, he had a plan. Because it was Sunday, he would take the children to the ranch. The day would be consumed with eating and visiting. Yes, he and Mercy might get a few minutes alone, but not enough. He had something more than that in mind. At the first opportunity he would ask Linette to watch the children and then take Mercy on a picnic.

He'd tell her all that was in his heart.

But first, he must bring in some more firewood before snow came and found him unprepared.

At church, Abel tried to concentrate on the talk Bertie gave and then later on the conversation about the new church, but with Mercy at his side and the knowledge of his plan, he continually had to shepherd his thoughts back from chasing after the idea of a picnic alone with her.

He accepted Linette's invitation to join them for dinner then wished he hadn't because several times Eddie gave him a studying look and Abel realized he had missed a question.

He could not keep his mind on the conversation.

All he wanted to do was arrange a picnic for himself and Mercy.

But the day passed without allowing him a chance to speak privately to either Linette or Mercy.

He would have delayed his departure, but he noted a heightened color in Allie's cheeks. The twins' needs must come first. He had to get them home before Allie got overexcited.

Chapter Seventeen

Mercy tried to think why Abel had been in such a hurry to leave Sunday but couldn't. Had she done something to disappoint him? She reviewed the past few days. She'd been as ordinary as milk. She'd watched Allie, though that was certainly no hardship. She only wished the child could be allowed to join the others at play. Maybe this doctor cousin of Miss Oake could look at Allie and say whether or not there was any damage to her heart.

Consumed by restlessness, she changed into her riding costume and took Nugget out for a long run. She came to a small lake, where she noticed a great honking flock of birds lifting off the water—geese and cranes. Majestic birds. They circled overhead, then returned to the water. She tied Nugget in the trees and sat to observe them. These birds were not ordinary though what they only did was natural for them.

A strange restlessness filled her, peppered through and through with a contrasting peace. Was she the Mercy she tried to be for Abel or the one she pretended to be to get her parents' attention? *God, creator of all this beauty, who have You created me to be?*

Peace swallowed up the restlessness and she sat watching the birds for a long time. Somehow she knew that God, who guided birds from north to south and back each year, would guide her on her own journey. She had only to follow directions—if she could only find them.

Finally, she slipped away, quietly so as not to disturb the flock.

At home she studied herself from every angle in her looking glass. She appeared to be an ordinary woman about to embark on an ordinary day.

Inside, her heart fluttered like a nervous bird. Would Abel look at her with dark blue interest and see how she longed to be accepted?

She shook her head. That wasn't what she meant. It sounded needy and immature. She only wanted—

"To be seen as a person of value," she said to her reflection. But even that didn't sound right and she spun away. Perhaps if Abel would accompany her to see the birds, they could, together, find the answers she sought. The peace she craved. But when she arrived at his cabin the next morning, she knew before she dismounted that he wouldn't. His horse was already harnessed to the stoneboat and Abel rushed from the cabin as soon as he heard her.

"Good morning." He slowed his steps, veered from his path toward the horse and headed in her direction. He looked into her face, his gaze lingering on her mouth. Did he see the woman he wanted her to be, she wondered? He brushed her cheek with his bare hand. "I

want to get a load of wood in while the weather holds."
With a fleeting smile he resumed his original direction.

Did he wish he could spend the day with her and
the twins?

She watched until he disappeared into the trees, then
went inside. Ladd and Allie rushed over to hug her.

"How are you feeling?" She studied Allie. The child
looked fit and eager for life.

"I'm not sick even if Papa thinks I am."

Mercy had thought the same thing many times.
"Nevertheless, you can't afford to take chances. We
wouldn't want anything to happen to you." She hugged
the little girl and tickled her, eliciting crazy giggles.

Together they washed the dishes and tidied the cabin.
Mercy brought out books and schoolwork but had more
trouble concentrating than the twins. The four walls
pressed too close. The stove overheated the small area.

She crossed to the window. The sky held only a few
gray clouds. The calm she'd felt watching the wild birds
on the little mountain lake had dissipated. How much
longer would the flock remain? If only she could see
them again and recapture the peace and assurance
she'd experienced. Why not? It was warm. The children would enjoy the outing. "Let's go on a picnic."

"Yah!" They both bounced off their chairs and hurried to her side.

"Help me get a lunch ready to take."

They did so eagerly and a few minutes later the three
of them rode from the yard on Nugget's back.

"Where are we going?" Ladd asked.

"It's a surprise." Despite their frequent asking, she
wouldn't tell them more. "Look around and enjoy the
journey," she said, pointing out moss on the north side

of the trees, a blue jay scolding from a branch nearby. They paused once to watch a V of geese honking overhead.

A little later they stopped and dismounted. "You have to be very quiet now." She held her finger to her lips and guided them silently through the trees. The trees opened up to reveal the lake. Fewer birds were there this time of day, and none of the huge cranes.

"Let's sit here and watch them," she whispered as she indicated a tree.

Their eyes sparkled with excitement and she knew they found the sight of so many birds as awesome as she.

They watched the birds take off and land. Allie covered her mouth to muffle her giggles as a duck skidded into the water.

And then a flock of the majestic cranes approached. Both twins sucked in air as the huge birds settled onto the water. When Mercy had described the birds—their size, the black tips on their wings and red crown—Eddie had said they were whooping cranes.

She whispered the information to the twins.

Mesmerized by the beauty of the birds and the noise coming from the lake, the three of them watched for a long time.

Ladd leaned closer to whisper, "I'm hungry."

Mercy nodded and led them back to Nugget. She found a grassy clearing and they shared the lunch.

"Can we watch them again?" Allie asked.

"Did you enjoy that?"

She nodded, eyes sparkling. "They're fun to watch."

So they tiptoed back to the lake. Mercy warned herself to be aware of the passing time. They must make it back before Abel. He would worry if he returned and they were missing.

After a while, she signaled the children to follow her back to Nugget. "It's time to leave."

As they rode away, the twins chattered nonstop about the birds.

They had only reached the trail when Mercy shivered as a cold wind suddenly blew in and whipped around them. She stopped and pulled a blanket from her bag and wrapped it around Allie. "Ladd, do up your coat and keep tight to me."

A glance at the sky revealed low-hanging black clouds. Rain clouds. If she hurried she might beat the storm back. But they hadn't gone five paces when the heavens opened.

She reined Nugget under the shelter of a tree and pulled the children down to the ground, wrapping them in a big black slicker she'd started carrying after Eddie said she ought to be prepared for bad weather. She silently thanked him for his advice as she held the twins close. At least they'd be dry. She leaned out to glance upward. Would the storm pass quickly or had it settled in for a long visit? She couldn't see enough of the sky to guess. She leaned back. How long could she stay here? The light would fade early if the clouds stayed.

She considered her options, which were limited to two—stay and hope the storm ended or endure the cold rain and get the children home.

The second seemed the most appropriate, though not the most pleasant for her.

She wiped the saddle with her sleeve and lifted Ladd then Allie to it. Ladd put his arms around his sister and held on. He would do everything he could to protect her.

Mercy meant to do the same. She wrapped the slicker around them tightly. "Is any rain getting in?"

"No," came Ladd's muffled reply. "It's dry in here."

"It smells funny," Allie said.

Mercy laughed. "You'll get used to it." She swung up behind the pair, pushed her wet hair out of her eyes and hunkered down for a long cold ride.

At least the twins were safe and dry. If Abel happened to return before they got back he would see how careful she was with the children.

She ventured a prayer. *God, could You please make sure we get back first?*

Abel shook the water from his coat. He had continued to work after the rain began but water dripped from his hat, trailed down his nose, ran under his collar. The stoneboat had a decent load. He better get it home before traction became a problem.

As he navigated the trail he thought of what lay ahead. He'd ask Mercy to wait out the storm. A picnic was out of the question, but he could leave the twins in the old cabin and take Mercy to the new one. Actually talking to her about the future in the place where his future would take place made perfect sense.

He rehearsed the words he would say as he made his way home. He arrived in the yard, unhitched the stoneboat and took Sam to the corral. Strange that Nugget wasn't there. Had she tied him in the trees to keep him out of the rain? It seemed like something she would think to do. He smiled as he pictured her running outside, unmindful of the rain, to take care of her horse.

Shaking off as much moisture as he could, he ducked into the cabin and put his hat on a hook. He turned.

"Mercy? Ladd? Allie?" Had they gone to the new cabin? He plopped his wet hat back on his head and jogged across the yard. He called them again. Nothing. He looked around the partitions, climbed to the loft and looked in the corners. Was this some kind of game?

He saw none of the three but searched the cabin again just to be sure. Finally convinced they weren't there, he jogged back to the other one. But they weren't in that cabin, either.

He went to the door and stared out at the pelting rain. Had they ventured outside and been caught unawares? "Mercy, Ladd, Allie," he roared at the top of his lungs.

Nothing but the sound of rain on the roof and water dripping from the trees.

Then it hit him. Nugget missing. The twins missing. Mercy must have taken them on one of her foolish adventures. His fists curled so tightly his knuckles creaked. He thought she'd changed. Just went to prove he didn't dare listen to his foolish heart. If this hadn't happened he might have asked her to—

Marry him.

The idea mocked him. Seems he had this unconscious wish to make his life miserable.

Thank God above he'd discovered his mistake before it was too late.

He circled the cabin, straining through the wet air for a glimpse of them.

Allie would surely catch a chill out there. He pressed a fist to his forehead. If something happened to her or Ladd...

He circled the cabin several times. Not until they were home safely would he go inside and shed his wet clothes. He deserved to be chilled to the bone for trusting his children to the care of a woman like Mercy.

As the minutes trudged by, his insides grew hotter. Would he have to ride to the ranch and ask for help searching for them? Wait. The ranch. Had she taken them there? Were they safe and dry?

He considered riding there, but he couldn't leave the cabin. What if one of them stumbled in needing help? The woods were full of dangers—mountain lions, bears, strange men. He couldn't be sure the man who shot the mountain lion posed no danger to his children.

He waited in the open doorway, his arms crossed over his chest, but his muscles twitched and he walked around the cabin again. Then he saw a shadow moving through the trees. Reaching for his rifle, he strained forward.

The shadow drew closer, materialized into a horse carrying a dark object.

He rubbed his eyes and blinked. Then he saw Mercy, her dress wet and limp, her hair a springy tangle. He bolted forward. "Where are my children?"

"Here." She indicated the dark shape.

He flipped back the slicker. Two pairs of eyes watched him. He grabbed them and set them inside the door. "Get into something dry and wrap up in blankets. I'll be right there." He had to spare a moment to speak to Mercy.

"Have you no regard for anyone but yourself?" Words spewed from his mouth. Words expressing his anger and fear. Even as he spoke them, he knew they were unreasonable. She wouldn't put his children as risk. He'd been as worried about her as them. His worry had grown until it was completely out of proportion.

He needed time to get his emotions under control. "I suggest you leave immediately."

The look she gave him could only be described as wounded. "You've never trusted me. And never will." She rode away without a backward look.

He swiped the moisture from his face before he hurried in to take care of the children.

The twins faced him as he closed the door.

"Papa, why did you yell at her?" Allie's voice rang with accusation.

"She shouldn't have taken you out in the rain."

"It didn't start raining until we were on our way home." Ladd crossed his arms and fixed Abel with a hard look. "Why did you say you didn't trust her?"

"It doesn't matter. Let's get you out of those wet things."

"We're dry." Ladd's stance suggested disapproval. "Mercy wrapped us up and looked after us." Ladd and Allie exchanged looks.

"And you sent her away wet and cold." Allie turned her back. She reached for Ladd's hand and they retreated to the bed. He wondered if they wished they could get farther away, but the small cabin made it impossible.

He touched Allie's cheeks, ignoring the way she drew back. She was warm and dry.

"You were rude to her." Ladd's look said quite plainly that he held his father in contempt.

Abel went to the window and looked out. He'd jumped to a wrong conclusion. Let his anger fuel hurtful words. "I made a mistake," he said.

"Then best you tell her." Allie was right. He had to tell her.

But the rain continued to sputter. He couldn't take the children out and do exactly what he'd accused Mercy of—putting his interests ahead of their well-being.

Ice encased her heart, more numbing and invasive than the cold rain soaking Mercy as she rode home. She'd tried. Tried to be an ordinary person, tried to show Abel how responsible she was, tried and failed.

He didn't trust her enough to even stop and look at the evidence before he'd said exactly what he thought of her. Plain and simple, he didn't trust her. Never would. What was the use in her even trying?

She reached the ranch and took care of Nugget before she headed up the hill to the house.

Linette saw her coming and greeted her with an armload of dry towels. "You get out of those wet things immediately before you get pneumonia." She hurried Mercy to her bedroom and threatened to personally undress her if she didn't get it done in what Linette deemed a "reasonable amount of time."

"Put on your warmest bedclothes," Linette added.

Mercy slipped out of her clothes and into a warm nightdress and dressing gown. She began to gather up the wet items. With uncanny timing, Linette stepped into the room.

"Leave it. I'll see to them as soon as I've looked after you."

She drew Mercy back to the kitchen and eased her into a chair close to the stove. She wrapped a warmed woolen blanket about Mercy's shoulders, then prepared a cup of hot, sweet tea.

With a throat choked by unshed tears, Mercy thanked

Linette. It was nice to have someone care that she was cold and wet. And bleeding inside as if a sword had been run through her several times.

Linette made clucking noises. "I can't believe Abel let you leave in this rain. What was he thinking?"

Mercy shrugged. She pulled the blanket tightly around her shoulders wishing she could likewise tighten a cover for her heart. She should have never opened the steel doors, but she had, and closing them would take some time and a great deal of emotional strength that she lacked at the moment.

Linette edged the cup of tea closer.

Mercy slipped one hand from under the blanket and picked up the cup and sipped slowly. The warm liquid stole down her throat. It began to melt the ice in the pit of her stomach, but did nothing to thaw the ice encasing her heart. That might never happen.

"Eddie brought home the mail. I had a letter from Grady's father. He sounded more interested in the boy than he has in the past. Oh, I almost forgot. There is a letter from your parents." Linette found it and handed it to Mercy.

Mercy tucked it into her pocket. She knew what it would say. "We trust you are enjoying your trip. We have had rain. Your father and I are well."

She didn't know why they bothered to write. Obligation, she supposed. Just as she replied out of duty.

A newspaper lay on the table and an advertisement caught her eye. The Greatest Little Wild West Show in the West Will Appear. She pulled the paper closer and read the entire piece. The show was coming to a rough frontier town to the north and east.

"The troupe will be heading south for the winter after their final show here."

She flicked the paper toward Linette. "I'm going there."

Linette read the news, then lifted worried eyes to Mercy. "I thought…" She shrugged. "What about Abel and the children?"

"His cabin is about ready to move into." Each word scratched her throat as if it came out sideways. She coughed but it did little to help. She did not attempt to say more.

"I see." Linette's quiet study made Mercy think she probably did see without further explanation.

Linette checked the date on the advertisement. "The show might already be gone."

"No. They were scheduled to do their last show on Saturday. I don't expect they'd pack up on Sunday. I might catch them before they leave. Or catch up to them. They won't have gone far. They won't go fast."

"I don't like the idea."

Mercy shrugged. "Everyone has been clear about that. Nevertheless, I intend to find them and join the show."

Linette slipped away. She must have informed Jayne and Sybil, for they both appeared within the hour and tried to persuade her to change her mind, but Mercy had already started packing. "I'll be off at daylight."

In the end, neither her friends nor Eddie could convince her to change her mind. She had to get away and this was the perfect escape.

When she saddled up the next morning, Slim rode to her side. "I'm to make sure you get there safe and sound."

"I'll be fine on my own."

"I have my orders."

"Very well." She would never admit that she welcomed his presence. This way she couldn't change her mind and ride to Abel's cabin, instead, demanding he look at her. Really look at her and see her for what she was.

Though she no longer knew for certain who that was.

Chapter Eighteen

Mercy stood in her stirrups and strained to see the town ahead. "They're still there." She pointed to the circle of tents and bunkhouses on wheels and horses penned nearby.

Relief surged through her and she sank back into her saddle. With no doubt but that she'd be accepted into the show, she could now face a future full of adventure and excitement, though her heart did not leap with anticipation. It sat heavy and unresponsive in her chest.

"You can still change your mind," Slim said as they turned in the direction of the gathering.

Only one thing would cause her to change her mind—Abel seeing her as someone he could trust. But he'd made it clear that wasn't going to happen. "My heart is set on this." She said the words as much for her benefit as his.

"I'll see that you're settled before I leave."

She started to protest but he cut her off. "Linette will demand to know all the details."

"Fine."

When she reached the area, Mercy reined in to listen and watch. A man worked with a pen of horses, waving a whip to direct them to do all sorts of tricks. Another man brushed a huge Clydesdale horse. Was he used to pull the wagons and movable bunkhouses, she wondered, or did he perform, as well? She watched for a few minutes, but the man simply kept brushing the animal.

The sharp scent of horse droppings mingled with the smell of canvas tents and wood smoke. And excitement.

This was what she'd wanted since she'd set foot in the West.

A woman in fringed leather strolled by.

"Hello," Mercy called, getting her attention. "Can you tell me who's in charge?"

"That would be Gus. Why? Who's asking?"

Mercy smiled at the woman's soft drawl and at her outfit and simply because she had arrived at her dreams. She quietly and firmly ignored the truth that she did this only to escape the pain of Abel's disapproval.

"I'd like to talk to him. Can you tell me where he is?"

The woman eyed her up and down, then shifted her gaze to Slim and studied him with such bold eyes that Slim shifted in his saddle.

"I suppose you want to join the show."

"I can ride and rope and do all sorts of Wild West tricks."

The woman gave a little laugh. "No doubt you can. And Gus is always on the lookout for performers to add to the show. You'll find him at that bunkhouse." She pointed toward one on the right. Then she held out her hand. "They call me Angel."

Before Mercy could ask if that was her real name or a stage name, the girl left.

Mercy turned toward the bunkhouse Angel had indicated. Slim followed, muttering about how unsuitable the place was. She ignored him and climbed the steps to knock on the door.

"Enter," a deep voice called.

Mercy hesitated.

"I'll wait right here," Slim said.

She opened the door and stepped inside. The room she entered held a desk covered with papers, two wooden chairs, a stove and cupboard and, at the back, a rumpled bed.

Her cheeks heated at the sight, but she drew herself tall. People must forgo certain rules of conduct living in such tight quarters. Not that it mattered to her. Rules were only made by fearful people and she wasn't afraid.

"How can I help you?"

She introduced herself. "I'd like to join your show."

His head jerked up, and she noticed his bold black eyes, an overlarge nose and a heavy mustache. He smiled, revealing a gold tooth. "I see. And what can you offer me?"

"Why don't I show you?"

He pushed to his full impressive height. "Show me."

She stepped aside and let him lead the way. Slim, still on horseback, followed.

Gus tipped a head Slim's direction. "Your husband?"

"No, he only escorted me here at a friend's insistence."

"So he'll be leaving?"

She nodded, her thoughts on the tricks she and Nugget would do. "You have to bear in mind that my horse has been on the road since morning."

"Let's see what you can do." He opened the corral

gate for her to enter, then leaned against the fence to watch.

She did rope tricks, gun-handling tricks and had Nugget do a number of the tricks she'd taught him. Then she halted in front of Gus and waited for his verdict.

He seemed in deep thought, his fingers stroking his mustache. Finally he nodded. "I do believe there is room in the program for you. You're hired. Can you be ready to join us today? We pull out tomorrow."

"I'm here to stay."

"Good to know. I'm Gus Seymor, the boss of this outfit."

She leaned over to shake the hand he offered. He held on a moment too long, forcing her to withdraw.

"Angel," he bellowed, causing several horses to neigh.

Angel trotted over.

"Take Mercy to your quarters. She'll be joining the show."

Something flickered through Angel's eyes. Mercy wondered if she resented Gus hiring another woman. But then Angel smiled and indicated Mercy should follow her. "Leave your horse here."

Mercy paused beside Slim. "You can leave now. Tell Linette that I'm okay."

Slim nodded but, rather than head for the trail, he dismounted. "Don't mind if I look around, do you?" he asked Gus. "Never been to one of these shows. It looks mighty interesting."

Gus gave him a hard look then waved his hand. "Go ahead. Have yourself a look."

Mercy followed Angel to one of the wooden structures on wheels and entered. Bunks for four took up most of the interior, crowded in with a wood heater, wash table and a wardrobe.

"Hang your things in there." Angel watched as Mercy did. "You got some mighty fancy clothes." Mercy had only brought two dresses. "You sure you're gonna fit in here?"

"I mean to."

"Even if you're asked to do things you don't want?"

Mercy stared at the other woman. "Like what?"

Angel shrugged. "Gus has certain expectations."

The skin on Mercy's spine did a snakelike crawl. She hoped Angel didn't mean anything other than shoveling manure.

"Never mind," Angel said. "Come on. I'll show you around."

They went from tent to tent meeting the others. Some were friendly. Others not so much. Several men leered at her and ran their hands along Angel as they passed.

Mercy couldn't tell if Angel liked it or not, but she vowed she'd make it clear she wouldn't tolerate such inappropriate behavior. At one tent two men made lewd suggestions.

Angel dragged her away. "Best you keep your distance from them."

Mercy glanced around for Slim. "Looking for your friend?" Gus asked, startling her with his sudden appearance. "He left a while ago. Said to tell you goodbye."

A little later the performers gathered round a table in a big tent and ate a meal. A man who'd been introduced as Bull squeezed in between herself and Angel. The four other women giggled as he patted Mercy's leg.

"Nice to have a new face in our midst."

A red-haired woman laughed raucously. "Bull, since when have you been interested in faces?" She winked at Mercy. "He's more interested in your body, if you know what I mean."

Mercy feared she did and her skin felt two sizes too small. "But I'm not that kind of woman."

Everyone except Angel laughed. Later, Angel pulled her aside. "Look, kid. You really aren't going to fit in here."

"Why? Just because I'm not interested in what Bull wants?"

"He's not your only concern." She looked about as if afraid someone would overhear her. "Mercy, you better think hard about this, because we pull out tomorrow and then there'll be no turning back."

"I'll be fine." But she vowed she would carry a loaded pistol with her day and night.

Gus invited her to his place later in the afternoon. "We need to discuss your performance."

Mercy glanced about. Angel had disappeared. She had no choice but to follow Gus up the steps. He closed the door behind him and ran his finger along her jaw. Funny how when Abel did the same thing, her insides got sweet like honey but when Gus did it, she felt like glass shattering on hard ground.

She shrugged away from his touch. "I'm not interested in that sort of thing."

Gus laughed. "All the girls say that to start with." He waggled his eyebrows and grinned as if she should appreciate his behavior.

"Did you want to discuss my act?"

He waved her question away. "Time enough for that. Why don't you sit down and tell me about yourself."

She reluctantly perched on a chair. He pulled the other one close enough to press his knees to hers.

"Tell me about your family."

She considered what she should say. Certainly not that she had no family in Canada. Nor that her parents wouldn't likely miss her if she disappeared. "Eddie Gardiner of Eden Valley Ranch is my guardian." Close enough.

"Never heard of the man. Is he rich?"

Again Mercy considered her answer carefully. "I couldn't say. I've never felt the need to ask regarding his financial status. He's a very important, powerful man though."

Gus laughed. And if the increased pressure from his knees was intentional or not, it made Mercy draw back. She slipped from the chair. "I better check on my horse. He's a valuable part of my act."

He didn't look happy but allowed her to leave. She found Nugget in a tiny corral, his hooves buried in wet manure. She poured some feed into a food bag for him but stopped when she saw the poor quality oats. It was the last straw.

She'd made a mistake. She didn't belong here. It was nothing like she'd imagined. The crowded conditions, the poor food…all of that she could tolerate. The advances by Gus and Bull she would not accept. She headed for the bunkhouse she shared with Angel and threw her things into her bag, then trotted back to Nugget. Several people watched her but no one said anything. She saddled Nugget and went to open the gate. Bull stood there, holding it closed.

"No one comes or goes without Gus's permission." His voice made it clear he would not let her by.

"I've changed my mind. I'm leaving."

He chuckled—a mean sound. "Like I said. You need Gus's permission."

"Then I shall get it." She stomped across to Gus's quarters and knocked. No one answered though she suspected the man was inside. She knocked for several minutes and called his name.

Angel found her there. "He's not going to answer. If he doesn't want you to leave, you won't."

She followed Angel back to their place. "He can't keep me here against my will."

"You came freely."

"Did you?"

Angel shrugged. "I guess I did. I had a cruel stepfather and joining a Wild West show got me away from him. You could do worse, you know. Gus won't beat you."

"I'm not staying." She opened the door. Bull sat nearby, watching. He touched the gun on his hip as if to warn her and she had a feeling he'd use it if necessary. She closed the door again. She would wait until after dark and slip away.

She pretended to be very busy coiling and uncoiling her rope. All the while, her mind raced. She had her guns. She could shoot at Bull but how far would she get? Likely all of the men were of the same mind. A shiver snaked up her arms. What had she gotten herself into?

Abel had to wait a full day for the rain to go from a downpour to a drizzle to nothing. He dressed the children warmly and then the three of them headed for Eden Valley Ranch.

"Are you gonna tell her you're sorry?" Allie asked, for the umpteenth time.

"When I get there, you two can stay with Mrs. Gardiner while I talk privately to Mercy." He'd about had it with their dark accusing looks and the way they shifted away from him every time he drew near. Even more daunting were his own thoughts, accusing and berating him. Why had he been so quick to judge her?

He did not like the answer.

Because he couldn't forgive himself for the mistake he'd made in marrying Ruby and his guilt made him see every woman as too much like her. Mercy wasn't. Even if she thrived on adventure. That was another thing. In his reaction to where his choices had taken him, he'd denied himself the things he enjoyed. He could afford to enjoy life a bit more, have some fun times with the children and Mercy. The picnic that had never occurred would just be the beginning once he'd apologized and told her how he felt about her.

Would she return his feelings?

They rode up to the big house and Linette came out to greet them. After the usual greetings he looked past her. "Can I speak to Mercy? Is she about?"

"I wish she was, but she's gone."

"Gone?" He'd never considered the possibility.

"Do the children want to come in and play with Grady?"

He recognized her subtle hint that she'd like to speak to him privately and lowered the twins to the ground, then dismounted.

She waited for them to go indoors and pulled the

door shut behind them. "Mercy left to join a Wild West show." She told him where the Mercy intended to catch up to the show. "We tried to stop her, but the best we could do was send Slim as an escort. I don't mind telling you I'm worried about her."

Abel reeled back on his heels. So this was her answer. She'd always wanted to do this. Nothing had changed.

Except it had. He couldn't let her go without telling her what was in his heart.

He loved her.

He wanted a chance to prove it to her. To win her heart in return.

"When did they leave? Is Slim back yet?"

They'd left yesterday, Linette told him, and Slim wasn't back.

"I don't know what happened between the two of you," she added, "but whatever it is, surely it's not so bad it can't be mended."

"How is it to be mended when she's left?"

She smiled gently. "Go after her. Persuade her to return. I'll keep the children."

He hesitated ten seconds as his head and heart warred over what to do. Couldn't he trust both? Hadn't she proved herself trustworthy? Fun yet responsible. "I'll go." He swung up to the saddle.

Linette caught her arm. "God go with you. I'll be praying."

"Tell the children I'll be back when I find her." He knew they'd approve of his decision.

"I'll let them know."

He rode from the yard and headed away at a gallop,

then realized he needed to slow down. He had a long trip ahead of him.

As the miles pounded away under Sam's hooves, Abel prayed. He prayed for forgiveness for the wild life he had chosen for a time, for the heartache he had caused his parents. One thing he meant to do as soon as he brought Mercy back was write his parents and tell them how sorry he was. He prayed that God would free him of guilt. *You've given me life to enjoy and I've been attempting to turn it into drudgery.* Most of all, he prayed Mercy would listen to him and accept his apology and his love.

The sun was high overhead when he reached the town where the Wild West show was supposed to be. But he saw no sign of it—no tents. Nothing. He saw a man crossing the street and rode up to him. "Say, did I hear there was a Wild West show around here?"

"Sorry, mister. You missed it. They pulled out this morning."

"Pulled out. What direction?"

"South. Along that road." The man pointed.

Abel sank back in his saddle. He'd missed her. But surely he could catch up to them. "Thanks." He headed down the street toward the road indicated. The smell of food slowed him. He should eat before he continued, but he couldn't spare the time. He must find Mercy.

The first night at the show, Mercy knew she'd made a mistake. She'd waited until after dark to crack open the door. She saw no one and quietly tiptoed out. Angel knew her plans and tried to dissuade her but promised she would not interfere.

One foot had reached the ground when a hand

clamped to her shoulder. Her breath caught in her throat. She tried and failed to control the jolt that shook her body.

"Gus thought you might be foolish enough to wander about," Bull ground out. "Says to warn you it isn't safe out there. It's my job to make sure everyone is safe, especially you pretty ladies. So be a good girl and go to bed." There was no mistaking the warning in his voice or the pressure of his hand meant to convey the same message.

She spun around and went back inside.

"I tried to warn you," Angel said. "Give it up and go to sleep."

But Mercy did not go to bed. She sat on a chair facing the door. Darkness made it impossible to see anything as she strained for any sound. Maybe Bull would leave. If he did, she'd be prepared.

What a fool she'd been to think she needed excitement and adventure. She didn't want either. She'd found all she needed in caring for Abel and his family. All she really wanted, all she'd really ever wanted, was someone to care about her. If only Abel had shown he did.

Did God care?

What had Bertie said? God sees us wherever we are. We could never go so far away that God wasn't with us.

God, are You here right now? Do You see me? She knew He did. *Can You help me?* She didn't know how He could but she trusted He would. Trust. Maybe that was the heart of her problem. She didn't trust her parents to love her. Maybe Butler's death had destroyed something in them so they couldn't. But she'd used the same measuring stick with everyone, including God.

Just as Abel used Ruby as the measuring stick for his life. She held back a chuckle. They were both so foolish.

God, please rescue me. All I want is a chance to show Abel I'm not Ruby. All I want is a chance to give the twins and him the love that I've longed for all my life.

Even if it took a long time, she would not give up.

The night hours slipped away. At times her trust in God faltered. But each time it did, she reminded herself that God was not like her parents to stop loving her.

She jerked to full attention. Had she fallen asleep? What time was it? What had wakened her? She strained to catch any sound. Then she heard it. A scratching at the door.

She bolted to her feet.

Did Bull or Gus intend to take advantage of her? Her hands shaking so badly her teeth rattled, she palmed her pistol. They'd have to deal with that before they touched her.

Chapter Nineteen

The doorknob rattled. *Help me, God. Protect me.* Mercy could barely make out shapes in the darkness. Couldn't be certain but it looked like the door cracked open.

"Miss?" The whisper was kindly enough, but Mercy didn't mean to take any chances.

"Don't come any closer or I'll shoot."

"Miss, I'm here to help you."

Help? Surely it was a trick. "I don't need any help."

"I think you do. You don't know my name so I won't give it but you've seen me plenty of times in the woods around Eden Valley Ranch. I shot a mountain lion that was about to attack your friend, Abel Borgard."

The man in the woods!

"You need to hurry. I don't think Bull will sleep very long."

Still Mercy hesitated, uncertain whom she could trust.

"Miss, your horse is waiting down the street."

Nugget. She could trust him. And God. Was this an answer to her prayer? Tucking her pistol in the waistband of her trousers, she grabbed the bags she had prepared earlier. "I'm coming."

"Be very quiet."

She stepped outside. A thin moon made it possible to see dark shapes. That bulky form near her door must be Bull. The loud snore made her jump but confirmed he slept. She tiptoed past him, following the shadowy figure ahead of her. Filling her mind were a thousand questions that would have to wait until it was safe to talk.

They crossed the yard. She sucked in air and stilled her anger and fear as they passed Gus's quarters. Her attention momentarily diverted, she stepped on a stick. The crack shot into the still air and she halted, holding her breath. When nothing happened she continued after the man from the woods.

They left behind the circle of tents and bunkhouses and stepped into the dark street. Still they hurried along as silently as possible. They turned a corner. Dawn streaked the sky, making it possible to see shapes.

A horse whinnied. Nugget. He stood at the hitching rail down the street and she ran to him and buried her face against his neck, choking back tears.

As soon as she could speak, she turned to her rescuer. "Thank you for helping me, but who are you? How did you know I was here?" She stared at the whiskered face as the elusive memory tugged at her brain. "Where have I seen you before?"

"You do remember me." He grinned. "I wondered."

She snapped her fingers. "I know where. I saw you at Fort Benton at the Wild West show." He'd been one of those grooming a big Clydesdale and then had raced a team of them pulling a careening wagon around the arena.

"Clay Morgan at your service, ma'am." He touched the brim of his hat.

"Pleased to meet you. But how did you end up at the Eden Valley Ranch? How did you know I was here?"

"I left the show at Fort Benton. Got tired of the stuff that goes on after the shows."

She had an inkling of what he meant.

"So I headed for the Northwest. Heard a man could find solitude and peace there."

She wondered if he'd found it.

"I saw you riding in the woods and recognized you. Watched you practice your riding and roping tricks. You got pretty good."

"Thanks." In hindsight it seemed foolish.

"I saw you ride home soaking wet the other day. Later, I started to worry about you and went to the ranch to see if you got back safely and were okay. A cowboy there told me you'd left to join this show." He grunted and stroked his beard. "I know this outfit. Didn't figure you'd find it to your liking."

"How right you were." She held her hand out. "I thank you. I believe God sent you in answer to my desperate prayers."

Their hands were still clasped so she felt the jolt in his arm.

"Miss, you think God can use an old reprobate like me?"

She heard the underlying question because it echoed her own of only a few hours ago. "God loves you. He loves me." The words filled her mouth with sweetness.

Clay pulled his hand to his side. "That's something to think on. Now you best be on your way." He scratched his chin through the mass of whiskers. "I suggest you avoid the roads for a while in case Gus decides to try and track you down."

Her insides tightened again. "Where can I hide?"

He grinned. "Best place to hide is in plain sight. Tie your horse behind the hotel and go to the lobby."

"I will. Thank you." But she didn't leave. "Will I see you again?"

"Could be. I've got a camp set up near the ranch." He sketched a wave and strode down the street.

She took up Nugget's reins and led him around to the alley behind the hotel, intending to stay out of sight in plain view until Gus and his show were a long way from town.

Now that she had escaped her foolish dreams, the enormity of what she'd done slammed into her and, with a moan, she bent over her knees. She had to get back to the ranch. If they'd let her back. Once Abel heard where she'd been and what she'd experienced he might never want her around the children again. He would be right. Her foolishness put not only herself but others in danger.

A question that had hammered relentlessly at the back of her mind insisted on attention. Were Ladd and Allie okay after their cold, wet adventure? Oh, how she ached to know they were both safe.

Would she ever see them again? Ever get a chance to prove to Abel the love that flooded her heart once she gave herself permission to believe she could be loved?

She waited with Nugget for an hour or so, not wanting to draw attention to herself by entering the hotel too early in the morning.

The longer she waited, the more the questions peppered her brain. *Oh, God, please give me another chance with Abel and the children.*

His stomach growled, protesting Abel's decision to forgo a meal. But he had to hurry along and catch the show before the day ended. Food could wait, he insisted again. Finding Mercy could not. As he reined about to resume his journey a woman stepped in front of him.

He jerked back on the rein, bringing Sam to a sudden halt. "Sorry."

The woman looked like Mercy. The way she walked, the tumble of mahogany hair down her back, everything about her.

He rubbed his eyes. Was he dreaming? Seeing her in every adult female? This gal wore trousers and a fringed shirt. No doubt a part of the Wild West show. He wasn't dreaming. It was Mercy, but why was she here? Had she missed the show? She moved with a purposeful step. Was she trying to locate the show, catch up to it?

He sat back on his saddle. If this was what she wanted, could he take it from her? No. He'd learned that lesson well enough with Ruby. But he couldn't let her go without talking to her, telling her how he felt.

"Mercy." His call rang out.

She drew to a halt and slowly turned to face him. Surprise and shock wreathed her face and then she gasped and ran toward him. He dropped to the ground to meet her.

"The twins?" she gasped. "Are they sick? Is Allie...?"

"They're fine. I came for my own sake." He grasped her upper arms and held her close but not too close. He must not be distracted by hugging and kissing. "Mercy,

I was hasty and wrong in accusing you of putting Ladd and Allie in danger. I know you wouldn't do that." He let the words sink in as he filled his lungs.

Her eyes widened as if she found it difficult to believe his words.

He rushed on, determined to make her understand. "I feared everyone would be like Ruby, putting their own interests ahead of the children. But more than that, I feared trusting what my heart said."

She tipped her head slightly to the side and studied him with guarded eyes. "What does your heart say?"

A smile drew his mouth wide. He drank in her features—her dark eyes, beautiful skin, lovely lips, then realized she waited for his answer. "My heart says..." He tried to sort out the many things he felt. "It says you are the best thing that ever happened to me. I can trust you. And enjoy life with you." His voice deepened. "Mercy, I love you and I want to share my life with you."

She laughed softly. "Took you long enough to figure it out."

"I had a lot to sort out." He stroked her cheek. "I know you want to join a Wild West show and I would never ask you to give up your dreams. But I'll come, too. I'll bring the children. We'll help you."

There was a sheen of tears in her eyes. "Abel, you'd do that for me?"

"I'll do whatever you need."

She lifted a hand and cupped his face, warm and possessive, and he turned into her palm.

"Abel, I found the show. I was invited to join them. It was awful." A shudder ran up her arm and he pulled her closer.

"If someone hurt you..."

"No. Our friendly woodsman rescued me." She filled in the details.

"I'm so grateful you're safe, but there are other shows."

She shook her head. "You don't understand. I don't want to join a Wild West show. I don't want to perform. I don't need the attention, because I found what I need with you and the twins."

"You did?" He ached for her to say she returned his feelings or at least welcomed them but he wasn't sure what she meant.

"Abel, I found acceptance with you. I found something worth being a part of."

He wanted more, but was he being greedy?

She chuckled. "Abel, just in case you aren't understanding what I'm saying, let me be clear. I love you. I want nothing else on earth but to share your life."

He stared. "You love me?"

She nodded, her eyes sparkling with joy. "You and the twins."

He leaned forward, but realized how very public the street was. "Let's find someplace private."

She led him to the back of the hotel where Nugget waited.

He pulled her into his arms, looked deep into her eyes. "Say it again."

Her soft laugh danced across his heart. "Abel Borgard, I love you and I want to share your life."

He caught the last word with his lips and claimed her mouth with a heart full of gratitude and anticipation of the future.

Cupping his cheeks with her hands, she offered him all her love in a kiss that threatened to explode his heart.

He eased back enough to smile into her welcoming gaze. "I love you, Mercy Newell. When can we change it to Mercy Borgard?"

She trailed her fingers along his jawline sending joy into every corner of his mind. "Do you suppose someone in this town could perform a ceremony?"

He roared with laughter. "You don't want to wait?"

"I have been waiting all my life." Her eyes filled with such need he hugged her tight to his chest and leaned his head against hers.

"You have my love now and always."

She clung to his shirtfront. "I don't want to ever leave you. Or have you leave me."

"I won't, except maybe to go hunting or get firewood."

She laughed.

His tension eased. "That's better." He wiped the tears from her eyes. "Wouldn't want the bride to appear teary." He tucked her in at his side. "Now let's go find a judge or preacher or someone to marry us."

She leaned her head on his shoulder. "I'm deliriously happy."

"Are you sure you aren't just overtired?" She'd told him how she'd sat awake all night waiting for a chance to escape.

"I'm wide-awake now. Thanks to your kiss."

They grinned at each other then restricted themselves to holding hands as they reached the street. They found the Mountie in his office and made their inquiry.

"You are indeed fortunate. The circuit judge is here

today to hold court. He'll be glad to perform a marriage ceremony." He directed them to the hotel.

An hour later they stood hand in hand while the stern-looking judge married them. "I now pronounce you man and wife. You may kiss."

She turned and wrapped her arms around her husband. He claimed her mouth in a gentle promise of forever.

Epilogue

"Do I look like a fancy riding lady?" Allie asked.

"You certainly do." Even more important, she looked the picture of health. Miss Oake's doctor cousin had visited and examined Allie and given the word that her heart was as sound as Ladd's.

Marriage to Abel was beyond anything Mercy had dreamed possible. He was thoroughly attentive, affectionate and caring. Within a few weeks, Mercy discovered she could think of her parents without the sharp pain she'd grown so familiar with she barely noticed it.

They had moved into the new cabin before the first snowfall. Mercy had made it homey with framed pictures, a collection of books and the quilts she'd finished for the children in time for Christmas. And what a Christmas it had been. For the first time since she was very young, Mercy celebrated the season with a heart overflowing with joy and excitement. The twins were so eager for the day that many times they brought chuckles to the lips of Abel and Mercy. Sharing the anticipation with the twins and Abel was the best Christmas gift she could ask for. With his ax, Abel had shaped a statue of a boy and girl sitting arm and arm on a bench. It was clearly the twins. She'd never seen anything more beautiful and told him so.

Every day she rose with a smile on her lips. Abel always traced the smile with his fingertip before kissing her.

She sighed.

Ladd tugged at her sleeve. "You gonna get ready?"

She brought her attention back to their task. "I'm about ready."

Abel worried so much about her not being able to join a Wild West show that she'd planned this surprise for him. "Let's go."

Allie rode Nugget while Ladd and Mercy walked on either side swinging lariats. They entered the area where Linette had staged her party after the roundup. They'd chosen a springlike day. It still amazed Mercy how the weather changed so quickly and unexpectedly.

The cowboys and residents of Eden Valley Ranch joined Abel for the show. Beside Abel sat Clay Morgan. They had located his crude camp after their return as a married couple. He had only a tent, which he had banked with earth to provide protection for the winter. Mercy and Abel had persuaded him to accept the use of the old cabin and, after a bit of demurring, he'd accepted.

They'd found him to be a good and trustworthy friend.

She and Allie and Ladd performed riding and roping tricks. Then as their finale, Allie stood on Nugget's back and rode around the enclosure. Mercy stayed at Allie's side, making sure she was safe.

When they were finished, they bowed to the sound of applause.

Mercy barely noticed. She sought Abel's gaze. They smiled at each other across the space.

She'd found what she wanted and needed in his love.

A little later, they walked with everyone to Linette and Eddie's house for dinner. Linette glowed with joy at the birth of their baby boy. Eddie was so proud he walked about with a swelled chest, Grady at his side imitating his every gesture.

As they reached the door, Abel pulled Mercy to one side. "Let the others go in first."

She gladly did so. Although she wasn't sure why he made the request, she trusted him so completely she didn't question it.

The door closed behind Roper.

Abel turned Mercy into his arms. "That was a wonderful performance. Are you sure you don't want to join a show?"

She shuddered. "Very sure. Besides," she said, and grinned up at him. "I don't think I'm going to have time. What with you and the twins and a baby to care for."

"A baby? Where—" He realized what she meant and touched her cheek gently. "Are you sure?"

"I'm sure. And it's about time. I want lots of little Borgards. I find my heart so full of love I fear I will smother you and the twins if I don't divide it up more."

He laughed. "My heart rests in your palm and it is safe. You have made my life everything I always wanted and dreamed of." He looked deep into her eyes. "I only hope I satisfy you as fully as you satisfy me."

She pulled his face close. "I don't mind letting you prove it."

He kissed her. "Does that prove it?"

She tucked her hand about his arm and reached for the door. "It's a very nice start, although I fear it will take a lot of kisses each and every day to make your point."

He pressed his chin to her head. "You are getting quite greedy."

"Hmm. Maybe not greedy. Just reveling in your love."

They entered the house amidst more applause. She wondered if they clapped for the show she and the children had put on or if they meant approval for the love that glistened from Abel's eyes and, she was quite certain, from hers, as well.

* * * * *

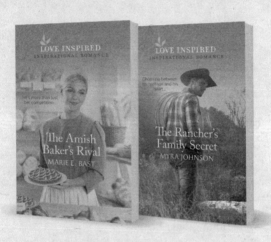

SPECIAL EXCERPT FROM

LOVE INSPIRED
INSPIRATIONAL ROMANCE

What happens when a tough marine and a sweet dog trainer don't see eye to eye?

Read on for a sneak preview of
The Marine's Mission *by Deb Kastner.*

"Oscar will be perfect for your needs," Ruby assured Aaron, reaching down to scratch the poodle's head.

"That froufrou dog? No way, ma'am. Not gonna happen."

"Excuse me?" She'd expected him to hesitate but not downright reject her idea.

"Look, Ruby, if you like Oscar so much, then keep him for yourself. I need a man's dog by my side, not some... some..."

"Poodle?" Ruby suggested, her eyebrows disappearing beneath her long ginger bangs.

"Right. Lead me to where you keep the German shepherds, and I'll pick one out myself."

"Hmm," Ruby said, rubbing her chin as if considering his request, although she really wasn't. "No."

"No?"

"No," she repeated firmly. "First off, we don't currently have a German shepherd as part of our program."

"I'd even take a pit bull." He was beginning to sound desperate.

"Look, Aaron. Either you're going to have to learn to trust me or you may as well just leave now before we start. This isn't going to work unless you're ready to listen to me and do whatever I tell you to do."

His eyebrows furrowed. "I understand chain of command, ma'am. There were many times as a marine when I didn't exactly agree with my superiors, but I understood why it was important to follow orders."

"Okay. Let's go with that."

"For me," Aaron continued, "following orders is black-and-white. My marines' lives under my command often depended on it. But as you can see, I'm having difficulty making that transition in this situation. We're not talking people's lives here."

"I disagree. We're very much talking lives—*yours*. You may not yet have a clear vision of what you'll be able to do with Oscar, but a service dog can make all the difference."

"Yes, but you just insisted the best dog for me is a *poodle*. I'm sorry, but if you knew anything about me at all, you'd know the last dog in the world I'd choose would be a poodle."

"And yet I still believe I'm right," said Ruby with a wry smile. Somehow, she had to convince this man she knew what she was doing. "I carefully studied your file before you arrived, Aaron, and specially selected Oscar for you to work with. I'm the expert here. So how are we going to get over this hurdle?"

"I have orders to make this work. How will it look if I give up before I even start the process?" He shook his head. "No. Don't answer that. It will look as if I wasn't able to complete my mission. That's never going to happen. I'll *always* pull through, no matter what."

Don't miss
The Marine's Mission *by Deb Kastner,*
available July 2021 wherever
Love Inspired books and ebooks are sold.

LoveInspired.com

LIEXP0621

LOVE INSPIRED
INSPIRATIONAL ROMANCE

UPLIFTING STORIES OF FAITH, FORGIVENESS AND HOPE.

Join our social communities to connect with other readers who share your love!

Sign up for the Love Inspired newsletter at **LoveInspired.com** to be the first to find out about upcoming titles, special promotions and exclusive content.

CONNECT WITH US AT:

f Facebook.com/LoveInspiredBooks

🐦 Twitter.com/LoveInspiredBks

Facebook.com/groups/HarlequinConnection

Get 4 FREE REWARDS!

We'll send you 2 FREE Books plus 2 FREE Mystery Gifts.

Love Inspired books feature uplifting stories where faith helps guide you through life's challenges and discover the promise of a new beginning.

FREE
Value Over
$20